Readers love JOHN INMAN

My Dragon, My Knight

"Every now and then, a book comes along that has everything I love… Such is the case with *My Dragon, My Knight*."
—Joyfully Jay

"*My Dragon, My Knight* is nigh on brilliant as a psychological thriller, and endlessly sweet and tender as a romance."
—The Novel Approach

Acting Up

"…*Acting Up* turned out to be unexpectedly sweet and enjoyable…"
—Just Love: Queer Book Reviews

"This was a quick fun read."
—Alpha Book Club

Ben and Shiloh

"This book was so full of humor and love. It was like a fun adventure…"
—Gay Book Reviews

"I highly recommend this series and this story. Pick them all up and get acquainted with some of the most delightfully quirky characters you will ever want to fall in love with."
—Scattered Thoughts and Rogue Words

By JOHN INMAN

Acting Up
Chasing the Swallows
A Hard Winter Rain
Head-on
Hobbled
Jasper's Mountain
Love Wanted
Loving Hector
My Busboy
My Dragon, My Knight
Paulie
Payback
The Poodle Apocalypse
Scrudge & Barley, Inc.
Shy
Spirit
Sunset Lake
Two Pet Dicks

THE BELLADONNA ARMS
Serenading Stanley
Work in Progress
Coming Back
Ben and Shiloh

Published by DREAMSPINNER PRESS
www.dreamspinnerpress.com

Love Wanted

JOHN INMAN

DREAMSPINNER PRESS

Published by
DREAMSPINNER PRESS

5032 Capital Circle SW, Suite 2, PMB# 279, Tallahassee, FL 32305-7886 USA
www.dreamspinnerpress.com

This is a work of fiction. Names, characters, places, and incidents either are the product of author imagination or are used fictitiously, and any resemblance to actual persons, living or dead, business establishments, events, or locales is entirely coincidental.

Love Wanted
© 2017 John Inman.

Cover Art
© 2017 Maria Fanning.
Cover content is for illustrative purposes only and any person depicted on the cover is a model.

All rights reserved. This book is licensed to the original purchaser only. Duplication or distribution via any means is illegal and a violation of international copyright law, subject to criminal prosecution and upon conviction, fines, and/or imprisonment. Any eBook format cannot be legally loaned or given to others. No part of this book may be reproduced or transmitted in any form or by any means, electronic or mechanical, including photocopying, recording, or by any information storage and retrieval system, without the written permission of the Publisher, except where permitted by law. To request permission and all other inquiries, contact Dreamspinner Press, 5032 Capital Circle SW, Suite 2, PMB# 279, Tallahassee, FL 32305-7886, USA, or www.dreamspinnerpress.com.

ISBN: 978-1-63533-471-5
Digital ISBN: 978-1-63533-472-2
Library of Congress Control Number: 2017900363
Published June 2017
v. 1.0

Printed in the United States of America
∞
This paper meets the requirements of
ANSI/NISO Z39.48-1992 (Permanence of Paper).

Prologue

The mansion is situated on a lonely mountaintop in the high desert outside San Diego, California, just a handful of miles from the US/Mexican border. Piercing a stuccoed exterior, the delving eye of our camera pans inward through burled walnut paneling, up a long winding staircase, past sconces and portraits and diplomas long yellowed with age, until we come to a damask-wallpapered bedroom on the second floor where Roger David Stanhope sits at his desk, staring down at his wizened old hands.

They are arthritic and unsteady, those hands, weak now and speckled with age spots. They had not always been so. He could remember those same hands in his youth. They had been lithe and strong once, firmly fleshed and sprinkled with golden hairs. He had taken them for granted back then as they chopped wood, deftly spanned chords on a piano, stroked a lover's skin.

In his youth, he had enjoyed a passion for carpentry. He remembered the feel of wood on his hands, be it the bark of a living chestnut tree or the smoothly sanded plank of cherrywood he had incorporated into a china cabinet to be proudly displayed in the dining room downstairs.

He had absorbed an entire lifetime through those very fingertips. His hands had not been palsied and hesitant in his youth. They had been skilled and exact, either gentle or strong, depending on the moment. They had not ached in the night or lost their grip holding the lightest of objects or grown numb for hours on end in cooler weather. They had served him well for decades, those hands. He had grown to trust they would be there for him to the end.

Which made their betrayal now all the more annoying.

Even the simple task of unpeeling a stamp and applying it to an envelope was a major undertaking. If it hadn't been so pathetic, he might have laughed at himself. For even at the ripe old age of ninety-three, he still had a few laughs on tap. They were dispersed rarely these days, but they were still there, stored away, ready to toss into the air like confetti at a moment's notice.

Before stuffing the letter inside the envelope, Roger David Stanhope perused it one last time. As he did, one of those hidden laughs, a mere chuckle really, sputtered up from his throat and bounced off the burgundy walls of the suite of rooms he rarely left these days.

His bedroom boasted an antique four-poster bed and other heavy, ornate pieces that had been fixtures in this house for more than a century; more than *two* centuries actually, having been delivered here by Roger's great-great-grandfather following a long sea voyage packed in the hold of a brigantine out of Liverpool. The same seaport would later launch the first and final voyage of the ill-fated *Titanic*. Happily, the brigantine had not suffered the same fate as the doomed ocean liner. The furniture it carried had been antique already when it safely crossed the Atlantic, rounded Cape Horn, and threaded its way through the Straits of Magellan before heading due north to San Diego Bay.

Today, while the brigantine was long gone from the face of the planet, the furniture was still here, and undoubtedly priceless.

But that did not impress the man holding the letter. He had wielded wealth far too long for anything with a high dollar value to hold sway over him now.

Remembering the *Titanic*, however, brought forth his second chuckle of the morning. He *was* the *Titanic* now, he suddenly realized, still a-sea upon his own maiden voyage. His own first and final adventure. He was about to meet his own fucking iceberg, whatever it might turn out to be. But he had a chore to accomplish before he let those metaphorical waves flood over him, inundating his holds, dragging him down into the cold dark depths where he would never be seen again by living eyes.

Well, not a chore, really. It was more of a larkish good deed. Thinking of it now, his old face crinkled into a merry smile that, had he a mirror handy with which to study it, might have brought forth the *third* chuckle of the morning. In that merry smile could be seen glimpses of the handsome young man he had once been. The business tycoon, the explorer, the lover of one man and one man only, who had shared Roger's life for seven decades, but who had slipped beneath his own waves two years earlier.

That parting had not been a sad one. Not really. Jeremy had been ill for several years before the cancer finally took him. He had suffered enough. And as Jeremy himself had said on the very morning that would be his last, eighty-nine years on this incredible planet, most of it spent in the arms of one wonderful man, was more than anyone deserved.

By the time that fateful morning rolled around, Jeremy had become a mere shell of the beautiful, swashbuckling rascal he once was. On that day, he had lain in the same four-poster bed where Roger now slept and taken Roger's hand for the very last time. His final speech came in fits and starts—it was such a torture for him to speak—but he finally wrested the words into existence.

They were words Roger would never forget. Nor would he forget the anguish Jeremy bore to utter them.

"We were lovely together in our time, Rog. Both of us handsome and strong and madly in love. Looking at us now, no one would ever believe how dashing we once were. I can still close my eyes and taste your beautiful young cock. I can still feel the heat of your juices spilling across my tongue. Your strong, sculpted body thrumming beneath my hands. And oh, how you relished me. Do you remember, Rog? Do you remember how well we fit together? How unconditionally we craved and savored each other?"

On that fateful morning, which was to be their last, Roger had squeezed the old hand he cradled. He was lying beside Jeremy in the bed, his head on Jeremy's chest. He lifted his head and pressed his bloodless lips to the throat of the man beneath him.

"I remember, Jeremy. I remember it all. Every day. Every moment. You made my life worth living."

"And you mine," Jeremy had answered, a gentle smile softening his mouth even as he tried to fight back the cough that rarely left him these days. It was in the very midst of that smile that his blue eyes dimmed and the breath slowly leaked from Jeremy's cancer-riddled lungs, leaving him at long last still and lifeless in the bed. His old fingers slowly relaxed in Roger's hair. The house grew silent around them but for the ticking of the Regulator clock in the hall. The bedroom, for the first time in decades, echoed with the beat of one heart instead of two.

Sensing that great silence settle around him, Roger had sadly smiled. It was the same gentle smile that Jeremy now wore in death. Pain free at last, his misery ended. Thank God.

"Good-bye," Roger had whispered softly into the silent air, his words lying listless in the space between the damasked walls. "Until we meet again, my love."

Later the tears would come, but at the moment of their parting, Roger felt only blessed relief to see Jeremy's beloved face calm and untortured by the traitorous body that had held it ransom for so long.

And now, on this morning two long years later, with the house *still* silent about his head, Roger wrenched himself from the memories and stared back down at the letter in his hand, his heart once again jovial, eager to begin this final chapter of his life. This final *escapade*. Hand-printed on the paper was the suggested wording for a help wanted ad. That's what the letter contained. Nothing more, nothing less. It would run in the *San Diego Union-Tribune* the following Sunday if all went as planned.

A simple ad. But not so simple either.

Roger's sweet old smile returned, once again casting youthful shadows over his weathered face as he read the letter one last time before slipping it into the envelope and sealing it shut.

Later, Mrs. Price, the old woman—and friend—who did for him, at least for a few weeks longer, would carry it down to the door and deliver it into the hands of the mailman, who would cart it away, thus setting the wheels of Roger's final adventure in motion.

And oh, what a splendid adventure it would be!

A flurry of hammering in a nearby room told him the technicians were still hard at work installing the cameras. Just a few finishing touches, they had told him, a few tweaks, and the system would be up and running. He had to give the tech guys credit. Not once had they asked the purpose behind installing hidden surveillance cameras in every room of the mansion, nor of the control panel with an array of monitors, which had been mounted in what had once been Roger's massive walk-in closet. Behind the high-tech installation sprang a tangle of fiber-optic cables and cathode-ray tubes, glisteningly new and shooting off to various parts of the mansion, concealed in baseboards and crown moldings. By manipulating a computer mouse, each high-resolution camera could be swiveled left or right, panned out to display an entire room, or pulled in tight for a close-up that filled an entire screen. The room housing the monitors was just off the master bedroom, not six shuffling steps from where Roger now sat in his silk brocade dressing gown with his white shock of hair still ruffled from sleep, surrounded by countless photos of Jeremy and himself, which were hanging on every wall and perched on every shelf.

As he sat, he softly hummed a tuneless song and turned the envelope over and over in his hands. Waiting for Mrs. Price to come and fetch the outgoing mail. Waiting for his final adventure to start.

While he waited, the smile never left his face.

Chapter One

It was an unassuming ad placed deep in the Help Wanted section of the Sunday issue of the *San Diego Union-Tribune*. Larry Walls spotted it while desultorily plodding his way through a breakfast of stale hamburger buns slathered with peanut butter, because he couldn't afford bagels and cream cheese, which would have been his preference. Well, no, actually his preference would have been to drag his ass down to the Denny's on the corner and scarf up a platter of waffles and sausage patties, but waffles and sausage patties cost money. And money was something Larry was a little short of at the moment.

Nothing new there, of course. Larry was always short of money.

Because of that, it was the first two words in the ad that had snagged his attention. Those two words really stood out, especially when glimpsed by someone like Larry Walls, who didn't have fifty dollars in the bank and who still had a week to go before his next paycheck would come along.

The two words, in all caps, were EASY MONEY.

Larry liked the sound of that. Not only did he have less than fifty bucks in the bank, the actual newspaper he was browsing through was stolen from the coin-operated kiosk down the street. Well, not stolen actually. The kiosk was faulty. Every time someone legitimately purchased a paper from it and closed the flap of the kiosk behind them, the next person to come along could open the flap without inserting any coins at all. But it only worked once, at least until the *next* person came along to stuff money into the slot.

This morning Larry had stood on the street corner for less than five minutes before a gentleman strolled up, stuck his two dollars' worth of quarters into the slot, and snagged a paper. Less than five seconds later, Larry moved in and snagged his own paper, free of charge.

So okay, if you wanted to get technical about it, Larry told himself, maybe the paper really was stolen. But hey, was it his fault the *Union-Tribune* people didn't keep their equipment in proper working order? And really, how much of a loss would the newspaper suffer by doling out a free Sunday paper to Larry Walls once a week? It wasn't like he stole a paper every day. Only Sunday. He liked the *New York Times* crossword puzzle, see. And the colored funnies. And sometimes the book reviews. Those things only came out on Sunday. The actual news in the newspaper was of very little interest to Larry. His own life was in too much turmoil for him to worry about what a mess the rest of the world was in.

Larry Walls slathered peanut butter over another stale hamburger bun and tore his eyes from the newspaper long enough to study the eviction notice propped against the saltshaker in front of him. He was behind on his rent. Again. Apparently, this time a simple apology wouldn't be enough to get him off the hook. While his manager liked him, she had also warned him that the owner of the apartment building was far less forgiving than she, and the next time Larry was late forking over the rent, he might very well be evicted.

She was right. And here in front of him was the eviction notice to prove it. He had found it hanging on his front door when he left that morning to run up the street to steal a paper.

Larry tore his eyes from the notice because it made him a little ill to look at it. It wasn't like he wasn't *trying* to pay his bills on time. It's just that the department store where he worked kept cutting his hours. He had tried to find another part-time job to fill the dead time, but when the store continually shifted his hours around as if on a whim, it was almost impossible to hold down a second job.

Weary of thinking about it, Larry tried to push everything from his thoughts, refocusing on the ad instead. And an intriguing ad it was too.

> *EASY MONEY. Wanted! Two gentlemen needed. Live-in. One to cook. One to run the house. Must be single and unattached. Need no references other than a ready smile and a gay, romantic heart. Kindness a must. Need for new beginnings a plus. Hunger for life an absolute necessity. Interviews one week from today at the address below.*

Larry stared at the ad so long his eyes began to ache. What the heck did "gay, romantic heart" mean? Was the hirer actually looking for gay men, or did they simply mean "gay" in the "cheerful, happy-go-lucky" sense? Was this some old man or woman expecting sexual favors along with cooking and a little light housekeeping? Or was the ad legit?

But "live-in"! Now there was a delightful phrase. "Live-in" would mean no rent. And for Larry Walls, no rent at the moment was a very appealing prospect indeed.

At twenty-three, with a mere high school degree and no college courses under his belt, Larry's prospects weren't exactly stellar. This ad could be the break he needed. It could help him get on his feet. It might also be a good way to keep his mind off Daniel, who after a six-month affair had just broken Larry's heart by dumping him for a barista, for Christ's sake. You know you're at the bottom of the slag heap when you've been replaced by a barista. And it wasn't even a barista at Starbucks. It was a barista at some shit-hole coffee shop on the wrong side of town with a B rating in the window and probably mouse turds in the muffins. Jesus.

Larry hadn't even known Daniel had left until he went to get something out of the closet and found all of Daniel's clothing gone. What kind of a lover would leave without saying a word? Or at least chucking something at your head as they stormed out the door?

Larry slumped in his chair, the hamburger bun in his hand forgotten. He closed his eyes and absorbed the silence in the apartment. The lonely, lonely silence. He had loved Daniel. He *had*. He had even been foolish enough to believe Daniel loved him back. At that embarrassing realization, Larry's throat tightened and tears sprang to his eyes. He tried to swallow away the urge to drop his head to the table and bawl like a baby. He was an adult. Adults don't do shit like that. Instead he sat there ignoring the tears streaming down his cheeks and stared out the kitchen window until the need to weep was vanquished.

A book Larry read in sophomore literature class suddenly came to mind. *The Scarlet Letter*. Larry wondered what tattoos cost, because he had just about come to the conclusion that he wanted a big scarlet *A* tattooed on his frigging forehead. Not for adultery, but for abstinence, which was how Larry was pretty sure he wanted to spend the rest of his life. Abstaining. Yes, at the ripe old age of twenty-three, he had already come face-to-face with the fact that being in love *sucked*. And being *hurt* by the people you love sucks even more.

Angry at himself for feeling as miserable as he did, but unable to do anything about it, he stuffed the rest of the hamburger bun in his mouth, thinking that might take his mind off his misery. Which it didn't.

"Fuck it," he said, rebelliously spewing the words out into the silent apartment on a cloud of peanut butter breath in an attempt to ease his pain, not unlike delivering a dose of antivenin to a snakebite. Then he upped the dosage. "Fuck it, fuck it, fuck it."

And with that rather feeble attempt at asserting his authority over life's miseries, he made a vow to himself. Never again would he fall in love. His heart was now off the market. *Forever.*

Larry sniffed up a wad of snot and studied his reflection in the dented, jelly-smeared chrome toaster sitting in front of him. Waiting for another hamburger bun to pop out, he eyed his red hair, which was in need of a cut and at the moment was sticking up all over the place because he had just crawled out of bed not thirty minutes ago. That was just before he stole a paper and returned home to find an eviction notice thumbtacked to his door. His blue eyes, warped in the chrome as if in a funhouse mirror, were bright enough. And since he wasn't wearing a shirt, or anything else for that matter, his bare shoulders were also reflected rather fetchingly in the toaster. He looked handsome enough to still reap some attention in the gay bars he occasionally frequented, when he could afford it. He supposed he wouldn't be frequenting them anymore, however, since abstinence was the game plan from here on out, or so he had resolved less than five seconds earlier.

He was sitting at the kitchen table naked, see, because once he returned home with the stolen newspaper in one hand and tore the eviction notice off the door with the other, and after coming to terms yet again with the fact that his lover had dumped him without even having the decency to say *good-bye*, for God's sake, he felt so hemmed in by the restraints of his miserable existence that he couldn't stand any *further* restrictions, not even *clothes*. They were currently scattered across the kitchen floor where he'd flung them in a fit of pique, which he had been throwing a lot of lately, now that he thought about it, which was *another* reason to abstain from men forever.

At that moment, the awaited hamburger bun popped out of the toaster. Larry smeared it with peanut butter and lazily gnawed away at it as he turned back to the ad.

The address in the ad was unfamiliar to him. He reached over and dragged his secondhand laptop off the counter. After punching a few keys and waiting for it to boot up, he was finally able to log in to Google Maps and see where the job interview was taking place.

Holy cow! It was way the heck out in the middle of nowhere, up on a mountainside south of the city. He ran his cursor over the little yellow man waiting patiently at the corner of the Google Map page and walked him up to the address displayed.

The screen opened up and there it was. A mansion! Larry leaned in closer. It really was. An honest-to-God mansion. With brick and brown-stuccoed walls and a confusing patchwork of gables and sloping adobe-tiled roofs and tall leaded windows. Flagstone chimneys poked up here and there off the roof, denoting, Larry assumed, fireplaces scattered throughout the edifice, and all of it surrounded by desert landscaping, with boulders and cactus and a gravelly macadam driveway leading to the house from the county road half a mile away.

To the left of the secluded mansion stood a greenhouse, with glass walls and a glass roof, it too tucked in among the boulders and cactus. The greenhouse stood in the shadow of the main house, like a poor relation cowering behind the skirts of a formidable old aunt. No glimpse of blossoms sprinkled colors behind the transparent greenhouse walls. The building stood empty, bereft of life and care and flora. Its glass panes, especially those on the roof, were yellowed with grime, as if a good rain had not swept them clean for many a long year. The glass structure appeared forlorn. Neglected. Sad.

Larry walked the little yellow man across the computer screen to see if he could catch a glimpse of what lay behind the mansion, but the little yellow man refused to go that far.

Since Larry was no five-star chef—his breakfast of hamburger buns and peanut butter was a good indication of that—he had to figure he would be applying for the caretaking part of the ad, not the cooking part. Judging by the mansion he could see on the computer screen, if he should turn out to be the only caretaker on the premises, he would have his hands full. Keeping the windows clean alone might well prove to be a lifelong vocation.

But surely there would be other servants around. Maids, maybe. Butlers. That would be interesting, Larry decided. He had never seen a real butler in his life, only the ones on *Downton Abbey* and *Upstairs, Downstairs*. He wasn't sure how well he would fit in with the snootiness of a household boasting butlers, but for free rent he was certainly willing to take a stab at it. And Larry wasn't afraid of a little work. He never had been. He could work like a pile driver when he set his mind to it.

He turned away from the computer screen and perused the ad one more time. While he studied the newsprint, he tried to decide what to wear for the interview, which more than anything told him he wasn't waffling anymore. He had decided to go for it.

The thought of waffling reminded him of the waffles he couldn't afford. With a sigh, because he still missed his lover who was most certainly never coming back, and since he was still as naked as a jaybird because he hadn't yet dressed to go to the job he hated at the department store, Larry slathered the very last glob of peanut butter in the jar over the very last goddamn hamburger bun and chewed it to a pulp.

While he chewed, he decided he'd wear his one and only suit to the interview.

At least in a suit he wouldn't *look* homeless, and homeless was what he'd be in exactly—craning his head, he checked the calendar on the wall—fifteen days.

Things were suddenly fairly desperate here, he realized. Perhaps he should even squander a portion of his last fifty dollars to spring for dry-cleaning the suit.

Oh God. How could his life so suddenly have gone spinning out of control like this?

Larry Walls closed his eyes, trying to shut out the day ahead, but it didn't work. When he opened them, the day was still there, waiting for him like a spider.

Resigned, he slouched off to the bathroom to shower and dress for work.

BO LANSING, at twenty-four, was a short-order cook at the 32nd Street Naval Station just south of downtown San Diego, where the Navy parked its ships. He was also a part-time student at the School of Haute Cuisine, located in Del Mar, just up the coast. He was attending classes at the school, because one day he hoped to rise above the funkiness of slaving away as a short-order cook to a bunch of sailors who would eat *anything* and enter the exalted realm of honest-to-God chefdom, where he could don a spiffy white toque and prepare delightful meals for people with discriminating tastes, and where he wouldn't be paid minimum fucking wage or get splattered with bacon grease and insults all day long.

Bo (which was actually short for Bobby, which was short for Robert—as he was fond of telling people) stood six feet tall, was as slim as an eel, graceful on his feet, and had the face of an angel, or so his mother always told anyone who would listen. He wore his dark hair buzzed down to nothing so it wouldn't fall in the food he prepared; that's how committed he was to becoming a chef.

Bo's eyes were green. The sort of green you see when the morning sun x-rays a fresh new leaf. Bo's green eyes were surrounded by long black lashes that any woman in the world would happily kill to call her own. In fact, Bo was such a handsome young man, not many women would be reluctant to call the entire *package*, from the crown of Bo's well-shaped buzz-cut head to the soles of his size twelve feet, her very own. Of course those women would be in for a rude awakening if they ever tried to bed him. Bo was not attracted to women. Bo was gay. And Bo didn't care who knew it. He was currently between lovers and apt to stay that way awhile because Bo was tired of being taken advantage of in affairs of the heart.

His last lover, Arturo, had moved out of Bo's apartment less than a month earlier. Well, he hadn't just *moved* out. He had been thrown out on his ear after Bo came home from school one evening to find Arturo with his tongue buried in the ass of a pizza delivery guy from Domino's. It wasn't the cheating that bothered Bo as much as the fact that there were anchovies on the pizza. At least that's what Bo told Arturo as he was tossing him, along with the delivery guy, through the door.

On this particular Sunday, of course, Bo was simply trying to concentrate on work. Or at least he was until the moment his cell phone rang. Bo laid his spatula aside, keeping one eye on the twenty-seven hamburgers he had sizzling on the grill and the two baskets of french fries he had crisping in the deep-fat fryer. He fished his cell phone out of his pocket while trying to ignore the long line of Navy uniforms standing in front of the counter, trays in hand, waiting for their lunch orders to be doled out and looking impatient at the short-order cook who seemed to think it was perfectly all right for him to bring the production line to a screeching halt while he answered his fucking phone. ("Fucking" was the only adjective sailors ever used, although oftentimes it was modified to a higher precision by sticking "Mother" in front of it. Bo had learned this, if little else, in his months of flipping hamburgers for the fleet.)

Bo checked the readout on his cheap Verizon flip phone and saw it was a fellow student of his at the School of Haute Cuisine. The fellow student's name was Bruce Something-or-Other.

"Make it fast, Bruce," Bo barked into the phone. "It's lunchtime. The swabbies are restless."

Bruce made it fast. "They've barricaded the doors and absconded with our tuitions."

Bo blinked back a bead of sweat that chose that moment to dribble down his forehead. "What? The school? The rumors were true?"

"Afraid so. And according to Mr. Turner, the sous-chef instructor, who has a really big dick by the way, they aren't returning anyone's tuition."

"How do you know he has a big dick?"

"I was sucking it after sauces class when he told me the school had gone belly-up, not unlike the position he was in at the moment he told me. There's more than one way to make a white sauce."

"Crap."

"Crap that I sucked Mr. Turner's dick before you got to it, or crap the school has gone belly-up?"

"Crap the school has gone belly-up. I don't care about Mr. Turner's dick. I'm not a slut."

"Ouch. That hurt."

Bo sighed. "What am I going to do?"

"What you're going to do," Bruce said, lowering his voice conspiratorially, "is check this morning's paper and answer the ad at the bottom of page twenty-six in the Classified section."

"Why would I want to do that?"

"Just trust me. Check the ad. And don't worry. I won't be there trying to snag the job out from under you. I'm moving to Iceland with Mr. Turner. He has a teaching position opening up in a cooking school there. Apparently he liked the way I sucked his dick so much, he's asked me to join him."

"But you only sucked his dick once!"

"Well, no. Sorry, Bo. I've kept it a secret from you, but Mr. Turner and I have been fooling around for weeks. Once between classes he even fucked me on a crate of frozen chipped beef in the walk-in freezer."

"That couldn't have been comfortable."

"Tell me about it. Gives a whole new meaning to the phrase 'shit on a shingle.'"

"Classy. And you still call him Mr. Turner?"

"Well, no. I call him Jack when no one else is around. Or pooty-pie. Anyway, the whole frozen chipped beef episode might prove to be fortuitous in that Iceland is so damn cold in the winter. I've sort of been broken in, temperaturewise, don't you know, fucking inside the walk-in freezer and all. Anyway, Bo, check out the ad. I think it's right up your alley."

One of the sailors standing in line cleared his throat. Another one coughed. A couple of others farther down the line began to grumble. On the tail end of a mumbled string of cuss words, the very first guy in line groused, "Hey, Beanpole, how about getting back to motherfucking work!"

Note the adjective.

While "fucking this and motherfucking that" didn't bother Bo, Beanpole was an insult he had heard before and one he didn't much appreciate, especially when it came from a pimply-faced Seaman Apprentice who probably made less money than the cook frying his cheeseburger.

"I gotta run, Bruce. Thanks for the heads-up. Have fun in Iceland. Don't get frostbite."

"I love him, you know," Bruce said. "Turner, I mean."

Bo grunted. "I should hope so if you're following him to Iceland." With that, he stuffed the phone in his pocket and started flipping burgers with a scowl.

Crap. Crap, crap, crap, crap, crap. He'd just lost eight thousand dollars in prepaid tuition. He'd be flipping burgers for the rest of his life if he didn't decide to end it all by hurling himself into the deep-fat fryer first.

But suicide wouldn't help. It was merely trading one level of screwed for another.

So he turned to the first sailor in line—the one who'd called him Beanpole—and forcefully molded a smile on his face, which at the moment was about as pliable as aluminum siding.

"Let's see now. You ordered a fucking double cheeseburger with fucking extra cheese and a motherfucking dill pickle. You want fries with that, numbnuts?"

MRS. PRICE had worked for Roger David Stanhope and Jeremy Miles Winston for almost thirty years. Upon Jeremy's death two years previous, she had politely suggested Roger give up the mansion and take up residence in one of the more exclusive assisted-living establishments peppered around the city. Roger had refused.

While still twenty years younger than Roger, Mrs. Price could not deny she now had her own old age to worry about, and her old age was not being as kind to her as Roger's was. Nor had it taken as long to arrive. While her arthritis became more worrisome with every passing winter, and with her husband gone these past twelve years and no longer sharing the workload, Mrs. Price had still managed to center her every waking moment on caring for her employer. She had seen him through the death of his partner, Jeremy, whom Mrs. Price had also loved as a friend, just as she did Roger.

But now, after thirty years of service, and with no children or grandchildren to brighten her declining years, Mrs. Price no longer had the strength to carry on. She was willing to try, since she had lived in the mountaintop mansion for the past three decades and considered it home, but Roger was not blind to the fact she could no longer attend to her duties as she once had, or maneuver the many staircases scattered about the mansion.

Loving the old woman like a sister, Roger finally came to the inescapable conclusion that he could not watch her struggle any longer. A month earlier, he had pressed into her hand a check for $200,000. That, along with the money she had saved during the past thirty years—three long decades during which she never once had to buy groceries or pay rent—left the woman damn near a millionaire in her own right.

Content she would want for nothing in her old age, Roger began to arrange for his loyal servant's retirement, and Mrs. Price didn't argue.

On this sunny spring morning, with an indeterminate period of employment remaining to her, Mrs. Price served her employer and friend chamomile tea and sugar cookies on the widow's walk atop the mansion's roof. The long spiral staircase leading up to the widow's walk had been augmented years earlier with a clattering elevator consisting of brass grates, accordion doors, and hazy mirrored walls. Without the elevator, neither of them would have been able to access the widow's walk at all. Or take in the endless view. Nor would they have been able to enjoy the healing sunshine while lolling about in chaise lounges, scarfing up cookies and sipping tea.

It was by long habit that Roger insisted Mrs. Price join him there. Together they would sit with their feet up, breathe in the clean mountain air, and chat back and forth like the old friends they were. Roger's pug dogs, Leo and Max, who in dog years were older than Roger himself, would sit snuffling at their feet, snatching up the occasional cookie fragment tossed their way and being congenial about it—as they always were.

This particular day was a bright one, the view down the mountainside endless and unobstructed by fog or mist as so often happened during the winter months. There was the sweetly bitter scent of sage on the easterly breeze that tickled Roger's old nose and made Mrs. Price sneeze now and then, foretelling the hay fever attacks that were bound to come later when spring truly set in.

"We're well into March," Roger said through a sad, commiserative pout. "Your allergies should be kicking in any minute now. No doubt you'll be bedbound before the week is over."

Mrs. Price nodded, pulled a silk hanky from the sleeve of her blouse, and patted her nose. The handkerchief had a red *P* embroidered in the corner, a gift from Roger and Jeremy on some long-lost Christmas morning so many years past that the handkerchief was now as flimsy as rice paper. Still, it was as well-loved by its owner as it was the day it was given. Mrs. Price was an appreciative soul who never forgot a kindness. She was also Irish, which meant she never forgot a slight either.

"Perhaps I can forgo the allergies this year," she said—rather plaintively, Roger thought. "Hopefully, I'll be long gone from here by the time the pollen gets heavy. I'll miss it, you know. Not the allergies, but the mountain. It's been a lovely thirty years living up here with you and Jeremy and my poor Tom. I truly will miss this house."

"And I'll miss your sugar cookies," Roger said, nibbling at one as he spoke. "And your pot roast. And the way you always hum when you ladle the soup." He reached out and patted her hand. "Most of all, my dear, I'll miss our chats."

She blushed, and then her old face turned pensive. "I wish you luck with my replacements. When are the interviews again?"

"Tomorrow," he said, gazing slyly over his glasses. "As if you'd forget. We have fifty-three applicants who have phoned in answer to the ad. Heaven knows how many more will show up who haven't called to confirm. As you know, all will be vying for only two positions. Housekeeper and cook. I'm sure we'll find a pair capable of doing what you've been doing alone since your husband died. But don't worry. I assure you I will not be suffering through my declining years, neglected and starved and covered with ants."

"Nor will I," Mrs. Price said with a grin, nibbling her own cookie after first dunking it in her tea. "You've left me a rich woman. I'll be hard-pressed to beat off the gold-digging old codgers at Frederica Manor."

"Where someone will be serving *you* tea. Won't that be nice?"

"It will indeed."

At that they both laughed. When they did, the pugs lying at their feet laughed as well, or at least their little tawny tails beat a happy drumbeat on the floor, which was about as close to laughter as they could come.

As the sound of house finches singing in the rafters replaced the sound of the two old friends laughing, Mrs. Price reached out and stroked Roger's hand.

"Do you still miss him?" she asked gently.

Roger looked honestly surprised by the question. He knew who she was talking about, of course. They spoke of him frequently. "No," he said. "Not really." He tilted his head back to study one lonely cloud, lazily scudding across the sky as if it had somewhere to go on this fine March morning but wasn't in any particular hurry to get there. At the same time, he flexed his bent, arthritic fingers, easing the pain in his ninety-three-year-old joints. "He'll be with me to the end, I think."

She nodded, understanding as perhaps only an older person can. "Just as it should be. You were barely ever parted in life. Why should death be any different?"

A gentle gust of wind lifted Roger's white hair off his forehead. A crinkle of merriment lit his eyes. "Why indeed?"

For a moment, he stared out over the mountain he loved so dearly. Then he continued, "No offense intended, Mrs. Price, but it will be nice, I think, to have some young blood roaming through the house. My two new employees may not do things the way you did, but just the same I feel confident the work will be done to your exacting standards."

"I'm sure it will. And the other part of your scheme? Do you intend to go through with that as well?"

Roger snatched up two more cookies before turning to Mrs. Price with an astonished expression on his withered old face. His wily smile spread so wide and the happy trenches around his eyes grew so deep that Mrs. Price had to swallow a joyful snort.

"My dear Mrs. Price," Roger said, innocent-eyed and jokingly appalled. "The other part of my scheme, as you so artlessly put it, is what makes the entire enterprise worthwhile. Why on earth would I *not* go through with it? I have no family, and I don't want to leave my fortune to some corporate entity that passes itself off as a charity, where the lion's share of my money will find its way into the pockets of a bloodsucking pack of lawyers. I'd rather the money bring happiness to just two people. Two kind, loving, committed people. Of my own choosing."

She clucked her tongue. "It may not be as easy as you think."

"What?" he asked. "Love? Love is the easiest thing in the world."

She gave a noncommittal shrug. "It's easy enough to land yourself in, I suppose. A little more difficult to inflict on someone else. Or make it stick."

At that, he did laugh. Loud and long. He laughed so hard he slopped tea in his lap and dropped a cookie. The cookie survived the fall, but it didn't survive the two pugs, who pounced on it the moment it hit the floor. As amused by the dogs as he was by Mrs. Price's concerns, he wiped happy tears from his cheeks. "Love is never an infliction, my dear. It is a blessing. And all I intend to do is help the blessing along. Tweak its progress a bit. Steer it in the right direction and give it a nice soft place to land when it falls. Maybe give it an encouraging nudge now and then as well. It only takes the proper flint and a little fuel to make a roaring fire, you know."

"And you've taken it upon yourself to personally handpick the flint and fuel."

"And create the spark. Yes, I have."

"Hopefully you won't burn the house down."

He barked out a laugh. "Yes. Hopefully I won't."

Mrs. Price eyed him askance, but not without amusement. "You're a sneaky old man."

"Thank you," he said, his expression victorious. "Here. Have another cookie. They're delicious."

"Of course they are. I baked them myself." She took the cookie anyway.

"I'll miss these, you know. I'll miss your snickerdoodles too."

Mrs. Price nodded. "I thought you might. I'll leave the recipe behind."

"Bless you. But they still won't be the same."

Mrs. Price lifted her chin and scanned the sky. Smug. "I know."

In the distance, they both heard hammering. The workmen were still hard at it.

"The cameras you're having installed are creepy."

"Don't be silly. They are a necessity. Nothing more. I need to see how my plan is progressing. I can't leave everything to chance, you know. I have to monitor the situation. Even love needs proper nourishing and oversight for it to bloom to its full capacity. Sort of like the orchids that used to grow in the old greenhouse at the side of the house. Remember? Jeremy loved them so. And he knew how to nurture them. As soon as Jeremy died, so did the orchids. A damned pity that was."

"Your new employees may not like being thought of as hothouse orchids."

"They'll never know, will they? And I'll be discreet. I promise."

She chuckled and shook her head. "Like I said, you're a sneaky old man."

He gazed at her with twinkling eyes, as if appreciating a compliment. "Thank you," he said. "I do my best."

A voiceless camaraderie settled over the two. It was a comforting silence bred of respect, affection, and long, long friendship. And yes, even love.

Mrs. Price broke the quiet with the very question Roger knew she would use for that purpose.

"Have you seen Jeremy lately?" she asked.

Roger smiled. "No. But he's around. One of the workmen has misplaced three screwdrivers and an electric drill."

Mrs. Price's face lit up like Fourth of July fireworks. Her eyes sparkled. She slapped her knobby old knee as a merry trill erupted. "Jeremy always did like his pranks."

They shared a look, then another spate of laughter. Roger's face twisted into a jolly mass of wrinkles like a gleeful sponge. "Yes, and he still does." After a moment, he added, "You know, I've always wanted an electric drill."

And at that they laughed all the harder.

Chapter Two

THE SUIT still fit. Larry Walls hadn't worn it since his mother married her old high school sweetheart after the death of Larry's dad four years earlier. The two seemed happy together, by all accounts, and for that Larry was grateful. Unfortunately, after the wedding the new hubby had dragged Larry's mom off to New Hampshire to live, and that made it a little difficult for Larry to approach his mom now about a loan to see him through the rough patch he was currently experiencing. Not that he would have asked her anyway. He might be poor and on the verge of being homeless, but Larry still had a little pride left. As he drove, Larry snatched up the ad from the seat beside him. The ad had run a week ago today. He had stared at the torn-out sliver of newsprint so often during the ensuing days, the inked words were smeared fuzzy and the paper was limp. EASY MONEY, the ad still read. Larry certainly hoped so. Especially since his car's engine was performing a new medley of disconcerting noises, he was a week closer to being evicted from his apartment, and his hours at the department store had just been cut *again*.

Larry wasn't a praying man, but he was seriously considering becoming one.

He tugged at his tie. Looking down at himself, he brushed an imaginary speck of lint from his jacket sleeve. With that out of the way, he leaned forward, squinting through the dirty windshield, trying to figure out just where the hell he was.

Larry was born and raised in San Diego, but he had never been on this lonely mountain road in his life, not even during the years of his adolescence when he'd steered his first car, a battered old '55 Chevy Bel Air, through every back alley and potholed gravel road the county of San Diego had to offer on endless nighttime excursions with his old buddy Hutch riding shotgun. Hutch, his best friend from elementary school on, had been even more of a loser than Larry—fat, lazy, and the funniest guy Larry had ever met, before or since. After a decade of friendship, Hutch had dumped Larry like a hot potato the first time he got wind that Larry just might conceivably be gay. That was about the same time Larry got wind of the fact himself, which pretty much showed what a loyal friend the fucker really was and how mind-bogglingly dense Larry could be. Most of Larry's homosexual acquaintances had known they were gay in grade school. Larry didn't figure it out until he was seventeen.

Hutch couldn't help Larry now anyway. Undoubtedly, he was even poorer than Larry at this point in his life. Poorer and uglier and still, no doubt, a homophobic dickwad. Served him right.

Larry chuckled, but his chuckle died quickly enough when his desperate straits came flooding back in to overwhelm him yet again, leaving him not only dismayed, but damn near breathless with dread.

Nor did his mood improve when he spotted his destination looming up ahead at a distance. The secluded mansion where his fate would be decided was just as stately and regal as it had appeared on Google Maps. Only now it was all but encircled by dozens of automobiles parked helter-skelter across the grounds and down the lane leading up to the property.

Automobiles driven, or so Larry assumed, by people answering the same ad as himself.

Larry's heart sank at the thought. It sank a little farther when he saw the caliber of applicants strolling up the driveway, heading for the portico in front of the venerable old mansion's front doors where everyone seemed to be congregating. They were all men, of course, for that was what the ad had stipulated. But Larry must have missed the memo stating the applicants should also be gorgeous. For most of them certainly were. As if that wasn't bad enough, most were also dressed far more casually—and far more stylishly—than Larry. He didn't see one suit in the crowd. Not one. He didn't see many cars as beat up as his either. And unless he was mistaken, his old Volkswagen Golf was the only one coughing up a steady stream of black smoke.

He parked behind a spiffy red Mazda Miata convertible, which somehow managed to piss him off just looking at it. Heaven knows which of the handsome young men converging on the mansion's front steps it belonged to.

Larry's inborn inferiority complex kicked in like gangbusters, and he suddenly had a better understanding as to why Daniel dumped him for a third-rate barista working in a fifth-rate coffee shop with a B rating posted in the window.

He sighed as he turned off the ignition, letting the car shimmy and rattle its way to silence around him. He climbed out, purposely avoiding the eye of a fellow applicant who at that moment strutted past in the latest Karl Lagerfeld creation like he was parading down a catwalk in Milan. Nice ass, though. It was a good thing Larry had sworn off men or he might be tempted to do a little window-shopping. Pushing all sexual thoughts aside, Larry waved the exhaust fumes out of his face, brushed a few more imaginary specks of lint from his suit, and headed toward the crowd of applicants gathering up ahead.

Someone eased alongside him and started talking, startling Larry so that he tripped over his own feet. He was spared the indignity of falling flat on his face by a strong hand that came out of nowhere and grabbed his arm, keeping him upright.

"Easy there," the stranger said. "I didn't mean to scare you." The stranger was not quite smiling.

Larry turned to study the guy. He was handsome and appeared to be about the same age as Larry. Tall, black-haired, green-eyed. Dressed casually like all the other applicants, he wore white slacks and a skintight black tee. A leather satchel hung draped over one shoulder and dangled down his back. A tiny loop of silver adorned one ear lobe. The guy might be thin, but judging by the bulges underneath the T-shirt, all of which were in exactly the right place, Larry figured he was also a gym rat. He was certainly built like one. A dangly bracelet comprised of small beads in rainbow colors encircled his left wrist. He was obviously not afraid to flaunt his gayness, which Larry admired. Of course, he was admiring other aspects of the man too. No sense denying it. If he and Larry had been standing in a bar on a Saturday night and Larry had had several shots of Southern Comfort coursing through his system, he would have been all over the guy like a quart of marinara sauce on a slab of lasagna.

As it was, the gorgeous hunk just made Larry feel more out of place than he already did.

"Hi," Larry managed to say, as if conversational budget restraints prohibited him from wasting any more words than one.

The stranger grinned. "You look nice," he said. "I should have worn a suit too."

Larry groaned. "I look like a turd on a tray of hors d'oeuvres."

The stranger threw his head back and laughed. "No, my friend. You look like the one and only applicant who cared enough to really put his best foot forward."

"I do?"

"Yes. But that's not the only reason I'm talking to you."

"No?" Larry asked, leery. "What's the other reason?"

"I just wanted to tell you to dump some STP in your gas tank. It'll make that beast you're driving smoke a little less, and it might even extend its longevity past next week."

Larry twisted his head around and gazed back at his crappy car. It still had a bilious layer of exhaust fumes hovering over it like swamp gas. "That bad, huh?"

"'Fraid so."

"Are you a mechanic?"

"No. I'm a chef. Well, no I'm not. Not really. I'm just a short-order cook who *wants* to be a chef, but I know a little about cars. My name's Bo. It's nice to meet you."

He stuck out a hand, and it took Larry a couple of heartbeats before he pulled his head out of his ass and shook the offered paw. It was also the moment he actually looked at the stranger again and spotted (for the second time) how handsome he was. Just Larry's type in fact, which under the circumstances, what with him swearing off men for the rest of his life and being on the brink of homelessness, was a rather pointless epiphany.

Shuttling the cruising, horny part of his brain into a back locker out of the way where it couldn't cause any further damage, Larry asked, "So is that Beau as in Beauregard?"

His new acquaintance blushed, which Larry found immensely appealing. "No, thank God. It's Bo. B-O. Short for Bobby, short for Robert. Lansing. Bo Lansing. That's your cue to cough up state secrets and tell me your name. I mean, if you want to. I realize we're sort of competing with each other here for the same job, which theoretically, in a shallower world, would make us enemies."

With an immense rush of relief, Larry realized that statement was incorrect. "Actually," he said, "I'm not *that* shallow. And we're *not* applying for the same job, since you must be applying for the chef's position. I'm not. Hell, I live on burned toast and TV dinners. I'm applying for the flunky position. You know, cleaning house and scrubbing toilets and being an all-around live-in gofer and wastrel, just like it said in the paper."

"Except for the live-in part, your ad must have read differently than mine."

"I'm paraphrasing." He stuck out his hand. Better late than never. "Larry. Larry Walls. It's nice to meet you."

Larry was pleased to see a very fetching smile spread across Bo Lansing's face, displaying a row of small white teeth and the tip of a merry tongue, which came out to lick the smile as if it needed lubricating. A similar smile spread his own mouth wide, which took him by surprise since he was so damn nervous about the interview.

"If I get this job," Larry said, "I'll try the STP. If I don't get this job, I'll just have to keep muddying up the environment with a miasma of tailpipe farts and continue to create more work for the EPA until my car explodes into a puffball of fairy dust."

"Fair enough," Bo said around a grin, and thinking they had probably held hands long enough, he released Larry's fist, and the moment he did, both men turned their attention to the mansion up ahead and the mob of beautiful young men still gathering in front of it.

"All these applicants must have done their research," Bo commented.

Larry gazed at him with a quizzical expression. "Huh?"

Bo pointed here and there at various eager hunks, each and every one looking hopeful and anxious. "These guys obviously googled the owner of this joint, and the minute they did, they started hearing greedy little wedding bells. You can see it in their eyes."

Larry was surprised he hadn't thought of researching the man himself. "Why? Who lives here? Who is it exactly who's advertising for help?"

"Roger David Stanhope. Well-known mega-multi-manytimesover-monstrously-moneyed millionaire, who earned his fortune by inheriting it, then quadrupled said fortune through some rather crafty real estate investments. He lived his life with the same lover for umpteen years until the poor lover died a couple of years back at the ripe old age of eighty-nine. If you read the ad with an agenda in mind, you might take it to mean the elderly gentleman is looking for a young buck to fill his lonely nights. Quite possibly even a second name to add to all the joint checking accounts and trust funds that must be currently up for grabs."

Larry stumbled to a stop. "Really? I didn't read any of that into the ad."

Bo stopped along with him, letting a few other well-dressed applicants with tight asses trail past in front of them. "I didn't read it that way either. I think the old man simply needs help. He's over ninety, after all. How randy can he be? He doesn't need tricks, he needs servants."

Larry gazed around at the others, all looking hopeful and straightening their clothes as they oozed and oiled their way toward the mansion's front steps. "So these guys think they are being auditioned for certain tasks other than cooking and housekeeping."

"That would be a delicate way to put it, but yes. I'm afraid they'll be in for a rude awakening if they are actually hired and suddenly find themselves scrubbing dentures and boiling pabulum and changing adult diapers in their Saks Fifth Avenue slacks and Tommy Hilfiger pullovers with their push-up Andrew Christian underpants fetchingly pooching out their privates for an audience that isn't there."

A sly grin split Larry's mouth. "A rude awakening indeed."

Bo offered up a self-deprecating shrug. "But what the heck do I know. Maybe they're really here looking for gainful employment like we are, but they're doing it with more panache. The bastards. Or maybe the old fart truly is shopping for a twink to liven his lonely nights, in which case I'm out of here."

"Me too," Larry hastened to agree. "Umm, did you say changing adult diapers?"

"A mere splash of whimsy. Hey, look!" Bo said, pointing to an upstairs window. "Someone's watching us."

Larry raised his eyes to follow where Bo was aiming his finger. There, in an arched window on the second floor, framed on the inside by what looked like red velvet drapes with braided gold tiebacks, stood an elderly gentleman with a shock of white hair, staring down at the gathering crowd through a pair of binoculars. Larry had the strangest sensation the old man was staring directly at the two of them.

"Prospective boss?" Larry asked, resisting the urge to run his fingers through his hair to make a neater appearance.

Bo shrugged. "Guess we'll find out soon enough."

Shuffling closer, but still at a distance, they could see the mob of applicants scattered across the mansion's broad front steps. And what a snooty bunch of individuals they were! It looked like snob night at the local gay watering hole, as with heads held high they haughtily ignored each other, standing around primping, tugging at their clothes, clandestinely smelling their breath behind their hands, sucking in their stomachs, trying to look casually unimpressed and failing miserably. As far as Larry could tell, he and Bo were the only two speaking to each other. Or not looking like assholes. Or so he hoped.

At the top of the steps stood closed oaken doors, eight feet high if they were an inch, with smoky windowpanes that prevented any prying eyes from peering inside. Overhead, the portico's roof blocked out the California sun, anointing the applicants with cooling shade. A breeze blew up, carrying the scent of honeysuckle from the surrounding mountaintop.

Jostled now and then by the dozens of souls surging toward the portico, Larry and Bo stood close together, shoulders brushing, still on the driveway under the burning sun, drawing comfort from each other, whether they actually admitted it or not. The other applicants milled about on the steps ahead, feverishly secluding themselves in their own private bubbles, determinedly self-quarantined from the crowd around them.

Larry would have been surprised to learn Bo was silently wishing he had worn a suit to the interview as Larry had. Larry would also have been surprised to learn Bo was just as desperate to acquire a domestic position in this marvelous mansion as he was, and that Bo's prospects in love and business and *life* were in just as big a mess as his own.

Or perhaps, unbeknownst even to them, that was why they had gravitated toward each other to begin with.

People began glancing at their watches. The time had come. An expectant hush fell over the crowd as they waited for the doors to open. A few straggling souls still jogged down the driveway behind them, hurrying to catch up, grateful they weren't too late.

Knowing his future was riding on what was about to happen, Larry nervously tugged at the knot in his tie.

Bo clucked his tongue and reached out to slap Larry's hands away so he could straighten the tie himself. "Leave it alone," he said. "You're making it crooked."

Larry smiled. "Thanks, Mom. Do I look nervous?"

Bo smiled back. "Yes. Do I?"

"Yes."

Both men snickered.

The humor suddenly fell from Larry's face. His eyes grew serious. As did Bo's.

Taking a deep breath and straightening their shoulders, they stepped forward and joined the throng on the shaded steps. Bo, trying to make room in the jostling crowd, climbed one step higher, so that Larry had to lift his face to speak to him.

Looking down, Bo swallowed hard. His eyes were as big as grapefruits. There was no longer any laughter in them. "I gotta tell you, Larry, I really need this job."

"Then I hope you get it," Larry said. "I really do." He was fairly astounded to realize he meant it.

Bo stared down at Larry's fiery red hair and pink-tinted cheeks. The somber countenance. He studied the spray of freckles across Larry's nose and wondered how they would taste against his lips. Then he shook that thought away and buried his gaze in the depths of Larry's worried, azure eyes. Those eyes, blue and bottomless, almost perfectly matched the afternoon sky sprawled across the mountain above their heads.

"Thank you," Bo said, honestly touched by what Larry had said. "I hope you get the other job."

Larry tore his eyes from Bo's face and peered around at the crowd. "The chance of even one of us getting hired is slim. The odds of both of us being chosen would be somewhat akin to winning the lottery. Twice. And then being incinerated by a bolt of lightning while cashing the check."

"By the way," Bo said. "Just so you know. My car's falling apart too. You don't have to be embarrassed by your piece-of-shit Volkswagen Golf."

"Really?"

"Really."

For the first time that day, an absolutely carefree smile lit Larry's face. He turned to the driveway behind them. "I have to see this for myself. Which one's yours?" he asked, craning his neck to see over the crowd.

Bo pointed down the lane behind them to a mid-80s Chevy pickup with a puke-green Earl Scheib paint job, sitting beneath a eucalyptus tree at the edge of the driveway not three cars behind Larry's. Even from this distance, Larry could see a cancerous spread of rust eating away at the truck's rocker panel and a dent the size of a medicine ball gouged into the back fender. It was the same fender that had a sheet of red cellophane duct-taped over a hole where an actual taillight once resided.

Larry laughed. "My God! Your vehicle may actually be *worse* than mine! At least I have taillights."

Bo groaned. "Thanks. That's just what I needed to hear. And by the way, I lied."

"About what?"

"STP won't fix your engine. It'll take an act of God. What you need is one of those big automobile smashers they use in junkyards that makes a suitcase out of a Pontiac. Then you could sell your piece-of-shit Golf for scrap and use the money to buy a Schwinn."

"Hurtful but astute," Larry said, his eyes no longer somber but squinting merrily.

The two men shared a communal chuckle, but the laughter died quickly enough when they heard the tall wooden doors swing open behind them. The humor fell from Larry's face in a heartbeat.

They spun around to see a thin old woman smiling down at the crowd beneath the portico.

"Everyone step inside, please," the old woman said, and a general rush ensued, with most of the applicants trying to squeeze their way through the doors ahead of everyone else. Only Larry and Bo stood back and let the mob flood past ahead of them. When they were the last two applicants standing on the stairs, they at long last allowed the woman to usher them inside.

Bo wasn't sure, but he thought he saw a look of approval on the old woman's face when she studied them filing past dead last. Maybe she appreciated the fact that they hadn't joined the throng in stampeding their way inside, pushing and joggling for position like a bunch of startled cows.

Or, Bo admitted, maybe it was just his imagination. He stepped quickly inside, staying close to Larry, who looked very handsome indeed with his dark suit and red hair and worried expression.

Bo tore his eyes from the back of Larry's head and studied the grand foyer leading into the mansion. One word crossed his mind. *Opulence*.

He gave a tiny jump when the entryway doors slammed shut behind them.

ROGER DAVID Stanhope stood alone at his bedroom window and tried to peer through the binoculars, which wasn't easy. His hands were too unsteady.

A voice—or was it a memory?—whispered in his ear. "A little palsied this morning, aren't you, my love. Here. Lean forward."

So Roger did. He leaned forward and rested the edge of the binoculars against the windowpane, steadying them. His vision became markedly less jittery. "Ah, yes," he said. "Much better."

Cars had begun arriving two hours before the time posted in the ad, and Roger had eyed each and every one of them as they pulled up his long driveway. As their drivers stretched long legs through car doors and made their first hesitant steps toward the house, Roger had eyed them too. It was after the fifteenth or twentieth applicant's arrival that Roger began to suspect these were not young men applying for strictly service positions. Many were obviously seeking far more than a paycheck and a place of employment.

He recalled the words of his ad and smiled. Yes, it did sound rather dodgy, didn't it? Asking for a "gay, romantic heart" and all. Those words should most probably have been left out.

Oh well. Too late now. The ad had run, and these young men had come to answer it. If they had the wrong idea, it was their fault, not his. He coughed up a chuckle or two. Little did they know he truly was seeking a "gay, romantic heart." Two, actually. He simply wasn't seeking them for the reasons they suspected.

It was about this time, after Roger had finally lowered himself into a chair, elbows propped on the windowsill to continue studying the arrivals through his binoculars, that he spotted the rattletrap Volkswagen chugging up the driveway, spewing a horrific cloud of black smoke in its wake.

He gave a reminiscent snort of amusement, recalling his own first car. A butt-ugly Nash, all rounded and bulbous. If he remembered correctly, it looked like a bigass turtle and smoked even worse than the old Volkswagen Golf down on his driveway. Roger stopped chuckling when the driver of the smokemobile stepped out of the car and straightened his suit.

Only then did Roger realize what should have been apparent to him earlier. None of the other applicants had worn a suit and tie. They had all gone for sexy casual. This young man alone, the man driving the environmentally disastrous VW, had been the only one to deem the occasion important enough to don an honest-to-God suit.

Roger liked that. He liked it a lot. He squinted, pressing the binoculars closer to his eyes, still resting them against the windowpane to keep them steady, so as to get a better look at the man in the suit. When he did, he gave a short intake of breath, startled.

The young man's hair was bright red. It caught the sunlight like a burst of flames atop his head. Just like Jeremy's hair! Jeremy had been a redhead too.

Memories flooded through Roger's mind of the first time he'd glimpsed that mop of red hair he would end up loving through the long expanse of his lifetime. And of the man who bore the red hair. The man who would love him back all those many, many years.

When Roger's vision began to blur with emotion—dammit, old people were *always* doing that—he set the binoculars aside and dried his eyes on a handkerchief he plucked from his dressing gown pocket. When his vision was clear, he pressed the binoculars back to his eyes, leaned them against the windowpane again to steady them, and continued his perusal of the young man below.

He witnessed the moment a second applicant approached his young redhead. The second applicant was casually dressed in white slacks and a black T-shirt. A very fit and handsome young man. Trim-hipped, graceful, with buzz-cut dark hair. Taller than the redhead. Stunning. The two made a lovely pair. That fact did not escape Roger's notice one little iota. And while he couldn't hear the words they exchanged, he could see the smiles they wore as they exchanged them. That was another good sign, was it not, that the first moments of their acquaintance should produce such handsome smiles.

A door opened behind him, and Roger turned from the window to see Mrs. Price approaching. She held a blue suit in her arms, freshly pressed, still draped from a hanger. Atop the suit rested a white shirt with the faintest blue pinstripe running through it, also on a hanger, with a selection of three ties to choose from.

Without a word, Roger pointed to the striped red tie in the center. Mrs. Price gave a nod and laid the clothes on the bed. Silently, she left the room with the other two ties in her hand, quietly closing the door behind her.

When she was gone, Roger turned back to the window. The two men were standing face-to-face on the driveway now. The young man in the white slacks and black T-shirt was straightening the redhead's tie. Roger smiled broadly, watching them, enthralled by the way the taller man took control of the redhead's necktie, as if he truly wished for the other man to put his best foot forward in his quest for employment, and coincidentally, pushing his own quest aside in the process. Roger's smile widened when he saw the black-haired fellow playfully slap the redhead's hand away, as if to say, "Let me do it. You'll just mess it up."

Roger sighed. Such a selfless, caring act.

Later, when the two turned away because the black-haired man was pointing at something down the driveway in the direction from which they'd come, it took a moment for Roger to understand what was happening. Then he laughed out loud, realizing the taller man was pointing to the only other piece-of-junk automobile parked along the drive. A rusted old pickup truck, which Roger thought, rather uncharitably, was damned near as old and beat-up as he was. Uncharitably, because in point of fact, the junky heap of a pickup was actually sixty-odd years *younger* than Roger. And wasn't *that* a revolting realization!

Roger's redhead and his new dark-haired friend were commiserating with each other over the fact that they both drove cars most people would be humiliated to be seen in at all, let alone own.

Just like Roger had been ashamed of his old Nash.

It was then that Roger set the binoculars aside. He hummed a tune softly in a fragile baritone, which rumbled up from the depth of his throat remarkably on-key. Slowly and painstakingly, he shrugged out of his dressing gown and pajamas and laboriously donned the blue suit with the white pinstriped shirt and the red tie.

It took a few minutes for his arthritic fingers to conquer a Windsor knot, but when he was finished, he sat at the edge of the bed and slipped into his shoes, grunting a bit when he did.

"We already know who it's going to be, don't we?" he said, rather conversationally considering the fact that he was sitting in an empty room.

The lampshade beside the bed gave a playful jiggle as a pen rolled off the dresser, clattering to the floor.

"Now, now," Roger said softly.

With a sigh that did absolutely nothing to lessen the merry gleam in his eye, Roger heaved himself from the bed, carefully bending to retrieve the pen and place it back on the dresser. He shuffled into the master bath to comb his hair, holding on for dear life to the metal handrails screwed to the wall along the way.

This was turning out to be a most interesting day. A most interesting day indeed.

While he combed his hair, Roger hummed a happier tune than the one before.

With his hair in place, he laid his brush aside and stepped back into the bedroom. Carefully navigating from one piece of furniture to another, always holding on to something in case one of his unexpected dizzy spells should attempt to knock him ass over teakettle, he crossed the room and stepped into what had once been a dressing room.

The cupboards and chifforobes and tall standing mirrors that had graced the room for decades were gone. They had been replaced by a bank of monitors, each displaying on twelve-inch screens a live shot of a different room in the mansion. Roger tucked himself into the rolling chair in front of the monitors, and after studying the controls for a moment, toggled a switch that brought up the monitor displaying the foyer downstairs, where the mob of applicants were now milling around.

As he slid the mouse around on the pad to redirect the camera, he scanned the faces on the screen. Most of the applicants seemed to be trying to ignore all the other applicants. After all, they were standing among a bunch of strangers—fifty souls competing for two positions, which Roger supposed didn't exactly lend one to strike up a friendship with the guy wanting the same job you did.

Roger studied the sea of anxious faces, going from one to the other with little interest. Little interest, that is, until he came to the two young men who had captured his attention out on the driveway. The redhead and his black-haired buddy.

They were still standing side by side. That was good. That was very, very good. A connection had already been made. How interesting.

Once he'd spotted them, Roger fiddled with another dial until the camera zoomed in on the two. He could not hear what they were saying, of course, but he could see them smiling together. He recognized the glint of easy camaraderie lighting their eyes, as if their growing friendship had deepened just in the last few minutes, when they had been out of sight while Roger dressed and combed his hair.

The two young men were now eying the chandelier and laughing.

Wondering what was so funny, Roger panned away and searched among the crowd with the camera's eye until he spotted Mrs. Price standing patiently on the stairs.

When Roger spoke, Mrs. Price laid a finger to her ear. Only then could Roger see the earbud tucked in among her gray curls.

Mrs. Price listened carefully to Roger's words, then lifted her eyes to the newly installed camera near the foyer ceiling, which was all but invisible if you didn't know where to look for it. She continued to listen to Roger's quiet words, then gave an understanding nod.

Dropping her hand from her ear, she gazed down at the crowd at her feet and sifted through the faces until she spotted the two Roger had mentioned. It wasn't difficult. The one young man's fiery red hair stood out like a signal flare.

"I hope you know what you're doing," she mumbled into the almost invisible microphone clipped to her collar.

"So do I," Roger answered through the earbud. There was a smile in his voice when he said it.

Carefully, Mrs. Price gripped the railing and descended the stairs to the waiting crowd below.

BO STOOD in the mob of applicants. Jostled this way and that by the crowd, he placed a hand on Larry's shoulder to brace himself. Larry didn't seem to mind. He was too busy staring about with wide appreciative eyes, just as Bo was.

Bo whispered in Larry's ear. "This looks like the foyer of the von Trapp mansion in *The Sound of Music*. I keep expecting to hear the shriek of a bo'sun's pipe and see a bunch of snobby, overdressed rich kids come thundering down the stairs."

Larry sniffed and happily warbled, "Doe a deer, a female deer."

An immense crystal chandelier hung overhead, lighting the marble floors and brass railings. Twenty feet above that, a massive skylight sprayed sunshine through the chandelier's crystal prisms. A broad staircase climbed upward at one end of the foyer, peeling off to connect to two bordering walkways on either side. Fifteen feet from the main floor, those walkways were lined with brass balustrades. The floors were gleaming white marble, the walls covered in satiny red wallpaper with fleurs-de-lis stenciled into it in what looked like gold leaf but surely wasn't. Mahogany accent tables lined the walls, three to each side. Atop the tables stood sprays of cut flowers, which undoubtedly changed periodically and cost a fortune to maintain. At the moment, the tall porcelain vases were filled with long stems of birds of paradise, their blossoms as yellow as the gold leaf on the walls, accented with great clusters of baby's breath.

Larry didn't care about the flowers. He had his head tilted all the way back, the tendons in his neck stretched tight, studying the chandelier above. In a low voice, he muttered, "How the hell would a person go about cleaning that thing?"

Raising his eyes to follow Larry's stare, Bo shook his head. "Don't ask me. I'm just the cook. Although I suppose you could squirt the dust off with a garden hose."

They grinned as their gazes drifted together.

"I have to pee," Larry said.

Bo grunted. "Sorry I mentioned squirting, then." He pointed to the flowers by the wall. "Use a vase, bro. Nobody'll notice."

They grinned again.

It was then that the old lady who had ushered them through the front doors came out of nowhere and laid a hand to each of their shoulders, making them quickly turn. "Come with me, please," she quietly commanded.

With that, she walked away while a surprised and considerably confused Larry and Bo followed along, staring down at the heels of the old woman's orthopedic shoes as they *thwapp*ed along in front of them.

You could have heard a pin drop as several dozen disgruntled and clearly jealous young men watched the three leave.

"Ooh," Bo whispered in Larry's ear. "We're first."

"Either that, or we're being evicted. They probably saw my car."

A moment later, they stepped through tall doors, which the old woman gracefully swung closed behind them, sealing out the staring crowd. Gazing around, they found themselves in a great ballroom, barren of furniture and music, with mirrored walls and parqueted floors and filigreed carvings adorning the distant ceiling.

"Mr. Stanhope welcomes you to his home," the old lady said. "If you'll step through the door ahead of you, you will find refreshments and a comfortable place where he can join you for a chat. There is a lavatory there as well, if you'd like to refresh yourselves. He'll be along shortly. Thank you, boys."

With that, she left the room.

"Thank God," Larry whispered. "A bathroom."

"Your sense of priorities is somewhat askew," Bo joked, following Larry across the gleaming ballroom floor and ducking through the doorway on the opposite wall as they had been ordered to do.

The room they entered was a massive library, with book-filled shelves lining every wall. Oddly for a library, there was a grand piano gleaming black in the middle of the room, and next to it sat an antique harpsichord. Chintz chairs were scattered about, and two long red leather sofas were parked around a huge flagstone fireplace dug into the wall to their right. On a credenza behind one sofa lay an array of pastries and a coffee urn.

On the floor in front of the fireplace lay two pug dogs. Real ones. They lifted their heads when the two young men entered and came running up to greet them, puffing and gasping and snorting for breath, as pugs are wont to do when they're having a good time and are perhaps a wee bit overweight.

While Larry set off in search of the bathroom, Bo said, "Don't forget to flush," then lowered himself to the floor. He stuck his legs straight out in front of him and allowed the two pugs to crawl into his lap, where they immediately offered up their bellies for a good scratching.

Deciding to go with the flow and try not to think about the fact that this was without a doubt the weirdest job interview he'd ever attended, Bo happily obliged, giving both dogs the belly rub of a lifetime.

When Larry returned, considerably more comfortable now that he'd spent a couple of minutes in the bathroom, he dropped to the floor beside Bo and claimed a dog of his own.

"The bathroom has a bidet," Larry casually mentioned.

"Ooh. Did you use it?"

Larry blushed. "Shut up." But a smile tried to worm its way through anyway.

Bo watched, intrigued, while Larry's face turned red.

"I really do hope you get the job, you know," Bo quietly said.

Larry's blush deepened, but he looked pleased. "Thanks. You too."

Now that they had survived their first embarrassing moment together, thanks to the bidet comment, they settled in with their new four-legged friends and waited for the interview to actually begin.

Little did they know that, for all intents and purposes, it was already over.

Chapter Three

"Yes, Roger, they are *quite* suitable."

"I'm not asking if they are suitable, Mrs. Price. I'm asking if you *like* them."

Mrs. Price eyed her old friend and thought he looked invigorated for the first time in months. Maybe he was right to be infusing the house with new blood. She answered his question with a businesslike nod, but at the same time she reached out and plucked a pale dog hair from his sleeve.

"Yes, Roger. I like them very much." It was true. She did. "Although I fail to see the gay magnetism at play between the two, which you profess to see. But then, I'm not a man with homosexual leanings. I might not recognize gay magnetism even if it rose up and bit me on the leg."

She had slipped away after leading the two applicants into the anteroom. She and Roger were now standing at his monitoring station in what had once been his dressing room, watching the two young men playing with the dogs in the library.

"God forbid gay magnetism should bite you *anywhere*," Roger snickered, with drooping eyelids and a droll gleam in his eye. "Be that as it may, Max and Leo like them just as much as I do." He leaned forward to better scan the monitor through his old eyes. "I guess that makes it unanimous for those who *matter*."

Mrs. Price chose to ignore that. "You have to speak to them, you know. You can't just hire help out of the blue without interviewing them a little. How do you know there aren't romantic entanglements that need to be ironed out? You don't want a bunch of paramours popping by at all hours. It would quite ruin everything. How do you know they are willing to completely relocate and move into the mansion as you wish? Good lord, Roger, how do you really know they are actually *gay*?"

At that last talking point, Roger snorted. "Trust me. They're gay. And they're drawn to each other, as well. I can see it in their stance. Their body language. I can see it in the redhead's eyes."

Mrs. Price sighed. She had dealt with Roger Stanhope for three decades. She knew when she was beaten. "Should I dismiss the others without you speaking to them at all?"

Roger frowned. "Won't *that* piss them off! But yes. Let them go. Thank them for attending and wish them the best. I've chosen. There's no point torturing the losers any longer."

Mrs. Price leaned in beside Roger, eying the monitor over his shoulder. The pugs were going crazy, wiggling around and grunting like pigs while the two young men tickled their tummies. All four creatures were laughing. All four creatures were having the time of their lives. As the men squatted on the parlor floor facing each other while entertaining the dogs, even Mrs. Price noticed the way their knees touched and how they made no pretense at all of avoiding the fact. She also noticed when the black-haired man playfully reached over and tousled the redhead's locks.

"Did you see that?" Roger asked.

Mrs. Price rolled her eyes. "No, Roger, I didn't see anything."

"Yes, you did. Don't play coy with me. What are their names?"

Mrs. Price had received at least that much information from the two as she led them from the foyer earlier. "The tall, black-headed one is Robert Lansing. He goes by Bo. The shorter redheaded man is Larry Walls." She smiled. "I especially like him."

Roger smiled too. "It's the suit, isn't it? *That's* why you like him."

"Yes. It's the suit. If nothing else, it shows he's serious about wanting the job." A beat of silence settled over them before Mrs. Price continued. "Both men are eager for a change in their lives. Both men are in dead-end jobs, unhappy with their financial situations, willing to commit to the enterprise of taking care of an elderly man for whatever time remains of his life."

"Ouch," Roger happily growled. "I'm standing right here, you know. You might have left *that* part out."

Mrs. Price ignored him. "The dark-haired man is applying for the position as cook. He has actually studied to be a chef, but the school recently closed, defrauding him of the money he paid in tuition. A horrible thing to do, in my opinion. The other man with the lovely red hair is applying for the servant's position. He currently works in a low-level retail job at a department store downtown, which means he knows how to interact with people. It doesn't necessarily mean he knows how to cope with a cranky old recluse with too much money, but I suppose he's willing to learn."

"How do you know all this?"

"I grilled them on the way into the ballroom."

"Well, you weren't long about it."

Mrs. Price lifted her chin and narrowed her eyes. "What can I say? I'm efficient."

Roger was hardly listening. He stared raptly at the monitor, a tiny grin playing at the corners of his mouth. "Look how well they get along," he softly said. "Look how well they fit together. Look how my dogs love them."

Mrs. Price *tsk*ed. "Those dogs love everybody. If I laid out tea for Adolf Hitler, Ted Bundy, and Attila the Hun, they'd be acting the very same way." She dragged her glasses down her nose and gazed over the rims at Roger's smiling face. "And why do I feel if I looked up the word 'conniving' in my trusty *Funk & Wagnalls*, I'd see a picture of you on the page staring back at me, sipping Metamucil and looking sneaky."

"Don't be silly. There's not a conniving bone in my body. And as for sneaky, well, that's just ridiculous. I'm not even going to acknowledge the Metamucil remark. There's a cruel streak in you, Mrs. Price. It's really most unbecoming."

At that, the old lady laughed. She didn't even try to hold it back.

After she got hold of herself, she said, businesslike once again, "You still have to speak with them. You can't just hire them out of the blue. We need to run background checks, get credit reports, make sure they aren't serial killers. For all you know, the FBI might be after them for duping little old gay men out of their fortunes." Her eyes turned serious. "Roger, you can't just hire people and move them into your home by looks alone. The formalities must be met."

"Fine," he said. "You take care of the formalities, while I go have a word with your replacements."

Mrs. Price harrumphed. "At least you have the good sense to know it will take two strapping young men to replace me."

"I never doubted it for a minute."

She headed off in one direction, Roger in the other. Behind them, the two young men and the two spoiled pugs played with each other on the screen.

LARRY GAZED around at the room they were in. Everything was spotless and far posher than anything he had ever seen outside of the movies. Some of the books on the shelves looked like first editions.

"I have a feeling we're in over our heads," he said. "Is it just me, or are we a couple of moth-eaten sweaters looking for hanger space among a rack of mink coats?"

Bo laughed. "Have a little respect for yourself! It's the owner of this mansion who sought us out, remember. Not the other way around."

Larry looked doubtful, even while he leaned down and blew a blubbery spout of air into the pug's belly, making the mutt wiggle and gasp like a tickled child. The dog's name was Leo. It was etched on his collar. A split second before the two men heard a door open behind them, the pugs squirmed out of their laps and took off running, tails whapping back and forth, tiny toenails tippy-tapping across the hardwood floor.

Bo and Larry hastily rose to their feet. Bo straightened his shirt while Larry frantically brushed pug hair off his pant legs. Only then did they lift their eyes to greet the man entering the room.

It was the man Larry had seen earlier, staring down at them through binoculars from the upstairs window as they stood on the drive. Up close now, they could see his true age. He did not appear feeble, exactly, although he was obviously old—*very* old. But he did display a certain amount of uneasiness on his feet. He leaned on a wooden cane with the body of a Chinese dragon carved along its length. The dragon's scales were painted a dull ocher, the color far lighter than the darkness of the cane itself, which Larry suspected was teak, polished to a high shine. Where the man gripped the cane with his scrawny old hand, the dragon's head was molded in what looked like bronze—it couldn't be *gold*, could it?—jaws agape as if the beast were feasting on the old man's fingers.

The two pugs bounced around at the old man's feet.

Larry quickly stepped forward and offered his arm to the gentleman, who gratefully took it.

Stepping carefully around the dogs, Larry led him toward a cluster of red leather chairs by the unlit fireplace. The old man lowered himself to a seat and motioned for the two men to join him in the other chairs.

When the three of them were comfortably seated and the pugs had plopped down side by side at his feet, Roger nodded toward the table where the coffee urn and pastries still sat untouched. "Are you sure you wouldn't care for a snack?" he asked. "The cookies were baked this morning, I believe."

Both Bo and Larry demurred.

The old man gave a brief nod and cleared his throat. "My name is Roger David Stanhope. This is my home."

"It's beautiful," Larry said.

"Beautiful," Bo echoed.

Bo and Larry turned their heads to a portrait hanging by the window—a man, perhaps in his forties, with red hair and a gentle smile twisting his mouth. He held a Chihuahua in his arms, the pup's tiny head tucked up under his chin.

"Is that you, sir?" Bo asked. "Is that you in the painting?"

Roger followed to where the men were looking. "No. That handsome creature is the man I spent my life with. His name is Jeremy. We have been lovers for almost seventy years."

Larry stared at the painting. "Wow," he breathed. Contrary to what Bo had told him earlier about the man's lover recently dying, the use of present tense in his comment made Larry ask, "And he's still with you, your lover?"

Roger smiled. "Only in spirit."

"I'm sorry," Bo said, more confused than ever.

At that, the old man happily scoffed. "Don't be. Sometimes a bit of spirit is quite enough."

Neither Bo nor Larry quite knew what to make of that, so they said nothing. The older gentleman got right down to business.

"I like you both. I've decided to hire you, if you are still interested."

Larry's mouth fell open. "What about the other applicants?"

"Mrs. Price is sending them away even as we speak." Roger chuckled lightly. "Surely you can hear them griping about it through the door."

Larry suddenly realized he could. The crowd outside didn't sound happy at all.

"Did you interview them at all?" Bo asked.

"No," Roger said. "Interviews were not necessary. You two were hired before you ever reached the house."

"It was you, wasn't it?" Larry asked, his curiosity overcoming his nervousness. "In the window. Watching us through the binoculars."

Roger laid his cane aside and scooped up the two pugs at his feet to position them in his lap, where they sat quietly, gazing up into his face, as worshipful as two disciples staring at the face of Jesus.

"Yes. I hope you didn't mind. I've always been hasty when it comes to making decisions, as well as in my judgment of people." He glanced at the painting over the fireplace. "I chose Jeremy as my lover over the course of a single night in a dive in Tijuana back in the days when you two were about fifty years short of being so much as a gleam in your fathers' eyes. I hate to dawdle over things." He coughed up a grunt of humor. "Except life, it would seem. I appear to be dawdling the shit out of that, being ninety-three and all."

Larry and Bo blinked at the old man's honesty, too surprised, perhaps, to laugh, although he was obviously cracking a funny.

It was about then that Roger David Stanhope leaned in and drew the two men toward him with a stare.

"I would like you both to work for me. The running of this great house will be a chore for both of you, I believe. I know I advertised for a servant and a cook, but I suspect you will have to help each other out a great deal if you are to be as efficient as the person who held the position before you."

"Mrs. Price?" Bo asked.

"Yes. Mrs. Price. And before he died, her husband as well. But he's been gone for a decade or more, so for the last ten years, Mrs. Price has done most of the work on her own. As far as the heavy cleaning goes, I have day help who come in occasionally to whip the place into shape. Once Mrs. Price retires, it will be only the two of you and myself in residence at all times. I don't like a lot of servants running around disrupting my days. Would that be satisfactory to you both?"

Bo and Larry glanced at each other.

Bo cleared his throat. "And the pay?"

Roger smiled. "Ah, a man with business sense." He pulled a slip of paper from his jacket pocket and handed it over. "The pay is more than sufficient, I believe. See for yourself. You will both receive the same stipend for the services you render. There will be no reason for discontent on that front, and also no chain of command between the two of you. You are equal under the eyes of God and myself. Ha-ha. Kidding. I have no idea how God judges his help, only how I judge my own. You will be friends, I hope. I like camaraderie in my house. The work will be time-consuming, I presume, but not overly strenuous. I want you to be as happy in this house as I am."

Bo eyed the paper, then handed it to Larry, who almost gasped at the figures scrawled down in spidery script, obviously scribbled by the old man himself.

The offered salary was more than generous, and after sharing a glance again, both men said so before handing the paper back. The old man crinkled it into a ball and tossed it into the fireplace.

Jokingly he said, hooking a thumb at the fireplace, "Don't light a fire in there. That piece of paper is the only proof you have of the salary I promised to pay. I'm old. I'm liable to forget and start doling out nickels instead."

Bo grinned. "Oh, I doubt it. I think you're pretty much on the ball."

Roger's old face squinted into a grin as well. "I'm glad you think so, young Bo." He studied each man in turn. "So are we in accord? Is the salary sufficient?"

"It is," both men answered in unison.

"There will be intermediate raises, of course. Cost of living and all that. Although of course you will reside here rent free, as was stipulated in the ad."

"Great." Again, Bo and Larry answered in unison, their synergy pleasing the old man no end.

"And can you both start right away?"

Larry and Bo shared another glance. This time they shared a shrug as well. "We can," they said, turning back.

"Good. If you need funding to buy yourselves out of leases where you currently live, I will supply it. If you have pets, as long as it isn't a rhinoceros or a porcupine or anything that eats pugs, you may bring them along. Leo and Max will throw a fit, of course, but they'll get over it."

"No pets," Larry said.

"Me either," Bo said.

"Do either of you have lovers in this world? Romantic entanglements, as Mrs. Price so delicately put it earlier?"

Both Larry and Bo thought it was an odd thing to ask, but they didn't consider it long. This whole interview was bizarre. One more little bit of weirdness didn't bother them much.

"I don't," Larry said.

"Neither do I," Bo agreed. "Ahem. I get the impression you are assuming we are gay."

"I am indeed," Roger said. "But please don't fear that I will try to take advantage of your good selves because of it. This is strictly a work proposition I'm offering. I wish to be clear about that. My days of diddling the help are long gone, not that I ever did diddle the help. Jeremy would have killed me, you see. Jealous, that one. Woo doggies. And I was just as jealous of him. We were a perfect match."

All three men smiled, one from fond memories and the other two from being charmed out of their socks.

"I wish we could have met him," Larry said, meaning it. Bo nodded in agreement.

The old man gave them a cryptic glance. "Be careful what you wish for."

His new employees wondered what the hell he meant by that, but neither said anything.

Bo looked suddenly anxious, which Roger noticed right away.

"Yes, young man? You have a question. Don't be afraid to ask it. I want everything upfront and aboveboard or our arrangement is never going to work."

Bo fiddled with the crease on his trousers. "Sir. About your health. Will we be expected to—"

Roger chuckled. "Ah, yes. You're afraid you'll be changing colostomy bags and clipping my toenails. Well, do not fear. Colostomy bags are a trial I've yet had to face, and believe it or not, I can clip my own toenails. At least at the present time. My plumbing still works, or most of it, and I'm still reasonably mobile, so neither of us will be suffering the embarrassment of diaper changes." He scrolled his eyes skyward. "Please God, let that forever be the case. If I require a doctor, I have one on call. I also have a nurse on call if the need arises. I despise them both with equal ferocity, but at my age one has to make a few concessions. So no. Health matters will not be in your domain. You may run an occasional bath for me or track down an errant pair of socks, but that's about as personal as things will get." He eyed first Bo, then Larry. "Is that acceptable to you both?"

"Quite acceptable," Bo said.

"Same here." Larry nodded. "Although, I think you should know, I do have first aid training. If anything should—happen—I can be of assistance until the medical experts arrive. I helped care for my father when he was sick with cancer."

The old man's eyes softened. "Your skills may indeed come in handy at some point, although I sincerely hope I won't be putting you through anything too dramatic. Still, thank you for letting me know. Tell me, son, did your father pass away?"

"Yes, sir. After a long fight, but that was several years ago."

"Still, I'm sorry."

For some reason Larry felt himself blushing. "Thank you." He blushed even redder when Bo reached over and patted his shoulder.

The gesture was not lost on Roger. He sat back in his chair, smiled down at Leo, who had crawled from his lap earlier and was now chewing diligently on the toe of his six-hundred-dollar Burberry leather wingtips. Straightening his tie in a businesslike manner, Roger asked, "So are we all in agreement, gentlemen? Would you like to come work for me?"

A moment of silence ensued while the question hung in the air. Then Bo said, "I believe we do, sir."

Larry added, his eyes eager and bright, "More than anything."

"Well, then!" Roger announced, rubbing his hands together as if closing a deal. "Your rooms are on the third floor at the opposite end of the house from mine. The rooms are furnished, of course. In this house you will find everything you need. If you don't find it, let me know, and I will see that it is supplied. If you have belongings or furniture you wish to keep but don't have room for in your rooms, you may store it in either the basement or the attic. This old house has endless storage space."

"Thank you."

Roger smiled first at one, then at the other. "Any questions?"

They shook their heads.

"Mrs. Price will arrange for moving vans or whatever you need. I realize it can't be easy uprooting your lives like this."

"We'll manage," Bo said.

"What about visitors?" Larry asked. "What about days off?"

"No visitors to the house, I'm afraid. Some of my belongings are quite valuable." He nodded toward a sketch over the fireplace of a male nude in a full state of arousal. "That's a self-portrait by Egon Schiele."

"Wow," Bo said. "Nice dick."

"Yes," Roger agreed. "Lovely erection, isn't it? And priceless, to boot. Worth an absolute fortune. There's also a Chaim Soutine in the music room, and in the dining room a Chagall. In the poolroom you'll find a rather marvelous collection of Warhol prints. There are other artworks scattered around as well, including a few pieces of Chinese cloisonné. So no liaisons with anyone from the outside, please. I'm talking about tricks, in case you're wondering. In my day we called them liaisons. Mrs. Price rather quaintly calls them paramours. Anyhoo, as for days off, they will need to be rotated, leaving one of you in attendance, if you don't mind. But we can discuss that over dinner, if you like. I'm getting rather tired."

"Certainly," both men hastily agreed.

"Thank you, boys." Roger eased the pugs aside and stood. Sticking out a hand, he offered a handshake to each of them. "I'm assuming it's a deal, then. Mrs. Price will show you to your rooms and your duties. Just so you know, I spend most of my time in my own wing of the house. It isn't easy being as old as I am. I find it takes a good deal of my time just to hold myself together."

Larry cleared his throat. "Will you ring for us when you need us?"

"Yes, son. And while we will share dinner together this evening, enjoying Mrs. Price's fine cooking, I might add, we will not be dining together often. I'm sure you won't mind. It isn't much fun watching an old fart like me gum a baked potato."

They all three laughed.

"You haven't asked about my cooking," Bo said.

Roger shrugged. "I'm not picky. Although I would appreciate it if you apply your skills to mastering the cookie recipes Mrs. Price will leave in your care. I would hate to approach the remaining days of my life without at least a *replica* of the good woman's snickerdoodles to augment my afternoon tea."

Bo smiled. "I'll do my best."

Roger reached out and patted the young man's cheek. "I know you will. Now if you'll excuse me."

They watched as Roger David Stanhope gathered up his cane, clucked his tongue at the dogs to beckon them to follow, and on his way out the door plucked a fistful of cookies off the table by the sofa.

"Later, gentlemen," he said, and he disappeared through the door.

Larry and Bo both jumped like they'd been poked with a pin when Mrs. Price appeared at their heels and announced, "If you'll follow me, I'll show you to your rooms."

They meekly followed, but inside they were leaping for joy, both men stunned to find their lives suddenly taking this monumental turn for the better.

Larry walked beside Bo. They trailed behind Mrs. Price as she threaded her way through the mansion from room to room and finally led them up a long staircase toward the third floor. Larry couldn't believe it. He honestly couldn't believe it. An hour ago he was on the verge of being homeless. Now, he was safe. He had a roof over his head, and he was about to begin working at the best job he'd ever held in his life. He no longer had to worry about rent every month or having his hours cut, and he was embarking on this new adventure with people he actually liked.

To his own surprise, he found himself fighting against a sob.

Rising tears suddenly burned his eyes, and mortified by the sudden welling of emotions, he sniffed and faltered on the stair.

Mrs. Price glanced back at him. She reached into her dress sleeve, plucked out a tissue, and handed it to him with a gentle "Cry all you like. I won't judge."

"Thank you," Larry said humbly before blowing his nose.

Bo tousled Larry's hair again as Mrs. Price turned away to resume climbing the long staircase before them. She had a tear in her eye as well, while Bo had only wonder on his face. Had he voiced his feelings, however, they would have been the same as Larry's.

He couldn't believe their change in fortunes either. If the truth were known, he wasn't far from shedding a few grateful tears of his own.

Mrs. Price, leading two very happy men and knowing it, glanced at the teeny red eye of the hidden camera hanging over the top of the stairs and smiled.

While she couldn't see it, she imagined Roger smiling back.

"HE SEEMS like a nice guy," Bo said, almost absentmindedly, studying the portraits and original artwork peppering the wall along the side of the climbing staircase. He eyed Larry beside him and saw that he was once again in control of his emotions. He too was eying the artwork as they passed.

"He's a wonderful man," Mrs. Price said, her hand on the rail as she carefully and slowly ascended the steps before them.

Bo was about to say something congenial when his eyes fell once again on Larry. He leaned in for a closer look. "Where's your tie?" he asked.

Larry slapped his hand to his throat and stopped dead in his tracks. Looking down at his own chest, he all but gasped. His necktie was gone!

Mrs. Price turned to watch this little drama unfold. She stared at Larry, then at Bo, then finally rolled her eyes toward the ceiling. "You devil," she muttered around a simpering smirk. "Give it back."

Larry and Bo stared at her as if she had just sprouted a clump of dandelions off the top of her head. Larry was still groping at his throat for the necktie that had somehow disappeared while Bo gazed around with a confused expression on his face like a guy who suddenly realizes he is on the wrong bus and is not quite sure how he got there.

Mrs. Price peered over the side of the balustrade, staring down at the foyer, empty now of all other applicants. There, draped across a bouquet of birds of paradise, hung Larry's tie. It was still neatly knotted as if the neck holding it in place had somehow dissolved, letting it casually slip away.

"Oh, there it is!" Mrs. Price announced gaily. "One of you boys go fetch it, will you? I go up and down these stairs enough in the course of a day. Your young legs will manage it better than mine."

Bo and Larry hung over the railing and stared down.

"Well, I'll b-be," Larry stuttered. He slapped his hand to his throat again. "How in the world do you suppose…?"

"I'll get it," Bo announced grandly and took off down the stairs like a shot. He returned seconds later with a silly glint in his eyes and handed the tie to Larry, who took it as if in a daze.

"Spooks." Bo smiled.

"Spooks indeed," Mrs. Price muttered to herself, and turning, she continued her slow unconcerned climb toward the third floor.

Larry stared at the knotted tie in his hand. It was still looped at the perfect size to fit around his neck. How in the world had it slipped over his head like that? And why the hell hadn't he noticed it when it did? At a loss to explain any of it, Larry stuffed the tie in his trouser pocket to get it out of his sight. While he did indeed enjoy the *New York Times* crossword puzzle every Sunday morning, this was a puzzle he'd rather consider at a much later date. If ever.

Bo took his arm and tugged him upward, both men trailing along behind Mrs. Price again like a couple of puppies. Mrs. Price was humming softly as if nothing untoward had taken place.

Larry patted his trouser pocket to make sure the tie was still there. Then he peered down over the side of the staircase again. He hadn't been in the foyer since he and Larry first arrived. He remembered wearing the tie when he was playing with the pugs because one of them had tried to chew on it. How could it have slipped from his neck still knotted without him knowing? Hell, how could it slip from his neck still knotted *at all*? And how did it find its way to the foyer when he hadn't been there since they had been called into the anteroom earlier?

Bo bumped him with his hip as they climbed upward, grinning wildly.

"You'll get used to the ghost," Mrs. Price blithely commented from up ahead. She stopped in her tracks as if suddenly realizing what she'd said. Taking a deep breath like she'd just climbed Mount Everest and pressing a hand to her hip as if her rheumatism was giving her a spot of trouble, she turned and smiled down at the boys behind her, clearly sorry she'd said what she had. "Kidding," she said. "About the ghost, I mean. There's nothing to get used to, I assure you. This house is old. It has shadowy nooks and things that thump against walls when you aren't looking. Odd occurrences happen. All of them can't be explained. But don't worry, there's nothing here that will hurt you."

"Like what?" Larry asked, one eyebrow arched high on his forehead.

Mrs. Price folded her hands in front of her bosom. She might have looked pious if not for the playful gleam in her eye. "Like anything. May I show you your rooms now, or would you rather stand here discussing the paranormal, which in my opinion is all a bunch of hooey anyway?"

Larry narrowed his eyes and studied her. *You're lying*, he thought. *But about what?*

Bo merely did a Three Stooges salami-salami-baloney bow and motioned for her to lead the way.

Mrs. Price chortled. "Cheeky rascal," she said. Turning, she stalked off, snickering and shaking her head. She was obviously having a good time.

Her followers did what followers are supposed to do. They followed—one glancing around like a tourist, and the other still looking fairly confused while continuing to pat the knotted necktie in his trouser pocket.

Just before they reached the top step and began following Mrs. Price down a long hallway that popped up in front of them, Bo stared bug-eyed at Larry and mouthed the words "I still say it's spooks!" He then threw his hands high in the air and made a perfect O with his mouth in a clever and quite horribly accurate parody of Munch's little guy in the painting *The Scream*.

Larry snickered and patted the necktie in his pocket one last time to make sure it hadn't wandered off again.

"HOLY COW! Is this the servants' quarters?" Larry asked.

"No," Mrs. Price answered. "These rooms are yours. This house was not built with servants in mind. It was never meant to house servants at all, in fact. That only came about when Roger and Jeremy—I'm sorry, Mr. Stanhope and Mr. Winston, began to age and required live-in help. Even then it was only my husband and myself. I began cooking for this house thirty years ago while my husband did maintenance about the place. Extra help has been brought in now and then as the years accumulated and we all grew old together, me included, but none of the extra help actually lived on the grounds. My husband, of course, has passed away. These days it's just Roger and me living on the premises. And now the two of you. As soon as I'm sure you are capable of caring for Mr. Stanhope, I will be gone too. I have my own retirement to look forward to."

She gazed about the suite of rooms. If Larry had not been so wrapped up in his own good fortune, he might have seen a spot of sadness in Mrs. Price's eyes. "So, Mr. Larry? Do you think you can be comfortable here?"

Before Larry could answer, he heard a gleeful *Whoop!* coming through the wall. It was Bo, checking out his own suite of rooms next door.

Larry patted his heart. He was a little breathless at the moment. It wasn't from climbing three flights of stairs, but because of the richness of the quarters Mrs. Price had ushered him into and because his life had taken a turn that he could never have predicted in a million years.

"I think I'll just agree with Bo next door," he said, his eyes wide, his voice not much more than a wheeze of wonder. "Whoop."

Mrs. Price seemed pleased. "You can bring some of your own furniture into your rooms if you like. That's entirely up to you."

"Why in the world would I want to do that?"

Larry gaped at the collection of polished antiques that made up his sitting room and bedroom. The silk divan by the fireplace. The leather armchairs by the ten-foot-high windows looking out on the grounds below. The four-poster bed made of cherrywood, hand carved with images of steeds galloping across the head- and footboards. Covering the bed, a beautiful handmade quilt in vibrant colors, which looked Amish in design, added a splash of warmth to the room. An array of ottomans, bookshelves, and posh accent pieces were scattered about.

Stepping closer to one of the bookcases, Larry ran his finger over some of the titles. Many of the books were bound in fine leather, obviously antique, most of them classics. Other books, more recent editions, Larry recognized from his weekly perusal of the Sunday papers and the *New York Times* Best Sellers lists, which made up part of the weekly crossword puzzle/comic page/Entertainment section fest he partook of every time he stole a paper from the kiosk down the street from his old apartment.

Those days were now over, he supposed. "Mind if I have the newspaper delivered?" he asked. "I'm addicted to the *New York Times* crossword puzzle."

She seemed taken aback by the question. "The master already takes it. He enjoys the puzzle too. I'll inform the delivery person to drop off two newspapers, otherwise you and Roger will be locked in mortal combat every Sunday morning. We can't have that. I have enough to do without forever keeping you two from killing each other over a silly crossword puzzle."

Following Larry's gaze, she too eyed the shelves of books with appreciative wonder. "The gentlemen were voracious readers in their day. Roger still is, when his eyes allow it. You saw the larger library downstairs. The books in this room are just overflow. I love to read myself," she added wistfully. "I'll miss these wonderful old books when I leave. I truly will."

Larry turned to study Mrs. Price more closely. "You've enjoyed working here." It wasn't a question. It was a heartfelt observation, and Mrs. Price accepted it as such.

She reached out and plucked a thin edition from one of the shelves. Larry saw it was an early printing of *Winnie the Pooh*. It was perfectly preserved but for a round coffee stain on the cover. Mrs. Price stared down at it. With her eyes misting over, she ruffled through the pages, stirring up the scent of old paper and memories, as only a well-loved book can do.

"I was reading this on the day my husband died." She stroked her thumb over the circular stain on the cover. "I found it two days later right where I'd left it in the breakfast room with my coffee cup sitting atop it. The stain won't come out. I've tried everything."

"Perhaps you should take the book with you when you go. Surely no one will miss it."

Mrs. Price straightened her back and poked the book back on the shelf from which it had come. "It's part of the house," she said stiffly. "It belongs here."

Larry heard a creak behind him. Turning, he spotted Bo, his head poking around a door leading off the bedroom. He was grinning.

"Oops," he said. "Didn't mean to intrude." To Larry he said, "Looks like we're sharing a bathroom."

"Yes," Mrs. Price said, first to Bo, then to Larry. "Your two suites are connected by a joint bath. I hope that is acceptable."

"Of course," Bo said, "but the fact that there aren't any locks on the doors is a bit of a mystery."

Larry joined him at the doorway leading into the communal bath. He checked the door, and sure enough, there was no lock. Nor was there a lock on the door on the other side of the bath leading to Bo's own suite of rooms. Nor a lock on the door leading out to the hall.

"The locks were removed throughout the house," Mrs. Price said. "By Mr. Stanhope's orders and the orders of his doctor. Is that a problem?"

"Even the locks to his own rooms?" Larry asked.

Mrs. Price nodded in agreement. "Especially those, yes. It is the only way to care for the elderly. Access must be available at all times. You understand, certainly."

"Yes," Larry said. "But why would that apply to *our* rooms?"

"It just does."

Larry's eyes met Bo's. They both looked a bit uneasy. "I guess I don't mind if Bo doesn't."

Bo's eyes went wide as he considered the question. Oddly, he felt a smidgeon of disappointment in the way Larry appeared to accept the inevitable. If he was intrigued by the idea that either man could walk into the other's quarters any time they wanted, either day or night, he hid it well. Bo wasn't quite sure why that irked him as much as it did. Then he laughed it off.

"I certainly don't mind," Bo announced. His gaze ricocheted over Larry's shoulder and spotted the bookcases on the wall. "Hey! You've got books!"

"You don't?" Larry asked, the matter of the unlockable doors already forgotten.

"No. But I've got a bigass TV." He slapped his hand over his mouth and cast a guilty look in Mrs. Price's direction. "Sorry. Didn't mean to embarrass you by cursing."

Mrs. Price pooh-poohed his apology as if shooing a gnat from a plate of potato salad. "My husband cussed like a sailor. Mr. Stanhope himself has been known to toss an F-bomb now and then. Trust me, there is nothing you could say that would embarrass me." She cast her eyes from one of them to the other. "So, may I take it that the two of you are satisfied with the living arrangements? Unlockable doors and all?"

Bo shrugged. "Okay by me."

"Sure," Larry said. "Why not? The rooms are gorgeous." He snagged Bo's attention and waved a hand toward the books at his back. "When you want to read, you can help yourself."

Bo brightened and hooked a thumb at the connecting door. "And when you want to watch TV, just pop on in."

Mrs. Price casually flitted her eyes toward the hidden camera at the corner of the ceiling, wondering as she did whether Roger was watching. Then, seeing by the teeny red light beneath the camera lens that he most certainly was, she checked a pocket watch on a chain she pulled from her dress pocket rather like a railroad conductor. "Good," she said. "Now that that is settled, I have just enough time to show you the rest of the house before I start dinner. If you'll follow me."

As Mrs. Price headed back toward the stairs, Bo leaned in and whispered in Larry's ear.

"I sleepwalk," he said. "I also sleep naked."

Larry stared at him. "Really?"

Bo gave him a gentle punch on the arm. "Nah," he said. "I don't sleepwalk."

Before Larry could ask if the *other* part of his statement was true, not that it was any of his business, of course, since he had sworn off men forever, being newly devoted to abstinence and all, (*Remember?* he chided himself),

Mrs. Price leaned around the doorjamb, and said, all business, "Come along, boys. Don't dawdle." She looked closer at Larry. "Your ears are red."

"Must be from climbing all those stairs," Larry mumbled, avoiding Bo's eyes.

"Yes, I'm sure that's what it is," Bo said, gazing innocently about the room.

Making a concerted effort not to dawdle, as Mrs. Price demanded, and to ignore Bo's flirting as well, if that's what it was, Larry hustled off to join the good woman. He left Bo grinning in his wake.

He also left Bo staring at Larry's ass as he walked away, but Larry didn't notice.

Roger, sitting one floor down in front of a monitor, smiling, most certainly did.

Chapter Four

Two days later, Bo's and Larry's new careers began in earnest.

Larry snatched his little travel alarm clock off the nightstand as the first ray of sunlight warmed his face. His ownership of a travel alarm clock was a bit of an enigma, really, seeing as how Larry spent most of his adult life never going anywhere other than home or work. Except for now, of course. Now he had moved into a spectacular mansion on top of a picturesque mountain out in the middle of nowhere. But that wasn't what amazed him at the moment.

What amazed him was the sense that he had somehow during the night been... touched. *Sexually* touched.

His cock was as hard as a flashlight and thrumming like a PSB subwoofer strapped to a 10,000 watt car stereo belting Tejano music inside a Latino homey's jacked-up '64 Chevy. I mean, Larry's dick was really humming. In fact, Larry thought maybe he was about three seconds away from shooting his rocks all over the nice clean sheets Mrs. Price had fitted to his bed the day before while he was moving out of his apartment in the city, putting most of his crap in storage in the mansion's six-acre basement, and then heading back to his apartment to reclaim his clothes and return his keys to the landlady before flying back to the mountain at the speed of light because he was pretty sure his damn car was about to conk out on him at any minute. Which, in the long run, it didn't. Not yet anyway.

But back to the boner.

Larry tried to blink the sleep from his eyes while squinting at the teeny munchkin clock in his hand. He breathed in the unfamiliar air. It was scented with fresh flowers and the heady, lemony reek of furniture polish, which seemed to be forever wafting from room to room. Needless to say, Larry had never *once* enjoyed the smell of cut flowers and furniture polish in his old apartment. All he had smelled there was poverty and the scent of Daniel's shampoo on his pillow. At least until Daniel split with the barista and Larry washed his sheets.

The thought of Daniel produced a sigh. And not a happy one.

Larry squinted against the rays of the rising sun stabbing through his bedroom window. He was pretty sure the morning light burned brighter on this mountaintop than it did down in the city. Or maybe it was just that the atmosphere was clearer, with fewer pollutants to muddy up the works. Larry narrowed his eyes to let his lashes filter out the glare and thought about the night from which he had just awoken—and the sensations he had awoken *to*.

He *still* could have sworn he'd felt hands on his body. Warm hands. Warm and lingering. And maybe even *lips*. Despite all the excitement of the day before, Larry had slept like a dead man. The antique four-poster bed in his room was exquisitely comfortable. The sheets luxuriously soft. Perhaps the warm, lingering hands he'd imagined feeling had been part of a dream. If so, it must have been a sexyass dream. Jeez, his morning hard-on really needed some attention.

Just as Larry accepted the inevitable and flung the covers back to reach for his cock to take it for a spin, a teeny red light went off on the camera far above his head, up in the corner of the ceiling. Since the red light was hidden within the carved cornices separating the wall from the ceiling, as was the rest of the apparatus except for the tiny glass circle that betokened a camera's lens, Larry didn't notice.

He was too wrapped up in other pursuits. Big, hard, horny ones.

He closed his eyes as his fingers circled his dick. A shudder went through his body when he arched his back and his ass came straight up off the bed.

Wow, he thought. *This won't take long.*

ROGER FLIPPED the Off switch posthaste.

"Oops," he crooned to Max, who was sitting on his lap as they both peered at the monitor in front of them. "Almost caught something we weren't supposed to catch."

Max wagged his tail, either in agreement or because he was feeling sociable. It's hard to tell with a pug.

Roger turned his eyes from the newly blackened monitor and eyeballed a second monitor to the left. There were nine monitors in all, laid out like a tic-tac-toe board.

In the second monitor, Roger saw Bo sitting on the edge of his bed in his underwear, rubbing the sleep from his eyes. In yet another monitor, he spotted Mrs. Price peeling fruit at the kitchen sink.

Watching Mrs. Price wasn't all that enthralling, so he shifted his gaze back to the monitor with Bo on it. Roger leaned in closer. The young man was so handsome with his lithe runner's body and neatly shorn head.

Roger watched as Bo brushed his hands over his buzz-cut hair, prompting Roger to touch his own hair and wonder how *he* would look with a buzz cut. Bo stretched his arms wide and yawned, showing luscious, lean biceps and sun-bronzed shoulders. His neatly muscled legs were just as bronze as his shoulders. Roger spotted a new addition to the room—a surfboard standing upright, propped in the corner. That explained the tan. Bo Lansing was a surfer.

Roger watched as Bo turned to gaze at the unlocked door leading into the bathroom and the suite next door. He seemed to be holding his breath, Roger thought, listening, perhaps wondering if the adjoining bathroom was occupied.

Roger gave a bark of delight. If only Bo knew what his workmate was doing at that moment.

Before Roger could ponder the question any further, Bo leaped from the bed, and in the space of a second and a half, shrugged out of his T-shirt and dragged his boxer shorts down over his slim hips and long legs and kicked them away, leaving him naked at the side of the bed, his lovely uncut cock at half-mast, swaying in front of him as he shook himself awake.

Roger hastily switched off that monitor as well.

He smiled down at Max. "It's going to be harder than I expected not to be a lecherous old fogy about this."

As if agreeing, Max gave him a commiserating pant accompanied by a congenial butt wiggle, making Roger laugh.

At that moment, both monitors flicked back on—just in time to show Bo stepping naked into the shower on the first monitor, and on the second, redheaded Larry, strong naked legs splayed wide on his bed, eyes closed, gasping for air, with a shimmering rope of freshly deposited come sparkling across his stomach.

"Stop that!" Roger barked, reaching to hastily switch off the monitors yet again. "You never did have any sense of propriety!"

"For which you were once most grateful," a breathy voice whispered in his ear. "By the way, young Larry has a perfect cock. Plump, firmly fleshed, all squiggly with veins, and tasty. Really quite tasty."

Roger cast a suspicious glance at the ceiling, the wall, the fireplace, the chair. "And how would you know that? Where the hell are you anyway?"

"Oh, I have my ways" came the lofty answer. "And I'm sitting on the poof."

"You *are* a poof. Tell me you weren't molesting the boy in his sleep."

"He was enjoying a rather erotic dream anyway, so I ducked my head under the covers to see what was going on. As long as I was already there, I figured a taste wouldn't hurt."

"Good lord!"

Grunting out a curse, which didn't have much sincerity behind it since he was trying not to laugh, Roger rose, eased Max to the floor, and headed off to begin his day.

He did his level best to ignore the chuckle he heard behind him in the empty room.

THUS BEGAN the first morning of Bo's and Larry's employment in the Stanhope mansion.

Their previous lives were now happily allocated to memory—happily because their most recent pasts had pretty much sucked and they both damn well knew it. With their old dead-end jobs severed and most of their meager belongings safely tucked away in storage three floors below their feet in the mansion's basement, they applied themselves eagerly to the learning of their new duties.

Both men were thrilled and grateful to have this chance. Their placement in the Stanhope household was a lifesaving turn of events. They intended to honor Roger Stanhope's trust in them by performing their duties to the very best of their abilities. Financially, their new positions were a godsend. A good salary, with no rent or utilities to pay, nor groceries to buy, and a luxurious home to live in—what more could they possibly want?

On that first morning, they met Mrs. Price in the kitchen, as had been arranged. While the three of them sat around a long kitchen table consuming their breakfasts of fresh fruit and scrambled eggs, she laid out their work schedules for them.

Once that was settled to Mrs. Price's satisfaction, Larry and Bo were given beepers to wear on their belts. If an emergency should arise and their employer should urgently need them, she said, the beepers would sound a horrendous wail, designed to catch their attention no matter *what* they were doing. To show them what she meant, she flipped a button on her own device, and it set off such a screaming, squelching cacophony of noise that both men jumped in their chairs.

It was a good system. The house was far too large for bells or buzzers. And bells or buzzers might not always be handy if help was needed in a hurry, or if Mr. Stanhope should fall and not be able to reach one. Roger was never far from his own transmitter because he wore it on a braided thong around his neck at all times.

For less urgent needs, the device would sound a simple beep, either one beep or two, depending on which of the boys the master needed. Bo's summons was one beep, Larry's two. Until her departure, two weeks hence, Mrs. Price could be summoned with three beeps.

"Since the delicate little beeps are not nearly as heart-stopping as the infernal banshee's wail the beeper makes for emergencies, neither of you will be startled into a heart attack by it," Mrs. Price said. "And that's a good thing. One patient in this house is plenty, trust me."

Larry and Bo assumed this was humor, so they dutifully smiled.

"While I'm thinking of it," Mrs. Price said, snapping her fingers, "the master would like you to park your two automobiles behind the carriage house at the back of the property. He didn't say it outright, but I believe he feared your rust-encrusted jalopies might decimate real estate values."

She said it with a straight face, which didn't surprise Larry at all, since it was probably the truth.

But Mrs. Price wasn't finished yet. "Roger said if you need to drive into the city on estate business, or if you need to carry him somewhere, as may happen now and then, doctor appointments and such, you may take one of the vehicles in the carriage house. There are four to choose from. Take your pick. For your own private affairs that need tending to on your days off, he would naturally prefer you use your own vehicles." She sniffed. "Such as they are."

Larry and Bo stared at each other.

Apparently Mrs. Price took their hesitation for doubt. Her back got a little straighter, as if the family escutcheon had been somehow besmirched. "No need to look so squeamish, you know. They are perfectly *nice* vehicles, I assure you. Not yours. Roger's." She looked over her glasses at Bo in particular. "Not a rust spot on any of them, as a matter of fact."

Bo stammered, "I'm sure they are quite lovely. Thank you."

"Yeah," Larry echoed. "Lovely. Can we see them?"

Mrs. Price harrumphed, still appearing vaguely offended. She dug through an apron pocket and hauled out a ring of keys. After sifting through them, she indicated the proper one and relinquished the entire ring to Larry.

Both men scooted away from the table.

"Take your beepers," Mrs. Price commanded.

They snatched up their beepers and attached them to their belts.

"Finish your milk."

Both men snarled under their breath and returned to the table to dutifully gulp down the remaining milk in their glasses.

"And hurry back," she added. "A tailor is stopping by in thirty minutes to measure you for uniforms."

Both men gaped. "Uniforms?" they said in unison.

"Yes. Uniforms. We can't have you serving the master in blue jeans and T-shirts."

"Why not?" Bo asked.

Mrs. Price merely narrowed her eyes in answer.

"*Now* you can go," she said, turning toward the sink to hide her smile.

Still wondering about the new uniforms, Larry and Bo were out the door before she could change her mind.

THE CARRIAGE house stood between the mansion and the greenhouse at the end of the circular drive that wound around to the back of the house from the lane out front. The structure could be accessed by a key in a metal box. When the key was turned, a series of garage doors rolled up into the ceiling, displaying six spaces for six automobiles. Only four of the spaces were occupied.

One held a 1963 silver Aston Martin DB5 in pristine condition that looked like James Bond had just parked it there a minute ago, then hustled off to beg a martini from Mrs. Price. Shaken, not stirred.

The car was beautiful. Larry almost got another hard-on looking at it.

In the second slot sat a 2016 ruby-red Lincoln Navigator SUV with tinted windows. Big. Butch. Businesslike.

In the third slot rested a Mercedes-Benz S550 with factory stickers still on the windows. The Mercedes was gleaming black with a pale leather interior and a grand total of 212 miles on the odometer. Bo knew this because he leaned inside to see. He closed his eyes, and in a rush of bliss that was almost sexual, sniffed the new-car smell while he was at it.

In the fourth slot sat a '57 Chevy Bel Air convertible with a shimmering metallic green paint job, buttercup-yellow interior, and a brown canvas top currently folded down into the compartment behind the back seat beneath a shiny bronze tonneau cover. The car had spinners on the wheels, a foxtail dangling from the antenna, and a pair of big fluffy dice hanging off the rearview mirror.

Larry and Bo all but drooled staring at it. This was the car they both longed to drive. When they turned to stare at each other, their bugged-out eyes confirmed that fact.

"We're in heaven," Bo said.

In the space between one heartbeat and the next, Larry forgot about the classic beauties parked in front of him and concentrated solely on his workmate instead. It was weird, almost as if he had never really noticed the guy before. He stared at the clean line of Bo's jaw. The well-shaped head beneath a mere shadow of black hair that couldn't have been more than a quarter of an inch long. The smooth skin, tanned to a healthy golden glow. The vibrant green eyes. The trim little ears. Ears, Larry thought, that were made to whisper earnestly into. Or at the very least, nibble on.

That last thought made him drag in a little gasp of air. The question was out of his mouth before he could stop it. "Did you come into my room last night?"

Bo blinked, surprised by the question. "Why would you think that?"

Larry remembered his morning boner, the tingling sensation on his skin from having either gentle fingers or warm lips caressing him in his sleep. And while a spate of blood rushed into his cheeks, he recalled whacking off practically the moment he opened his eyes and the explosive orgasm that followed.

"Never mind," he said, turning back to the cars.

Bo laid a hand on Larry's shoulder. "Was someone in your room last night?"

Larry was afraid to look at him. He wasn't sure why. He glanced uncomfortably in Bo's direction. "It must have been a dream," he said.

"Pity," Bo muttered around a sly smile. When Larry didn't respond, Bo turned his attention back to the carriage house. "I guess we'd better bring our clunkers around and get them out of sight. Property values and all that."

Larry latched on to the suggestion like a drowning man grabs a life preserver. "Yeah, I guess we'd better," he said.

But what he remembered *later* was the one teeny word Bo had uttered, and the breathless way he had uttered it, when Larry told him he must have been dreaming the night before when he thought someone had been in his room. What was it he said? Oh, yes.

"*Pity.*"

"I'M SORRY, Bo, but you may not have much opportunity to show off your culinary skills. Roger prefers simple fare. In fact, a ninety-three-year-old digestive tract rather requires it. Of course, you will also be feeding yourself and Larry, so perhaps you can experiment there."

They were standing in the kitchen with Mrs. Price again.

Bo looked rather less than appeased by her announcement, so Larry cast him a sympathetic glance. Larry's sympathy was quickly forgotten when Mrs. Price thrust the master's bed tray into his hands.

The tray held a soft-boiled egg in a porcelain cup, two croissants, a jar of marmalade, a frugal wedge of brie, a glass of orange juice, and two bowls of what looked like cubed chunks of liver, bloody and raw. Larry stared down at the bowls, then back at Mrs. Price. "What is he, a vampire?"

Mrs. Price squinted, obviously unamused. "The liver is for the dogs."

"Oh. Do I knock before entering?"

"Yes."

"Will he dine in bed?"

"Yes. And stop by the front door to retrieve the morning paper as you go."

"He follows the stock exchange?"

"No. He likes to read Dagwood. Be sure you open his drapes. He prefers natural light in the morning."

"I'm nervous," Larry admitted.

Mrs. Price tutted. "Don't be. He puts his pants on just like you do. Only slower." She glanced down at his blue jeans. "And the master's pants don't have raggedy cuffs and a faded spot on the crotch."

Bo chuckled at that, but when Mrs. Price turned a cool, appraising look in his direction, he stifled it quickly enough. He was wearing blue jeans too and his weren't in any better shape than Larry's.

She turned back to Larry and nudged him toward the door. "Hurry now, while the egg is still warm. After they eat, take the dogs outside."

"On leashes?"

"No. They won't run away."

"Fine. Should I take the elevator I saw in the second floor hallway?"

"No. That elevator only goes to the widow's walk on the roof."

"Oh."

"Hurry along now. While you're doing that, I'll give our new chef a tour of the kitchen and pantries."

Bo rubbed his hands together. "Goody."

The two young men shared a smile. Then Larry straightened his shoulders, swallowed hard, glanced down to make sure his shirt was tucked in, and headed for the kitchen door, careful not to slosh the juice. He crossed the foyer and set the tray at the foot of the stairs long enough to hustle off to the front door to grab the newspaper off the front step. After placing the paper carefully on the tray among the food, he headed up the long staircase, trying to ignore his thumping heart.

On the second floor, with no table handy on which to rest the tray, Larry tapped lightly at the master's door with his toe.

"Come in," a soft voice answered.

Larry sucked in a bracing gulp of oxygen to calm his jangly nerves, juggled the tray around to free a hand so as to twist the doorknob, and stepped through the door.

ROGER SAT propped up in bed, a welcoming smile on his face. He felt a blush rise to his weathered cheeks when he thought of the young man before him lying naked on his bed earlier, legs splayed wide, gasping for air, and with a goodly amount of come sprayed across his belly. He quickly pushed that thought away. And yes, it must be said, he pushed it away rather reluctantly.

"Good morning, young man. Still getting settled in?"

Larry too had a blush on his cheeks. Roger wasn't sure why. Perhaps it was the whole master/servant thing. Roger didn't mind really. This all had to be such a new experience for the boy it was understandable that it would take a while for him to adjust.

"Yes, sir," Larry said, carefully setting the bed tray across Roger's lap like he was laying a roadside mine outside of Aleppo. His blush deepened when he saw Roger watching him. "I...."

"Yes?" Roger asked, helping the young man position the bed tray properly, then shaking out his napkin and spreading it over his chest. "Did you want to say something, son?"

Larry stepped back from the side of the bed, gazed down at his hands, then looked back up to Roger's face. "I just wanted to thank you one more time for this opportunity. I think.... Well...."

"You think what?" Roger asked, not unkindly. While he waited, he studied the handsome face before him, the unlined forehead, the spray of golden freckles across the neatly carved nose, the strong young hands sprinkled with golden hairs and bulging blue veins. They were beautiful hands, he thought. Competent hands. Sexy. He remembered what Jeremy had said about visiting the young man while he slept and a surge of jealousy shot through him. *Holy damn,* he thought, *who knows what other interesting pastimes you can get up to when you're dead as a mackerel.*

Larry killed Roger's musings by nervously clearing his throat. "I think, sir, you may have saved my life."

Roger sat there staring up at the young man before him, soaking in his sincerity, knowing beyond all doubt that it wasn't feigned. There was no duplicity in the boy's eyes. Not an ounce. At that realization, Roger's heart gave a gentle lurch. A lurch of longing. A lurch of... *respect.*

"Open the drapes, please, Larry," Roger said softly.

Larry snapped to attention. "Of course! I forgot!"

He bustled off to pull the drapes aside from every window in the room, of which there were several. Roger lay in his bed, his breakfast forgotten, watching him. He watched too as the streaming morning sunlight tore its way through the panes of each freshly uncovered window and stirred his new employee's red hair into an eruption of carroty flames.

"It is so like mine was," a voice whispered in Roger's ear.

Roger nodded. "Yes, it is."

Larry turned. "I'm sorry, sir. Did you say something?"

"Not a peep," Roger lied.

He tore his thoughts from all the memories Larry's flaming hair had stirred up and refocused his attention on the tray before him. With his knife, he tapped away the tip of his soft-boiled egg. His hands were fairly steady this morning, he noticed. For that he was grateful. Sometimes they were not.

At the first sound of the drapes being pulled, the two pugs, Leo and Max, came squirming out from under the blankets at Roger's feet. Roger placed the two bowls of chopped meat, one to either side of his outstretched legs, and the dogs dug in. With that chore complete, Roger turned his attention back to Larry.

"How did I save your life?" he asked, as if it all meant very little to him. But he was listening. Oh yes. He was listening with every ounce of concentration his old brain could muster.

He waited, his nerve endings sparking like electrodes as he stared up into that youthful, sincere face. Was it his imagination, or did he truly see a shimmer of tears sparkling in those heavenly blue eyes?

"Tell me," Roger urged, barely breathing out the words. "Please. I'd like to know."

Larry opened his mouth to speak, then turned aside, aiming his gaze into the shadows of the unlit fireplace at his feet. Tiny white teeth gnawed his lower lip for a moment. The azure eyes flitted once to Roger's face, then back to the grate.

"Y-you just did," Larry stammered, so embarrassed now he couldn't have raised his eyes from the fireplace if he'd tried.

Roger eyed the boy warmly—intrigued by his shyness, moved by his candor. "Perhaps another day you can explain it to me."

"Yes," Larry said. "I will." He looked immensely relieved.

Roger reached out from the side of the bed and took Larry's hand with a playful twinkle in his eye. "But don't think you're off the hook. You owe me an explanation. I always collect what I'm owed."

Larry nodded, finally able to raise his eyes to the old man's face. "Yes, sir. I promise."

Roger's merry eyes veered away from Larry and took in the expectant expressions on the dogs' upturned faces. Their bowls were empty, their butts wiggling with eager apprehension.

"Off you go, then," Roger said gaily, and the two pugs flew off the bed, heading for the door.

Larry stood there watching them until Roger said, "That's your cue, son. Take them outside, if you please. They enjoy a run across the grounds in the morning. Keep your eye on them, but don't worry. They won't run far. They'll let you know when they want to come back in."

Larry almost jumped out of his shoes. "Of course! Walk the dogs. Got it. Umm—see ya." And he ran off after the dogs, who had already pattered through the open door and were thumping and thundering toward the stairs. They knew where they were supposed to go even if Larry did not.

Before Larry could leave the room, Roger stopped him with a gentle "Ahem."

Larry froze at the door, turning back. "Yes, sir?"

Roger studied the boy before him. "I just wanted to tell you that I like both you boys. It might just be possible that you've saved my life as well. Or at least given it some sort of purpose."

Larry blinked. "I—I don't understand."

"No, I don't suppose you do." Without explaining himself, Roger flipped his fingertips toward the door, shooing Larry away. "Best catch up with the dogs, son. They'll be in Tijuana before you know it."

Feeling rather fatherly, Roger David Stanhope fondly watched the clearly confused young man hurry off, then began spooning brie over one of his croissants.

"The lad was a perfect choice," he said softly, not really knowing if he was alone or not and not really caring. "Can I pick 'em or what?"

Bo stood at the kitchen window and stared out at Larry and the two pugs. All three were running in circles on the lawn, Larry obviously having as much fun as the dogs. Mrs. Price came up behind him and rose up on tiptoe to rest her chin on his shoulder so she could look through the window too.

"He's a fine young man, I think," she said softly.

"Yes," Bo agreed. "I like him very much."

"Unless I'm mistaken, you've only known each other since you met at the interview three days ago."

"Actually, it didn't take three days. I liked him in the first three minutes."

"Roger was right, then," Mrs. Price said. "Sometimes I wonder how he does it."

Bo eased himself out from under the woman's chin and faced her. "Right about what? And you wonder how he does what?"

Mrs. Price stepped away and began clearing the breakfast dishes from the table. "How he claims to know people at first glance."

"Does he?"

"Yes. And he's always right. He always *does* understand people immediately."

Bo took the dishes from Mrs. Price's hands and rinsed them under the faucet before placing them in the dishwasher. "I'm almost afraid to ask, but did he say he knew *me* at first glance too?"

While Mrs. Price wiped down the kitchen table, Bo gathered up all the remaining dishes, loaded them into the dishwasher, and added soap before locking the lid and turning on the machine.

Mrs. Price answered over the hum of sluicing water. "He understood you first. He understood you the moment you straightened Larry's tie out on the driveway shortly after the two of you arrived for the interview."

"He saw me?"

"Oh yes. Roger never misses an act of kindness. It is through those spontaneous acts of generosity that he judges the people around him."

Bo considered that. He glanced at Mrs. Price, who turned away from the breakfast table and gazed at him in the same moment. "I was wondering…," Bo ventured.

"Yes?"

He turned back to stare out the window again. Larry and the pugs were nowhere in sight.

"I was wondering why the ad asked for applicants with a 'gay, romantic heart.' Seems a strange qualification for employment, don't you think?"

The sun was coming through the kitchen window now. It would be a hot day. Mrs. Price reached around Bo and drew the blinds, blocking out the light and heat. She chewed on her cheek for a moment, then clapped her hands together, all business.

Ignoring his question, she announced, "You have so much to learn. We'd best get started."

She moved off toward the walk-in pantry that abutted the kitchen, but Bo didn't follow. He stood his ground at the sink, watching her. Waiting.

When she realized he wasn't with her, she stopped and turned. She studied his face for a moment, then expelled a puff of air.

Wiping her hands on her apron, then crossing her arms in front of her chest as if settling in for an argument, she said, "Mr. Stanhope is the one who should be asked that question, not me. Although if you'll take my advice, you won't ask him either. After all, it's really none of your business, is it? When Roger wants to explain things to you, I'm sure he will. In his own time. In his own fashion. What you should be doing, young man, is learning your job and becoming friends with your workmate. The two of you will be thrown close together from here on in. A certain amount of camaraderie might come in handy. You'll be helping each other perform your duties, and hopefully you will enjoy the closeness. Roger expects a congenial attitude among his staff."

Bo sighed. "But what does that have to do with possessing a gay, romantic heart?"

"You'll have to figure that out for yourself," she said with a frown. "Now, then, let's get back to work."

With that, she clutched his arm in a grip that was strong enough to strangle a rhino and tugged him toward the pantry. By the time he got there, he was laughing and saying, "Ouch, ouch, ouch, ouch."

Mrs. Price regally ignored him. She was laughing too, of course, but it was all on the inside where it didn't show.

THAT EVENING, when the hour was late and after Bo and Larry had shared a quiet dinner at the mansion's kitchen table, barely speaking three words to each other because they were so tired and had so many things on their minds, they retired to their own rooms. Bo to watch TV and Larry to read.

Larry drew on a ratty old pair of lounging pants and a T-shirt that had seen better days, then plucked a book from the bookshelf. It was a well-thumbed copy of *Tom Sawyer*, which he hadn't read since he was a kid. Through the adjoining bathroom doors, he could hear Bo's television emitting the sounds of some sort of reality show, which Larry detested, thinking they were the dumbest things ever. He was surprised, and a little disappointed, they would appeal to Bo. The guy seemed more cerebral than that.

Larry rolled his eyes, making fun of himself. *What a snob I am*, he thought before glancing at the nightstand to make sure the beeper was handy in case Mr. Stanhope needed him. Reassured on that account, he immediately forgot about Bo and his stupid TV show and settled back to immerse himself in the world of Tom and Aunt Polly and Peter the cat, grateful for a little downtime from reality.

After twenty minutes or so had passed, and Peter had sailed through Aunt Polly's window after Tom poured the painkiller down his throat, there came a soft tapping at Larry's bathroom door. It was obviously Bo. Who else would it be?

"Come on in," Larry called out, closing his book, and a moment later, Bo stuck his head through the door.

"Am I interrupting anything?" Bo asked. His green eyes skittered around the room as if expecting to see a stranger or two lurking in the corners.

It took a bit of effort for Larry to drag his eyes upward to Bo's face rather than let them hover around his long naked legs poking out from beneath a pair of baggy white boxer shorts, which was apparently the attire Bo liked to lounge around in when he wasn't working. Not that Larry minded. He appreciated a nice pair of legs as much as the next guy. Well, the next *gay* guy, at any rate. There also seemed to be something with substantial weight to it swaying behind the front of those boxer shorts every time Bo moved, but Larry tried not to think about that.

After all, he reminded himself, he *had* only recently devoted his life to abstinence.

"Come on in," Larry said again, setting his book aside and forcing his eyes off Bo's legs and crotch. *Dammit*, he told himself. *Look at the face. Concentrate on the face.*

Bo stepped inside, leaving the bathroom door open wide behind him as if thinking maybe Larry would feel less put-upon if he didn't feel they were locked in together.

Larry found the gesture faintly charming, and quite perceptive. For Bo. "Pull up a chair," he said, amiably enough.

But to his surprise, Bo stepped directly to the fireplace. "I guess you haven't figured this out yet," he said cryptically. He pressed a button above the mantle, and jets of gas flames erupted among the ceramic logs on the grate. With just that one simple act, Bo brought the room to life. The flames were beautiful.

"Wow," Larry said, staring into them. "How cool is that? Thanks."

With the flames to break the ice, Bo did finally snag a chair and sit across the fireplace from Larry. He stretched his long legs out and wiggled his toes in front of the fire. He looked so comfortable doing it that Larry did the same.

"How was your day?" Bo asked.

"It was great. How was yours?"

"Perfect. Although I didn't see the master. I guess you'll be the one spending more time with him. Not me."

Larry smiled. "He likes you, though."

Bo dragged his gaze from the flames. "How do you know that?"

"Just do."

"Really?"

"Yes. He likes us both. He told me so."

Bo sat quietly for a minute, considering that. He was staring into the flames again. "I'm glad," he finally said in a gentle hush. "At least somebody likes me."

Larry turned to him with a start. "What do you mean by that?"

Bo shrugged, playfully avoiding his eyes, staring at the walls, the ceiling, then back to the fire. "Dunno."

Larry frowned. "You must know what you meant. Why would you say it if you didn't?"

Bo once again tore his eyes from the flames. He focused his attention on Larry, and for some reason Larry felt a nervous tug inside his chest. What the hell was that all about?

Bo didn't give him time to wonder about it. "I'd like us to be friends, Larry."

Larry's frown deepened. "I thought we were friends already."

"Really?"

"Yeah."

"Then why do you keep your distance?"

Larry felt a blush rising to his cheeks. He tried to ignore it. "I didn't know I was."

"Oh please."

Larry sighed. "Okay. Maybe I am. I'm sorry. But I've never been in a situation like this before. We're workmates. Who knows how close we should be?"

"Do you like me?"

Larry blinked. "Of course I like you. You haven't pissed me off *yet*."

Bo grinned. "Well, that's good to know. You don't still think I was in your room the other night, do you?"

At that, Larry began to understand a few things. He rolled his eyes toward the ceiling. "Oh Jesus. Is that what this is about? I told you it was just a dream. A sexyass dream."

A broader smile played at Bo's mouth. "Exactly how sexyass was it? Wanna tell me about it? Share the details?" He wiggled his eyebrows like Groucho Marx.

Larry tried not to smile back, with varying degrees of success. "No, I do not wish to share the details."

"Darn."

Bo yawned and stretched and slid his hands along his bare thighs, stirring the hair there and pretty much welding Larry's eyes to the motion. The light brushing of dark hair on Bo's legs made Larry stare as if he had never seen anything as mesmerizing in his life. For the umpteenth time in the last few minutes, he forcibly dragged his gaze up to Bo's face, where he found Bo staring right back.

A silence settled around them, which wasn't entirely uncomfortable.

"I'm not shooting for anything more than friendship here," Bo said. "I mean, if that's what's worrying you."

Larry aimed his eyes at the fire, just to tear them away from Bo's legs. "I-I didn't think you were."

"Besides," Bo explained. "I'm just getting over a broken heart. I don't need to start working on another one."

"Right," Larry agreed, a little too eagerly, with a little too much animation. "Me too. Getting over a broken heart, I mean. I've just sworn off men forever, in fact."

"Well, sure," Bo said, bobbing his own head up and down now as if he couldn't agree more. "Me too. Men suck."

Before he could stop himself, Larry snerked, "If you're lucky."

The two had a good laugh over that, some of it forced, some of it not. But it did serve to defuse the situation and relieve the tension of both men wondering if they had said too much or had perhaps attempted to insert themselves a little too forcibly where they were clearly not wanted.

Finally, Bo heaved a long sigh and slowly rose from his chair. He went through the motions of stifling a yawn, which was obviously fake. He stretched his arms high in the air, dragging his shirt up enough to expose a tiny belly button that boasted a very attractive treasure trail leading downward to where it ducked beneath the waistband of his boxers. The fact that Larry was watching was not lost on Bo.

"I guess I'll leave you to your book," he said, without much enthusiasm.

"Oh," Larry said, torn between relief and disappointment that Bo was about to leave. Once again he tried rather unsuccessfully to command his eyes to work their way up to Bo's face, since the man was standing there in front of him like a half-naked god, the light from the flames in the background limning the edges of his long legs as it shimmered through the fuzz that coated them. And that treasure trail! Holy Christ, that treasure trail! "G-good night, then."

"Good night," Bo said, smiling, brushing his hand across his stomach, and dragging the shirt up even higher.

A second of silence settled around them, interrupted only by the sputtering of the gas jets in the fireplace. The quiet was finally broken when Bo reached out, letting the shirt fall back into place, and tousled Larry's red hair. Only then did he draw back his hand and turn away.

With the feel of Bo's fingers still burning on his scalp, Larry watched Bo stride lazily toward the bathroom door, turn for a final wink of good-bye—looking mischievous as hell—then softly pull the door closed between them.

Just before the door shut completely, Larry shot out his hand as if to ask Bo to stay a little longer, but it was too late. The latch clicked shut, sealing Bo out and Larry in.

Larry sighed, turning his eyes back to the fire.

"Probably for the best," he muttered to himself, staring into the flames.

Chapter Five

Days passed. March became April.

After their brief interlude in front of the fire in Larry's room, the two new Stanhope employees forged a wary camaraderie, each trying not to overstep his bounds or insert himself into the private space of the other. Larry thought of that night a lot. He knew he was drawn to Bo. My God, how could he not be? The guy was gorgeous. He also suspected Bo was drawn to him. He was pretty sure Bo would respond favorably if Larry chose to reach out in a manner that might not be exactly businesslike, but the fear of where that might lead prevented Larry from going past the imagining phase.

Plus, this job was the best break he'd ever had. He didn't want to do anything to jeopardize it. Who knows what his boss would think if he found out his two helpers were diddling each other in the off hours? Would he care? Would he *not* care? Would he throw them both out on their ears? Larry didn't want to find out, and he was pretty sure Bo felt the same way.

Happily, there was plenty to learn and enough to keep them both busy as they absorbed what was expected of them in the Stanhope household. Larry didn't have to dwell on Bo as much as he might have otherwise. What Bo dwelt on was Bo's business. Larry wasn't going to worry about it.

So he stayed friendly, but not too friendly. Warm, but not effusive. Larry tried his damnedest to keep all sexual thoughts at bay. The last thing he needed was another broken heart.

With these considerations in mind, Larry and Bo quickly settled into their respective routines of service, and they did it with very little drama. There was a calmness about the way Mrs. Price ran the estate that eased their fears and misgivings considerably. Not a moment passed when they did not appreciate how lucky they had been to have claimed their positions over all the other applicants without a nerve-racking interrogation to sit through or so much as a burp of upheaval to their own lives.

Mrs. Price had not yet departed to begin her luxurious retirement at Frederica Manor when a day came that found Larry in closer proximity to the master than he had ever been before. The result of that first extended visit with Roger Stanhope might have gone poorly, but happily for Larry, and it would seem for Mr. Stanhope as well, their being thrown together quickly produced the seeds of a burgeoning mutual respect. Larry had, of course, served Roger his meals in his room many times. He had even begun to understand the complexities of the way Mr. Stanhope preferred his clothing be laundered and arranged, and how he seldom required help dressing but did sometimes need a hand, due to his arthritis, with the knotting of ties and the tying of shoelaces. Larry knew how and when to walk the dogs. He had learned the art of polishing silver (which he hated) and the trick of flattering Mrs. Price's hairstyle (which he got a kick out of) when she nagged a bit too long regarding his shortcomings, of which he seemed to be blessed with many, at least in her eyes. And he had even acquired the ability to artfully ignore the master at those times when he seemed to be speaking to someone who wasn't there, which Larry assumed was simply one of the many vagaries of old age.

All that aside, however, Larry found himself continually astonished that he should take such pleasure in the company of a man as old—and as *rich*—as Roger David Stanhope. Even from the beginning, to Larry's amazement, there was very little master/servant attitude to be seen from the man signing his paychecks. In fact, he comported himself more like a loving old uncle than a boss.

For his part, Roger was not surprised to find himself enjoying the new help's company as much as he did. He had seen the goodness in Larry that very first day through a pair of jittery binoculars long before they ever confronted each other face-to-face. So matters on the home front were progressing as Roger had hoped.

Their growing friendship was cemented on a day a few short weeks after Larry and Bo took up residence beneath the Stanhope roof. It came about because Mrs. Price's allergies had finally landed her in bed, as they did almost every spring. While Bo saw to her needs, Larry attended the master's.

That day Larry and Roger came together for the very first time on the widow's walk high atop the venerable old mansion, a place Larry had yet to visit.

It was coming on to evening. While a crystal California sky sprawled unblemished across the heavens, a rimmed, reddish sun hung low on the western side of the mountain. From its position there, teetering on the brink of the horizon, it would soon welcome the night ahead by blinking itself into oblivion and releasing the stars above. A freshening breeze sighed among the eaves. The air was heavy with the scent of sage, poor Mrs. Price's downfall.

Roger had napped in the afternoon, so he was enjoying his tea and cookies later than usual. For the first time, he would be partaking of them without the jovial Mrs. Price to keep him company.

While Mrs. Price recuperated downstairs, Larry stepped out onto the widow's walk, arriving there in a clatter of metal inside the rickety elevator, which Larry had never experienced before either and didn't much care for, if the truth were known. The tiny elevator was a little too confining for Larry's taste. A little too claustrophobic. A little too groany and rattly and wobbly. Larry didn't like elevators anyway, and this one was clearly a death trap.

When he stepped through the grated doors and planted his feet back on solid flooring, he did so with considerable relief.

Roger was already waiting. In fact, it was the beeper at Larry's belt that had summoned him to the master's side. At Mrs. Price's orders, muttered between sneezes and a flurry of tissues, Larry bore a tray, balancing it carefully. The tray contained a teapot of brewing turmeric and ginger tea, a plate of homemade cookies, and two cups and two saucers. Larry wasn't sure who the second cup and saucer were for until Roger invited him to sit and relax for a while.

Larry poured the tea. Before dutifully plopping himself down in the chair beside Roger's, he stepped up to the railing to stare out at the mountain sloping away in the distance, bluish now with the haze of a spring evening moving in. Even with a bank of fog rolling up the hill toward them, the view was breathtaking, with the golden lights of the San Diego city skyline shimmering far off in the distance, and beyond that a muted line of blue water—the grand Pacific Ocean.

"Wow," Larry said. "This is beautiful!"

"Thank you," Roger said as he arranged cookies on his plate, tucking them painstakingly around the edge of his teacup with trembling fingers. His hands were weak this evening. "When it's less hazy, you can see the ocean off in the distance a little more clearly. It's one of the reasons I love this house."

"I can understand why," Larry said, awed by the endless beauty stretching from one horizon to the other. He finally turned his back on the view and leaned against the rail, awkwardly balancing the delicate saucer and teacup in front of him. China teacups and saucers were a new experience for him. He was more used to slurping instant coffee out of big fat mugs.

Roger gazed up at him and smiled, amused by the uneasy way Larry handled the china but happy to learn his new employee enjoyed the view as much as he did.

Roger's smile became an apologetic cluck of sympathy when Larry, pinky up as Amy Vanderbilt had decreed and trying not to spill, took his first dainty sip of tea. Larry instantly made a face like a kid who has found a worm inside his Snickers bar. He even did a wee tap dance of disgust, he was so taken aback. When Larry stopped jumping around and making faces, he stared down at the cup he was holding, appalled.

"Holy crap."

Roger tried desperately not to laugh but didn't succeed. "Sorry about the tea," he finally sputtered. "It's vile, son, I know. But the turmeric and ginger are supposed to be good for me. Mrs. Price's cookies should make up for it. Have a seat and help yourself."

Larry cast another horrified glance at his cup, then took a last peek out across the mountainside before lowering himself to the chair his boss was pointing at. He immediately took Roger's advice and gathered up a fistful of cookies from the platter on the table and sat munching them as they talked, happily dispelling the taste of the tea.

Roger studied him, his old eyes wide and friendly. "Do you miss being in the city?" he asked. "We're rather secluded up here, I'm afraid. A young man like you must find it tedious."

Larry's eyes slid to Roger, then just as quickly moved away. He still wasn't accustomed to the casual relationship Mr. Stanhope appeared to nurture with his employees. He appreciated it, but he wasn't used to it. "No, sir. I don't miss the city at all."

"Do you miss your friends?"

Larry shrugged. "I didn't have many."

"Why do you suppose that was?"

At a loss as to how to answer that question, Larry merely remained silent.

Roger's smile widened. "You don't talk much, do you?"

Larry let his eyes drift to Roger's face again, and this time they stayed there. A tiny, teasing smile twisted the corner of his mouth. "Give me a six-pack of beer and I never shut up."

Roger threw his head back and laughed. "One of those! My lover was like that. Three beers and it would take a bazooka to shut him up. I'll have to tell Mrs. P to order some beer."

Larry watched as the old man sat chortling to himself. Still smiling, Roger turned away and stared out at the horizon as if suddenly lost in memory. Larry gave him a moment of peace to enjoy his thoughts, whatever they might happen to be. While he waited, he devoured a couple more cookies.

The humor gradually faded from Roger's face. He turned to gaze at Larry once again. Larry sat up straighter when those delving eyes fell on him. He had to remind himself he was actually working here. It might not be wise to let his guard down completely. He didn't want the old gentleman to think Larry was becoming too familiar. Or not showing enough respect.

Roger looked away long enough to dunk a cookie into his tea. "Will you tell me now why you think I saved your life?" Roger asked quietly. "You said you would tell me one day." He waved a hand expansively across the heavens. "Today would appear to be as good a day as any, don't you think?"

Larry choked down another sip of tea. The stuff really was disgusting. He scooped a few more spoonfuls of sugar into it, hoping that would help. When it didn't, he ground up a cookie in his fist and dumped that in, much to Roger's delight. Finally Larry faced the fact that he was stalling for time. Figuring he had milked his cup of tea for all it was worth, he glanced up at Roger and said, "I'm not very proud of the story, sir."

"Tell me anyway," Roger said. He gazed about, taking in everything; the mansion below, the sky above, and most of all the young man sitting next to him. When he felt the universe was in the order it should be, he reached out and patted Larry's arm. His eyes were kind. "There are no judges here, son. You may always speak freely with me."

Larry nodded and stared out over the rail at the approaching bank of fog still oozing up the mountainside. Soon it would touch the grounds around the mansion, and the air would turn cool and damp. Even his rooms would be chilled as the night wore on, but a nice comfy fire would remedy that. Larry almost smiled at the thought. Then his face sobered, and he looked down at his hands. "Well, sir, on the day I saw your ad, I had just found an eviction notice on my front door because I was late paying the rent. It wasn't the first time. I guess the landlord had finally had enough." Larry heaved a sigh. "I was working, see, but it was a dead-end job and paid practically nothing."

"So you were unhappy," Roger said softly.

Larry tried to ignore the blush he felt rising to his cheeks. "My lover had just left me too. I was…. I was…."

"Heartbroken?" Roger gently prompted.

"Yes. Heartbroken. Pissed off. Feeling sorry for myself. Whatever your problems are in life, it seems that love only complicates them. I hope I never have to suffer through it again. I hope it never comes crawling out of the woodwork to ambush me like it did the last time. I hope… I just hope…."

"Yes? You just hope—what, son?"

Larry dropped his eyes to the cookie in his hand, gazing at it oddly, as if he couldn't quite remember how it got there. "I hope I never fall in love again."

Embarrassed by the way the words had started pouring out of him and hoping to maybe stem the tide a little bit, Larry took a long sip of tea, forgetting what it tasted like. When his eyes flew open in surprise, Roger reached over and plucked the cup from his hand.

"The next time you serve me tea on the roof, I think you'd better bring a beer along for yourself. I won't tell Mrs. Price if you won't."

Larry blinked back his embarrassment. "Really?"

"Yes. And while I'm thinking of it, you might bring a beer along for me as well. You're not the only one who hates this fucking tea."

Larry's jaw dropped; then he immediately perked up. "Yes, *sir*!"

Roger gave Larry a gentle perusal. "And don't be so quick to give up on love. Sometimes it's all that stands between us and the abyss."

Larry shook his head. Adamant. Determined. "Nope. It's not for me. Never again."

Roger eyed him sadly, but not so sadly either. Actually he was eying him more like a particularly troublesome crossword puzzle that he was determined to solve no matter what it took to do it. "Oh dear," he said, playfully drumming his fingers on his teacup.

"Huh?"

Roger gazed off at the setting sun, its flames paler now, dulled by the encroaching fog. "Never mind, son. I may have to rethink a few things. That's all."

"I don't understand."

Roger turned back to the boy and smiled. "No, I don't suppose you do. But then, how could you? Let's just say I've suddenly spotted a roadblock in my well-laid plans. Now I need to find a way around it."

"I still don't understand."

Roger clucked his tongue in sardonic sympathy. "Poor boy."

Larry had noticed that for the last few minutes, Mr. Stanhope had been rubbing his eyes as if they bothered him. Peering closer, he thought he detected the reason for it. Mr. Stanhope's eyebrows had grown ragged and long. He wondered if he was being presumptuous, but he decided to ask anyway.

"Sir, your eyebrows are so bushy they are getting in your eyes. You're starting to look like Gandalf the wizard. I can trim them for you, if you like. I mean, if you don't mind."

Roger stopped chewing his cookie and stared at the boy. "Why—no, son. I don't mind. In fact, I would appreciate it. My eyes *have* been bothering me lately. I just wasn't smart enough to realize what the problem was."

Larry's face lit up. He dumped his saucer and cookies on the tray, held up a finger, and said, "Stay right there. I'll get my scissors."

With that, he took off on his young legs, bounded through the door that led to the elevator, and disappeared with the distant clanking of the hated apparatus as it lowered its excited cargo into the bowels of the building.

Roger sat chuckling as he listened to the rattling car drop away to silence.

A melodic noise immediately hummed in Roger's ear. It might have been the whispering whine of an insect, but Roger knew it was not. He knew because insects rarely mutter actual words.

"Don't go falling in love with him, Rog. You still belong to me."

The old man chuckled. "But he looks so like you with that stunning red hair. And his laugh. His laugh is like yours too. And his hands. Did you see his beautiful hands?"

"Don't care," the voice buzzed. "Don't do it. I'll pitch you both off the roof if you even think about it. Won't hesitate for a minute."

Roger dropped his head to his chest and laughed quietly. "You always were a violent chap."

"I may need to do a bit of gentle prodding, though," the voice said, and Roger lifted his head.

"You mean with him and me?"

"No, indeedy. You two are getting close enough. I mean with him and the cook."

"Ah, yes. He did say he never wants to fall in love again, and we can't have that, now, can we? Think you can fix it?"

"Perhaps. An idea or two come to mind."

"Don't you go crawling under Bo's blankets in the middle of the night. I let you get away with it with Larry. The next time you engage in sexual meanderings with the help, I'll call a priest and have your spectral ass exorcised."

"Snippy," Jeremy said. Then silence fell. It didn't last long. "He's coming back. Remember what I said, Rog. Don't go falling in love with the lad. I don't want to see you on the flagstone path below surrounded by broken cookies and a shattered teacup. I bought that china pattern in Hong Kong, if you remember."

"I do indeed," Roger said around a smile. "I remember we laughed about it at the time. Buying china in China. We were amused easily back then."

"Asshole."

Roger barked out a laugh, and at that moment, Larry returned, a little out of breath, looking handsome and triumphant.

"Got 'em," he said, flashing a tiny pair of scissors that looked like the sort a first grader might have stowed away in his school desk for art class. "Who were you talking to?"

"Myself, of course," Roger said rather defensively. "Who did you *think* I was talking to?"

Larry thought about it for a moment. "Ghosts, maybe?"

Roger sat smiling inwardly, refusing to respond. He could have orated for twenty minutes in reference to what the boy had just said, but he knew he'd better not. He was fairly certain his young house servant thought the new boss was dotty already. No sense convincing him completely.

In the end, Roger didn't answer the ghost comment, so Larry gave him a questioning little moue. When he did, a most agreeable pair of crinkles appeared around Larry's eyes, which Roger found quite lovely.

Larry tucked a napkin around Roger's neck and gently eased the old man's head back. "Close your eyes, sir," he said. "This won't take but a minute."

Roger did as he was asked. He sat there with his eyes closed for what seemed the longest time, but nothing happened. He finally eased one eye open to take a peek.

"What's wrong?" he asked.

"I'm nervous," Larry said. "My hands are shaking. I don't want to hurt you."

"Just because I'm old, son, doesn't mean I'm fragile. Do your worst. I can take it."

"I don't want to blind you."

"With your young eyes, I'm sure you won't," Roger said, tapping his fingertips on his chair arm, growing a bit impatient. "I trust you completely. Go ahead. Shear me like a sheep."

Larry sucked in a deep, pensive breath. Shielding Roger's eyes with one hand, he began carefully snipping away at the long eyebrows that were impeding his boss's vision.

Roger sat perfectly still while Larry worked. Only once did he reach up and rest his fingertips to the hand that shielded his eyes from the falling hair and snipping blades. Larry ceased cutting at the touch.

"I wasn't always old, you know," Roger said, gazing up into Larry's face. The words seemed to be something he needed to say. Something he had been *longing* to say. A proud sadness showed in the narrowing of his lips, the stubborn line of his sagging jaw. "There was a time when I was young like you, son. I want you to know that. I wasn't always feeble and helpless. I didn't always hide from the world as I do now."

Scissors poised in midair, Larry gazed down into the old man's eyes. The lines on his brow relaxed. Compassion flared in Larry's eyes. Roger sat speechless and humbled in the warmth of that kind gaze. His fingertips still rested on the boy's hand.

"No, sir," Larry said, easing back the snow-white hair from Roger's forehead with a gentle nudge. His pliant fingers remained there, resting at Roger's temples. "I never thought you were, sir. I never thought you did." Quietly, he added, "Close your eyes now, please. I'm almost finished."

Roger did as he was asked and felt Larry's warm breath on his face as Larry blew the clipped hairs from around his eyes. Larry's breath smelled of cookies and youth. The scent of it filled Roger with memories of another's breath, another's gentle scent and heat. Another's kindly touch.

It was at that precise moment that their friendship was born. Although as yet, only the older man was truly aware of the fact.

MRS. PRICE lay wrapped in a cashmere bed jacket with a twist of tissue protruding from each nostril, rather making her resemble a skinny old walrus. Breathing through her mouth, she was trying not to sneeze again for what had to be the one hundredth time in the last ten minutes. She stared piteously at Bo through rheumy eyes, her nose as red as a strawberry. Then she gazed self-pityingly at herself in a hand mirror she kept tucked at her side, plucking the tissues out of her nostrils as she did. With a *tsk tsk tsk*, she focused her attention back on Bo.

"I'll bet when you woke up this morning, you didn't know you'd be spending the day picking snotty tissues off the floor around an old woman's bed."

Bo grunted as he bent down and scooped a couple of errant wads of Kleenex from beneath the antique dresser perched against the wall. Then he spotted two more behind a potted plant by the window and crawled across the floor to gather those up and stuff them in the trash can he was holding. The receptacle was already overflowing.

"Wasn't even on my radar," he said with a grunt. Heaving himself to his feet, he gazed down at his patient. "I've never in my life seen anyone leak as much mucus as you. It isn't normal. It's like fodder for a horror movie. *Night of the Living Snot.* Or maybe *The Fall of the House of Phlegm.*"

She gave a nasal snort that in certain alien cultures might have denoted a laugh. In this culture it sounded more like a note from a dyspeptic oboe. "As Mr. Stanhope ages further, you may be required to do worse things than pick up an old lady's snotty tissues. You realize that, I hope."

Bo grunted again, just for the hell of it. "The fear strikes me with unrelenting frequency."

Mrs. Price laughed and simultaneously cleared her nasal passages into a fresh swath of tissue. This time the sound she produced was akin to that of a mating yak. She knew it and Bo knew it, but both were too embarrassed to mention it. "Well, it's been a while since you started working here. How are you getting along with Larry? Roger wants the two of you to enjoy the time you spend together."

Still clutching the wastebasket filled with snotty tissues, Bo propped his ass on the windowsill and stared at Mrs. Price lying in the bed in front of him. "I like him well enough. He's a little hard to get close to. Not sure if he likes me or not."

"Men are so silly," she said. "If you aren't sure he likes you, then do something to *make* him like you. Be proactive. Throw caution to the wind. Hurl yourself at his feet. It might be to your benefit, you know."

Bo cocked his head and gave her a leery once-over. "I'm sorry. Are you asking me if Larry and I are getting along, or are you giving me tips on how to get him into bed?"

Mrs. Price pretended to act shocked. "Why, I'd never!" A moment later her expression mellowed. "But you like him," she said, batting her eyes and trying to look innocent. Then she coughed up a wad of crap the size of a baby turtle and spit it into a Kleenex, which pretty much dispelled the illusion of innocence.

"Does Mr. Stanhope know you do this?"

"Do what?" she asked, as guileless as a newborn.

"Play Cupid with the help."

"As long as I'm part of the help myself, I guess I can do whatever the hell I want."

Bo grinned. "I guess you can."

"Besides, I'm on my way out. What's he going to do, fire me?"

Mrs. Price plucked a tissue from the tissue box, then stared into the hole. The box was now empty. It was her third box in three days. She handed it to Bo as if his sole purpose for existing was to stand there and relieve her of it.

He clucked a sympathetic cluck while cramming the empty box into the sea of damp tissues in the waste can. The sympathetic cluck was for himself. "So when *are* you leaving?"

"Not as soon as you'd like, I'm sure. Nor as soon as I thought," she said. "The woman who was supposed to die at Frederica Manor and hand over her rooms to me has decided to be difficult and not kick the bucket quite yet. It's somewhat of a medical miracle, they tell me. Until either she or someone else on the premises departs the place toes up, I'm stuck right where I am."

"Damned selfish of the woman," Bo said, commiserating.

Mrs. Price's eyes twinkled. "That's what I thought. The bitch."

"On the bright side, I'll be able to enjoy your cookies a while longer."

She smiled. "What a sweet thing to say. You're not such a meanie after all."

Bo ignored the jibe and lowered himself to the edge of the bed. He sat there staring out the window. He finally cleared his throat and asked, "Seriously. Why are you so interested in how well Larry and I are getting along? If I didn't know any better, I'd swear you were trying to matchmake the two of us."

"Is matchmaking so bad?"

He glanced at her, then just as quickly looked away. His face got sneaky, but she was too busy blowing her nose to notice. "Tell me," he said. "Does this have anything to do with the way Mr. Stanhope worded his ad for help? You know, the whole 'gay, romantic hearts' and 'new beginnings' and 'hunger for life' business he was spouting. Know anything about that?"

"Not much."

He sniffed. "I'll bet." Bo sat quietly for a moment. "I do find him interesting, you know. Larry, I mean. I like him a lot. I just don't think he's interested in anything other than a working relationship."

"Are *you*?" Mrs. Price asked quietly, folding her hands in her lap, trying to maybe not look quite as eager as her question might imply.

Bo let her two little words hang in the air, purposely refusing to answer them, mainly because he wasn't sure what his answer would be if he did. He glanced at the ceiling, then over at her, then back out the window. "Wonder what Larry and the boss are talking about up there on the roof."

"Probably you," Mrs. Price drolly commented, then sneezed with enough force to rattle the blinds.

Bo ignored the sneeze. He'd gotten used to them by now. However, he was surprised by her answer. "You think they're really talking about me?"

"Yes. Indubitably. Just like we're talking about them. There is only a small contingent of us in residence. Potential for gossip is limited."

Bo considered that for a moment, then stared down at his hands. "It must be hard for him. Mr. Stanhope, I mean. Losing his lover after so many years. Being alone now. Yet he doesn't seem lonely. Mr. Stanhope is quite an exceptional guy, I think."

It was Mrs. Price's turn to cast her gaze in the direction of the widow's walk overhead. She did it fondly. "Yes, he is. Sweet, kind, generous. A loving soul." She sat more erect in the bed and reached out to snag Bo's hand. When she did, he turned his eyes to her with a vaguely offended look—or the pretense of one.

"I'll have to sterilize that now," he said, gazing down with mock horror at his hand covered by hers. "I'll have to dunk it in a bucket of lye and scrub it with a wire brush."

She smiled. "Oh, shut up." She took a moment to erase the humor from her face. "I hope you and Larry will take good care of him," she said. "If he asked, I would stay, you know. But the truth of the matter is, I simply can't do the work anymore. If I can't be of service, there is no need for me to remain in this house, even though I love it like my own."

"He wouldn't mind, I'll bet. I've seen how close you two are. Lord knows the house is big enough. Hell, if you didn't tell him, he'd probably never know you were still here."

She clucked her tongue as if it was pointless to argue. "The path is set. No sense forging a new one now."

Bo studied her. There were tears in her eyes. Bo wasn't sure if the tears were from the allergies or from the emotions the two seemed to have dredged up in each other. Actually, he didn't much care *why* there were tears in her eyes. He was still considering more important matters. More important... *mysteries*.

For the first time, Mrs. Price grew uncomfortable beneath his stare. "Run along now. It's almost time to start dinner. I think I'll sleep for a while. Don't forget to listen for the doorbell. The tailor is scheduled to deliver your uniforms today. Heaven knows it's taken him long enough."

"Oh God."

"Don't worry. This isn't a fashion shoot. You boys will look fine. And you won't have to worry about ruining your own clothes." She eyed him up and down, regarding his blue jeans and T-shirt with something less than relish. "Not that you really could."

Bo shot off a sarcastic little military salute and rather presumptuously patted her foot before leaving the room.

He was no more than three steps down the hall when he heard the front doorbell jangling away in the distance. He immediately sprang down the staircase to answer it. Mrs. Price was right. The uniforms had come.

EXPECTING THE worst, Larry and Bo stood on either side of the doors to their adjoining bathroom and tried on their new uniforms in the solitude of their own rooms. While they did, they yelled back and forth through the closed doors.

Neither noticed the teeny red camera lights shining from their ceilings.

Bo, in socks and underpants, stood in front of the full-length mirror in his room and pulled on the crisply ironed white chef's smock. It fit perfectly. Then, because pants are boring, and because he had waited to see himself in one of these for as long as he could remember, he tried on the billowy white chef's toque that came with the new uniform. He perched it on his head and stood smiling in the mirror.

"This is great!" he announced through the door.

"Glad you're happy," Larry returned, laughing.

"What did you do today?" Bo called out, making conversation.

"I had tea and cookies with the boss. He's really a nice guy. What did you do?"

Bo grunted with considerable disgust. "I got to watch Mrs. Price shoot snot through her blowhole like Moby Dick with a head cold."

"Lovely."

"Not really." After sorting through their new duds, both men were surprised to learn they'd had two separate sorts of uniforms prepared for them, with three changes of each outfit. Both men received blue dungaree pants and shirts for more physical work. Then for Bo, a chef's uniform, classic and snow-white except for an *S* (for Stanhope) embroidered on the smock. For Larry, neat black trousers with a red shirt and a black vest to be worn while serving the master. His vest too had a crimson *S* sewn neatly into the fabric.

Larry tried on the dungarees first. They looked great from the front. After neatly tucking in the work shirt, he turned his back on his mirror and craned his head around to see that his ass looked pretty good in the dungarees too. Well, that was a bonus.

"Not bad at all!" Larry called out through the door. Then he peeled off the dungarees and shook out the dressier service uniform, trying the vest on first, just for the hell of it. He stood admiring himself in the mirror in nothing but socks, jockey shorts, and the vest. He sucked in his gut and ran his hand through the reddish-blond fuzz on his stomach before turning to check out his ass again. With just the black vest on his back and his slim-cut briefs hugging his ass atop his strong hairy legs, he thought maybe he could audition for Chippendales—if he had a tan and at least a modicum of rhythm. Then he laughed at himself, although if the truth were known, he was actually thinking, *Well, huh. That's kind of sexy. Even for me.*

Bo opened his bathroom door and crossed to the other door. He rapped on it with his knuckles. "Can I come in? I want to see!" He was still wearing just the smock and chef's hat. His trousers seemed to have been forgotten.

Without waiting for an answer, Bo pushed through the door and found Larry in the black vest and little else, admiring his ass in the mirror.

Larry jumped three feet straight up in the air, and his face turned cherry red as he spun around and clapped his hands over his crotch.

"Jesus!" he bellowed. "Haven't you ever heard of knocking?"

Bo fought back a laugh, but couldn't have stopped looking if he'd wanted to. He swallowed hard and said, "Wow. Nice vest."

"Twit!" Larry grumbled. He snatched the black dress slacks off the bed and started pulling them on as fast as he could.

ONE FLOOR down, in the room that used to be a vast walk-in closet but now held a bank of security monitors rather like the President had in his War Room, Roger sat with his chin in his hand, enthralled, staring at the screen. His two boys had finally found themselves in the same room without pants. *This is certainly a step in the right direction*, he thought.

"Not good enough," said a voice in his ear. "Watch this."

"No, wait!" Roger wailed. But he knew it was too late. The resident spook was off and running.

WHILE BO continued to rudely stare at him from the bathroom doorway, Larry stuffed his bare legs into the trousers and started hopping around, trying to yank them over his ass.

"You have no sense of propriety whatsoever," Larry bitched, tripping, stumbling, and almost landing flat on his face when one foot got tangled in the trouser cuff and the other leg, still completely uncovered, was forced to tap-dance around to keep Larry balanced.

Bo still had a grin on his face. Politely turning away was the last thing on his mind. "I don't. I really don't. No sense of propriety at all. Never did have any, as a matter of fact. Probably never will. Say, Larry. Anyone ever tell you that you have really nice legs?"

Larry took a second out of his humiliation to glower at Bo, realizing for the first time that *he* wasn't wearing trousers either. "So do you!" he snapped. "But what the hell does *that* have to do with anything?"

At that, Bo finally laughed. "Well it certainly opens up a world of opportunities."

"Ass," Larry snapped.

"So I noticed," Bo said, ogling Larry's red briefs.

Furious, Larry managed to free his trapped foot and continue pulling the slacks all the way up over his ass, hastily buttoning them in the front. He reached for the zipper tab, gave it a yank, and... nothing. It wouldn't budge. His zipper was stuck.

"Jeez," Bo said, delighted. "Is this my lucky day, or what?"

"YOU DIDN'T," Roger said.

"I most certainly did," said Jeremy's voice in his ear. "Just like dead lovers, wardrobe malfunctions have their uses too."

"You always were devious."

"Thank you."

"But I won't have it."

"Oh pooh. Try to stop me, you old twit."

Roger reached for the control panel to turn off the cameras, thinking things were about to get steamy between his two new employees—and wasn't *that* a most amazing development? Still, he thought it would be the gentlemanly thing to do to remove himself from the equation. Unfortunately he found an invisible force preventing his hand from reaching the Off button.

"No, wait," Jeremy said. There was a chuckle in his voice now. It was a happy voice. A diabolically merry voice. For a ghost. "Let's see what happens."

"Pervert," Roger muttered around a grin. Bowing to the inevitable, he allowed himself to be coerced into staring at the monitor for just a little while longer, leaning forward now, his old eyes bright and eager. To his surprise, he found a snickerdoodle in his hand that had been there for the last three minutes. He had forgotten all about it.

"Fuck!" Larry sputtered.

"Well, if you think we have time," Bo simpered, batting his lashes like Bugs Bunny in high drag singing opera in front of a furious Elmer Fudd.

When Larry stabbed him with a stare chock-full of hatred, Bo tried to mold his face into a semblance of concern. If he didn't look too closely, the casual observer might have even believed it was sincere.

"Let me help you with that zipper," Bo said, solicitous as hell.

Before Larry could argue or scream or cuss Bo back into a neutral corner, the guy had crossed the room and dropped to his knees in front of Larry's crotch. Slapping Larry's hands impatiently away, he started tugging on the stalled zipper.

Larry stood frozen. Afraid to move. Afraid to breathe. Afraid he'd get a boner.

Still working at the zipper, Bo cast his green eyes up Larry's naked chest until they found that handsomely blushing face staring down. Bo offered a lascivious smile. "Do you have any idea how sexy you are in that vest? Especially from this angle. There are so many possible scenarios crashing through my brain right now about how this might turn out, I don't know where to start sorting through them."

Larry's Adam's apple bobbed up and down. They both heard an audible *gulp*. "Just hurry and fix the fucking zipper."

"Gotcha."

With a little more manipulation—during the course of which Larry held his breath again because Bo's clever brown hands were continually bumping his dick and balls, and dammit, it actually felt pretty good—the zipper finally broke free from whatever the hell was holding it and slid neatly upward into place.

The moment it did, Bo managed to look both victorious and crushed at the same time. Once again, he lifted his eyes to gaze up at Larry's face, trying to stare past Larry's fuzzy flat stomach without ogling it too much. He rested his hands on Larry's knees to brace himself.

"Don't," Larry said, tensing up even more than he already was.

Bo tilted his head, still locked on to Larry's gaze. "I'm not doing anything." The bowl of his puffy new chef's hat billowed down over his forehead, and he impatiently pushed it out of the way. His glance so burned into Larry's bare chest and midriff, Larry thought he felt the heat of it scorching his skin.

Larry fought to find his voice. When he located it, after a moment's desperate search, it sounded breathless even to his own ears. "Stop it."

"Honest," Bo said again, a tiny smile twisting his mouth, which was maybe four inches from Larry's crotch. "I'm not doing anything."

"Yes, you are."

Bo still made no move to rise. "I like your uniform. Does it have a shirt too?"

Larry reluctantly pointed to the bed, where the red checked shirt lay in a ball. He noticed his finger was shaking. "There," he managed to squeak. He was squeaking because not only was Bo's heated glance burning his skin, but now Bo's warm breath was blowing over his belly, and wasn't *that* a mesmerizing sensation.

"Nice," Bo said, mirroring Larry's thoughts, and giving Larry's knees a gentle squeeze with his fingertips, he hauled himself to his feet. But instead of stepping back, he moved closer. His hands came up as if to test the feel of the fabric of the vest Larry wore, and the backs of his fingers brushed the hair on Larry's chest. Both men shuddered at the touch. When he inched even closer, Bo's bare legs brushed Larry's slacks. By the startled look in Larry's eyes, Bo immediately knew he had gone too far.

"That's enough," Larry whispered. "Please." He breathed in Bo's clean scent, feeling Bo's body heat wafting over him. Or was that his imagination? And if not imagination—what? Wishful thinking?

What had previously been indecision, and possibly intrigue, immediately morphed into anger and maybe even a little fear. Larry wasn't ready for this, and Bo damn well knew it.

Larry pressed his hands to Bo's chest and pushed him away. Not hard enough for Bo to lose his balance, but with enough force to let Bo know he meant business.

Only then did Bo realize what he'd done. He gave Larry a contrite look, and the same blush that was still shining in Larry's cheeks rose to his own.

"I'm sorry," Bo said. "I didn't mean to do that."

"It's all right. Just go, okay?"

Bo nodded and, without speaking another word, moved to the bathroom door and hurriedly stepped through.

Larry stared at the back of Bo's strong bare legs until Bo latched the bathroom door quietly behind him, giving Larry the privacy he wanted. Or at least the privacy Larry *thought* he wanted. Now, of course, he wasn't so sure. Alone, Larry inhaled a great gulp of air to calm his nerves, and only then did he look down to see that he had an erection. There was even a spot of precome darkening his slacks. Christ, he really *was* turned on!

At that very moment, unbeknownst to him, the camera light over his head blinked out.

ONE FLOOR below, sitting in front of a bank of monitors now dark because he'd flicked them off, Roger glared into the empty room, his eyes ricocheting from one wall to another, never lighting anywhere. Searching.

"You've made matters worse," he hissed. "Now they're barely speaking to each other."

"Hmm."

"So fix it."

"Okay, okay. I'll fix it."

"You'd better," Roger groused, and heaving a sigh, he shuffled off to the bedroom to rest before dinner.

Chapter Six

Bo stood all by himself at the L-shaped kitchen island. Its tiled surface gleamed beneath him, and the doughy scent of fresh mushrooms flavored the air about his head. Happily chopping away at everything from bell peppers to cilantro, he chewed on a carrot stick and doo-wopped an old '50s tune so horribly off-key that even he was appalled by the way it sounded. With an array of sparkling brass pots and skillets and crepe pans dangling from hooks above his head, he energetically sliced and diced ingredients for vegetable soup, which would be the main course for that evening's meal. What with Mrs. P bedbound by allergies and Mr. S requesting mild fare for his ninety-three-year-old digestive tract, it was the simplest dish Bo could think of, but that was no reason it couldn't be delicious. For Larry and himself, and their younger and greedier appetites, he had prepped burgers and baked potatoes to augment the soup.

Having the sprawling Stanhope kitchen all to himself made Bo feel a bit like the lord of the manor. The kitchen was exceptionally equipped with the very best tools of the trade, and Bo loved it. Mrs. Price had stinted at nothing, which told Bo she must surely love to cook as much as he did. Even the Zwilling knives Bo wielded at that very moment were of high-carbon German steel, exquisitely balanced and as sharp as a harpy's tongue. They all but danced in his hands, shooting sparks of light across the room like fireworks while he worked. The larder too was continually stocked with fresh fruits and vegetables, the finest cuts of prime meat, and a goodly selection of sweets as well, including an astonishing twelve varieties of ice cream tucked away on a shelf inside the huge walk-in freezer. Bo suspected the master must have a sweet tooth.

For the first time in his life, Bo wore a newly tailored chef's uniform while he worked, something he had dreamed about for years. All but for the puffy *toque blanche*, that is. Having that fat, billowy thing parked on his head made Bo feel more like an actor than a chef. He had worn it for a while, imagining himself suave and urbane, sort of a reincarnated Emeril Lagasse with three decades shaved from his age and ten or twelve pounds peeled off his ass. Bo had stuffed the hat in a drawer after catching a glimpse of himself in the stainless steel refrigerator and realizing he simply looked silly. With his locks shorn down to nothing, it wasn't like Mr. Stanhope would be pulling Bo's hair out of his soup. Frankly, the toque made Bo feel pretentious and an imposter. It embarrassed him. After all, he wasn't *really* a chef. When it came right down to it, he was still nothing more than a short-order cook—albeit a short-order cook with pricier tools, far better pay, and an enjoyable lack of sailors yelling at him to hurry the fuck up with their motherfucking onion rings.

Bo's thoughts were interrupted by the happy clatter of toenails rat-a-tatting his way. Looking toward the door, he spotted the two pugs, Leo and Max, bustling into the kitchen. They were panting up a storm, their little tongues dangling free, and looking everywhere at once as if they owned the place—which in a sense they did. They seemed to be under the misapprehension that Bo had left a couple of T-bone steaks lying around for their dining pleasure.

"Sorry, boys," Bo said. "Nothing to see here. Move along."

Max and Leo plopped down right at his feet, haughtily ignoring the suggestion, so Bo went back to work.

While he chopped a few more vegetables, he eyed the perfect white rose that protruded from a slim crystal vase and currently sat on the kitchen windowsill where he had placed it earlier. Bo had discovered the rose, freshly cut and lying on the floor by his bedroom door when he left his room that afternoon to start dinner.

He had carried it with him down the stairs, cradling it between his fingers, breathing in its fragrance, as he descended to the kitchen, wondering all the while what the hell a perfect white rose would be doing lying outside his bedroom door. He had gone up to his room to fetch his cell phone because he had the soup recipe saved on it. The rose wasn't by the door when he went into his room, but it was there when he came out, no more than ten seconds later.

In the kitchen, he had rummaged through the cupboards until he unearthed a vase. So now there they both sat on the windowsill, the rose and the vase, looking all hopeful and fresh and enigmatic. Enigmatic because Bo still didn't know where the flower came from, or who had presented it to him.

Of course, the list of possible culprits was far from long. It had to be one of three people, in fact: Mrs. Price, Mr. Stanhope, or Larry. Those were the only three people on the premises, and two of those were laid up with health issues and far too old to be presenting flowers to *anybody*. Ergo, weeding out the two *least* likely candidates for putting a rose in front of his door wasn't much of a chore.

It was obvious Larry had placed the rose there. The only real question left was... *why?*

Was it Larry's way of apologizing for throwing Bo out of his room last night? Of course, Bo had deserved it. He knew that. But still, the gift of a white rose spoke of more than a simple apology, didn't it? In most circles it would be considered—what? A romantic overture?

As that thought crossed his mind, Bo stopped chopping for a minute and just stood there chewing up another carrot stick and deriding himself for being a sap. Larry had made it monumentally clear he wasn't interested in any sort of "romantic overture" when it came to Bo. He didn't even seem open to a simple *sexual* overture, which was actually what Bo had been shooting for with that stellar performance of dropping to his knees in front of Larry's crotch and grabbing the poor guy's recalcitrant zipper tab. He had been trying to get a rise out of Larry. Literally. And he hadn't been particularly subtle in the way he went about it.

So Bo stood here now. Fixing dinner. Chopping veggies. Glancing now and then at the rose on the windowsill. Remembering that luscious expanse of bare belly that had been smack in front of his face the night before.

Jeez. Even now his fingers itched with the need to touch the man, stroke that fuzzy chest, lay his lips to Larry's skin, and breathe in the scent of him. And then do more. Much more.

Like *that* was ever going to happen. Apparently.

Disgusted with himself, he tossed a fistful of diced tomatoes into a saucepan and growled. Only Leo and Max, milling at his feet, heard. And they didn't know what the hell it meant. Or care. They were still waiting for the human in white clothes to drop something tasty on the floor.

ROGER STANHOPE sat in front of a fire in one of the high-backed leather chairs. He had an ottoman tucked under his aching knees and a book in his lap. The book was currently closed, and he was using his index finger as a bookmark. He had just been interrupted in his reading by the clearing of a throat in the grate, which sounded somewhat like a sardonic "Ahem."

Until the clearing of that throat came along to interrupt his reveries, Roger had been happily reading and contentedly absorbing heat because his joints were acting up and nothing waylays arthritis like the soothing heat from a nice fire. Now, of course, he was simply staring into that fire with a scowl on his face.

"There you are," Roger said. "Did you fix the problem?"

"Yes. I gave him a rose."

There was nothing as obvious as a floating ghost's head staring back at him from the flames, but Jeremy was most certainly there, nevertheless. Roger could not only hear his voice, he could sense his presence. Just as Roger had understood Jeremy perfectly in life, he now understood him perfectly in death. Their love had spanned seven decades, after all. It spanned it on both this and the other side of mortality. Which wasn't to say Roger couldn't still be surprised by him now and then.

Roger leaned forward, peering more closely into the crackling fire as if he thought a ghostly head *should* be in there somewhere, tucked in among the flames.

"Did you say you gave him a *rose?*"

"Trust me. The cook'll love it."

"His name is Bo."

"Whatever. He's staring at the rose now while he's working in the kitchen. You're having vegetable soup for dinner. Sigh. I miss soup. And crackers. And blowjobs."

"Oh, hush. So where's the other one? Where's Larry?"

"He's been working on the lawn all afternoon, pulling weeds from the flower beds. At the moment he's in the shower cleaning up for dinner. Let's turn on the camera and watch him. He's quite lovely, you know. Very scrumptious. Nicely assed, if you take my meaning."

"No, I most certainly do not! You've ogled the man enough. And why is he doing yard work? Don't we have a gardener for that?"

"The gardener quit over a week ago. Mrs. Price has been too ill to interview another one."

"Well, I don't want to deal with it either. We'll let Larry do it."

"Come on, Rog. He'll be naked. Let's turn on the camera in the bathroom and snoop."

"Pervert," Roger said, trying not to grin. "You have no sense of decorum."

"I remember a time when you didn't either."

"Yes, well, I've matured. Even *death* didn't make *you* grow up."

"You mean I'm *dead*?"

At that, Roger barked out a laugh.

WITH THE sun teetering precariously on the horizon and the shadows of nightfall dimming the mansion's interior, Larry flicked on a few lights here and there while delivering a tray of soup to first Mrs. Price, then the master, both of whom were still under the weather—Mrs. Price with her allergies and Mr. Stanhope with his arthritis—and reluctant to leave their rooms.

"How is Mrs. Price?" Roger asked as Larry arranged his dinner on the table beside his chair, where he was still soaking up the heat from the fire.

"Snotty," Larry answered.

Roger chewed on a smile, all the while grunting in sympathy. "Attitudinally or medically?"

"Medically. Well, both actually."

"I was afraid of that. Look, I don't want to disturb her," he said, "nor do I want you to feel you need to assist in maintaining the grounds, Larry. That isn't your job. You have enough to do catering to me. Call around and see if you can hire a new gardener. The grounds require at least one man three days a week, I should think, to keep it decently groomed. Or four if they think they'll need it. Don't pay more than fifteen dollars an hour. Think you can handle that?"

"Yes, sir," Larry said, shaking out the linen napkin and spreading it over Roger's lap.

Roger patted his hand. "Thank you, son. You look nice in your new uniform. It's to your liking, I hope."

Larry twisted toward a full-length mirror in the corner and glanced at himself in his new duds. Dark slacks, red checked shirt, black vest. They were the first tailor-made clothes he had ever owned. He was still rather astounded by how perfectly they fit. He turned back to Roger and offered his best smile. "They're great. Thank you."

The worry in Roger's face dissolved. "How sweet you are." He gazed down at his dinner, then back up to Larry. "You may go now, son. Thank you. I can take it from here. Please leave the door ajar for the dogs."

"Yes, sir," Larry said. He glanced one last time at the dinner tray to reassure himself everything was the way it should be, then quietly left the room.

His heart quickened as he neared the kitchen. He wasn't sure what sort of reception he would receive. When he'd picked up the two prepped dinner trays for the master and Mrs. Price, Bo had been nowhere around. Upstairs showering away the grime of the day, Larry supposed. This morning Bo had been away from the kitchen as well, visiting with Mrs. Price, Larry presumed, leaving him to snatch up a fistful of croissants and some lunch meat and eat breakfast on the run before starting the yard work. All this meant, of course, that the last time he actually saw Bo was the night before when Bo had been half-naked and on his knees in front of him with his hands at Larry's crotch, gazing up at Larry's face with a sexy, hopeful leer in his eyes prior to Larry throwing a snit and tossing him out of his room.

And then there was the hard-on, but Larry didn't want to think about that. Hopefully, Bo hadn't noticed.

Larry rolled his eyes. *Yeah, right.*

By the time Larry stepped through the kitchen door, he was already blushing.

Bo was there. He was in his civilian clothes again and looking freshly scrubbed. The kitchen table was neatly set for two with the everyday Stanhope china—not the expensive stuff. There was even a white rose in a vase in the middle of the table. The delicious aroma of sizzling hamburgers and baked potatoes filled the air, making Larry's mouth water.

Or was it the sight of Bo standing at the stove, gazing over his shoulder at him, looking embarrassed.

"I wasn't sure you'd come," Bo said. "After last night and all."

Larry shrugged. "Gotta eat."

Bo's face fell. "Of course."

Larry blinked at Bo's reaction. "No! I didn't mean it that way! I'm not mad about last night. Things just got—*weird*. That's all."

Bo leaned his hip to the stove and stared. "I didn't think it was weird. I thought it was nice."

"Well, yeah," Larry fumbled. "That's what I meant. Nice. In a weird sort of way."

At that, Bo couldn't help but laugh. "Jesus, kid. Sit down and I'll serve dinner. You must be starved. I saw you slaving away in the yard all afternoon. You didn't even come in for lunch."

Larry looked away. "I was busy."

Bo turned back to the stove, and Larry breathed a sigh of relief. Maybe the dinner wouldn't be as uncomfortable as he had feared. He dragged out a chair and parked himself at the table, shaking a napkin into his lap. "Roger wants me to hire a gardener. I've never interviewed anybody in my life."

Bo cast a little sympathy his way. "I'll help you if you want."

Larry dragged out his first honest smile of the evening. "We'll see. Thanks."

Bo dumped a plate in front of him with two hamburgers, piled high with every garnish imaginable, and a humongous baked potato steaming between them, smothered with sour cream. Then Bo parked another plate with the same dinner on his own side of the table. He swung a leg over the back of the chair, plopped himself down, and dug in. A moment later, so did Larry.

Mouth full, Bo garbled, "There's soup too, if you want."

"No, this is plenty. Thanks."

Oddly, at that moment, Bo noticed Larry was no longer blushing, although he suspected *he* might be. He felt a definite burning in his cheeks. He stared at the flower between them, then redirected his glance to Larry's face.

Sensing the stare, Larry gazed back. "What?" Larry asked. There was a smear of ketchup on his lip, which Bo would have enjoyed licking off.

"Just wanted to thank you for the nice flower."

Larry stopped chewing. "Huh?"

Bo pointed at the rose. "The flower. Thanks."

"I didn't give you the flower."

"Sure you did. You left it by my door."

Larry gulped down a mouthful of hamburger just to get it out of the way. "No, I didn't."

"Then who did?"

Larry shrugged. "Beats me."

"God, I hope Mrs. Price isn't trying to woo me."

Larry snorted.

Bo snorted back.

Then both men sat frozen, their smiles fading as they stared at the offending rose.

It was Bo who finally broke the silence. He gave himself a shake like a wet dog and tore off another bite of hamburger. His face was still red. He could feel it. Larry's face was now just as red as his was. Must be something going around.

"I really am sorry about last night in your room, Larry. I didn't mean to—"

"S'okay. Nothing happened. It's all right. Let's just forget it."

That answer didn't seem to be to Bo's liking. He didn't take many pains to hide the fact either. "If that's what you want," he said coolly.

Trying his best to ignore the attitude, Larry executed a little drum roll on the table with his fingertips. "Still friends though, right?"

"Sure," Bo said. "If that's what you want."

There wasn't a lot of warmth bundled up in those words. Larry knew he had made Bo mad. Or hurt his feelings, which was even worse. Especially since Larry wasn't even sure why he was being such a dick about last night. It wasn't like he was that shocked to find a man on his knees in front of him. Heaven knows it had happened a few times before. And besides, would a pass from Bo be such a horrible development? After all, Larry found the guy sexy. He freely admitted it. Maybe it was just the *playfulness* of what had happened last night. The casual way it came about. Larry knew all too well what sort of heartache that could lead to. He and Daniel had started their affair joking around, and the next thing Larry knew, he was sitting alone in his apartment back in town, staring at four walls and wondering when his heart had exploded into a big ball of pain inside his chest. That's why he had sworn off love. *Remember?* he chided himself.

Then he stared across the table yet again at Bo, who was avoiding his eyes now. Yep. Larry had definitely hurt Bo's feelings.

A silence settled over the two men. In the hushed kitchen, the only sound they could hear now was the ticking of the clock on the wall behind them.

In that silence, without warning, came another sound. A sound— *and a movement*—directly in front of them.

They stared in horror as the vase with the white rose standing in it slid three inches across the table. *All by itself.*

A chunk of hamburger fell out of Larry's mouth and landed on the table. The fork in Bo's hand tilted and fell from his grasp, clattering to the floor. Both men stared at the rose. The vase. Waiting for it to move again. But it just sat there. Motionless. Just like it was supposed to.

"Am I crazy," Bo asked, "or did that thing move?"

Larry's mouth was still hanging open. He made a concerted effort to flip it shut before any more food escaped. He had never stopped staring at the rose. It took him a minute even now, but he finally wrenched his gaze from the damned vase and aimed it at Bo instead.

"Uh-huh. I saw it. I was staring right at it when it slid across the table toward me."

Bo's voice was breathless. Awed. "Good. For a minute there, I thought I was nuts."

At that, Larry dredged up an uneasy smile. "If you're nuts, so am I."

Together now, their eyes wandered back to the rose. They sat there considering it, like maybe it was actually a snake about to strike. Or a stick of dynamite ready to explode.

Bo took another bite of his hamburger. I mean, what else was he supposed to do? "So I guess we got ourselves a spook," he muttered.

"Looks like it."

"Maybe it was even the spook who left the rose by my door."

"Well, like I said, it wasn't me."

Bo tore his eyes from the flower and centered them on a far more pleasing target: Larry's face.

"And you forgive me for last night? We're still friends?"

"Yes," Larry said. "Still friends."

"I enjoyed it, you know."

Larry's eyes widened. "Enjoyed what?"

"Last night."

Larry sat there as the silence deepened around him. The only thing he could hear was the *whoosh*ing of the blood sluicing through the arteries in his head. At least he was pretty sure he could hear that.

The silence stretched out. Both men's dinners were forgotten as they gazed at each other. They weren't even thinking about the haunted vase anymore. They were simply staring into each other's eyes. Staring. Staring.

Just as the silence and the staring started to get awkward, Larry tore his gaze away from Bo's face and stared through the kitchen window instead, studying the darkness outside, the mountain buried in mist. Even the stars were absent. *Perfect*, Larry thought. *Not only do we have a ghost, now a bank of horror movie fog has moved in for atmosphere.*

"Did you hear what I said?" Bo asked, edging forward in his chair. "I said I enjoyed last night. I suppose that pisses you off."

Still eying the creepy night outside, Larry tried to ignore the heat he felt rising to his cheeks and ears. That heat had nothing to do with ghosts or fog or horror movies, and everything to do with the night before. Closing his eyes, he said softly, "No, it doesn't piss me off. I enjoyed it too."

Bo's eyes lit up. "Really?"

At that moment, both beepers, one clipped to Larry's belt and the other lying on the countertop by the kitchen sink, erupted in a wail of sound that sent both men flying out of their chairs. A glass toppled to the floor and shattered. The vase with the haunted rose tipped and rolled toward the table's edge. Even in the shock of the moment, Bo had the common sense to reach out and snatch it out of midair, standing it upright before it could follow the shattered glass to the floor.

The two beepers wailed excruciatingly on, signaling an emergency. Somewhere above their heads, they heard another wail. This one a living sound. It was one of the pugs, either Max or Leo, howling, getting his two cents' worth into the racket. Not to be outdone, the other dog joined in as well. Apparently they didn't like the wail of the beepers any more than Bo or Larry did.

It was the dogs' cries that spurred Larry and Bo to action. They both dove for their beepers, desperately punching buttons and all but shaking them to silence. With the sound abated enough that they could actually *think*, they hurled themselves through the kitchen door, then tore up the long staircase to the second floor. They thundered down the hall, then flung themselves side by side toward the master's bedroom door.

Behind them they heard the padded shuffle of Mrs. Price's house slippers hot on their tail. She was adding her own noise to the melee, screeching nasally, like a banshee with a head cold. "Oh lord! Oh lord! What's the man done? Oh lord!"

All three of them dove for the master's door at once, each trying to squeeze in first, jockeying for position and all but bonking heads together in their panic.

Popping through together, they stumbled to a stop and stood there staring.

Mr. Stanhope sat in his chair, his feet still propped up in front of the fire. He had a croissant protruding from his mouth, and he looked even more startled than they did.

"What is it?" he asked innocently. "What's wrong? Why was the alarm sounded?"

It was Mrs. Price who answered, and she did it with a huff of annoyance.

"Somebody's playing tricks," she said. "And if he wasn't already dead, I'd kill him myself."

Roger plucked the croissant from between his teeth, chewed up and swallowed the part that fell inside, then let his face split wide in a grin.

He was staring at Bo and Larry, standing there in front of him.

"Well, look at you two," he said, his hand coming up to pat his own heart as if it was all just too romantic for words.

Mrs. Price faced the two boys to see what Roger was talking about. Since Larry and Bo didn't know what the old man was talking about either, they turned to each other with the same purpose.

Much to their amazement, gazing down between them, they saw their hands clasped tightly together.

Roger swiveled his head to stare at the fire in the grate, aiming a jovial wink into the flames.

There was laughter in his voice when he said, "Well played, my love. Well played."

"What was that all about?" Larry asked.

He and Bo were standing in the hall outside their rooms. The mansion was silent around them again. Peace had been restored. The dinner dishes were being scrubbed and scalded to within an inch of their lives by the industrial-strength Amana dishwasher down in the kitchen. The dogs were tucked under the bedclothes in Mr. Stanhope's bed, undoubtedly dreaming of pot roast while they waited for their human to join them. And poor Mrs. Price, still vibrating with outrage (or was it glee?), lay in her bed hawking up snot balls, wondering if she'd ever get back to sleep.

"More importantly," Bo said. "Who were they talking about? Who was Mrs. P threatening to kill if he wasn't already dead? Who was Mr. Stanhope addressing in the fireplace? If I didn't know any better, I'd say there really *is* a ghost on the premises and they both know it."

Somehow Larry couldn't get too wound up about the ghost. In the first place, he didn't believe in ghosts. In the second place, he had more pressing matters to consider.

"And why were we holding hands?" he asked.

Bo stared down between them. "The more imposing question, I think, is why are we *still* holding hands?"

Larry lowered his gaze to where Bo was looking and saw it was true. They *were* still clasping hands. When he realized it, he yanked his own away.

The moment he did, Bo clucked his tongue. "Don't do that," he said and immediately reclaimed Larry's hand, snatching it back like he had every right in the world to hold on to it.

Larry's heartbeat shot from 33 RPM to 78. If he had possessed an internal turntable, Edith Piaf would have been sounding like Alvin the Chipmunk about now. He wasn't sure, but he thought maybe he could hear his heart thumping away inside his chest like a tom-tom.

When Bo reached up and slid a gentle fingertip across Larry's lower lip, Larry's heart pounded all the harder.

"I like you, you know," Bo said, his voice a gentle hush.

Larry tried to ignore a sudden tremor in his knees. He was also trying his damnedest not to close his eyes and lean into Bo's touch. "I like you too. But we're both gonna live to regret this."

"Maybe not. If we don't do anything stupid."

Larry's face went beet red. "I don't seem to have much control over that. I *always* do something stupid."

"Then I'll try to ignore it when you do."

As if he had no steerage capabilities over his own feet, Larry found himself taking a half step forward. Now they were so close together their toes were touching. He was starting to shake. He wondered if Bo could sense it.

"You're shaking," Bo whispered, laying that question to rest. Bo shuffled closer just as Larry had done. His fingertip left Larry's cheek, and he slipped a hand around Larry's waist, resting it lightly at his back, holding him in place as if afraid Larry was about to run.

Instead of running, Larry closed his eyes.

Bo held his face only inches from Larry's. Each man's warm breath flowed over the other—Bo's in lazy exhales, sexy and in control, Larry's in nervous little gasps. Since he didn't know what else to do with them, Larry raised his hands and gingerly seized Bo's arms. He thought maybe that way he wouldn't shake so much. It didn't work. It actually made him shake more. He opened his blue eyes and lost himself in Bo's green ones. *He's not smiling anymore*, Larry thought.

Bo's voice was a fragile thing, as if he had just dredged it up from the bottom of the ocean and exposed it to the light for the first time in decades. "It's pretty obvious the master wants us to be together. I'm not sure why, but he does."

Larry gave a shuddery exhale, expelling enough carbon dioxide to keep himself from passing out. Suddenly the inner workings of his body seemed to teeter on the very brink of dysfunction, like maybe he needed a tune-up or something. Or maybe his spark plugs were shot.

"Why would he care about that?" Larry asked.

"I don't know. I'm more interested in what you might think about it."

"You mean you and me?"

"Yeah."

"Isn't this kind of sudden?"

"I've been flirting for over a month, trying to get somewhere with you with little or no result. It hasn't exactly been the bullet train to Happyville, if you want to know the truth."

Larry blinked. "Sorry."

Bo's green eyes bored deeper. "Are you just not interested? Is that what it is?"

"N-no."

"No you're not interested, or no that's not what it is?"

Larry shuddered amid another nervous gasp. He wanted to pull away. Or did he? Somehow he couldn't bear the thought of stepping away from Bo's heat, or moving out of the line of fire of Bo's sweet breath blowing over his face. Or not having Bo's strong hands holding him in place.

"Every time I do this, I end up getting hurt."

"Every time you do what?"

"This. Don't be coy, Bo. You know what I'm talking about."

Bo inched closer. Larry hadn't been aware there was enough space left between them to *get* closer until Bo closed the gap even farther. "I've been hurt too, you know. It's no reason to stop trying, Larry."

"I-I know."

"I'm not declaring my undying devotion here. I just want to be closer. I want to get to know you. Biblically."

Larry took that at face value. He didn't even smile. "I know."

Their kneecaps were pressing together now. Larry figured it would only take an adjustment of a silly centimeter or so before their crotches came into contact. It would be all over then, of course. He knew that much. He was as hard as a hammer down there already, and he suspected Bo was too.

"Larry?"

"What?"

"I don't want to chase you anymore. I want you to walk through this door and get into my bed."

"You mean now?"

"Yes. While you're still trembling."

"I'm not trembling."

Bo's mouth molded into a sexy, sweet smile that sent a rush of endorphins shooting through Larry's body like a surge of electricity. If he had been a computer, his memory banks would have been sizzled clean.

"Liar," Bo said with a kindly sneer.

"I know," Larry sighed, accepting the truth for what it was. Knowing he couldn't fight it anymore, and not *wanting* to fight it anymore, Larry shuffled forward even *more*, closing that final knife edge of distance between them. He gripped Bo's hips and tilted his head up. Rising on tiptoe, he laid his mouth over Bo's, claiming his first kiss.

As much as Bo had been wanting this, he still gave a tiny jerk of surprise when Larry's lips found his. He squeezed his eyes shut, tasting Larry for the first time. Their tongues met inside the moist heat of that kiss, and Bo's heart sped faster.

Their crotches bumped, and just as Larry suspected, there were two hammers down there now, and they were snuggled right up next to each other, one just as hard as the other. Simply feeling their two dicks together made Larry's knees buckle.

Two seconds later, Bo was dragging him on his wobblyass knees through the bedroom door.

At that moment, the camera light at the corner of the hallway ceiling blinked out.

One floor down, an old man and his dead lover sat giggling. If more than one of them had possessed any real substance to his being, they would have been high-fiving each other and tossing down celebratory shots of brandy.

Chapter Seven

"I'm going to regret this," Larry said.

"No, you won't."

"I'm regretting it already."

"No, you aren't."

Larry shuddered uncontrollably, as if proving Bo right.

He was shuddering because of the lips at his neck. The hands at his back. The cock pressed against his own through *way* too much fabric.

As if reading his mind, Bo went to work removing some of that fabric immediately, while at the same time he stuck his foot out behind him and kicked the bedroom door shut, sealing them in.

Larry toed his shoes off while Bo peeled away Larry's uniform vest and tossed it in a corner. With the vest gone, he went to work on the buttons of Larry's shirt. As he did all this, his lips never left Larry's throat.

While Bo tore at Larry's clothes, Larry didn't just stand around waiting to get naked. He went to work himself, fumbling with the snap on Bo's jeans, pulling them apart. Since he couldn't reach any farther at the moment, what with Bo's mouth on his throat, he tugged Bo's T-shirt over his head and flung it away. At that same moment, Bo's hot fingers pushed Larry's shirt back off his shoulders and let it drop to the floor behind him.

Their mouths came together yet again as their naked chests lay suddenly one against the other.

"Oh man," Bo mumbled into the kiss before dropping to his knees and pressing that same kiss to the crotch of Larry's pants.

"I'm starting to see a pattern here." Larry smiled down. "Me on my feet, you on your knees."

"Deal with it," Bo gasped. With shaky fingers he unclasped Larry's belt, unsnapped the button holding Larry's slacks shut, and without asking permission or shooting off an application by mail or anything, he tugged Larry's slacks straight down to the floor.

He rocked back on his heels and admired the bulge inside Larry's jockey shorts. Since that bulge seemed to be doing everything it could to claim its freedom, Bo decided it would be ungentlemanly of him not to give it a little help. Without further ado, he slid his hands up inside the leg holes, relishing the warm skin of Larry's thighs, and when his hands were inside Larry's underpants all the way up to the elastic, where his fingers suddenly popped out into the light, he took hold of the waistband and stripped the shorts straight down Larry's gorgeous fuzzy legs until they were covering nothing but Larry's ankles.

Suddenly freed, Larry's cock sprang up, bonking Bo on the chin, eliciting a smile from both men.

"Well, now, look at this," Bo said, his dimples boring deep holes in either cheek.

Larry squeezed his eyes shut. Then he peeked downward to find Bo's handsome face pointed upward toward his. Larry's cock lay nestled against Bo's cheek as if it had come home to roost, which indeed it had.

Splaying his broad hands across Larry's stomach, Bo pressed a kiss to the nest of hair encircling one of the most beautiful cocks he had ever seen in his life. It rose up before him, long, fat, and proud. The thatch of pubic hair it stood anchored in was fiery red and coarse, audibly bristling at Bo's touch. The bristling of that coarse red hair was the most erotic sound Bo had ever heard. With his nose buried deep in Larry's pubes, Bo breathed in the intoxicating scent of testosterone-laden maleness, with just a soupçon of body lotion, perhaps, or maybe body spray, sweetening the mix.

The heft and fiery heat of Larry's thick shaft lying against his cheek made Bo utter, "God, Larry. What a hunk you are."

Larry ran his palms over Bo's shorn scalp and, cupping the sides of Bo's face, pulled him gently to his feet. The moment he was standing, it was Larry's turn to venture south.

Dragging a long unbroken kiss along Bo's torso, from throat to belly button, he settled comfortably to his knees and, too eager to waste time, gripped Bo's jeans and pulled them the rest of the way open. Leaning forward, he laid a kiss to the heated skin just below Bo's belly button. With Bo's pubic hair tickling his chin and Bo's hands clutching his head, pulling him even closer, Larry pushed the blue jeans down those long, lean legs until they were puddled at Bo's feet. Bo's cock slapped his cheek. While he braced himself by clutching Larry's head,

Bo stepped out of his pants almost lazily. Only the trembling in his legs gave him away.

The moment Bo stood completely naked before him, Larry slipped his hands around to cradle Bo's ass, and at the same time he pushed Bo's cock to the side and slid his tongue over Bo's balls, tasting him, prodding gently, leaving moist swaths of saliva in his wake. From there his tongue traveled up Bo's erect shaft, licking and savoring along the way. With a fingertip, he tilted the unbending shaft downward to where he could get at it and, with a groan of ecstasy, tucked the head of Bo's magnificent cock between his lips.

Bo spasmed, and his fingers tightened in Larry's hair. While Larry gently cupped Bo's balls in the palm of his hand, he dragged Bo's dick ever deeper inside his mouth. Savoring the girth of it. Relishing the rubbery fat corona against his tongue, his cheeks. Tasting already the seeping fluids oozing from the slit.

Larry's cock was so hard now it was starting to hurt. He had reached down to grasp it, to stroke it into pleasure because there was no way he could ignore it another second, when Bo leaned forward, slipped his hands in Larry's armpits, and pulled him to his feet.

"Bed," Bo breathed. "Now."

His mouth moist from Bo's juices, Larry lifted his eyes to Bo's face, seeing the smile there, the lazy, hungry eyes staring back at him. Bo gently circled Larry's cock with his fingers. He brought his mouth forward to sample the moisture on Larry's lips. Their tongues met again.

Rising on tiptoe because Bo's hand felt so wonderful around his dick, Larry almost lost his balance, and losing his, he almost knocked Bo down as well.

They both laughed while Bo pulled Larry toward the bed, being none too gentle about it. "Hurry," he said. "Before we break our necks."

A moment later Larry fell through the air and landed with a crash on Bo's bed. In Bo's arms. Their strong legs wound together. Their mouths joined once again in a kiss. Their arms hungrily pulled each other close. Bo clutched him so tightly Larry had to struggle for a breath of air, but at the same time he returned the grasp with all the strength he could muster, matching Bo's need with needs of his own.

"Swing around," Bo pleaded.

"Oh, yeah," Larry gasped, getting the gist immediately, and flipping himself to face the opposite direction, he squirmed down in the bed until he had Bo right where he wanted him. The moment he took Bo's cock into his mouth, Bo eagerly consumed Larry's as well, drawing it all the way down his throat until Larry gave a cry and arched his back like a drawbridge.

Fearing things were going too fast, Bo eased up. Using his hands now as much as his lips, he continued to pleasure Larry's beautiful cock, but he did it gently, his hands never ceasing to move, exploring the vast plains and luscious valleys of Larry's smoothly muscled body. And while he explored Larry's terrain, Larry explored his.

Long minutes of pure wonder passed. Once again their movements, their proddings, their *savorings*, began to grow more fevered.

Larry pawed at the satin skin covering Bo's rib cage as he once again arched his back to meet Bo's hungry mouth, driving his cock deeper into those worshiping lips as Bo silently pleaded for him to do.

Around Larry's cock, Bo whispered, "Come for me."

"You too," Larry murmured, still relishing Bo's iron dick.

Seconds later—or was it hours?—the two knew they couldn't hold off any longer. Lying in each other's arms, hanging on for dear life, their hearts began hammering a frantic tattoo. Larry stiffened first, then Bo. An instant later, their backs rose in unison. They cried out as hot lava suddenly flowed through their cocks and over their tongues at the exact same moment. Clutching each other blindly, they savored the juices spilling into their mouths and held on tight as each bucked and gasped and emptied himself into the hungry, eager mouth of the other.

The bucking went on and on. Even when their juices were spent, they still clutched each other, their hips moving as if in perpetual release, their bodies shaking, their mouths still drawing yet one more drop of delicious nectar from the other. One more taste. One more treasure.

As their cocks began to soften on come-soaked tongues, their bodies slowly relaxed. Their thundering heartbeats slowed. Yet their hands still moved, still languidly explored, still clutched and prodded and stroked and kneaded. But gently now. Lazily. Contentedly. The feeding frenzy calmed. The desperation of their own desires abated. For now.

As Larry's moist, softening cock slid from between Bo's lips, Bo pressed those same lips to Larry's stomach and breathed in his scent yet again. He listened to the quieting heartbeat thudding inches away. The gentle intake of breath, less desperate now. Less flurried.

"Thank you," Bo mumbled against Larry's skin, still thrilled by the feel of that hot, hairy stomach against his face.

Larry answered by clutching Bo tighter against him. Bo's depleted cock rested softly against Larry's lips, right where Larry wanted it to lie. It still seeped crystal liquid, which Larry happily tilted his head to lap away. Savoring Bo's taste with every new smear of juices on his tongue.

Never moving from their positions, the two men lay in situ, neither wanting to pull away.

Before they knew it, sleep crept in on quiet feet and claimed them, drawing them down into its contented depths, where the taste and scent of each other still laid claim to their senses even while their awareness of each other's presence had slipped away. Although they didn't know it, neither relinquished the other even in sleep, holding on tight till morning.

LARRY OPENED his eyes to a gray dawn spreading bluish shadows across an unfamiliar room. He suddenly remembered he was sleeping in Bo's bed. No wonder the room was unfamiliar. He felt a warm weight pressed to his sternum. It was Bo's arm, draped across his chest, holding him in place. Sometime in the night, they had shifted position and now lay side by side, although Larry didn't remember it. Bo was snuffling in his sleep, his slack mouth pressed to Larry's bicep. There was moisture on Larry's skin, like Bo had maybe slobbered while he slept.

Larry grinned. A little slobber couldn't hurt. It wouldn't be their first sharing of body fluids.

Fully awake now, Larry was inundated by a cornucopia of sensory overloads. The delicious scent of Bo's sleep-warm skin. The gentle, childlike sounds Bo made as he slept. The bristle of Bo's leg hair scraping against his own. Bo's sharp toes pressed against the ball of his foot. The overwhelming presence of Bo's long body snuggled up against his, both of them as naked as the day they were born.

Then Larry felt another sensation—the flutter of Bo's eyelashes against his shoulder—and noted the altered cadence of Bo's breathing as he wormed his way out of sleep.

Larry was staring right at him when Bo's eyes opened. The immediate smile that lit Bo's face on seeing Larry there in his arms made

Larry's heart give a startled patter. It had been a long time since anyone had looked at him that way first thing in the morning.

All Larry could think to say was "Yo."

Fighting back a yawn, Bo dragged Larry closer, pulling him over onto his side to bring them face-to-face. With their chests lying snug together, each could hear and feel the thumping heartbeat of the other. Bo bent his head into the crook of Larry's neck and pressed his lips to the tender skin beneath his ear. Larry closed his eyes to better savor the sensation. Their morning erections bumped heads down below, both cocks iron hard and doing a sensuous dance of reunion that caused the two men to grind their hips together, the mechanics of it beyond their ability to control.

Bo's voice was deeper than usual. Raw from lack of use. Or from the exertions of the night before. "Thank you," he muttered.

Larry snuggled closer, enjoying the sandpapery feel of Bo's buzz-cut hair against his tender lips, almost uncomfortable but sexy as hell anyway. He splayed his hands wide against Bo's back and explored the knotted muscles, still hot from sleep. The skin, the bone, the slumbering strength of Bo's lean body thrumming with life beneath his fingertips. He could feel Bo smile against the side of his neck. Bo kissed him there, and a second later Bo's heated tongue shot out and licked the kiss away, as if erasing all evidence of it, causing Larry to shudder yet again.

Bo eased himself away far enough to direct his eyes at Larry's face, studying him, admiring him. He pushed Larry's hair off his forehead, then left his fingers there, tangled in Larry's morning mass of curls.

"I've wanted this for so long," Bo said.

Larry struggled to find his voice. "Wanted what?"

"You. Being here. Like this. Ever since the day of the interviews. Down on the driveway. Remember? Tell me you've wanted it too. Tell me I'm not the only one who felt this way."

Larry's eyes skidded away. Still leery even after their amazing night together. Still afraid of being hurt. Being used. Rushing into things he wasn't ready to cope with. "Bo...."

Bo freed his fingers from Larry's hair and tucked a finger under his chin, dragged Larry's gaze back to him. "Tell me you enjoyed last night at least. It won't kill you to tell me that much."

Larry laid his hand against Bo's cheek, gently cradling Bo's delicate ear in his fingers. "You know I did."

"You're so beautiful."

"I should go," Larry said, but he smiled when he said it as if he knew the words were a lie. He didn't want to go, and he was pretty sure Bo knew it.

Bo smiled, proving him right. "You don't mean that any more than I *want* you to mean it. Admit it."

Larry ducked his head and pressed his mouth to Bo's throat. He wasn't sure if it was to taste him yet again or simply to hide his own embarrassment. "No," he said softly. "I don't want to go."

As if he had said enough to satisfy Bo, at least for the moment, Bo let the silence of the approaching dawn flow back in to surround them. While their stiff cocks still hungered down below, aching with need yet again, both men were lazily contented enough not to let the sensations tear them from each other's arms—at least for the moment.

When Bo cleared his throat to speak, his voice was stronger, no longer fractured by sleep and disuse. Still, the timbre of his words was so soft as to barely flow across the pillow from his lips to Larry's ear, as if Bo feared to be overheard—or was simply reluctant to share the words with anyone but the man in his arms.

"We're secluded here. I thought it would be lonely living on this mountain, but it isn't. Thanks to you, I haven't spent a lonely moment inside this house." A grin played at his mouth. "Frustrated, maybe. Horny. But never lonely. Tell me I won't have to feel those things anymore. Tell me I won't have to look at you from a distance anymore."

"What are you asking, Bo? What is it you want?"

Bo heaved a shuddery breath. He had pulled back again, just far enough to study Larry's face, Larry's expressions. It was the only way he could map the direction he wanted his words to go. If he made a wrong turn and began to scare Larry off, he would know, and then he could redirect his path. This was important. He didn't want to get lost. Or worse, lose Larry along the way.

Once again he recalled the words of the ad that brought them here. The words he continually found himself obsessing over. The words that were never out of his head. He also remembered Mrs. Price's evasive answer to his questions about the ad. She was hiding something. Bo was sure of it. For now, until he knew exactly what it was, he had to tread carefully.

Draw Larry in. Keep him close. And with a grin that never quite surfaced, Bo thought, *There is too much at stake. Maybe even a fortune if my suspicions are correct. Could it be? Is that what this is really all about?*

He forced his attention back to the man in his arms. The luscious feel of Larry's body against his. No matter if his suspicions about the ad were true or not, the game would be fun to play. And the sex wouldn't hurt either.

"I want us to open up the doors between our rooms," Bo said. "I want to go to bed with you at night and wake up with you in the morning. Every night. Every day. I want us to make love. I want us to get to know each other completely. I want you to miss me when I'm not close, and I want you to know I'm missing you. I want us to build a friendship and take that friendship wherever it leads us."

Larry ducked farther down in the bed and pressed his lips to Bo's nipple. He circled it with his tongue until it hardened in his mouth. Then he rose up on one elbow and gave Bo a playful leer. "I think you might be jumping the gun. Is this because I'm the only other person in the house who isn't drawing social security?"

Bo growled with mock fury and snatched Larry into his arms, dragging him high until it was Larry's nipple now in *his* mouth. Ticklish, Larry tried to squirm away. He only stopped squirming when Bo's fist gently circled Larry's cock.

"Sweet Jesus," Larry mumbled, trembling with a sudden rush of desire.

Bo gazed up at Larry hovering over him. His free hand cupped Larry's ass and pulled him higher. When Larry's fuzzy stomach was in kissable distance of Bo's mouth, Bo pulled Larry close, pressing his face into the hot skin and inhaling Larry's smell.

"There's nobody else here for you to have sex with," Bo said, now exploring Larry's belly button with his tongue. "You might as well settle for me."

Larry giggled and squirmed and tried to wrench himself away from that probing, tickling tongue. And maybe he was trying to squirm away from the words as well, although he tried not to show it.

Bo flipped Larry onto his back and flattened him with the weight of his own body. "You'll pay for that silence," he said, pinning Larry beneath him, grinding their cocks together, and finally burying Larry's mouth under his own until Larry almost forgot he had reservations about all this.

Almost.

Larry closed his eyes. He would let Bo's sweet mouth, Bo's delectable body, carry him into the coming day. He would even allow himself to enjoy it.

But that was all he would let Bo do.

It was no big mystery why, either. As far as being in control of his own heart, Larry knew exactly where this sudden well of strength came from. It came from this mountain, this house. But mostly, he knew, it came from the kindness of his employer.

Somehow being hired by Roger Stanhope, being *trusted* by Roger Stanhope, had given Larry the self-esteem he needed to stand up for himself again. He flat-out refused to let himself be hurt anymore. Right now, right this very minute, he felt truly in control of his life for the first time in a long while, and being in control meant he refused to let himself be dragged into an unwanted romance. Not this time. This time he had the strength not to let it happen.

And that was a good feeling indeed.

"YOU LOOK chipper."

Larry looked up from making the master's bed. Roger Stanhope sat at the window in one of the high-backed leather chairs. He was still in his pajamas. His breakfast was laid out on a tray table before him, but he wasn't paying much attention to it. Instead, he kept a keen eye on Larry. Accompanying the keen eye was an indulgent smile.

Something about that smile made Larry blush.

"I guess I *am* chipper," he said, averting his eyes while fluffing a pillow and smoothing out the bedspread.

"Well, good, son. I like seeing happy people."

"Yes, sir," Larry said for lack of anything wiser to say. Then he blushed even redder.

Thinking he might shift the conversation from himself to a little manor business instead, Larry added, "I found a gardener to start working on the grounds, as you asked. I interviewed him over the phone and he sounded experienced. I was wondering, sir, if maybe you would mind if I tried to spruce up the greenhouse. Grow a few flowers for the house.

It would save you some money on florist's bills since you seem to enjoy fresh flowers all over the place. I'll only do the work in my free time. And even then I'll have my beeper handy to attend to your needs. Just a couple of hours every day in the afternoon should do it. Certainly not much more than that. Maybe the gardener will even help."

"That sounds fine," Roger said, looking up from buttering his croissant.

"He starts in a few days. His name is Jimmy Blackstone. He made it a point to tell me he's Kumeyaay Indian. Hope that's all right."

"Which one?" Roger asked. "That's he's a Kumeyaay Indian or that he starts in a few days?"

Larry smiled. "Either one. There's something else."

"Yes?"

"Jimmy will be working four days a week, like you said. He asked if he could stay on the premises."

"You mean live in the house?"

Larry shuffled his feet. "Well, no. He'd like to park his camper out back and stay there."

"Have you seen this camper? What does it look like?"

"Jimmy said it was an Airstream Flying Cloud. One of those rounded aluminum numbers. He also said he renovated it himself, and if he can't bring the trailer with him, he can't take the job."

Roger chuckled and glanced through the window, as if seeking old memories. "Well, I can certainly understand that. I've always been partial to my vehicles too. And Airstreams are classics. Maybe he'll give me a tour."

Larry thought of the beautiful automobiles in the carriage house downstairs and the fondness in Roger's voice when he spoke of them. His mouth twisted into a wry smile. "Yes, sir. I'm sure he'll give you a tour."

Roger swiveled his gaze back into the room, straight at Larry's face. "I'm intrigued, son. The Kumeyaay are a beautiful people. I can't wait to meet him. Tell our new gardener he may most certainly reside in his trailer while he's working here. You may also tell him if he's interested, he can take on the job of maintaining my cars as well, if he's mechanically inclined. If he can restore an Airstream, he must know his way around automobiles. The '57 Chevy ragtop especially needs a little engine work. Tell him if he accepts my offer, we'll up him to full-time.

There are water hookups and electrical outlets on the outer wall of the carriage house. He may plug his Airstream in there."

"Thank you, sir. I'm sure he'll appreciate it."

Roger sat there fiddling with the fork in his hand. He still hadn't eaten anything. He was too busy studying the young man in front of him, considering all they had talked about. "You've done fine, son. Once you hire this young man—he *is* young, I presume."

"Yes, sir. My age. Twenty-four."

"Good. Good. Once he's settled in, I think it would be wonderful if he could help you whip the greenhouse into shape as well. I'd love to see it operational again. I used to spend long happy hours in it myself, you know. Jeremy and I both." He gave a wistful sigh. "If only I could join you."

Up until this point, Larry had been fretful about asking if he could work in the greenhouse. He thought Roger might think he was trying to shirk his real duties. But with Roger's permission, he brightened immediately.

"There's no reason you can't, sir! I'd love your company. Jimmy would too, I'll bet. I can wheel you down in the wheelchair, and once there, you can move about well enough, I think. You might enjoy the fresh air."

Roger nodded. "That's very sweet of you, Larry. I appreciate it. We'll see, all right?" At that moment, a spark of mischief lit his eyes. "Back to this 'chipper' business. Is there anything I should know about?"

Larry refluffed the pillow. It was the fourth time so it didn't need it, but he did it anyway. "Nothing I can think of," he said, averting his gaze again.

"Getting along with Bo?" Roger asked, tilting his head and trying to appear innocent, which, on a ninety-three-year-old face, doesn't always succeed. There's too much mileage there for innocence.

Larry thought so too. While he ignored a fresh infusion of blood rushing to his cheeks, he chewed on his lower lip for a second, trying to gnaw away the smile wanting to form there. Although it was a good impersonation, his show of innocence was just as false as Roger's, especially after last night. "What exactly are you asking, sir?"

Before Roger could answer, there came a soft tapping at the bedroom door. Both men turned to stare.

"Must be Mrs. Price," Roger said. "Best let her in before she takes a screwdriver to the hinges."

Larry chuckled, then moved to the door and pulled it open. To his surprise, it was Bo. He was wearing his white chef's uniform. As a concession to visiting the master's quarters, he even had the hated *toque blanche* perched rakishly on his head. He held a folded newspaper in his hand.

Roger sat patiently in his chair by the window, content to watch the two young men come face-to-face in his doorway. He saw Bo's expression soften when they gazed at each other. He saw the tip of Larry's pink tongue come out and moisten his lips while Bo laid his strong brown hand to his own chest as if a sudden flurry of heartbeats had unsettled him. But he wasn't *too* unsettled, if the way his dimples popped into view was any indication.

"Come in, son," Roger said, breaking the spell with an inward chuckle, causing Larry and Bo to give a little jump as if they'd been caught doing something they shouldn't.

Roger flapped a distracted hand in front of his face at the feel of playful, invisible fingers ruffling his hair. "Oh, shoo," he whispered, too softly for anyone else to hear, but he appeared pleased by the touch anyway. Jeremy was such a card.

Bo stepped inside the room, brushing lightly against Larry as he did. The master was sitting by the window, gaily twiddling his thumbs and looking extremely pleased with himself. Bo was pretty sure he understood the old man's glee. Especially if his theory was correct.

"Your newspaper was delivered late, sir. I thought I'd bring it up. I know you enjoy the funnies in the morning."

Roger's eyes slid from Bo to Larry, then back again. "How lovely," he said, wiggling happily in his chair. "I have both my young men in my bedchambers at once. We can have a chat! Sit, boys, sit." He pointed his index finger like a gun, directly at the newly made bed.

Larry and Bo shot a glance at each other. Larry's glance was uneasy, Bo's as pleased as punch. Victorious, even. Since the master had all but commanded it, they parked their asses on the edge of the bed, facing him. They sat close enough for their legs to touch, and that tiny detail made Roger all the wigglier.

Roger leaned forward over his croissants and brie, rather like a mother eagle eying her chicks. Bo had that wide-eyed look of cool control that all confident men wear so grandly, while the best word to describe Larry's demeanor was "disconcerted." He wasn't comfortable at all.

Roger found it all intensely amusing.

"How are you two getting along?" he asked. "Are you happy with your positions? Is there anything I can do to make you more comfortable? I'm quite pleased with your work, you know. I don't want you to feel anxious on that account. Quite pleased indeed. I just want you to get along. Be close. Be friends. Have fun."

He sat there, eyes propped open wide, still shooting for nonchalance, waiting for an answer while both men gazed down at their shoes, then at each other, then up to him.

"We're friends," Larry said.

"We're having fun," Bo said with an interesting light in his eyes that intrigued Roger all the more.

An awkward silence ensued while Roger continued to stare and Larry continued to fidget and Bo continued to sit there looking more and more in control.

"Can't think of a thing we need," Larry said, more to fill the silence than anything.

"Well, maybe *one* thing," Bo said, causing Larry to look startled.

Suddenly all eyes in the room were on Bo.

Bo ignored the fact that Larry had tensed up beside him, and he wasn't too bothered that Larry was now staring at him like he might stare at a rogue elephant, not quite knowing when it would trample him to death. Bo was less interested in what Larry was worried about, and more interested in Roger's obvious fascination by what he'd just said. He leaned forward, and in response, Roger leaned forward in his chair as well. They couldn't have looked more conspiratorial if they'd tried.

Roger beetled his eyebrows, looking delightfully inscrutable. "What is it, son? What exactly do you need?"

To Larry's horror, Bo claimed his hand. Larry tried halfheartedly to pull away, but Bo wouldn't let him, so Larry finally stopped tugging. He sat there, his neck and ears crimson, nailed to the bed by Bo's strong grasp, and wondering just what the hell Bo was about to do.

Bo cleared his throat and gave Larry a glance before centering his attention back on the boss.

"Sir, I want to ask your permission for Larry and me to begin an affair. We'd like to share our rooms as a suite rather than separate bedrooms. We're asking you in advance because we don't want there to be any awkwardness in case you see us perhaps canoodling in the hallway or something."

Roger stared at him. He might have been staring at a two-headed chicken, he was that interested. "Canoodling. Interesting choice of words. Implies romance, I think."

"Yes, sir. Indeed it does."

Roger turned to Larry, who was looking a little green around the gills. "How do you feel about this, son?" Roger asked.

"Appalled," Larry said.

Roger laughed. "Didn't know it was coming, huh? I mean Bo's request, not the romance."

"Actually I didn't know either one was coming. They've both hit me broadside. And I'm not sure I—"

Larry was suddenly furious that Bo was gripping his hand. When Bo worked to more firmly intertwine their fingers and scoot a little closer to Larry on the bed, Larry got even madder. And scared shitless.

"But you share your friend's sentiment, I presume?" Roger asked. "He hasn't asked me for anything you don't want to occur, has he, Larry?"

Now all eyes in the room were on Larry, and he damn well knew it. Bo's fingers tightened around his. Every muscle in Larry's body was drawn taut. If he'd been a guitar string, he would have snapped by now.

Larry avoided Bo's eyes, avoided the master's kind gaze even more. Staring at their two hands clenched together, his own trapped inside Bo's, he mumbled, "I don't know what I want."

At that moment, flames sprang to life in the unlit fireplace. Roger barely paid attention to the newly erupted fire, while Bo and Larry stared at it slack-jawed.

"What the fu—" Bo gaped.

"Oh, how nice," Roger cooed, unperturbed. "A fire."

He spread his fingers in front of the flames as if enjoying the heat already. "Permission granted, boys. You may indeed cohabitate the premises. Just don't 'canoodle' too enthusiastically with Mrs. Price present or you may find yourself smacked upside your two handsome young heads with a rolling pin. She's a bit old-fashioned, our Mrs. Price." He stared fondly at Larry, then more seriously at Bo. "I'm sure you'll both work your feelings out. I hope you will, anyway. It's funny, but there hasn't been young love in this old house for many a long year. And when it *was* here, it was mine. Mine and Jeremy's. Now run along," he finished up, snatching a napkin off his tray and blowing his nose. *God*, he thought, laughing at himself, *I hate how old people get so emotional.*

"Nobody mentioned love," Larry said between tight lips, stubbornly refusing to be dismissed quite yet.

Bo eyed him but remained silent. He still had one dimple on display. Just one. His expression might best be described as leery.

Roger twisted away from the fire to study Larry's face. His eyes burned as brightly as the flames on the grate. "Sometimes love doesn't *have* to be mentioned," he said, sounding for all the world like a wise old Buddha spouting the lessons of life. "It just is. Like sunlight."

"Yes, sir," Larry said, taken aback by the passion in Roger's words, but resenting it a little bit too. "Still…."

Beside him, Bo nudged him with his elbow. "Hush, now," he quietly said.

Larry turned to face him. His eyes were ice. "Excuse me?"

Roger studied them both, his brow furrowed as he gazed deep into each of their faces as the two men glared at each other. *Best let them work it out themselves*, he thought. He watched them both a bit longer and finally decided he had seen what he hoped he would see. There were feelings there indeed. It was too soon to name them, maybe, and Larry seemed a little unsure, but they were there nevertheless. With the merest twitch of his head, Roger signaled for the boys to go.

"But before you leave," he said, averting his eyes from Larry, who still looked unhappy, and directing his words to Bo to try to lighten the mood. "I just want you to know, son, you don't need to wear that chef's hat if you don't want. It looks kind of silly. Mrs. Price's idea?"

"Yes, sir."

"Then toss it."

"Yes, sir!"

Bo flashed his teeth in a radiant smile as he ripped the toque off his head and crumpled it in his hand. Two seconds later he and Larry were out the door.

Once again alone, Roger turned away from the door. After fiddling with his breakfast for a moment, he at last gave in and bit off a healthy chunk of croissant, then sat there happily chewing it to mush. He cocked his head as if listening to a voice only he could hear.

The fire in the fireplace erupted with a *whoosh*. The flames licked at the brick lining, the flue. The gas jets flared and the flames shot higher.

Lifting his eyes to the ceiling, Roger barked out a laugh. "Don't burn the house down, Jeremy. And yes, I know I'm a genius. There's really no need to blather on about it. I do believe, however, the next few weeks should prove quite interesting."

Humming softly, he clutched the eggcup to steady it. Decapitating his soft-boiled egg with a smooth, decisive swipe of his knife, he grinned to see his hands working properly for a change.

He gave a gleeful snicker, as once again invisible fingers ruffled through his hair. Their touch was as familiar on his skin as the taste of milk on his tongue—the taste of brie. When those invisible fingers slid across his scalp and caressed his ear, Roger closed his eyes. A gentle purring sound emanated from his wrinkled throat.

"You rascal," he said softly. "And stop worrying about Larry. I'm sure he'll come around. Bo can be quite persuasive, I imagine."

He offered a risqué wink to the empty room.

IN THE hallway, Larry hurried away, refusing to look back. Bo had to jog to catch up. He grabbed Larry's arm, tugging him to a stop.

"Wait," he said.

Larry turned to face him, his eyes furious. "You shouldn't have done that."

Bo pulled back from that angry glare. "I-I thought we wanted to get to know each other. That's what old man Stanhope wants. If we play our cards right—"

"I don't know what the hell you're talking about, and I don't care. You didn't have to make a grand announcement about it, Bo. I never said I was ready to live with you yet. We've spent one night together."

There was sadness on Bo's face when he said, "It was a great night."

At those words, Larry relented. A bit. "Yes, it was. But it was still just one night. And it wasn't love, it was sex. A couple of blowjobs. A little cuddling. You might want to keep that in mind."

Bo stepped backward. Like a man who has just been slapped, color rose in his face, and his pulse pounded visibly at his temple. He ran a hand over his closely shorn hair, trying to think what he should say. Nothing came to him. He simply stood there, silently wondering how things could have suddenly gone so wrong.

"I have work to do," Larry said, and turning aside, he hastened away, heading for the stairs. A moment later Bo heard the front door slam shut.

He heaved a sigh and headed for the stairs himself. No matter what sort of mess he had made, there was still work to be done. Mrs. Price's breakfast. Prepping lunch. Maybe trying out one of Mrs. P's cookie recipes to take his mind off everything else.

He knew one thing. He wasn't going to let Larry ruin this for him. No way in hell.

At the sound of Mrs. Price's bedroom door opening farther down the hall, he hurried away, headed for the kitchen. Then, on a whim, he ducked into a shadowy corner instead. Tucked behind a grandfather clock, which sat silent and unwound, he waited for Mrs. Price to walk by. Bo watched as she passed, smoothing her skirt as if she had just dressed. A second later, she tapped at the master's door, waited for a response, then slipped inside, closing the door behind her.

Bo stepped softly, being sure to stay on the carpeted runner to silence his footsteps, and approached the master's door. With his heart galloping, he pressed his ear to the door and listened. Mrs. Price was just inside the door. If she decided to quickly leave, Bo would be discovered. Still, and for reasons even he couldn't explain, he had to know what they were talking about.

It was the old woman who began. "Do you still think you should go forward with your plan?"

The master's voice was farther away. He was probably still sitting by the fireplace. "And why wouldn't I? Things are progressing swimmingly, I think. One is leery, but the other is determined. That's certainly a step in the right direction, don't you think?"

"Is it worth gambling your fortune on?"

"Well, I'm not dead yet. We'll still monitor the situation. I admit it isn't time to contact the lawyer and change my will. Let's watch and see a bit longer, shall we?"

"Of course. Whatever you say."

Those words sounded like a prelude to Mrs. P exiting the room, so Bo took off in a patter of muffled footsteps. He didn't stop until he reached the foyer at the bottom of the stairs. With his hand still on the newel post, he gazed back up the staircase with a victorious leer on his face.

They were talking about changing the will!

Bo remembered the enigmatic wording in the ad. How did it go? Oh, yeah... single and unattached... gay, romantic heart... need for new beginnings....

...need for new beginnings....

The old man had no family. What else was he going to do with his money? Making Larry and Bo fall in love was a game to him. And if they played it properly, if they could convince the old fart they had really fallen in love, it would all be theirs. The entire Stanhope fortune. Holy shit!

At the sound of the master's bedroom door opening and closing up above, Bo scuttled off, heading for the kitchen, a dozen questions still tumbling through his head. A dozen questions and one very astonishing possibility.

A triumphant glow lit Bo's face. A greedy flame flared in his eyes. *I was right. I knew it.*

Abruptly his eyes narrowed. With clenched fist, he smacked the wall, but not loud enough to be heard by anyone upstairs. He stood trembling. Suddenly furious. Suddenly desperate.

And Larry's going to spoil it all.

Chapter Eight

THREE DAYS later, a little wobbly but feeling better than she had in weeks, Mrs. Price sat at the kitchen table guzzling a pot of tea and ravenously demolishing a cheese omelet and an enormous mound of country-fried potatoes. Bo stood at the sink with his back to her, washing a chicken carcass, whistling a breathless little tune, and impatiently nudging Leo away from his feet. Leo loved chicken, and he was being a real pain in the ass about it. The only sound in the air, other than Bo's whistling, was the clatter of Mrs. Price's cutlery.

"What are you making?" she asked around a mouthful of food.

"Chicken croquettes for the master's lunch."

"Are you using my recipe?"

"No. I'm using my own."

"Hmm."

The *screech* of a knife on china. "These fried potatoes are delicious. Palm oil?"

"Canola. Lower in saturated fat. I would prefer to use macadamia oil. It has a nutty taste that's really delicious, but with the master's high blood pressure, canola is better." *Like I give a shit*, he thought.

"You served Roger fried potatoes?"

Sigh. "He requested them. Said he smelled them when I made them for Larry and me a couple of weeks back."

"Not once in thirty years did he ever ask *me* for fried potatoes."

Bo grinned, turning to her. "Do I detect a pang of disgruntlement?"

"Of course not. How are you and Larry getting along?"

Turning his back to the woman again, Bo glowered at the chicken carcass lying dismembered in the sink. *Now why would she be interested in that, pray tell?* "We're getting along fine, Mrs. Price. Why do you ask?"

She wiped her plate clean with a crust of toast, averting her gaze. "No reason. There's a hickey on your neck, you know. It's been there for three days."

From the one and only time Larry and I had sex. "It's probably a mosquito bite."

"Yes, I'm sure that's what it is."

Bo gazed down at Leo, who had flopped over on his back on top of his foot and was currently gnawing at Bo's pant cuff, his little paws waving in the air, his tail sticking straight out behind him like a rudder. Bo wondered what sort of shitstorm he would release if he stomped on the little fucker's head.

You're still playing the game, Bo said to himself. *Don't forget you're still playing the game.*

"I think he's afraid of me," Bo said quietly. It wasn't all pretense either. He truly was still astounded by the way Larry had shut him out.

Mrs. Price looked up sharply. "What do you mean? Who's afraid of you?"

Bo still leaned against the sink, staring down. He rubbed Leo's belly with his other foot, shooting for gentle rather than homicidal. When he spoke his eyes never left the dog. "Larry. He's not admitting it even to himself, but I think he's afraid I'm going to break his heart."

Mrs. Price sat perfectly still, watching him. "And are you?"

Bo frowned. "Of course not. At least I hope I won't."

"Perhaps you're rushing the relationship. There's no hurry, you know. You're both young. The master should be around a while longer. You have all the time in the world."

Bo stared at her, his eyes eager, his words innocent. "What does the master being around have to do with anything?" *Like I don't know.*

Mrs. Price stammered a reply. "I-I just meant that as long as the master's still alive, you and Larry can keep working together and getting to know each other better. So there's no rush. That's all I meant to say."

Nice save. "I see." A sardonic smile wanted to bend Bo's face, but he aborted it before it came to life. He had less luck in keeping his words neutral. "I get the impression Larry and I have been pushed together from the very beginning. Not that I mind, of course. But it's odd, don't you think? Why would the master—or *you*, for that matter—care about us being together?"

"Maybe we just want to see you happy."

"There's more to it than that, I think."

Mrs. Price was fidgeting uncomfortably now. "Don't be silly. How could there be more to it than that?"

"I don't know," Bo said. "But there is." *And you damn well know it.*

Mrs. Price pushed herself to her feet. Crossing the kitchen to stand directly in front of Bo, ever mindful of the dog at their feet, she rested her hand on his arm, and with the other hand tilted his face in her direction. "Don't worry about the master or me. Worry about Larry. If you want to be with him, just do what you can to make him happy. Give him room to be himself, but always let him know you're there for him when he's ready to let you in. Love is a two-way street, Bo. You have to give as much as you get back."

Thank you, Confucius. Unable to stop, Bo slitted his eyes in a triumphant leer, but he looked away before Mrs. Price could recognize it for what it was. "I didn't say anything about love, ma'am."

Mrs. Price ducked her head to stare at him over her glasses, eying him like she might a kid who's been caught in a lie. A small lie, maybe. But still a lie. "No, I guess you didn't," she said, her voice little more than a whisper.

"Where *is* Larry?" Bo asked. He wasn't particularly interested, but it seemed a good idea to sound like he was.

"He's introducing the new gardener to the grounds. You may be cooking for one more from here on out. I'm not sure. He'll be staying in a trailer out back. Roger okayed it, although I have no idea why. Sometimes I wonder if that man is getting senile."

"What's the new gardener's name?" Bo asked.

"Jimmy," she said. "I expect you to make him welcome."

Bo glanced over at the woman. "Of course. Why wouldn't I?"

Mrs. Price offered Bo a wily glance of her own.

"Oh, no reason," she said, averting her eyes. "No reason at all. Except he's awfully handsome."

Bo stared at her. *Great. Just what I needed. Competition from the fucking gardener.*

LARRY GOT his first glimpse of the new gardener as he wheeled his Airstream up the long driveway. Both the pickup he used to tow the trailer and the trailer itself were coated with dust, and Larry remembered the new employee had driven in from the desert to take the job.

Jimmy Blackstone waved a friendly greeting and leaned out the window. "Hop onto the running board!" he cried out, bonking the door with the palm of his hand. "Show me where to park!"

Larry did as he was asked, while Jimmy slowed the pickup just enough for Larry to climb on without breaking his neck. Since all their business dealings had been conducted over the phone, the first time he shook hands with the new gardener was through the driver's side window of a moving vehicle. That was unexpected.

Seeing what might have been a slightly worried expression on the face of his passenger, Jimmy offered him a conciliatory smile. With his arm out the window, he took a fistful of Larry's belt buckle and held him in place. "You won't fall. I gotcha."

Larry stared down at the hand clutching his belt. The move was so unexpected, and that hand was so close to his dick, he tried not to gawp.

Jimmy saw his surprise and laughed. His laugh was a bawdy one. "Don't worry. I'm not going for the big prize. Just trying to keep you safe."

Larry found himself smiling back, much to his own surprise. "Oh, well, uh, thanks, then."

Sticking his other hand out the window and leaving the truck to steer itself, Jimmy said, "Pleased to meet you, Larry."

Larry took the hand with a dawning smile, trying to do it quickly so they wouldn't either drive straight through the greenhouse or clip the corner of Mr. Stanhope's mansion and unintentionally ventilate the joint. "You too."

Jimmy shot him a wink and turned back to peer through the windshield. "Thisaway, I presume."

Once again, Larry dragged his eyes up from the hand at his belt. "Uh, yeah. Right around the corner of the house. I think you'll find everything you'll need there."

Jimmy considered him through a pair of wide brown eyes. Taking a firmer grip on Larry's belt, he said, "Trust me, I don't need much. Electrical outlet, water spigot, enough room to unroll my awning. Somebody to share a beer with now and then. That oughta do it."

Larry beamed back, no longer uncomfortable. Just sort of... *fascinated*. My God, the new gardener was a hunk. And a friendly one to boot. "I think we can supply all that."

"Then we're in business."

Even if Larry hadn't been told Jimmy Blackstone was an American Indian, he would have known it, what with the acorn-colored skin and high cheekbones. His smile displayed an array of snow-white teeth that seemed to be permanently on display and would have graced any toothpaste commercial on TV. Larry could tell Jimmy smiled a lot. That smile sat too comfortably on Jimmy's handsome face not to be a frequent visitor.

Speaking of commercials, the shampoo industry could have done worse as well. The new gardener's hair hung straight down each side of his face without a bend in it. It was long enough for the tips to reach the flaps on the pockets of the western-style shirt he had on. That thick mane of hair, wind-tossed now from the drive out here, shone like polished onyx. Not a split end in sight. Jimmy occasionally pushed it absentmindedly off his face with a sweep of his brown hand in an almost elegant gesture that enthralled Larry every time he watched it.

Peering through the side window, Larry saw that Jimmy was dressed in jeans below his western shirt, and below the jeans, down around the gas and brake pedals, he had on a pair of battered pointy-toed cowboy boots. The sleeves of his shirt had been torn off, leaving a few threads dangling here and there and exposing a pair of beautiful biceps that it took Larry a considerable amount of willpower to pull his eyes from.

It took Jimmy less than twenty minutes to park the Airstream at the side of the carriage house, unhook it from his truck, run a few wires to the outside outlet, attach the water hookup, and unroll the awning at the front, which made for a nicely shaded veranda. The last thing he did was kick open two lawn chairs and place them in the newly constructed patch of shade by the Airstream's front door.

Jimmy stood back and proudly surveyed the results of his labors.

"Wow," Larry said, impressed. "You've got it down to a science."

After making a final adjustment to the locking mechanism on the awning, Jimmy rolled his head around to swing his hair out of his eyes. "It ain't much, but it's home."

"No, it's great!" Larry wasn't just being polite, and he wanted Jimmy to know it.

Jimmy gave him another one of his blinding smiles. "Okay, then," he said, rubbing his hands together. "Give me a tour. Let's see what I've got myself into."

Before Larry could answer, Jimmy gazed up at the roofline of the mansion. "This is quite a spread, isn't it?" He strolled around the corner of the house with Larry at his heels, eying the grounds. Tutting sadly in passing over a stretch of dead hedge Larry hadn't known what to do with, he moved around to the front of the mansion and stopped. Standing with his hands on his hips, Jimmy studied the property.

"Who's been doing the work lately?" he asked.

"I did as much as I could," Larry said, "I mean between my other duties. I didn't make many improvements, I'm afraid. Just tried to keep the weeds from taking over. There isn't much grass, as you can see, since it's mostly desert landscaping, but still it takes more than I have time for to keep it looking good."

Jimmy patted his back. "No, I think you did great." He turned away from the grounds and studied Larry's face. "Do you like working here? The boss isn't a dick, is he?"

Larry didn't hesitate. "No, the boss is great. I love working here."

Jimmy's eyes crinkled into another one of his smiles. "Then I'm sure I'll love it too."

"Um... the master was also wondering if you would help me get the greenhouse in order." Larry immediately felt guilty and shuffled his feet. "Well, no. That's a lie. Refurbishing the greenhouse was my idea, but the master okayed it. It's back around by the carriage house."

"I saw it," Jimmy said. "Was wondering why it was so neglected. You can tell the master I'd be happy to help." He gazed up at the house again. "Anybody else around I should know about?"

Larry followed his glance as if seeing the house for the first time. The fluttering of a curtain in a second floor window caught his attention. "There's one of them right there," he said, pointing. "That's Mrs. Price. She used to work here, but she's winding down to retirement and will be leaving soon. At the moment, she's laid up with hay fever."

"Snot city, huh? Been there, done that."

Larry waved at the woman staring down at them, and she waved back. She had a handkerchief in her hand. Jimmy went through the motions of doffing an invisible hat and bending low in the woman's direction. Both men saw Mrs. Price giggle, pat her hair, and flap her hand at them as if shooing them away for flirting. She disappeared in a flurry of curtains. Far off in the distance, they heard a horrendous sneeze.

"Yep," Jimmy said with something between a chuckle and a sympathetic cluck. "That's hay fever, all right."

"You've got a fan there, I think." Larry grinned.

"Well, good. Not much sense making enemies. So who else is on the premises?"

"Well, there's Bo. The cook. You'll meet him at dinner." Still annoyed with Bo, Larry opened his mouth to say more, then flapped it shut.

"And that's all?" Jimmy asked.

"That's all. Except for the master himself. Mr. Stanhope is the one who'll be signing your paychecks."

Jimmy bounced his eyebrows up and down. "Then I'll be especially nice to him."

Larry laughed. "I thought you might."

Jimmy glanced at the second floor window again, but Mrs. Price was good and gone, the curtains unmoving, no faces behind the glass. He turned his eyes back to Larry. "Not many people for such a big place. But don't look so worried. That's a good thing. I'm not much on crowds. The fewer people around, the better, as far as I'm concerned."

"Me too," Larry agreed. As if some hurdle in their new friendship had been met and successfully navigated, Larry hooked a thumb back in the direction they'd come. "Come on. Let's finish the tour."

Mrs. Price's appetite might have recovered, but the woman herself was still red-nosed and bleary-eyed from her battle with hay fever. Bo urged her back to bed as soon as she finished breakfast. He was tired of listening to her sniff and snort and honk. Besides, he needed to be alone. He wanted to think.

Pouring himself a cup of coffee, he stood at the sink and peered through the kitchen window at the Airstream trailer now parked out back. So the new gardener was here, as Mrs. Price had said. It hadn't taken him long to make himself at home either. Bo hadn't seen the guy yet, and he wasn't curious to see him now. He had more important matters to consider.

Mr. Stanhope's will was at the tippy-top of the list. Obviously, the master had been pleased that Bo made the overture of asking his permission for him and Larry to share living quarters. *Now why would that be?* Bo wondered, activating his sardonic wit. Of course, Larry had pretty much killed the idea with his lack of enthusiasm. Still, Bo was sure he could bring Larry around. He remembered all too well the ease with which he had bedded the guy. Sure, it might have taken a while, but once between the sheets, Larry had been putty in his hands. Enjoyable putty too.

Smiling, Bo sipped his coffee. *Since I now know there's a fortune at stake, it might just be time to try a little harder.*

"OH MAN, oh man, oh man."

When Jimmy Blackstone discovered the lineup of gorgeous automobiles in the carriage house, his face lit up like Times Square on New Year's Eve. Larry couldn't remember the last time he'd seen a happier human. Even the guy's fingers were working like spider legs, as if he was eager to start overhauling an engine or two right there on the spot.

They had just toured Jimmy's Airstream, and Larry had been amazed by how perfectly laid out the interior of that classic aluminum bubble was. Clean too. Despite the veneer of road dust on the outside, Jimmy's trailer on the inside was way cleaner and more organized than Larry's bedroom. He didn't figure he needed to admit *that* to the new gardener anytime soon.

"And you restored the trailer yourself?" Larry asked, more than a little awed.

Jimmy gave an affirmative grunt. "Everything from the axle bearings to the foldout bed to the microwave over the sink."

"So you're a mechanic as well as a gardener."

"I guess I know as much about one as the other."

Knowing he was about to infuriate Bo, Larry cleared his throat and forged full speed ahead. "Then can I tell Mr. Stanhope you'd be willing to take over maintenance of his fleet of cars?"

Jimmy turned blazing brown eyes in Larry's direction. With one hand he swept his long hair back off his face, and with the other hand he reached out and pumped Larry's paw for about thirty seconds. "Hell, yes! I'd probably do it even if he *didn't* offer a full five day's wages. The chance to piddle under the hood of that Aston Martin would be enough to sway me. Not to mention the ragtop. And the Navigator. And holy shit, the Mercedes! Jeez, this is a grease monkey's wet dream."

Larry grinned even though his fingers were going numb in Jimmy's excited grasp. Teasing, he said, "A grease monkey's wet dream, huh? I'd rather not explore the mental image that expression conjures up, if you don't mind. I'll just drop it down a notch and assume you like piddling with cars."

Jimmy grinned back. "I was born with a wrench in my hand."

"Your poor mother," Larry said.

"Yeah. It was a big monkey wrench. Worst labor pains ever." Both men laughed.

Jimmy finally released Larry's hand. "Okay," he said happily, punching the button on the wall to make the garage doors scroll down with a screech and seal off the lineup of Mr. Stanhope's automobiles. "I'll oil that door too," he said, then faced off with Larry once again. "What's next, Chief?"

Both men's eyes drifted to the greenhouse next door. Jimmy immediately frowned. "Poor thing," he mumbled.

Poor thing indeed. The greenhouse had been ignored for almost a decade. There were weeds growing in the corners, the benches where Roger said orchids had once bloomed under Jeremy's loving care were dusty and scattered with empty terra-cotta pots, half of them broken. The dirt floor was as dry as desert dunes. Puffs of dust rose up under Jimmy Blackstone's well-worn cowboy boots as he clomped through the place. Sealed off for so long, the air was hot and dead around them.

Jimmy stood in the middle of the structure and stared up at the glass ceiling and walls, yellowed now with neglect and the scum of countless untended seasons. Larry stepped back and quietly studied Jimmy as the light that passed through the grimy panes of glass surrounding them cast a yellowish pall over his copper-colored face. Jimmy's laughter had died the moment he stepped inside the neglected greenhouse, but Larry still had a smile playing at the corners of his mouth, watching him. Something about Jimmy Blackstone made Larry happy. His exuberance, maybe. Or simply the fascination he displayed with everything he came across. Even the sorrowful way he considered the greenhouse pleased Larry. It was sort of the way Larry felt every time he crossed the dusty threshold—as if a flower had been left untended to wither and die from neglect. The greenhouse must have been beautiful once, and with a little bit of work could be made beautiful again. Even in its current state of dilapidation, it didn't take much effort for Larry to imagine it filled with blossoms and fine tall greeneries reaching high along the walls, absorbing crystal beams of sunlight through newly scrubbed panes of sparkling glass.

"I'm going to enjoy working in here," Jimmy said, studying the ceiling overhead, the way the light tried to shine through, but couldn't. "We can grow new plants for the grounds. Give them a good start in life before we transplant them into the yard. I'll have to clean the glass first. Inside and out. Then we'll sow the flowers. Plant some succulents and cactus. Tend them. Watch them grow. Let their fragrance fill the air. Leave the doors open for the bees to come in." He turned to Larry, his chiseled face once again lit with excitement, his eyes as bright as a cloudless dawn. When he spoke, his voice was breathless, the spark in his eyes almost childlike. "I can't wait to get started."

"I'll help you," Larry said. "We'll do it together."

Jimmy nodded. "I'm glad. It's great to share stuff like this. It's... *important*, I think."

"Important?" Larry asked.

"Yeah." Jimmy smiled. "It's nature. Nature's always important."

He hooked his thumbs in his belt and once again stared at the dingy panes of glass overhead, the feeble light seeping through, the dust motes floating in the dead, dry air around them. "I think I'm going to like being on this mountain. Hiking it on my days off. Getting to know its secrets." His eyes found Larry. "I'll bet it has 'em, you know. There are secrets everywhere if you know where to look."

Larry blinked, mesmerized by the intensity in Jimmy's eyes. "Are there?"

Jimmy answered with a simple nod.

Stepping toward the door, Jimmy draped an arm over Larry's shoulder and steered him outside. "I'd like to meet the boss now. Think that would be okay?"

"Certainly," Larry said, lost in the sudden overwhelming *nearness* of the man standing beside him. A gust of sage-scented wind tore up the side of the mountain and lifted Jimmy's long hair. When the hair whipped across Larry's cheek, Jimmy apologized. Gathering his hair in his fist, he dragged it over to his other shoulder in one thick rope and held it there while the wind thrashed on.

"Sorry," Jimmy said. "My hair gets away from me now and then."

Larry ignored the apology. "I don't mind," he said. Then to his own surprise and horror, he added, "It's beautiful." To cover up what he'd just said, he tried to strike a more businesslike tone. "Follow me."

"I'm hot on your heels," Jimmy said softly, peeking at the man beside him, surprised by what Larry had said about his hair, but pleased as well.

At the mansion's front doors, Jimmy dusted off his jeans and scraped his boots on the mat before allowing Larry to usher him inside. The moment he crossed the threshold, he slapped his hand to his chest as if a chill had shot through him.

Larry touched his arm. "You okay?"

Jimmy nodded. "It was just a shock, is all."

"*What* was a shock?" Larry asked. He gazed about the foyer. There was no one near, nothing to be shocked *about*, as far as he could see.

Jimmy still stood rooted, barely one step inside the door. His eyes were closed and Larry watched as Jimmy's nostrils flared, as if breathing in an aroma he hadn't expected or fully understood. He stood straight, his back unbending. When he released his hair from his hand, it flowed free, rolling like a wave, flattening out across his shoulders. Slowly, framed again in that luxurious mane of hair, Jimmy's face began to relax. A tiny smile appeared. The brown eyes opened. And when they were open all the way, they centered on Larry's face, but somehow Larry knew he wasn't seeing anything. Not yet. They were still a sleepwalker's eyes.

"There's love here," Jimmy said, his voice hushed, the words lazily dragged from his throat. "It never left when it was supposed to."

Larry reached out and laid a hand to Jimmy's arm. "I-I don't understand what you're saying."

At the touch of Larry's fingers on his bare skin, Jimmy's eyes focused. He blinked and took a step backward as if momentarily confused; then a look of determination crossed his face and he stepped farther into the foyer. The wind blew the door shut behind them, causing both men to jump.

Jimmy recovered first, laughing at himself.

"What happened?" Larry asked. "You felt something. What was it?"

Jimmy ignored the question. Letting his gaze traverse the stairs in front of him, he said, "The master's upstairs, I think."

"Yes," Larry said. "The second floor. He hardly ever leaves his rooms."

As if suddenly out of breath, Jimmy whispered, "Show me."

ROGER STOOD at the window of the sitting room that connected to his bedchamber. He stared through the pane at the two men standing side by side in the greenhouse below.

"He's handsome, isn't he?" a voice whispered in his ear. "The new gardener."

Roger nodded. "I wonder if this will complicate matters," he pondered aloud. "Do you suppose he's gay?"

"I don't know. Would you like him to be?"

"I don't know. But Larry likes him. That much is obvious."

"Larry is a gentle soul. A kind man. He likes everyone."

"I know."

Roger eased around from the window and faced the empty room. There was a fire burning on the grate, and since the flames were the only movement in the room, he let his eyes rest there for lack of a better target. "Larry fought back when Bo asked if they could room together."

"It was too early," a voice said. It was the voice Roger would never forget as long as he lived. Jeremy's voice. The voice he was glad to have still sharing his life. "Bo shouldn't have moved that chess piece yet. He jumped the gun. Larry wasn't ready. I'm not even sure Bo was ready. I wonder...."

Roger cast his eyes about the room, still seeking the well-loved face that went with the voice, but as always, it wasn't there. Only the voice remained. "What do you mean, Jeremy? Then why did Bo ask if they could move in together?"

"I'm not sure. Quiet, now. They're coming up."

"What? Who?"

The voice was suddenly at Roger's shoulder. He almost imagined a human breath blowing across his ear. A *familiar* breath. A breath that even now in his old age stirred Roger sexually like no other breath ever had. "Larry is bringing the gardener up to meet you, Rog. I'd better leave."

That surprised Roger more than all the conversation that came before it. "Why should you leave? What possible difference could it make if you are in the room or not? You can't be heard by anyone but me."

The room lay silent for a moment, as if Jeremy's spirit was weighing his response. In the end, he said simply, "I can't be heard by anyone but you *so far*."

And before Roger could question that odd statement, he sensed beyond all doubt, in the space of time between one tick of the wall clock and the next, that Jeremy was gone.

Roger stood alone.

At the sound of approaching footsteps, he turned toward the door. With unsteady hands, he straightened the collar of his robe, tightened the belt, and gave his hair a pat. A moment later, he heard the hushed whisper of voices in the hall and a quiet knock.

He listened for the sound of Jeremy among the furniture, behind the paintings, inside the fire. But he knew it was pointless. Jeremy was truly gone. At least for the moment. For some reason, the things Jeremy had said, and the way he said them, unsettled Roger, although he couldn't imagine why.

With a voice not quite as steady as he might have wished for a lord of the manor, he faced the door and announced, "Come in."

THE FIRST time he stood in the same room with Jimmy Blackstone, Roger froze under the new gardener's gaze like a deer in headlights. When the young Kumeyaay's warm, friendly eyes stopped browsing the walls of the sitting room and centered on Roger's face, Roger sucked in a breath of air as if his old lungs suddenly needed more oxygen. The long black hair, the strong high cheekbones, the tip of a pink tongue moistening a crisp welcoming smile on that astonishingly open face—it all drew Roger in. And he liked the boy immediately.

There was no cane in Roger's hand, but he stepped forward, as unsteady on his feet as ever. Raising his hand in greeting as if meeting a long-lost friend, he moved toward the young man. Before he could take two steps, Jimmy saw what he was doing and rushed forward to fill the gap between them first.

Larry still stood at the door, lagging respectfully behind, as the two men came together for the first time—one so beautiful and tall and perfect—the other shriveled with age but with an air of ancient kindness and wisdom that brought another kind of beauty to the meeting. Larry watched as Jimmy carefully grasped Roger's outstretched hand, then eased the older man into a gentle embrace. Over the thudding of his own heart, Larry heard Jimmy's voice, barely above a whisper, speak soft words into the old man's ear.

"Thank you for welcoming me into your home, sir," Jimmy said, and as he spoke, Roger rested his eyes over Jimmy's shoulder on Larry standing across the room.

With the slightest tilt of his head, Roger leaned in for one brief moment to press his nose to Jimmy's long hair, inhaling the scent of it, enjoying the softness of it against his cheek. A moment later, Roger pulled back from the embrace while the two still clutched hands. It was then that Roger's eyes left Larry's face to study Jimmy's.

A long silence filled the room as the three men stood mute.

"You are most welcome," Roger finally said, suddenly remembering his manners, pushing the silence away, in control of himself once again. He wasn't quite sure why he hadn't been in control all along, except that something about Jimmy Blackstone had literally taken his breath away. Still did, although now that Roger had reclaimed his senses, he was more adept at hiding it. But his eyes never left Jimmy's face. He seemed to find solace there. Or was it simply intrigue?

"I understand you are Kumeyaay," Roger said. "Your ancestors used to live on this mountain, you know."

Jimmy still cupped Roger's hand, his thumb stroking the back of the old man's wrist. "Did they?"

"There are caves farther down the mountainside where they lived for many generations hundreds of years ago, I believe. I'm afraid I can't show them to you. My days of hiking the steep trails are long over, but I can tell you where they are. I explored them many times when I was younger."

"You and your lover," Jimmy said.

Surprised, Roger nodded. "Yes. Me and my lover. How did you know? Did Larry tell you?"

"No," Jimmy said. "I just... knew."

Roger glanced at Larry, who was still standing by the door, and by the slightly confused look on Larry's face, Roger immediately knew it was true. Larry hadn't told Jimmy anything. Jimmy had simply known.

Jimmy, still holding Roger's hand, pointed his chin at a chair by the wall. "Let's sit."

Roger laughed. "Before I fall on my face, you mean."

Jimmy's face split into a wide grin. There was laughter in it, but there was kindness too. "Something like that."

At that moment, Larry stepped forward and the two young men helped the older man to the chair. When Roger was comfortably seated, and admittedly glad to be off his unsteady legs, Roger waved a hand, indicating all the choices of other seats in the room. "Sit, boys. Anywhere you like."

To Larry's surprise, Jimmy dropped to the floor at the old man's feet, crossed his legs, and was immediately relaxed and comfortable. He gazed up at Larry and patted the floor beside him.

Larry joined him without thinking twice. Together the two gazed up at Roger Stanhope. Both Jimmy and Roger were smiling. Soon Larry's smile joined the other two. Gradually, Roger focused solely on Jimmy's face, but before he could speak, the clamor of tiny footsteps thundered down the hall. Leo and Max tore into the room, gave a friendly sniff to Jimmy and Larry sitting on the floor, then stood on their back legs at Roger's knees, tails wagging, whimpering, begging for a seat.

"Do you mind?" Roger asked, and Jimmy quickly lifted both dogs, one after the other, into Roger's lap, where they settled in right away. Roger smiled indulgently down at them, then turned his eyes back to Jimmy.

"It's an Indian thing, isn't it?" Roger asked. "Your knowing, I mean."

A furrow formed in Larry's forehead. *What* was an Indian—er, Native American—thing? He turned to Jimmy to see if he knew what the master was talking about, and apparently he did.

"Yes, sir," Jimmy said, amused and a little charmed by the elderly gentleman's naive way of bucking political correctness by calling him an Indian. The harm of a word is in intent, not simple utterance. And with Mr. Stanhope, Jimmy somehow knew he was in safe and respectful hands. "Or so my grandmother tells me."

"Do you sense him in the room now?" Roger asked.

"No, sir, but I felt him when I stepped through the door downstairs. When he wants to, I'll bet he can fill this house from floor to ceiling, from the basement right up to the gables on the roof."

Roger lost himself in the boy's brown eyes, then threw his head back and laughed. "He can indeed! You should have seen him when he was alive. His personality filled the sky. His laughter could light the world like a bolt of lightning."

Jimmy's face softened. "I'll bet it still could."

A tear sparkled in Roger's eye as he remembered. He nodded once, and with a voice softened by memory, he said, "Yes. Yes, it still can."

Both Roger and Jimmy turned to Larry, a matching twinkle in their eyes. "Keeping up?" Jimmy asked, and Larry looked so confused Roger barked out another laugh.

"Are you gay, son?" Roger suddenly asked, every ounce of his attention centered once again on Jimmy Blackstone's face.

Jimmy nodded. "A hundred years ago they might have called me two-spirit. But yes, in this century I am gay."

"You hide it well."

At that, it was Jimmy's turn to laugh. "Sir, I'm not trying to hide *anything*. I am what you see."

"I know," Roger said, stroking the dogs in his lap, his eyes never leaving Jimmy's face. "You are you and nothing else. That's another Indian gift, I imagine. One that other people would do well to emulate." He shot a glance at the flames in the fireplace, then flicked his gaze back to the two men in front of him—first Larry, then Jimmy, who he finally focused his full attention on once again. "I'm glad you're here, young man," he said quietly, his old fingers gently twiddling Max's ear. "This mountain has needed you, I think."

Jimmy humbly nodded, then reached over and patted Larry's knee. "And I look forward to exploring it, sir. Maybe Larry and I can explore it together." He suddenly twisted his head to glance back over his shoulder at the hallway door behind them. "We're no longer alone."

Roger shifted his eyes to the fire. "Is it—"

"No," Jimmy said, a spark of mischief lighting his eyes. "I think it's the living this time."

Roger leaned forward and peered at the door as if trying to activate his X-ray vision. "Ah, yes. Someone's eavesdropping, then."

"It would seem so."

A moment later came the distinct sound of footsteps retreating down the hall. Whoever had been at the door must have heard they'd been discovered.

A familiar voice whispered in Roger's ear. "A little competition never hurts."

The voice was so unexpected, Roger clutched his chest, startled.

Jimmy gave the old man a knowing look, as if he too had heard the whispered words, although he hadn't. "I think maybe it's not just the living who are eavesdropping," he said with a smile.

"I think you may be right," the old man answered, grinning back.

Larry, meanwhile, was totally confused. He hooked a thumb toward the hallway door. "Should I go see who was snooping?"

Roger refocused his attention on the dogs, but his words were directed at Larry. "Let it go, son. It doesn't matter."

"Oh. Okay," Larry said. Unsure *what* to do, he cast his eyes at Roger, then Jimmy, then back toward the door.

It was at that precise moment when Larry gave up all interest in trying to understand what the hell was going on. He figured he was so lost by then he would never catch up anyway. He just sat there looking more befuddled by the minute.

Roger beamed down at the two young men in front of him, one clearly confused, the other calmly sure of himself. The other presence in the room, the one only he and Jimmy knew was there, didn't need to direct Roger's attention to the fact that Jimmy's hand still rested casually on Larry's knee. That presence didn't need to mention that Jimmy's hand looked like it belonged there either.

Roger figured that all out by himself.

"WAS THAT you?"

Bo faced the stove where he was stirring a pot of boiling pasta. He didn't bother turning around. "What are you talking about?"

"Upstairs," Larry clarified. "Just now. By the master's sitting room."

Bo never for a moment stopped stirring the pot. "Nope. Wasn't me."

Larry grunted as if unconvinced, then dragged his social graces reluctantly into play. "I'd like you to meet Jimmy Blackstone, the new gardener and all-around psychic phenomenon of Stanhope Manor."

Jimmy poked him in the ribs and said, "Stop it," with a grin. Turning his attention to Bo, who had finally faced the two, albeit grudgingly, Jimmy stuck out his hand. "Pleased to meet you."

Bo ignored the hand, which didn't come off as *too* antisocial since, after all, he was holding a steaming pot lid in one hand and a dripping wooden spoon in the other. He might have at least said "Hello," but he didn't. He simply stood there.

Backing away and tossing Larry a wink, Jimmy said, "Brr. There's a chill in the air."

With that, Jimmy turned and walked out of the room whistling.

Larry glared at Bo. "What the hell was that all about? Why were you being such a dick?"

"Larry," Bo ventured, ignoring the question and working his way up to an apology for what had happened earlier, "about us rooming together—"

Larry interrupted with a disbelieving shake of his head.

"Don't," he said. "Just don't." And without waiting to hear anything further, Larry spun and followed Jimmy out the door.

He snagged an apple off the counter along the way.

Chapter Nine

The old Regulator clock in the hallway bonged out ten o'clock. The mansion was silent, on the verge of sleep. With Roger Stanhope quietly reading upstairs, all cameras were turned off. For Roger, it might have been better had this not been so. He might have learned a few things. Not that he didn't have other sources—more *ethereal* sources—for finding things out. One floor above, Larry lay naked in his bed with the window open, the mountain breeze blowing cool across his skin. He needed the night air to wash away unwelcome thoughts. He could hear Bo moving around in the bathroom next door. Larry's eyes occasionally skittered to the bathroom door, leery of Bo simply walking in unannounced. Again.

The only light in the room came from a small lamp on the nightstand, which barely pushed back the darkness.

Larry thought of Bo, naked in his arms. The taste of Bo. The *feel* of him. Their night together had been a trip. Enjoyable as hell, in fact. No two ways around it. Still, it left Larry feeling—not quite right. Ashamed, maybe. Cheapened. Even so, those erotic memories swelled his cock now as he lay in bed among the shadows with the night air washing over him.

He thought of Jimmy. His smile. The way his long hair had lashed across Larry's cheek when stirred by a gust of wind that afternoon. The clean softness of it. The way it shone in the light. The way it perfectly framed Jimmy's handsome face.

Larry closed his eyes and tried to push both men from his mind while at the same time attempting to ignore the growing weight of his rising hard-on. He fought against the urge to touch himself. To take his cock into his fist and make it thrum all the more.

Determined, he settled back into the pillow. Squirmed around on the bed, trying to relax. Tried not to think of his own body and how easily it could betray him.

Along with the wind, country music playing softly flowed through the bedroom window from the trailer parked three floors below at the edge of the carriage house. Larry threw the sheet aside, swung his bare legs off the side of the bed, and stepped to the window to peer out. He had to close his eyes for a second; the night air felt so delicious on his heated skin. When he opened his eyes, he gazed down through the darkness to Jimmy's Airstream.

There were lights burning both inside the trailer and outside the front door, illuminating Jimmy's makeshift front porch. Larry couldn't see under the awning, but he imagined Jimmy sitting there in his jeans and cowboy boots, sipping a beer. Shirtless, maybe, enjoying the night air as much as Larry was.

It was that thought alone—the thought of Jimmy sitting bare chested down below—that shattered Larry's willpower. Unbidden, his hand slid down his stomach to cup his balls. His cock was half-hard, stirred by the air and by the thought of Jimmy in just jeans and boots not thirty feet away. Larry had to admit the guy was sexy. Bo was sexy too, and Larry had enjoyed the night he spent in his arms, but he also regretted it. He regretted it a lot.

Bo seemed to think they had made some sort of pact. That an agreement had been settled upon. But it hadn't. Not in Larry's mind.

Especially after meeting Jimmy. Larry knew all too well where his interest now lay. Jesus. Was he fickle or what?

He remembered how Roger Stanhope had known immediately that Jimmy was gay. Larry hadn't. He recalled how Roger asked Jimmy about it point-blank, and how unhesitatingly Jimmy admitted the truth. Jimmy had not just been unashamed. It was as if he knew Roger had known and had every right to ask. Hell, it would probably have taken Larry a month to build up the courage to ask even if he had suspected, which he hadn't.

Larry continued to cup his balls while his cock kept on swelling, the heated weight of it sliding up his wrist as it grew in length and thickness. Eyes closed, Larry stood enjoying the play of cool air across his belly and bare legs, the wind stirring through his pubic hair, caressing his thighs. His other hand touched the base of his throat, his forefinger resting in the little triangular indentation there. That spot had a name, but Larry could never remember what it was. His hair shifted in the breeze, and he pushed it back from his forehead. He was fully erect now. He could feel it. Opening his eyes and glancing down, he licked his lips as he saw the shimmer of precome sparkling on the tip of his cock.

Squinting into the breeze, Larry stared yet again at the world outside his window. The trailer below shot beams of golden light through the thrifty little windows onto the sandy grounds surrounding it. The moon lay on the horizon, not yet high enough in the sky to reach the eaves overhead and disappear from view. On the moon's surface, etched among the shadows of craters and valleys, Larry could clearly see the outline of the lady his father once told him about—the lady who sat at her dressing room mirror brushing her hair. Around her, stars dotted the heavens like teeny spotlights, illuminating the moon lady's evening ablutions.

The scent of sage filled the air, tickling Larry's nose. While it was the bane of poor Mrs. Price, Larry rather enjoyed the smell. It smelled clean to him. It smelled... *wild*. As if the scent of sagebrush wasn't wild enough, somewhere off in the distance a coyote howled. Then farther away, another bayed in answer.

The creatures' plaintive wails brought Larry back to his senses. He peered down yet again at the grounds below—the dark edge of the carriage house, the Airstream trailer parked alongside it. There, alongside the broad bar of light that shone out across the grounds from beneath the canopy over Jimmy's front door, stood Jimmy!

He was dimmed by the darkness, tucked in among the shadows, but still Larry could see him well enough. He was standing just as Larry had imagined. Shirtless. Clad in jeans and boots. He held a bottle of beer in his hand, and while Larry stared down at him, Jimmy lifted the beer and took a long drink.

As he drank, he stared directly at Larry standing naked in the window above his head.

And there Larry stood with his cock in his hand, looking for all the world like the biggest slut ever!

Larry stepped away from the window so quickly he almost stumbled. He yanked the drapes closed, his face going red. Christ, what the hell had he been thinking?

At that moment, there came a knock on his door. The bathroom door. It was Bo. Shit.

"Let me in, kid," Bo pleaded through the door. "We need to talk."

Larry snatched the sheet off the bed and wrapped it around himself. "Wait," he called out, but it was too late. Bo was already peering around the edge of the door.

"I told you to wait!" Larry snapped, furiously tucking the sheet across his chest like some half-assed toga, trying to gather the folds together to hide his hard-on poking out down below.

"Oops," Bo said. "I'm sorry." But he didn't look sorry, which made Larry even angrier. It didn't help that Bo was standing in the doorway in nothing but a pair of saggy pajama bottoms so stretched out of shape they barely clung to his hips, exposing a fluff of pubic hair in the front and the swell of his ass in the back, which Larry couldn't miss when Bo turned to close the bathroom door behind him, sealing them into the room together. That was the *third* thing to piss Larry off.

Larry's anger jumped a gear and went straight to fury when Bo strode across the room and scooped him into his arms. Without thinking, Larry slammed his hands to Bo's chest and pushed him away.

Bo, caught off guard, stumbled backward. Pinwheeling his arms, he tried to regain his balance, but it was too late. He landed on the floor with a crash, flat on his back.

Now it was Bo's turn to get mad. "What the fuck is wrong with you?"

"You," Larry said. "*You're* what's wrong with me."

For the briefest flash in time, Bo's eyes got mean.

"That's not what you said when you had your dick down my throat."

Larry didn't have to worry about his hard-on anymore. It was long gone. He sucked in a deep breath in an attempt to lower his blood pressure. Like that was going to work. "Look, Bo. We tricked. It was fun. I'm pretty sure you enjoyed it as much as I did. Still, it doesn't mean we're lovers. You can't just walk in here anytime you want."

Bo still lay on the floor, his PJs pulled even lower from the fall. He propped himself up on his elbows and stared up at Larry, long legs akimbo, chest heaving, belly flat.

"Larry. I'm sorry. I-I won't do it again. I shouldn't have done what I did in front of Mr. Stanhope either. I know that now."

"No, you shouldn't have."

"I was wrong. I-I just like you is all." Bo let a smile tease its way across his mouth. His hand slid across his bare stomach, his gaze wandering over Larry's sheet-clad body. His green eyes turned molten. "Let me make it up to you," he said softly. The hand on his stomach slipped lower, his fingers dipping beneath the waistband of his baggy pajama bottoms.

If he thought that would turn Larry on and make him forget everything that had happened, he was sorely mistaken. In fact, it did the opposite. It made Larry even madder.

He aimed a trembling finger at the door. "Get out, Bo. I mean it. Get out now!"

Bo's eyes narrowed. "Don't be stupid. I don't think you know what's going on here. I think maybe we've got a chance to really make a killing."

Larry was still trying to calm down. He was even having a little bit of luck at it. Not much, but a little. "I don't know what the hell you're talking about, Bo, and I don't care. I just want you to go."

Bo's face fell. The mean glint in his eyes reappeared, but only for a second. He quickly blinked it away, knowing it would be counterproductive. There was too much at stake here. He had to calm the hell down. Slowly, Bo pulled himself to his feet, hitching up his PJs as he did.

A new wave of country music poured through the bedroom window. Ignoring Larry's demand for him to leave, Bo stepped past Larry and pulled the curtain aside to look out.

"I'm not going to ask you again," Larry said quietly behind him.

Bo turned once again to face into the room. His eyes lit up like he'd suddenly seen the light. He hooked a thumb at the window behind him. "You mean you'd rather go after *that*?"

It was too much even for Larry. His voice turned cold. "Let me get this straight. We trick once and you ask the boss if we can move in together without consulting me first. Now you've decided to play the jealous lover and start accusing me of trying to bed the gardener? What is this, a Lady Chatterley novel? Jesus, Bo, you're more fucked-up than I am. Get the fuck out. Now. I mean it."

Bo stepped directly up to Larry and only stopped when their faces were inches apart. He slid his finger across Larry's chest, then dipped his finger in his mouth as if testing the icing on a cake.

"Come to me tonight," Bo said, his voice warm and pleading. "Let me make love to you. You don't even have to reciprocate."

"Please," Larry said, closing his eyes but refusing to budge, "just go."

"What if I told you Mr. Stanhope wants us to fall in love?"

That caught Larry's attention. Unfortunately for Bo, it caught it for all the wrong reasons.

"You're not only fucked-up," Larry groaned, "you're crazy."

Taking Bo's arm, he dragged him toward the bathroom door. Bo didn't resist. By the time Larry had pulled the door open and stepped back to wait for Bo to walk through it, he was surprised to see Bo smiling at him. The smile was one of Bo's sexy numbers. It had melted Larry before, and obviously Bo had hopes of it doing the same again.

"We had a great night together, Larry. You have to admit that much."

"Yes," Larry said. "And that's all it was. Good night, Bo."

Gently, yet *not* so gently, Larry pushed Bo through the door. Just when Larry had decided to close the door softly, as befitting an adult, Bo shot him a wink.

So much for being an adult. Larry slammed the door so hard, the pictures rattled on the wall. If Bo had been standing an inch or two closer, it would have flattened his nose and probably taken out a few teeth.

Even so, Larry heard Bo chuckling on the other side of the door.

Which infuriated Larry even more.

ROGER WOKE with two words tumbling through his head. He wasn't sure if the words were residue from the dream he had been dreaming, or just the slipped cog of an old man's addled thought processes.

He repositioned the book in his lap, the one that had put him to sleep a few minutes earlier. It was no easy matter placing the book where he needed it for comfortable reading, since his lap was also filled with two snoring pugs.

After taking a moment to stare into the fire, then glance through the window at the moon rising across the mountain, he refocused his attention on Stephen King's latest.

It was then that he heard the two words again. They didn't come from a dream this time. And they didn't come from an old man's imagination either. They came floating on the air around him.

The words were "He knows."

It was Jeremy who uttered them. Softly. In his ear.

Roger closed the book and peered around, confused.

"That's impossible, my love. How could he know?"

TWO DAYS later, Mrs. Price sat perched on a bench in the side garden, crying. The dogs were playing among a stand of yucca, abloom now with tall bell-shaped clusters of creamy white blossoms. The sun was beaming down as hot as fire, promising a toasty summer to come. Not four feet away, an alligator lizard sat atop a boulder doing push-ups, heaving its little body up and down, trying to cool off.

She turned at the sound of footsteps crunching through the pebbles behind her. It was Larry. In his hands he held two tall glasses of lemonade, ice-cold and sparkling with condensation. She forced a welcoming smile.

"Aren't you sweet," she said, hastily brushing tears from her cheeks.

Larry handed her one of the glasses and joined her on the bench.

She took a sip, then pressed the cool glass to her forehead. "That feels good," she sighed.

Larry watched her, sipping at his own drink. He spotted the lizard on the rock and pointed.

Mrs. Price nodded. "Jack LaLizard," she said, and they both chuckled.

Larry focused his attention back on her. He gave a sympathetic *tsk*. "Are those sad tears or allergy tears?" he asked kindly.

Mrs. Price slid her eyes to him momentarily, then hurriedly looked away as if ashamed. Her gaze fell back on the rock, but the lizard was gone. "I'm afraid a little of both," she said.

"Anything you want to talk about?"

She took another sip of lemonade and carefully set the glass beside her on the arm of the bench. She gazed across the grounds, out over the landscaped desert lawns, and farther out, down along the slope of the mountain. In the distance, the mountain view shimmered in the heat like a mirage, but it was real enough, she knew. She had been staring at the same view for thirty years and had never grown tired of it yet.

"I'm going to miss this place," she said. "It's been my home for so long. I've been tucked away here for three decades, you know. I don't have many friends left down there." She lifted her chin, indicating the hazy city skyline, wavering in the heat, barely visible, miles and miles away. "Roger, too, I'm afraid. We've both cocooned ourselves in this house—on this mountain—for so long, we've almost forgotten there's another world out there at all."

Larry reached over and laid his hand on hers. While sweat sparkled both their foreheads from the sun crashing down on their heads, their hands were cool and moist from the drinks. Mrs. Price's slim fingers felt like brittle sticks of ice against his palm, so delicate he was almost afraid he would snap them off like icicles if he squeezed too hard.

As if on cue, both pairs of eyes settled on Jimmy Blackstone, once again clad in only jeans and boots, down on his knees at the edge of the shrubbery bordering the grounds, maybe a hundred yards away. His brown back was lean and strong. Even from all the way across the property, they could see his skin shining with perspiration, see the muscles knotting and unknotting as he worked at tugging something from the ground.

"I fear he needs lemonade more than we do," Mrs. Price offered.

Larry nodded. "When we're finished talking, I'll take him some."

Mrs. Price turned her attention back to the young man beside her. "I heard you quarreling with Bo."

Larry blushed. "Oh, that. Do you think the master heard?"

She tucked in her chin and smiled sadly. "Probably not. Usually by that time in the evening, he's removed his hearing aids and lost himself in a book."

"I never knew he wore hearing aids."

She tapped her ear. "They're inside where you can't see them."

"Ah."

Her eyes still studied Larry's face. "Is everything all right now?" she asked. "With you and Bo? We're pretty much a family up here. When people don't get along, everyone suffers."

Larry looked away. "We'll be fine. It was just a misunderstanding."

Mrs. Price smiled. "You're lying. He likes you, you know."

"Yes," Larry droned, his eyelids at half-mast. "I know." And as the words left his lips, his eyes never left Jimmy's sweaty back. For the first time, he noticed Jimmy had his long hair tied back in a ponytail. It made a clean elegant line flowing down the back of Jimmy's neck. Even with Mrs. Price at his side, he found himself wanting to press his lips to the heat of that sleek neck, feel that wet skin, cooled on the surface with sweat, lying salty beneath his kiss. He wanted to grasp Jimmy's sun-browned shoulders and twist him toward him, brushing the long hair aside, pulling him to his feet, and claiming the man's mouth with his own.

With those images swirling through his head, he found Mrs. Price staring at him quizzically as if wondering what he was thinking.

Larry blushed some more and laughed at himself. "Daydreaming," he said. Of course, he had no intention of letting the good woman know what he was daydreaming *about*.

Before she could figure it out on her own, Larry nudged the conversation back to her.

"Any word from the place you're moving to? Anybody kicked the bucket yet?"

She huffed. "No. They're all on their last legs, but still they refuse to keel over."

"I'm sorry they aren't dying quicker."

She laughed.

Larry laughed too. "No, really. I am."

She eased her hand from his grasp and wiped her cheeks with the handkerchief again. She was wiping sweat this time, Larry noticed, not tears. For that he was glad. Maybe he'd actually cheered her up a little.

"Roger likes having you here," Larry said. "I'm sure he'd be just as happy if you never left at all."

Mrs. Price studied his face, trying to look appalled but not really carrying it off very well. "Well, he is a friend. I suppose he'll miss me a *little* when I go. But then you and Bo would have *two* geriatrics to care for."

Larry shrugged, teasing her with a grin. "Maybe they're like cats, geriatrics. Two being no more work than one."

Mrs. Price shot him a disbelieving grimace. "That's what you think."

Across the grounds, they both watched Jimmy rise to his feet. As soon as he was up, he put his hands to his hips and stretched. Turning, he spotted them in the distance and waved. They waved back.

"Look how handsome he is," Larry said softly.

Mrs. Price turned to stare at Larry, but he was so raptly watching Jimmy, he didn't notice.

"Bo's handsome too," Mrs. Price said a little too casually.

Larry nodded absentmindedly, and she realized he wasn't even listening.

She let her eyes wander back to Jimmy, sweating in the sun, his knees dirty, his hair pulled back from his face and tied off with what looked like a strip of leather.

"He looks like he could use that lemonade now," she said softly.

"Yes," Larry said, his voice dreamy, drifting. "I'll take it to him, then."

Larry rose and walked away, leaving his own glass of lemonade forgotten on the bench.

Mrs. Price shook her head, listening to his footsteps crunch across the pebbles as he plodded his way toward the house. When she was all alone, she stared at the boy in the distance. The other boy. The one working in the yard. He was back on his knees again, but he wasn't digging in the earth this time. He was staring over his shoulder, watching Larry walk away.

Mrs. Price gave a weary sigh, but she didn't look unhappy. Just resigned.

"So much for well-laid plans," she muttered to herself, and looking down, she noticed the little lizard was back. This time he was not alone. Another lizard, slightly smaller, was stretched out on the boulder beside him. They were both doing push-ups, hoisting themselves up and down in unison, cooling off. Reptilian gym class.

"Hello there, Jack," Mrs. Price cooed to the first lizard. "I see you found a new friend."

Smiling, she reached for her glass. As she sipped, her eyes traveled back to Jimmy Blackstone.

"It would seem you're not the only one," she mumbled to herself.

ROGER ASKED that dinner be served for two in his sitting room at eight o'clock that evening. Bo prepared Italian cuisine, as was requested. Apparently, Roger Stanhope was in the mood for lasagna.

Knowing Mrs. P would be Roger's dinner guest, Bo went all out, hauling out his favorite lasagna recipe. For a side dish, he chose escarole and white beans. For bread, homemade sourdough buns garnished with fresh garlic and goat's butter.

Upstairs, Roger sat at the console in what was previously his dressing room and stared at the monitors before him. He was watching Larry stroll up and down the hallway outside Roger's bedroom door not ten feet away as if working himself up to knocking and asking to be let in.

"What's up with him?" Jeremy asked in Roger's ear. "He's as jittery as a cat in a firecracker factory."

"I imagine he's building up his courage to speak to me," Roger said.

"About what?"

Roger shrugged. "No idea."

He turned to another monitor. The camera for this screen was placed high on the exterior of the mansion, toward the back. It looked down upon the rear of the grounds, including the exterior of the carriage house and the gardener's trailer. An occasional shadow passed behind the trailer windows. Jimmy was inside, his workday over.

Mrs. Price, Roger knew, was secluded in her room, where no cameras had been installed. He grinned, remembering how she had expressly forbidden it.

"I'll not have you watching me don my unmentionables!"

"Like I'd want to!" Roger had shot back.

Now, with everyone present and accounted for, he switched off all the cameras and the monitors went dark. "Our romance has stalled," Roger intoned, rising and toddling toward the bathroom where he still had to tie his tie before dinner. Otherwise, he was dressed.

"Which romance might that be?" Jeremy asked.

"Don't start," Roger grumped. "I like Bo. We need to get our boys together again."

"I'm not so sure. I told you he knows."

Roger stopped messing with the tie. His arthritis was bad today anyway, the Windsor knot fighting him tooth and nail. He had just about decided to forgo a tie altogether, then decided he wouldn't. He flexed his aching fingers and tried again. "What do you mean by that? *Why* do you think he knows?"

"He as much as said so to the other boy—to Larry."

"Are you referring to our… *itinerary*?"

Jeremy snorted. "Is that what we're calling it now?"

"Oh, shut up."

"I have another news flash for you, Rog. You might be interested to know that interests have shifted."

"What the hell is *that* supposed to mean?" Roger cursed. "Oh, damn this tie!" He flung it across the room. At that very moment, he heard a knock on his bedroom door. Whatever Larry had been freaking out about, he seemed to have resigned himself to getting it out in the open.

"Leave us," Roger said.

"Say *what*?" snapped the voice at his ear. A moment later, a long string of toothpaste shot out of the tube at the edge of the sink, splattering the wall, the commode, the towel rack.

Roger rolled his eyes. "*That* was peevish," he muttered, hobbling toward the door. Pulling it open, he found Larry standing there just as he knew he would. There weren't many surprises to be had when you installed cameras all over the place.

"Hello, son," Roger said. "I didn't ring."

Larry cleared his throat, shuffled his feet, and tugged at his uniform vest as if he thought maybe it was hanging crooked.

Before he could explain the reason he was there, Roger interrupted, pulling him into the room and closing the door behind them. "Good lord, son, you're as fidgety as a salamander. I'll not bite your head off. Just tell me what's troubling you."

Larry cleared his throat one last time. "It's Mrs. Price."

"Why?" Roger asked, looking resigned. "What has she done now?"

Larry blinked. "Huh? Oh, nothing! It's just—"

"Just what? Whatever it is, I suggest you spit it out soon. She's joining me for dinner in a few minutes."

"Yes, sir. I know. I'll be serving it."

"Oh yes. So what is it? And while you're here, would you mind tying my tie for me? My fingers aren't working very well this evening. You'll find it on the floor in the corner where I fucking threw it."

Larry blinked again. "Oh, uh, sure." He scurried off to fetch the tie, shook some imaginary dust off it, and planting himself six inches in front of Roger's face, proceeded to drape it across the back of Roger's neck and carefully adjust the lengths of the two ends in front. He found it easier to speak while concentrating on the knot. Swallowing hard, he took the bull by the horns and just blurted it out.

"Mrs. Price would stay here if you asked her to."

It was Roger's turn to blink. "What do you mean? Stay where?"

"Here, sir. In the mansion. Lord knows you have plenty of room."

Roger studied the young man's face, looking a bit shell-shocked as he did, then he chortled rather unkindly. "I'm afraid you're hallucinating, Larry. Mrs. Price is going to Frederica Manor, where they will wait on her hand and foot. It's only fair, since she's been doing the same for me for the last thirty years. Now it's her turn to be pampered. She's earned it."

"I know," Larry said, still working diligently at the knot, which wasn't exactly his forte since he had actually worn a tie maybe three or four times in his whole life. "But just because she's going, doesn't mean she *wants* to go."

A silence settled over the room while Roger studied Larry's face. The boy stood there in front of him looking studious and concerned, still concentrating on the stupid tie. It was an honest face Roger stared at. An honest, caring, and *kind* face. The fact that it was also handsome seemed less important than it once had.

"Did she tell you this?" Roger asked softly.

"Not in so many words, sir, no."

"But you believe it? In your heart, I mean. You think she wants to stay?"

"There you go," Larry said, patting the tail of the newly knotted tie, then giving it a little tug to tweak the knot before lifting his eyes to meet Roger's. "And yes. I believe it in my heart, sir. My heart, my liver, a couple of lungs, adenoids, toenails. Mrs. Price doesn't want to go. She thinks of this house as her home. She thinks of you as her family." Larry stared back down at the knot at Roger's throat as if afraid to lift his eyes again, second-guessing himself, wondering if he'd said too much, said too little, should have stayed out of it completely.

Roger patted his own chest, as if his heart was suddenly doing somersaults under his freshly pressed shirt, which Larry himself had ironed not two hours earlier. "Help me to the chair," he said.

"Certainly." Larry took Roger's arm and steered him to his favorite chair by the fire. "Are you all right?"

"I'm fine." Gazing up, Roger eyed the young man standing solicitously before him. Then, patting the ottoman at his feet, Roger said, "Sit, son. Please."

Larry sat, looking for all the world like a young boy sitting at his grandfather's knee waiting for a story to unfold.

"I know it wasn't my place—" Larry began, but Roger waved him to silence.

Roger stared down at his hands, twisting the wedding ring on his finger. Surprised as always by the spiderweb of capillaries drawn across his crepe-papery skin. The age spots. The tremor that never completely went away. Wondering at what point in his life had those hands grown so old and feeble. When he found his voice, his whispered words were barely audible.

Larry had to lean in close to hear.

"Jeremy bought me this wedding ring in San Francisco almost seventy years ago. It's never been off my hand once. Look at it. It's worn as thin as paper. You wouldn't think silver would do that."

"It's still beautiful," Larry said, his voice just as soft as Roger's.

The flames on the grate crackled. For a moment it was the only sound in the room.

"Jeremy told Mrs. Price once that she would have a home with us for as long as she wanted. I wonder if she remembers that."

"Maybe it only matters that *you* remember it," Larry said, reaching down to lift a pleading Leo from the floor and place him on Roger's lap. Max immediately became jealous and hopped up under his own power, causing Roger to chuckle.

"Little scamps," he muttered.

Larry checked his watch. "I need to go, sir. Bo will be finishing your dinner. I still haven't set the table in your sitting room. I just...." He hesitated, unsure what to say next. "I just wanted to let you know about Mrs. Price."

"Neither Mrs. Price nor I are getting any younger, Larry. It would mean more work for you and Bo," Roger said, "having another full-time guest in the house."

"No more work than it is now," Larry answered. "Plus, I like Mrs. Price. I hate to see her sad."

Roger's eyes opened wide. "Is she sad?"

Larry simply nodded. He pushed his hair back off his forehead. A nervous habit.

Roger reached over and patted his knee, although he had to work around a couple of pugs to do it. "I would hate to see her sad too," he said, straightening his tired shoulders, his stooped back. "In fact, I won't have it. I'll speak to her at dinner. Would that be all right?"

A broad smile lit Larry's face. He tried to stifle it but didn't succeed very well. "Hey," he said, drawing in a shuddery breath, lifting his hands in a helpless shrug, "you're the boss."

Roger laughed. "Yes, well, sometimes one wonders about that." With a wink, he tipped his head toward the door. "Mrs. Price will be here soon. Beat it. Get back to work. And don't worry, I won't tell her you're the one who spilled the beans."

"Thank you, sir. She'd probably kill me if she knew."

Roger patted the knot at his throat, reassuring himself it was straight. "Yes, I'm sure she would. She kills people regularly, I hear. It's one of the things I most admire about her."

Larry laughed. Nodding good-bye, he stepped into the hall and quietly closed the door behind him.

The old man watched fondly as Larry disappeared from sight. "What a wonderful young man. If only I were seventy years younger—"

Somewhere overhead he heard the crash of broken glass. A mirror knocked from a wall perhaps. An expensive vase petulantly tipped off the edge of a table by unseen hands.

"—and not already spoken for," Roger hastily added.

"Stop cruising the help and come with me," a voice whispered in his ear.

Roger jumped and slapped a hand to his heart. "Christ, Jeremy! You scared me to death."

"Not quite, or you'd be here with me now, prancing through the afterlife instead of wishing you could bed the butler."

"I'm far too manly to prance, and Larry's not the butler. Exactly. Anyway, what is it? Where do you want me to go?"

"The monitor room, Your Butchness. I've laid a trap. Let's see what we catch."

"Huh? You know, you're more confusing dead than you ever were alive."

"Really?"

"Well, maybe not."

Roger snatched up his cane from where it leaned against the chair and made his way toward the monitors. The last time he had been in this room, he had turned the monitors off. Now, one was lit. On that screen he saw Bo down in the kitchen, working at the stove, looking as handsome as ever in his white chef's outfit. He never wore the toque anymore, and Roger thought the young man's buzz-cut black hair was quite sexy. Bo did, after all, have a nicely shaped head. Of course, his body wasn't bad either.

Jeremy, it seemed, could read minds. "You're cruising again. Besides, it's what *inside* the head that matters," he said, while Roger positioned himself in front of the monitor, setting his cane aside and leaning forward to watch more closely.

"What am I supposed to be seeing?" Roger asked. "He's fixing my dinner. That's what I pay him to do."

"No," Jeremy said, his voice no longer a whisper, but as loud as if he were a living soul standing at Roger's side, not a corpse that had been dead for two years. "You pay him to fix your dinner, be forthright and honest, and bring dignity to the Stanhope name."

Roger chortled. "All that, huh? And you're saying he's falling short in some way?"

"Honesty is an important character trait, you must admit."

Roger was becoming annoyed. "Yes, of course. What is all this about? Get to the point. Are you implying my new cook is less than honest?"

Jeremy whispered conspiratorially in his ear, "Watch closely and judge for yourself."

Roger sighed impatiently but did as he was asked. He stared at the monitor. It was rather eerie to watch people through the hidden cameras without sound. Roger almost wished he had laid out the extra $20,000 to place microphones around the mansion as well as cameras. But it was too late to worry about that now.

Bo stood at the island, prepping what looked like sourdough bread. Homemade. Roger's favorite. He could almost smell the delicious yeasty scent of it three floors up. Bo seemed absorbed by what he was doing. His eyes occasionally skimmed to the stove, where a tray of lasagna steamed and bubbled, having just been taken from the oven. Turning back to the bread, Bo held his mouth in such a way that Roger suspected he was whistling while he worked, just like one of Snow White's dwarves. Roger smiled at the whimsy of that thought.

His smile faded quickly enough when Bo turned to grab something from a cupboard to his left and froze, staring down at the floor in front of him.

Roger squinted at the screen. "What *is* that?"

His question was answered quickly enough when Bo bent and picked up what looked like cash. Three bills. It was too far away for Roger to clearly see the denomination with his old eyes.

"Are those...?"

Jeremy tittered. "Hundred-dollar bills. Yes."

Bo stood there staring at the bills—the bread, the lasagna, all the rest, clearly forgotten. The young man's eyes shot toward the doors, first one, then the other. Then he twisted to peer through the window, as if thinking perhaps someone might be spying on him from outside. Convinced he was truly alone, Bo stared back at the three bills in his hand. He gave them a shake as if testing their reality. Slowly, a sneaky smile lit his face, and he stuffed the three bills in his trouser pocket.

He turned back to the bread on the counter.

Roger sat watching, baffled. He finally tore his gaze from the monitor and glanced around the room, knowing it was pointless even as he did it. Jeremy was as invisible as he always was.

"What the hell was that all about? Why was there money on the kitchen floor?"

"I stole it from your safe. Community property, you know."

"Community property is for the living. You're as dead as last week's—wait a minute! You can access my *safe*?"

"I can access anything. I'm a ghost. Besides, I'm the one who bought that safe in 1967. I still remember the combination. My mind, as it was in life, is a steel trap, don't you know."

"Don't brag. But why would you steal money from me to see if Bo would steal money from *you*?"

"To test our young cook's honesty."

Roger drummed his fingernails on the ledge in front of the monitors. "So you honestly think he's dishonest."

"Nice play on words. And yes. I've just proven it, have I not?"

"Perhaps young Bo will ask around about the money later. He's in the middle of preparing dinner, after all. He can't just drop everything and...." Even as Roger blathered on, he knew he was whistling Dixie. The look on Bo's face when he stuffed the money in his pocket told the true story. The money was gone. It belonged to Bo now. He could see it in the greedy light that had blossomed in Bo's eyes. Young Bo wasn't *about* to attempt to seek out the true owner of that money.

"Maybe he needs it," Roger said. "He was in financial straits when he came here to work for me. Maybe he's still trying to get his head above water."

"Do you really believe that?" Jeremy sighed.

"I would prefer it over the alternative." Roger thought for a moment, then shook his head as if his mind was made up. "No. I'll not believe it. Let's give the man a chance. I'm sure he'll ask around and try to discover who the money truly belongs to."

"Are you really sure?"

"Well...."

"Uh-oh."

"What now?"

"Mrs. Price is coming to join you for dinner. Toodles," Jeremy piped, and within the space of a single heartbeat, Roger knew he was alone.

A moment later there came a knock on the sitting room door.

Chapter Ten

Days passed, accumulating one by one into weeks. The weeks became a month, and still Bo did not ask if anyone had misplaced three one-hundred-dollar bills. In fact, aside from Roger and Jeremy, the three hundred dollars was never mentioned again. It was as if the money had not appeared at Bo's feet at all.

At the same time, the fate of Mrs. Price's planned relocation to Frederica Manor was dealt a welcome deathblow when Roger asked her to remain at the mansion with him until such time as they carried her off the mountain toes up, just as they would with Roger one day. She had agreed—not only with surprise, but with wholehearted enthusiasm and gratitude.

"All those years we were together," she said, tears glistening, "you really *were* a friend."

Roger laid his palsied hand to her cheek. "My dear Mrs. Price," he said. "I always was and always will be."

On a Saturday evening in the first week of June, Larry stood at the greenhouse door, staring in at all he and Jimmy had done in the past couple of weeks to whip it into shape. The evening air still shimmered with heat. Larry's hair lay damp and curly on his head after showering away the day's labors. His work finished, Larry was decked out in a pair of baggy running shorts and a T-shirt, with a pair of beat-up tennis shoes on his sockless feet.

Roger Stanhope, Larry knew, was safely ensconced in his upstairs suite of rooms, freshly fed and cared for and nose-deep in a gay romance from Dreamspinner Press. Mrs. Price sat huddled with a collection of poems in the library on the first floor, where she spent most every evening, lost in Dickens or Twain or one of her other favorite authors.

Then there was Bo. On this evening, Bo had driven into town since it was his day off. He would probably come home drunk. Lately it had become somewhat of a habit with him. Larry sighed, wondering if Bo would yet again come pounding on his door in the middle of the night, trying to worm his way back into Larry's bed—into Larry's heart.

It had not been easy, dealing with Bo these past few weeks. Many days, Larry took his dinner in his room so he wouldn't have to suffer Bo's hurt looks, which seemed to be Bo's new game plan—acting hurt rather than accusatory about Larry's refusal to resume their affair. Although truthfully, it had only been a one-night stand to begin with, never an affair. Stubborn to the end, Bo steadfastly refused to see it that way.

Larry closed his eyes, willing these thoughts to go away. Eventually, through sheer perseverance on Larry's part, they sort of did.

So once again, here he stood, breathing in the mountain air and staring through the greenhouse door.

Newly cleaned and renovated, the greenhouse was alive now with greenery and the heady musk of freshly tilled earth. Hibiscus, the sweet blue pinwheels of chicory, California fuchsia, beavertail cactus, Indian paintbrush, and the scents of a dozen other species of desert flora sweetened the air. Today, with Jimmy's help, Larry had repotted trays of newly purchased California poppies into crockery pots, their yellow blossoms already rolled shut for the night. The poppies, once properly rooted and healthy enough to be moved, would replace a bed of dying succulents along the front walk. As Larry stared at them now, their golden blooms, wrapped tight until morning, slept in the light of the setting sun streaming through the newly sparkling panes of the greenhouse walls.

Larry heard footsteps approach and recognized the cadence immediately. When Jimmy laid a hand on his shoulder and reached the other arm around to offer him a beer, Larry took it without comment, although he did offer a smile of gratitude.

Jimmy stared into the greenhouse over Larry's shoulder. "We did good," he said, speaking softly in Larry's ear. "Just look at this place."

"It's beautiful," Larry said, as the air around him was suddenly infused with all new smells. More exciting smells. Soap, shampoo, a hint of mouthwash. Jimmy was obviously just out of the shower too. Damp hair. Freshly scrubbed skin. Scrumptious.

Jimmy stepped around him and leaned against one of the long shelves that ran down the length of the building. He wore his usual boots and jeans. His shirt was an old flannel work shirt that he wore untucked and unbuttoned, exposing his hairless brown chest and flat stomach. His long hair was damp from the shower just like Larry's was.

Larry cast a furtive glance in Jimmy's direction, admiring the expanse of russet skin, the tiny belly button, and the one exposed nipple, as brown and round as a penny. Tearing his eyes away, he sipped his beer and stared out at all the newly potted plants. Some in bloom. Some not. All looking healthy and vibrant and well-tended. Just like the man beside him.

"I wonder if the orchids will blossom," Jimmy pondered, sensing Larry's eyes on him and enjoying the sensation, but sensing Larry's reticence too.

Unaware of the true thoughts tumbling through Jimmy's head, Larry studied the small array of orchids they had potted. Larry hadn't forgotten Roger telling him that Jeremy had loved them so.

"We'll see," Larry said, tasting his beer for the first time. "I hope they'll bloom, for the master's sake." Glancing at Jimmy again, he was confused by an empty feeling. An empty feeling he *always* had lately when Jimmy was around. He tried not to stare at Jimmy's bare chest. He wanted to turn away but couldn't quite do it.

While he fought a silent battle within himself, their gazes fused and they stared at each other, one confused, one content, and neither really admitting even to himself how he truly felt. The pattering of Larry's heart ratcheted up a notch, as if he'd been suddenly infused with adrenaline.

"I know Bo is gone," Jimmy said quietly. "Do you have your pager in case Roger needs you?"

Larry patted his pocket. "Sure. Why?"

"Walk with me," Jimmy said. "Just down the mountain a little way. We won't be gone long. I just want to watch the sunset away from the house."

Larry glanced up at the side of the mansion, then back into Jimmy's eyes. "All right. But just for a while."

After closing the greenhouse door behind them to keep out any night critters that might come calling, they set off across the grounds.

"I found a game trail," Jimmy said. "It's right over here. There's a ledge of rock farther down where we can sit and watch the sunset. It's only a few hundred yards from the house."

"Okay," Larry said, once again patting the beeper in his pocket. "Lead the way."

The trail was narrow, obviously made by tiny feet. Raccoons, possums, rabbits, maybe the occasional coyote. Jimmy led the way and Larry followed directly behind him. The light was quickly fading since sunset was only minutes away, but there was still enough light for Larry to lose himself watching Jimmy's blue-jeaned ass in front of him. Knowing he would not be seen, Larry reached out his hand and lightly touched Jimmy's flowing shirttail, surprised by the spark of imagined electricity that shot up his arm as he did.

When Jimmy stopped in front of him without warning and turned quickly around, Larry plowed right into him. Jimmy's arms came up and circled Larry's waist, as if to keep either one of them from falling flat. Both men froze.

Jimmy grinned from an inch and a half away. "Sorry. Hope you didn't spill your beer."

"N-nope," Larry breathed. "Still got it."

A tiny smile played at Jimmy's mouth. "Am I too close?"

"N-no."

Jimmy's smile widened as if he didn't quite believe it. "Good. I've been watching you, you know."

Larry swallowed hard. "You have?"

"Yes. I like the way you move."

Larry tried to step back, but Jimmy's hands held on to his hips, keeping him right where he was. Larry didn't struggle much. He didn't want to move anyway.

"It's because I'm a klutz, right?" Larry asked.

Jimmy grinned. "No, that's not it at all. Well, maybe a little."

Both men offered up an embarrassed laugh.

Their laughter rang softly over the mountainside, and at the sound of a catbird trilling somewhere in the bushes along the edge of the trail not three feet away, they both quieted, as if their own voices didn't really fit in with the sounds nature could make. The gentle scent of desert wildflowers rolled over them. A breeze brushed their skin. It felt cool on their damp scalps.

Larry trembled. "Y-you said there was a rock? Where you wanted to watch the sunset?"

Jimmy studied Larry's eyes, delving deep, each man's warm breath flowing over the other. "There is," he said. "But there was something I wanted to do first."

"What's that?" Larry asked, his voice weak, almost inaudible.

"This," Jimmy said, and ever so gently, he leaned in to lay his lips over Larry's mouth. The kiss was almost casual. Lazy, unrushed, as soft as cotton. Larry's eyes automatically closed while his pulse pounded in his temple and his hands came up to rest on Jimmy's bare chest.

The kiss went on and on. No pressure. No tongues. No urgency. Just softness. Sweet softness. And all the while the kiss continued, the feel of Jimmy's bare chest against the palms of his hands made Larry burn inside.

When Jimmy at long last ended the kiss and eased back, his eyes stayed on Larry's face. He was watching when Larry's eyes slowly opened and a palpable shudder raced through his body. Teetering off balance, Larry gripped the flaps of Jimmy's shirt to keep himself upright.

"I've been wanting to do that," Jimmy whispered.

Larry ran his tongue over his lips, retasting the kiss. "I'm glad you did. I-I've wanted it too." His mouth still moist from their kiss, Jimmy took Larry's hand and released him from his arms. "Come on, then. Let's watch the sunset."

"But—"

Jimmy gave an innocent tilt to his head, studying Larry's face. "But what?"

Again Larry slid his tongue across his lips. Lingering. Finally he shook his head and whispered, "Never mind. Show me your sunset."

THEY SAT on a spur of rock overhanging a precipitous drop so steep it made Larry's toes ache. They could see past a bank of chaparral that clung to the cliff's edge down to a scatter of boulders and scree below. The boulders had undoubtedly been cast there eons earlier in the upheaval of some long-forgotten seismic Armageddon. The mountain wasn't really that high. Still, this section was sheer enough to scramble a few neurons if you tumbled down it. The outcropping of stone they sat on, side by side, was granite, Larry thought. At least it looked like granite. The stone had absorbed a lot of sunshine through the course of the day, and the heat of it was uncomfortable on the back of his bare thighs. He was kind of sorry he hadn't worn long pants.

The view was spectacular. Miles away, before the half dome of a setting orange sun, they could see the spires of the downtown skyline. Larry used to live there, work there, among the high-rises and bustling city streets. It seemed odd, seeing it from this quiet stretch of mountainside, with the warbling of wrens in the bushes, and somewhere in the underbrush at their feet, the skittering rustle of some small creature perhaps setting out for the evening hunt. Traffic sounds, the honk of car horns, the milling of crowded sidewalks, was just a memory here. A memory unmourned.

Larry loved the quiet solitude of the mountain.

He ventured a cautious glance in Jimmy's direction, their kiss still hot and fresh in his mind. He longed to reach over and lay his hand on Jimmy's leg, but he fought the urge. He had hated it when Bo moved too fast. He refused to act the same way, no matter how much he wanted to.

Jimmy's voice tore into his thoughts as easily and as painlessly as deft fingers plucking a weed from the greenhouse floor.

"I used to look at this mountain from the reservation where I was raised." He hooked a thumb over his shoulder. "That was from the other direction, of course. We couldn't see the city from there. This little mountain was just big enough to be in the way."

Larry closed his eyes, as much to erase the tempting sight of Jimmy as to better feel the evening breezes blowing across his face, still flushed from the kiss. "What was it like? The reservation? Were you happy there?"

Jimmy made a little grunting sound deep in his throat. "I was. Being a kid, I didn't know any better. I imagine if you asked my parents the same question, they'd give you a different answer. For them, it was a hardscrabble life. Forever trying to find work that lasted more than a day or two. Wanting to get away, but having nowhere to get away *to*. Being strapped with a kid. Living on commodities. Driving a car that was on its last legs so that even if they *found* jobs for the two of them, they'd be hard-pressed to get to them."

"You were poor, then?"

Jimmy chuckled. "We sure as hell weren't rich."

"Are your parents still living?"

Jimmy nodded. "Yeah. They're still there. Still struggling. Now that I'm working steady, I send them money every week. They don't want to take it, but they don't have much choice. They know they need it as much as I know they do."

Silence settled over them, along with the shadows of approaching dusk. The colors of the mountainside softened from silvers and golds and radiant greens to grays and blues and muted lavender where the shadows lay deepest. The air grew cooler by the minute.

To Larry's surprise, Jimmy's hand came out of nowhere and rested on his bare leg, just above the knee. Almost absentmindedly, Jimmy squeezed him there. Gently, just once, then left his hand to rest in stillness. The hair on Larry's leg bristled against Jimmy's palm, and sometimes Jimmy's thumb would move, just a little bit, as if enjoying the feel of it.

"Say something," Jimmy said, staring out across the foothills. "I'm doing all the talking."

It had been minutes since they'd gazed at each other. Perhaps they were afraid to. Instead, they stared out at the blazing sunset, watching the flames of it slowly burn down to darkness.

"Tell me why you kissed me," Larry said, his words so softly uttered they barely carried on the air.

Jimmy turned and studied Larry's face. "Because I wanted to. Actually, I've been wanting to kiss you for a long time. Hope you didn't mind."

"I didn't mind."

Jimmy smiled. "Good."

The view was lost to Larry as he sat staring down at that strong brown hand resting atop his pale, fuzzy leg. Jimmy's hand and arm were almost hairless, veins etched beneath the skin, muscles and tendons moving with life even at the slightest motion. Jimmy's fingernails were broad and neatly trimmed, although one thumbnail was torn ragged, probably from working in the earth. Larry picked up that thumb and rolled it between his fingers, running his own thumb over the roughness of the nail. He gently clasped his hand around it, and with Jimmy's thumb still in his fist, he lifted his head to stare out at the sunset once more.

"How are you getting along with Bo?" Larry asked. "I never see you two together."

Jimmy leaned over the rock and spit, watching it land on a rock thirty feet below. "He's jealous. Haven't you noticed?"

Larry turned to him. "Jealous of us?"

Jimmy snickered. "Hell, yes. You aren't exactly on the ball when it comes to romance, are you? After all, I've been wanting to kiss you for weeks now and you missed all my not-so-subtle clues. Bo wants to get you in the rack, and you seem to be missing all his clues too."

"No," Larry said on a sigh. "I didn't miss them completely. Bo and I slept together once. It was way back before you came. I'm not proud of it, but we did."

It was Jimmy's turn to stare. "Just once? Why'd you stop?"

Larry shrugged. "I'm not sure. He gets a little intense. Asked me to share a room with him right off the bat. Even asked Mr. Stanhope if it would be all right."

"And you didn't like it."

"No," Larry said. "I didn't like it at all."

Jimmy cast him a sad little smile. "And now you've got me rooting around after you, grabbing you on the trail and kissing you without permission."

"It isn't like that."

"What's it like, then? Should I be apologizing?"

Larry stroked the back of Jimmy's hands with his fingertips. When he lifted eyes to Jimmy's solemn face, his heart gave a lurch. He struggled with the words for a second but finally got them out. "Don't ever apologize to me, Jimmy. You have no idea how long I've wanted you to do that."

Jimmy moistened his lips with his tongue. "Really?"

It was Larry's turn to smile. "I guess you're not so big on subtle clues either."

Jimmy's face squinted into a grin. "Jeez, maybe I'm not."

They stared into each other's eyes, letting the silence move back in. Sort of like the cool evening, it settled over them, enveloping them in a bubble of contentment. Sometimes in past relationships, Larry had been uncomfortable with the silences. With Jimmy, not that it was a relationship or anything, he realized right away that the silences between them didn't scare him at all. In fact, they were comforting. They seemed to—*belong*. And he belonged inside them. They both did.

They sat without speaking a while longer. By now the sun had dropped below the horizon. Dusk was just a short breath away from night.

"Are you hungry?" Jimmy asked.

For lack of anything smarter to say, he said, "I could eat. You asking me to dinner? After all, our cook is off. We're pretty much on our own."

"Okay, then," Jimmy said. "Have dinner with me in my trailer."

Larry shrugged for show, but deep down inside he was thrilled. "Sure. Whatcha serving?"

"Pemmican?"

Larry's mouth dropped open. "Wow. Really?"

Jimmy threw his head back and brayed out a honking laugh. "No, dumbass. I'm not that much of an Indian. How about peanut butter and jelly sandwiches and another beer? I might have potato chips for a side dish."

"Even better."

"It really is," Jimmy said. "Pemmican tastes like crap, in case you're interested."

Larry stared at Jimmy's face, almost lost in shadow now but for the crystal-white flashes of his eyes and teeth as the darkness settled around them. "Trust me," Larry said quietly, "I'm interested."

The intensity of his words and the gentleness of his voice quieted Jimmy's laughter. He lifted his free hand and brushed his thumb along the line of Larry's jaw, his eyes wide, amazed by what he was feeling.

"Would you be interested in one more kiss before we go?"

Larry drew breath with an almost imperceptible shudder. Afraid to speak for fear of what he might say, he merely nodded.

For only the second time in their lives, their lips came together in a kiss. This one lasted even longer than the first.

When it was over, they opened their eyes and were surprised to find the darkness had fallen completely. Still tasting each other's lips, they strolled back to the mansion in the deepening shadows, holding hands. Stars appeared one by one above their heads. As they walked, neither said a word, except for an occasional warning from Jimmy about uneven spots on the path.

Neither minded the silence or the darkness at all. They hardly noticed anything but the feel of the other's hand.

THEY LAUGHED all the way through dinner. Jimmy warmed up a pan of sloppy joes over a two-burner gas range, served the glop over toast, and apologized for not having french fries to go with it.

Larry praised Jimmy's Airstream. The compactness of it. How clean it was. The neatly made double bed at one end, the miniature kitchen with everything anyone could need at the other. The dining area with the oblong table and the built-in bench seats. The aluminum walls, the touches of warmth like the cougar throw on the armchair by the bed, and the sunflower-colored towels in the tiny bathroom.

They sipped another beer while they ate. Larry talked about his lousy job at the department store and how lucky he was to find employment with Mr. Stanhope. Jimmy told him of the dozens of jobs he had held, everything from yardwork to carpentry to auto mechanic. He mentioned in passing, as if it was of very little importance to him, the prejudice still to be found in the world for people of darker color.

"I'm sorry," Larry said, sensing the subject was not as idly mentioned as Jimmy would like him to believe.

But Jimmy laughed off his own complaints. "Sometimes," he said, his eyes burning bright while he studied Larry's face, "sometimes, I meet people who make up for all the others."

Larry blinked at the sincerity in Jimmy's voice—at the feelings he unashamedly laid open for Larry to see.

"I hope I'm one of them," Larry said, his voice blending with the muted strains of Patsy Cline playing from the CD player in the corner.

Jimmy nodded shyly. "You are."

Their meal finished, they sat at the little oblong dining table and worked their way through another beer. While they quietly chatted about this and that, Larry was never unaware of Jimmy's foot resting against his beneath the table.

After a lull in the conversation, Jimmy said, "I'm glad we're working together."

Larry fought the urge to say more than he should. It wasn't the beers that were trying to free his tongue; it was the feelings that had been welling up inside him all night. Not just sexual longings related to the man across from him, but other feelings too. More complicated feelings. In the end, he said, "I'm glad we're working together too," and left it at that, although it practically killed him to do it.

As night deepened, they moved out to the two lounge chairs under the awning. Crickets were cricketing from the flower beds at the edge of the mansion. A heat lamp left burning inside the greenhouse for the newly rooted orchids cast a pinkish light over the grounds. That pinkish light was so beautiful, Jimmy turned off the light outside his front door and let the heat lamp and the climbing moon overhead do all the work of illuminating the night around them.

Jimmy eyed the sky, sniffed the air. "It's going to storm before morning."

Larry looked around and didn't sense anything of the sort. "You're crazy."

Jimmy gave him a supercilious eye roll. "Hey, I'm an Indian. We know these things."

"Yeah, okay, Mr. Roker."

They sat close, their chairs nudged up next to each other. After a while, Jimmy's hand came to rest on Larry's forearm, and Larry felt his cock slowly lengthen inside his running shorts. He laid his arm in his lap to hide it. He wasn't sure if Jimmy knew what he was doing, but even if he did, he didn't remove his hand from Larry's arm or stop brushing through the hair there with his fingertips.

"Bo's going to hate me even more," Jimmy said.

The statement took Larry by surprise. "What do you mean? I'm sure he doesn't hate you."

Jimmy took a long pull from his beer. "Oh, he hates me all right. And when he finds out I'm trying to get close to you, he's going to hate me all the more."

"Is that what you're doing?" Larry asked quietly. "Trying to get close to me?"

Jimmy chuckled and gave his head a shake. "It's taken me a month to get this far, but yeah, that's what I'm doing. Guess I'm not doing it right, if you aren't noticing."

"Oh, I'm noticing."

Jimmy lifted playful eyes. "Well, that's a relief."

Larry watched Jimmy's very kissable lips spread wide in a self-deprecating grin. He reached out and tucked Jimmy's long hair behind his ear on the side closest to him, so they could see each other better.

"Listen!" Jimmy said, cocking his head. His aura of contentment dissolved like smoke. His body suddenly tensed. "Your buddy's coming home."

Larry heard it then. Bo's old pickup truck, rattling along the drive, the motor straining hard as it climbed the slope. A pair of headlights stabbed across the property, illuminating the grounds, the house, the trailer. A moment later the old pickup trundled past, radio blaring rock, and then silence descended as Bo parked alongside the carriage house and killed the engine. When the motor died, the music died with it.

They heard the squeak of a truck door, first opening, then banging shut. Shortly after, footsteps approached, crunching through the gravel. Jimmy stood and reached in the front door of the Airstream to turn on the porch light. Returning to his chair, Jimmy rested his hand on Larry's arm exactly the way it had been before. Together, he and Larry waited.

A long pair of blue-jeaned legs came into view. Then a shirt, half-untucked. And finally, there was Bo, standing in the glow of Jimmy's porch light. He didn't look particularly drunk, but he didn't look particularly sober either. Just somewhere in between.

He opened his mouth to speak, then saw Jimmy's hand resting on Larry's arm. Lifting his eyes, he studied first Larry's face, then Jimmy's. His eyes went cold. The smile that had been on the verge of springing forth disappeared as if blown away by the freshening breeze, which, now that Larry thought about it, *did* smell a little like rain.

"Cozy," Bo said with a mean twist to his mouth. An anxious silence hung on the air for long seconds, until with a final glare in Larry's direction, Bo wheeled and stalked off toward the house.

That anxious silence lasted a few beats longer. Finally, Larry said, "I'd better go."

Jimmy's hand tightened on his arm. "No. Let him get to sleep first. While you're waiting, we can have another beer. Please, Larry. Don't go. He'll pick a fight if you do. He was itching for one. I could tell."

"All right," Larry said, relieved. The last thing he wanted to do was ruin this incredible night by facing off with Bo. "I'll stay for a while if you'd like."

"Thank you," Jimmy said, laying a hand to Larry's cheek and stroking it gently with his thumb. "I didn't want you to leave anyway."

Larry leaned into the touch but said nothing.

HIGH ON the greenhouse wall, a tiny speck of red light shimmered in the darkness, unnoticed by either man.

Only Bo, cowering in the mansion doorway, spying from the shadows, saw the blink of red. Seeing it, he knew immediately what it was. A security camera.

He was amazed he hadn't noticed it before. Were there others? How many? Were there only exterior cameras, or were they placed inside the mansion as well? He had to know.

Easing through the door, he entered the kitchen. Weeding his way through the familiar shadows, he fumbled for the drawer that held a myriad of objects not really related to cooking. One of those objects was a penlight. He shuffled through the junk until he recognized it by feel. Extracting the penlight, he held it unlit as he studied the pitch-black shadows over his head. Along the walls, in the high corners, above the valances over the vertically blinded windows.

He saw nothing. No red lights.

Switching on the penlight, he again studied the ceiling overhead. This time he saw it immediately. A sparkling circle of light shining in the penlight's beam. Not red, just a crystal spark of silver light reflecting off a spot of glass. A camera lens. It had to be.

Bo was so intent on his search now, he had sobered himself up. He stepped into the dining room and cast the penlight's beam around the cornices until he spotted another spark of white reflected light.

The sitting room was the same. Also the library and poolroom. All accessed by security cameras. Apparently the only one switched on at the moment was the camera watching Jimmy and Larry down by the trailer.

Bo stared up at the ceiling once more. This time his imagination carried him up to the second floor to Mr. Stanhope's suite of rooms. There were no security personnel in the mansion. It must be Stanhope who was accessing the cameras. Playing with his puppets down below, maybe? Following their games, their romances, their simple daily routines? Pulling the strings? Directing the drama?

Bo smiled in the darkness. The smile was amused, but it was not kind.

And why would he be doing that, I wonder?

JIMMY SERVED them each another beer. Only when they resumed their seats by the trailer's front door and Jimmy returned his hand to Larry's arm, did the light from the camera perched high on the greenhouse wall go out, still unnoticed by either man. High above their heads, also unnoticed, the light in Roger's bedroom window went out as well. The mansion grew still.

Thirty minutes later, with their beers empty and barely a dozen words shared between them, Larry finally said, "I guess I should go."

"I wish you wouldn't," Jimmy whispered, watching him with gentle, pleading eyes.

"I know," Larry said, and reaching out once to brush his fingers through Jimmy's long hair, he turned his back and walked away.

At the mansion's back door, he stopped. Without looking back, he said, "Good night, Jimmy."

"G'night," Jimmy said. He raised his hand, but Larry was already gone.

Chapter Eleven

STILL DRESSED in his running shorts and T-shirt, with only his tennis shoes kicked off, Larry lay restless on his still-made bed. He had left Jimmy's trailer hours ago. He'd dozed for a little while, but now, thinking about everything that had happened, his eyes were wide open, the possibility of any more sleep not much more than a pipe dream. Through the window beside his head, he watched intermittent flashes in the night sky. Lightning. Jimmy had been right. A storm was moving in. It was still a ways off but approaching fast. Larry could smell it on the breeze, could feel it in the wisps of damp air that stirred his bedroom curtains and washed raw across his bare skin.

Through the connecting door, he could hear nothing. Bo must be asleep. Or passed out. Thank God. Larry wasn't in the mood for a confrontation. Or worse, a fight. He had other things on his mind.

He rested his forearm across his eyes, blocking out the present, focusing his thoughts on the evening he had spent with Jimmy. Their walk down the game trail. The simple dinner they shared. The sweetly hesitant way Jimmy had of letting his interest in Larry be known. So different from Bo, who had plowed ahead like a freight train at every step. Commanding, sexy even, but in the end, unnerving. Pushy.

Infuriating.

The light touch Jimmy had wielded through the course of the evening, the way he carefully felt his way along, testing the waters as he went, never going too far, never saying too much—it made Larry smile now as he lay in the darkness on his lonely bed. He could still feel Jimmy's gentle fingers stroking his arm, touching his cheek, the weight of his foot against Larry's ankle under the tiny dining room table inside the camper while they ate. The sight of Jimmy's bare chest, so beautiful that Larry even now couldn't stop thinking about it.

Jimmy's kiss.

In the darkness, in the silence, Larry could taste that kiss all over again. He could remember every little thing about it. The way his hands had rested on Jimmy's warm chest, and how Jimmy's hands had effortlessly clutched his hips, holding him close. Keeping him near. The way Jimmy smiled into the kiss when Larry began relaxing in his arms.

The way their heartbeats pattered when Larry finally let himself go and started kissing back.

He opened his eyes now and rose from the bed on trembling legs. Stepping to the window, he gazed out at the grounds below. The lights in Jimmy's trailer were out. The only illumination down there was the heat lamp in the greenhouse that still cast that weird pinkish light on the flowers inside, spilling out through the glass walls to shimmer on the shiny aluminum exterior of the trailer, to light the path from the mansion's back door to the carriage house beyond. Straight to Jimmy's front door.

The path Larry knew he had to take. Now. Right now.

Without thinking about it, without letting his fears get in the way like they usually did, Larry stepped away from the window at the very moment the first drops of rain began plunking against the glass. Still barefoot, grabbing only his beeper from the dresser beside the bed, he left his room, quietly closing the hallway door behind him. He padded silently down three flights of stairs through the sleeping mansion to the kitchen below. From there, he passed through the back door like a wisp of shadow and stepped out into the night.

Holy crap! What had begun as a light sprinkle had already become a downpour. Larry gasped as the cold wind hit his bare legs. He squinted breathless into the frigid needles of icy rain that suddenly peppered his face. Larry's hair was drenched in seconds, his shorts and T-shirt plastered to his skin. He stood in the yard, staring up at the rain coming down as if he had never seen such an amazing thing in his life.

Still he burned inside. Burned for Jimmy. The rain didn't douse that fire at all.

Shivering in the cold, he hurried down the walkway, splashing heedlessly over rain-soaked cobblestones. When he ducked under Jimmy's awning, he shook himself off like a dog. Teeth clattering from the frigid, wet wind on his drenched skin, his bare feet feeling like two big clumps of ice, he stood there staring at the door in front of him, suddenly afraid to knock.

The trailer was silent. Or was it? He thought he heard a noise. Footsteps maybe. Then, before he could react except to stiffen in surprise, the trailer door flew open and Jimmy stood there staring out. He was in a flannel shirt. Nothing else. The shirt was long and covered his crotch, but by a swaying movement there behind the fabric, Larry knew Jimmy was naked beneath it. His lean legs protruded below and soaked up every ounce of Larry's concentration.

Jimmy stepped through the door and stood on the top step, looking down. "Larry," he said, his eyes bright, his hands clenching the doorsill.

Without thinking, without wondering if he knew what he was doing at all, Larry stepped forward and dropped to his knees on the top step, wrapped his arms around Jimmy's legs, and laid his face against the warm skin of Jimmy's thigh. He closed his eyes, breathing in the scent of Jimmy's skin, feeling the heat of his smooth hairless leg against his face. Larry kissed that silken skin, caressing it softly with his lips. His fingers stroked the tender skin behind Jimmy's knees, and then he leaned his head back and stared up past the shirt to Jimmy's face.

With his lips still pressed to Jimmy's thigh, he watched Jimmy's eyes staring down from above. He watched Jimmy smile, and with that one simple offering, he knew everything would be all right. Jimmy's hands came out and stroked the wet hair off Larry's face, squeegeeing it back away from his forehead, and Larry knew everything would be even *better* than all right.

"Let me in," Larry whispered. "Before I catch my death."

"Yes," Jimmy said. "Yes." And pulled him through the door.

JIMMY TUGGED Larry into the kitchen. Along the way, he grabbed a bath towel from the rack in the bathroom. Larry stood obediently shivering on the kitchen linoleum, the rainwater puddling around his feet. Jimmy gave him a pathetic *tsk*, and without asking, peeled Larry's T-shirt over his head and flung it into the sink. Taking a moment to stare deep into Larry's eyes, as if asking for forgiveness, maybe, but not really caring if he got it or not, Jimmy dropped to his knees in front of Larry, slid the soaked running shorts down Larry's hips and legs, and plucked them from around his feet.

When Larry stood naked before him, clad only in rainwater and goose bumps, Jimmy rocked back on his heels and muttered, "My God, you're beautiful."

Larry's continued shivering was his only response, and Jimmy quickly stood and wrapped him tightly in the towel.

"Rub yourself dry," he ordered. "Your teeth are chattering."

While Larry obeyed, Jimmy snagged a dishtowel from the kitchen counter and began drying Larry's hair. When it was as dry as it was ever going to get on the spur of the moment, Jimmy tossed the hand towel away and took command of the bath towel.

Vigorously massaging Larry's back and chest with the towel, getting the blood moving, trying to warm the man up, Jimmy pulled Larry close and simply held his naked body tight against the warmth of his flannel shirt. The wet towel fell at their feet, and Jimmy massaged Larry's back with his bare hands now, squeezing his waist, roughly kneading his skin, outlining Larry's shoulder blades with warm fingertips, offering heat, offering comfort.

Larry closed his eyes and buried his face in Jimmy's long hair. With a trembling hand, he pushed Jimmy's collar aside and laid his mouth to the crook of Jimmy's neck.

"Baby," Jimmy muttered, and ever so gently he tugged Larry toward the bed. "Let's get you warm," he said.

With his eyes closed and his lips still pressed to Jimmy's neck, Larry whispered through still-clattering teeth, "Please, Jimmy. Take off your shirt."

Jimmy smiled, but Larry didn't see it. Larry's eyes were still closed. He couldn't stop quaking, but it wasn't only because he was chilled. His cock was an iron shaft that occasionally brushed Jimmy's leg, and now Jimmy's cock responded. Larry longed to drop to his knees and take Jimmy into his mouth, but he was still shivering so he thought he'd better not. The way his teeth were chattering, it would be like sticking a hot dog in a Cuisinart.

If he wasn't so damned cold, he would have laughed at that thought.

"I will," Jimmy said. "Trust me. This shirt's as good as gone. Just let me get you into bed first."

Larry nodded and let himself be led toward the bed. The covers were already a mess. Jimmy must have been sleeping when Larry arrived. After easing him down to the mattress, Jimmy gently laid Larry back and pulled the covers over him. Larry reached out and clutched the back of Jimmy's knee. "No," he said. "Don't go."

Jimmy smiled down at him. The trailer was dark but for a nightlight in the kitchen and intermittent flashes of lightning strobing through the windows.

"I'm not going anywhere." With hurried fingers, Jimmy unbuttoned his flannel shirt. He shrugged out of it, letting it fall to his feet. In the dim light, Larry could see him naked now for the very first time, his body brown and lean, his cock erect and uncut.

Larry slid his fingers along the length of that magnificent cock and cupped Jimmy's balls. At Larry's touch, Jimmy rocked on his feet and damn near toppled over. He barked out a laugh and dove under the covers next to Larry, pulling the blankets tight around them, pressing their unfettered bodies together, his arms snaking around Larry's waist, dragging him close, offering heat and anything else he could offer.

Still shivering, Larry tried to relax and let the warmth of Jimmy's flesh flow through him. He couldn't tell now if he was shaking because he was cold or because he was so turned on he was about to have a stroke.

Before he could decide, Jimmy claimed his mouth in a kiss and all questions were obliterated from his mind.

Slowly, oh so slowly, Larry's trembling subsided. He rested one hand on the creamy softness of Jimmy's ass, while his other arm was trapped between them, that hand resting on Jimmy's chest a little above his heartbeat. Or was that Larry's own heartbeat he was feeling?

"I'm glad you came back," Jimmy whispered, their lips still joined in a kiss.

Larry bit Jimmy's bottom lip with a gentle nip of his teeth and said, "I had to."

Jimmy pulled him closer. "Yes. You did."

Their two cocks scraped against each other, and Larry's body convulsed at the sensation of it. His hips pitched and he pushed himself closer. Jimmy's hand slid down across his stomach, and warm fingers circled Larry's cock. Larry convulsed again.

"You probably shouldn't do that," Larry gasped. "I'm not exactly in control of things at the moment."

There was a tightness in Jimmy's voice. A breathlessness Larry had never heard there before. "Who's asking you to be in control of things?"

Larry hesitated, then muttered, "Your body. You feel so good."

"So do you."

Larry felt eyelashes brush his face as Jimmy blinked. Jimmy's warm tongue slid across Larry's lips, caressing him in a kiss. "I want to taste you," Jimmy muttered. "Not just your mouth. I want it all."

"M-me first."

"Sorry, Larry. It's my bed. My house. I'm pulling rank."

"Fucker," Larry gasped.

"Maybe later," Jimmy said. There was a smile and a promise in the words that made Larry tremble, but he didn't have time to think about it long.

Scooting beneath the covers, Jimmy slid his lips across Larry's furry chest, tasting each nipple as he passed. Farther down, Jimmy dipped his tongue in Larry's belly button. Larry laughed, and at the same time he clutched Jimmy's long hair like reins, steering that heated mouth ever farther south.

"You want this as much as I do, I think." Jimmy laughed. And before Larry could respond, before Larry could do *anything*, Jimmy tilted Larry's stiff cock toward him and drew it between his lips.

Larry stifled a cry. Arching his back, he drove his cock deeper into that well of delicious heat. Every muscle in his body clenched as his fingers tightened in Jimmy's hair.

Jimmy's attentive tongue probed and stroked as his fingers gently manipulated Larry's balls. Soon his mouth slipped away from that delicious cock long enough to drag his tongue across Larry's testicles, one by one.

Larry enjoyed that so much he accidentally banged his head against the headboard and damn near knocked himself out. Taking pity on him, Jimmy once again sucked that long fat shaft into his mouth, smiling now as he tasted leaking juices. "Yummy," he mumbled, while Larry buried his trembling hands in Jimmy's hair and both men's heartbeats thundered in their ears.

"Oh no!" Larry cried.

Jimmy let Larry's long cock slide free from between his lips. He laid its moist heat against his cheek and slid it across his face, relishing the hard spike of flesh against his skin. "Let it go," he whispered. "Let it go."

"I'm too turned on. I'm sorry. You'd better stop, or else!" Larry half laughed, half sobbed, partly embarrassed, partly more turned on than he'd ever been in his life.

"What if I don't want to stop?" Jimmy giggled. As if to prove his point, he stuffed Larry's swollen cock back down his throat and took control of it for the final ride.

Larry thrashed around, his legs now wrapped around Jimmy's shoulders as Jimmy brought him to the brink of orgasm, then eased off for one torturous second before coaxing him to the brink all over again.

"No more!" Larry gasped, and at that moment his entire body froze. His back tensed. He curled himself into a ball, hugging Jimmy's head, and before he could cry out one more time, his seed erupted, filling Jimmy's eager mouth. He trembled and shuddered as hot jets of come tore out of him like buckshot. Jimmy happily claimed every drop as Larry spasmed beneath him.

Slowly, Larry relaxed. His body collapsed back on the bed. His cock began to soften between Jimmy's come-soaked lips, and as it finally slid free, sated, drained, Jimmy gently caressed Larry's stomach. His mouth, hot and moist with Larry's juices, laid kisses at Larry's waist, across his ribs, down his thighs.

Before Larry could coordinate his trembling muscles to crawl down in the bed and begin reciprocating, which was what he wanted to do more than anything in the whole wide world, Jimmy eased him onto his stomach. Too weak to resist, Larry stared back over his shoulder, watching Jimmy in the moonlight as he caressed Larry's ass, easing the heel of his hand between Larry's cheeks, sliding a gentle thumb over Larry's opening.

"Oh man," Larry gasped, and at that moment Jimmy ducked his head and pressed his mouth to the heated opening, his tongue sliding over it, *into it*, his lips still moistened with Larry's come.

Strong fingers spread Larry's ass, and Jimmy slid his probing tongue even more hungrily across Larry's hole, claiming it as his own. Again, as if he hadn't just come at all, Larry started to tremble. He spread his legs wider, giving Jimmy all the access he needed. Too busy to say thank you, Jimmy probed ever deeper with his warm tongue, rimming hungrily, tasting, savoring. He lifted Larry's hips with strong fingers, carrying his ass closer to Jimmy's worshiping mouth.

Larry reached around behind him and once again grabbed a fistful of Jimmy's hair.

"Baby," Jimmy muttered, and there was a question in the muttering.

"Yes," Larry breathed. "Do it. Fuck me."

Jimmy slid farther up in the bed, laying his long body over Larry's, pressing his wet mouth to Larry's ear.

"Are you sure?" Jimmy breathed. "Is this really what you want?"

"Yes. Please," Larry arched his neck, tilting his head back to bury his face in Jimmy's hair.

Jimmy answered with a kiss, then pulled gently away.

After a brief moment filled with the sounds of a nightstand drawer opening and a foil wrapper being torn, sure fingers spread cool lotion over Larry's opening. Larry lay shivering as he felt the first careful piercing. Just a gentle reconnaissance with an exploring fingertip. A moment later, a deeper delving. Then another finger. While Jimmy explored, easing the way for bigger things to come, his warm mouth laid kisses at the edge of Larry's hole. Gentle stirrings of breath and sweet mutterings accompanied every kiss. A sexy rumbling purr issued from deep in Jimmy's throat.

"I'm ready," Larry whispered, quaking, his knees bent under him now, his ass in the air as eager as it had ever been. "Jimmy, please. Don't make me wait any longer. I want you in me *now*."

Jimmy eased Larry's legs flat on the bed. Spreading them wide, he stretched out over him again, pressing his lips to the back of Larry's neck. With a tender, unending pressure, he eased his long cock ever so slowly into Larry's heated depths. Larry lay trembling beneath him, forcing himself to relax, his hands reaching back, clutching Jimmy's thighs, pulling him ever deeper. His breath came in frantic gasps; his pulse thundered inside his head.

Larry's mouth lay against Jimmy's forearm as Jimmy held him in place beneath him. Slowly, Jimmy began to move. His hard cock rocked forward, sliding deep, then lusciously pulled away, leaving an emptiness behind that he then immediately refilled. Time and time again. Larry's labored breathing fell into rhythm with Jimmy's movements.

"My baby likes this," Jimmy whispered in his ear, and Larry could only nod.

Larry had never felt a defter touch than Jimmy's. Never before had he been penetrated with such sweet care and tenderness. Never before had he been so lost in the erotic pleasure of it.

"I love this," he mumbled into Jimmy's wrist, made almost drunk by the delicious taste of Jimmy's fevered skin on his mouth while Jimmy plumbed his depths from behind.

Jimmy smiled against the back of Larry's neck, his breath hot on Larry's skin. "I'm going to come," he whispered, his voice cracking with desire. "You feel too good. I-I can't hold off anymore. Oh, God, your ass is like silk."

"Do it," Larry said. "Please. But let me watch. I want to see."

Jimmy's moist tongue pierced Larry's ear. He offered breathless words, the delicious scent of hot, sweet kisses. "Whatever you want," he rasped, on the verge of release. "Whatever you ask, Larry. That's what I'll do."

Jimmy rose up on his knees, driving harder now, plumbing deeper, but still gentle, still careful not to inflict pain. While Larry shuddered and rocked beneath him, enjoying every stroke, Jimmy felt his release roiling in his balls. His entire body tensed as the moment of truth neared.

Just as he reached the point of no return, he pulled his cock free and in the same moment, flipped Larry onto his back beneath him. Plucking the condom away, he knee-walked up Larry's chest and rested his balls over Larry's mouth. Taking his cock in his hand, Jimmy pumped the length of it while he threw his head back, the tendons in his neck stretched taut.

When his legs spasmed and clenched around Larry's shoulders, Larry lifted his head and laid his lips to the underside of Jimmy's cock. He raised his hands high and stroked Jimmy's smooth chest, damp now with perspiration, played his fingertips along Jimmy's finely muscled arms. He kissed the length of Jimmy's pulsing cock, licking, tasting, relishing the heat of him, loving the weight of Jimmy's balls on his chin, loving the way Jimmy's entire body shivered and quaked above him.

Suddenly Jimmy flung his head back and cried out. A geyser of sweet come tore out of him, splashing Larry's hair, spattering Larry's face, as hot and thick as molten metal.

Jimmy emptied himself while Larry clung to his cock, pleading for more, lapping away the delicious strings that had fallen across his mouth, finally taking control of Jimmy's cock altogether and tipping it between his lips as the flow of come began to abate.

His muscles still as tense as piano wire, Jimmy held Larry's head in his hands, holding him motionless, letting Larry's mouth do all the work now, giving Larry exactly what he wanted, just as he had promised he would.

Slowly, Jimmy's body shrank in upon itself. His thrusts slowed. His muscles relaxed. His torrent of come ceased to pour.

With a shudder of contentment, he opened his eyes and stared down at Larry beneath him, drenched in juices. Jimmy's softening cock rested comfortably against Larry's chin now. His eyes still afire with hunger, Larry smiled up, his fingertips still stroking Jimmy's smooth stomach, his long, lean thighs.

Doubling up, Jimmy collapsed over him and Larry's arms came up to hold him tight. They rested like that for the longest time. Jimmy on top. Larry beneath, cradling Jimmy, his face against the heat of Jimmy's stomach, Jimmy's juices still smeared across his face. Eventually, they stretched out on the bed and their lips found each other. They kissed.

When their hearts had quieted inside them, when their desires were fully laid to rest, at least for a while, Jimmy led Larry to the tiny shower where they stood side by side on wobbly legs, washing each other down.

Later, they lay in bed and watched the lightning shoot across the sky, listened to the thunder tumble through the heavens, while the staccato patter of raindrops peppered the trailer's roof.

By the time the storm had ended and the rain had stopped, they were sound asleep in each other's arms.

They stayed that way till morning.

THE SAME morning would find Bo with a thumping head and his mouth tasting of too many shots of last night's Wild Turkey. It would also find him standing naked and horny in the doorway leading from the bathroom into Larry's bedroom—staring at Larry's unslept-in bed.

Through the haze of a drunken fog, he remembered Larry and Jimmy the night before, sitting outside Jimmy's trailer sipping beers. He also remembered that as they sat there side by side, Jimmy's hand had rested on Larry's arm.

As if Jimmy was letting Bo know he had laid his claim!

Fists clenched, eyes cold, Bo forced himself to rein in his anger and turned away from Larry's empty bedroom, quietly closing the door behind him.

He remembered the speck of red light atop the greenhouse wall. He remembered his search. His discoveries.

Playing his fingers down his bare thigh, Bo strode back into his bedroom and collapsed naked on his bed. Closing his eyes, not bothering to search for a speck of red light in the corner above his head, he grasped his erect cock in his fist and slowly stroked himself to orgasm.

Finished, he dipped his finger in the spend and laid it to his tongue.

Chuckling inwardly, he thought, *Let the old queen watch that.*

Chapter Twelve

Bo slid a plate of bacon and eggs in front of Larry when he walked into the kitchen. Bo's greeting of "Good morning" sounded casual on the surface, but Larry knew better.

"Morning," Larry warily answered back. He parked himself at the kitchen table and tucked into his food right away so he wouldn't have to say anything else.

The ploy didn't work. "Where's your friend?" Bo asked. "Eating in his trailer this morning?"

Larry gnawed at a strip of bacon. "Yes. He cooked for himself. He wanted to start tearing out the dead hedges down along the drive. It's a big job. He thought he'd get a head start on it while the ground is soft from the rain."

"You didn't eat with him?"

"N-no. Why would I do that?"

Bo tossed a skillet into the sink with a clatter. He turned his back to Larry, staring out the window. "Don't play innocent with me. I waited for you. I wanted to talk. I tried again this morning and realized you didn't come back to your room all night."

"Sorry," Larry said. "What did you want to talk about?"

"Us," Bo said.

Larry sighed. "There is no us."

"So I gather," Bo muttered. Turning from the window, he leaned against the sink. There were dark smudges under his eyes from all the drinking he'd done the night before. His face was a little pale, his eyes tinged with red. He let the silence carry them through an awkward moment or two, then asked softly, "Are you really going to do this?"

"Do what?" Larry asked with as much innocence as he could muster, sopping at his over-easy eggs with a swatch of toast.

Bo shot a glance upward at the ceiling. The red light was off. They were not being watched.

"Throw it all away," Bo said, turning back to Larry. "I tried to tell you the other day. There's a reason the old man ran the ad the way he did. I heard him and Mrs. Price talking—"

"Were you spying on them?"

Bo jerked his head up, piercing Larry with a glare. "What?"

"I asked if you were spying on them. And he's not the old man. He's Mr. Stanhope, the very *nice* man, in case you've forgotten, who pretty much saved our lives by bringing us here to work. I'm sorry things didn't work out between you and me, but we're still better off than we were when we lived in the city. Bo, please don't do anything to get us fired. I-I like it here. Especially now."

Bo coughed up a nasty little laugh. "Especially now, you say? Don't you mean, especially after last night?"

"Bo—"

Bo heaved himself away from the sink and stalked toward Larry, where he bent down, his face inches from Larry's, his knuckles white on the edge of the table, eyes flashing with fury.

He kept his voice low. A desperate hiss. "He wants to leave us the money, you stupid fuck. Roger. He wants to leave it to you and me."

Larry stared at him. "You're crazy."

"What else is he going to do with his millions? He wants to leave it to two people who love each other. He's a romantic. He wants them to love each other because he set the whole thing up. He's playing matchmaker, and if we go along with it, the payoff will be *huge*. There's a ghost in the house too. Did you know that? I think it's his ex-lover, but I'm not—"

Larry stared at Bo, his breakfast forgotten. He tried not to grin but didn't completely succeed. "You're as crazy as Jimmy. He thinks there's a ghost too."

Bo's fist came down and banged the table. Silverware clattered. Larry's milk sloshed from the glass. "Fine. Don't believe me about the ghost. I don't care."

Taking Larry by surprise, Bo gathered up Larry's vest in his fists and yanked him to his feet. "Goddammit, Larry, the money is there for the taking. I know it. All we have to do is fool the old—fool Mr. Stanhope into thinking we're in love and he'll leave it all to us when he dies. Everything. The money, the mansion, the works! What do you want to do? Throw it all away because you'd rather fuck the gardener?"

Larry slapped Bo's hands away and smoothed the wrinkles from his vest to stall for time. Thinking. Thinking. Then he lifted his eyes and studied Bo's face. The guy was still handsome, dammit. But who knew anybody could look like that and still be such an asshole?

Larry was so mad, his knees were shaking. "If you must know, I didn't fuck the gardener. He fucked me. Which has absolutely *nothing* to do with you, so keep your nose out of my business. And what if you're right about the money? Roger could live for years. What do you want to do? Playact our way through an affair for the next decade or so waiting for the big payoff at the end of it? Or did you think maybe you'd hurry things along somehow? Push him down the stairs? Strap a bomb to one of the dogs? Sprinkle a little cyanide over Roger's croissant?"

Spit flew as Bo snarled, "It's *millions*! Aren't you tired of being poor? Aren't you sick of clawing around to make a life? This money is ours for the taking, I tell you. It's being *freely offered*, for Christ's sake."

Larry forced himself to calm down, forced his teeth to stop gnashing together, forced himself to stop thinking about bonking Bo on the head with a fucking skillet.

"Look, Bo. I like Mr. Stanhope. He gave me my life back. I'm not going to lie to him and I'm not going to cheat him."

"I like him too!"

"No, Bo. I think maybe the only person you like is yourself."

Bo stepped closer, sliding a fingertip across Larry's chin. "I like *you*," he said softly.

Larry's laugh was not kind. "Yeah, right. If what you say is true, then you only like me for what you think you can get by being with me. Look, Bo. Do what you think you have to do. Just leave me out of it. I'm not going to play a part in your bilking Mr. Stanhope out of his fortune. I don't know what I'd do with a fortune anyway, except maybe get as far away from *you* as I possibly can."

"Very funny! And it's not *bilking*! He wants to *give* it to us! He wants to make us the heirs to the Stanhope fortune! All he asks is that we love each other." Bo's eyes grew mean. He furiously spat the last words out. "Or at least *pretend* to."

Larry sucked in a deep breath while his eyes foraged around the kitchen simply because he couldn't stand to look at Bo anymore. He couldn't think about what Bo was saying. He didn't want to. It didn't even interest him. His thoughts were still taken up by Jimmy. The gentle probe of his long cock moving inside him. The taste of him. The sound of his voice when he first awoke this morning, sweet, hoarse, purring as he snuggled close to Larry in that ridiculously tiny trailer with the cloud-laden dawn barely lighting the day outside the window.

Larry wiped a hand across his face, not erasing the memories, just setting them aside until he could be alone to relish them better. "I'm not hungry anymore," he said, his voice flat. "Just give me Mr. Stanhope's tray and I'll take it up to him. After that, it's my day off. I think I'll help Jimmy with the hedge."

"Fine!"

Bo whirled around, grabbing things from the counter, the fridge, the cupboard. He threw the master's breakfast tray together—croissants, soft-boiled egg, brie, butter, juice, clattering silverware. From the microwave he extracted two warmed bowls of fresh liver prepared earlier for the dogs. He carelessly tossed the bowls on the tray, not caring if it spilled or not.

Larry avoided Bo's hard raptor eyes as he straightened the items, making the master's tray presentable.

Before he could lift it from the counter, Bo came up behind him and spun him around, holding him close, his fingers harshly squeezing Larry's arms, fingernails digging deep.

"You liked it when we had sex. I know you did."

"You're hurting me," Larry seethed. "Let go."

Bo ignored the words and pulling Larry close, smashed his mouth over Larry's in a jarring kiss. Their teeth clacked together. Larry bit his own tongue, and the moment he did, his knee came up in a reflexive action that caught Bo smack in the nuts. That was the end of the kiss. Bo doubled over with a groan.

Appalled by what he'd done, still Larry glared down at Bo without a speck of sympathy. Slouched at his feet with his eyes bugged out, Bo clutched his aching balls while a string of saliva dribbled off his chin and he gasped for air like a grounded fish.

A drop of blood shimmered on Larry's lip where Bo's teeth had torn into it. He wiped it away with the back of his hand and grabbed the breakfast tray off the counter.

Without another word, he carried the tray through the kitchen door and up the stairs.

Passing Mrs. Price on the stairs, Larry nodded and tried to smile, all the while avoiding her eyes.

Mrs. Price stopped in her tracks and watched him retreat behind her. She called up the stairs. "Larry, you're bleeding. Your lip is swollen."

"It's nothing," Larry said, not turning back, not slowing his climb.

"Well, if you're sure...." Mrs. Price mumbled to herself, still eying him uncertainly.

A moment later, stepping through the kitchen door, she spotted Bo leaning against the sink, still doubled over in what was clearly agony. When he quickly straightened and tried to hide his pain at the sound of her footsteps behind him, Mrs. Price acted as if she didn't notice.

"I'll serve myself," she said quietly, and nodding, Bo left the room.

THE ROOTS of the old hedge were as tough as baling wire. Both men were sweating bullets, even though the sun had yet to make an appearance. The air was cool, the sky gray. The two pugs were enjoying the company of both humans, and as if that wasn't enough to make the dogs happy, they were at the moment chasing a rabbit across the grounds, not that they had a hope in hell of catching it. Leo and Max were far too well-fed and much too short-legged to be chasing down bunnies.

"You felt like warm milk last night," Jimmy whispered, a secretive smile playing at his mouth. He had just rocked back off his knees and squatted there in the dirt, eying Larry beside him. He brushed his long hair away from his face with a leather-gloved hand. There was a smudge of dirt on his nose.

Larry had never seen anyone so handsome in his life.

Unable to think of a single thing to say, Larry simply blushed.

Jimmy's brown eyes flared with tender heat, watching him. "I'll never want to sleep alone again, you know. You've spoiled me for life."

Larry reached out with his own gloved hand and dragged a thumb across Jimmy's nose, trying to remove the dirt. What he actually did was make it worse.

"Thank you," he stammered. "I've never...."

A single dimple formed in Jimmy's cheek. "What?" he asked kindly. "You've never what?"

But Larry couldn't say the words. He merely gave his head a shake and blushed all the redder.

"Stay with me tonight," Jimmy said, his voice as smooth as cream, the heat in his eyes now burning hotter.

Larry didn't even think about his answer. "All right," he said. "Whatever you want."

At that, Jimmy flashed white teeth, and the opposing dimple popped into view as well. Almost as quickly as it did, his smile faded. His eyes turned serious.

"What did Bo say? Did he know you spent the night with me?"

Larry peeled off the gloves and stretched his fingers. The cool air felt good on his hands. To tell the truth, he wasn't used to such physical work. He was too embarrassed to mention it, but he was actually getting a blister. "He knew," Larry said. "He got mad. And then—he kissed me."

Jimmy faced Larry more directly, all humor gone from his face. "What did you do?"

"I kneed him in the nuts."

Jimmy blinked. In less than a heartbeat, his smile was back full force. Almost every tooth in his head was visible.

"I guess that'll teach him," he said, impressed. He scratched his head. "Makes me a little fearful for my own safety, however."

Larry didn't laugh. "It isn't funny. I don't want to start a big war. I love this job. And this morning I—"

"You what?"

Larry trailed his eyes to Jimmy's face and locked gazes. "This morning I found myself liking it even more."

Jimmy brushed his hand over Larry's shoulder. "In case you're wondering, so did I."

Larry cast him a grateful smile. "Actually, I *was* wondering. Thank you."

"Maybe I should talk to him."

Larry wrapped his fingers around Jimmy's arm. Even that simple touch sent a surge of desire shooting through him. "No. Please don't. Just let it rest. He'll come around. He doesn't have much choice. I mean, you know. If we continue to—" Larry suddenly appeared trapped, as if he'd talked himself into a corner he didn't know how to get out of. His hand dropped away from Jimmy's arm. His eyes grew hooded, embarrassed.

"Continue to what?" Jimmy asked a little too innocently. "Continue to do what we did last night?"

Larry stared out over the grounds, unable to make eye contact. "Yes," he finally said. "That."

Jimmy's words were gentle, but there was a sweet fervor in them too. He reached out and claimed Larry's hand, tucking it inside both his own.

Again, a shiver of desire shot through Larry's body.

"Don't worry," Jimmy said, his voice hushed. "We'll get through this. And I won't let you lose your job. I love working here too. Especially now."

Larry lifted his gaze and grinned. He ignored the blush rising to his cheeks. "It really was a hell of a night."

Jimmy leaned in and rested his forehead on Larry's shoulder. For just a tiny moment in time, both men closed their eyes.

Jimmy edged closer and laid his lips to Larry's neck. "Tonight will be even better."

WHILE MRS. Price ate her breakfast in the empty kitchen, her brow furrowed with worry, Bo stood at his bedroom window three floors up and stared out over the grounds at the two men huddled by the hedge. While he watched, he was ever mindful of the unblinking red light shining down through the ceiling cornice. He knew when it came on. He would know when it went off.

He knew now that cameras were scattered throughout the mansion. He knew they were being spied on. All of them.

And he was pretty sure he knew why.

When Jimmy pressed his mouth to Larry's neck down below, Bo's fists clenched. He clutched the curtains at his window, squeezing them so tightly the wrinkles would last for days. Suddenly mindful of the camera's eye, he forced his hands to relax their grip.

But the camera couldn't see inside his brain. The camera didn't know what he was thinking.

Furious thoughts shot through Bo's head like gunfire. His eyes narrowed to burning slits as he stared at the two down below—Larry's red curls gleaming in the light, Jimmy's long black hair shifting as the wind swept through it, stirring it across his shoulders.

He wondered what his chances were of bedding the guy himself. Making Larry jealous. Worming his way between them until he broke their connection altogether.

But no. He would simply wait. Maybe it was just a onetime fuck. Maybe Bo didn't really have anything to worry about at all.

He let the curtains fall into place before him, blocking his view. Bo's hatred didn't feel so all-consuming when the two were out of sight.

Bo stood there, shaking his head, trying to understand how Larry could just blow off the revelation about the Stanhope money maybe falling into their hands. Even the fact that it had been planned from the very beginning—pushing him and Larry together in the hope of making them fall in love—hadn't made Larry understand the opportunity they were being given.

The Indian must be one hell of a lay if Larry would rather ball the guy than take control of a fortune.

Maybe what Bo needed right now was a little finesse. A lighter touch. Give the two time to let their little fuckfest peter out on its own. In the meantime, Bo would do what he could to ingratiate himself back into Larry's favor. From there he could weasel the guy back between the sheets. Once there, Bo knew he could control him completely. Larry had loved Bo's body once. There was no reason he couldn't love it again.

Mind made up, Bo grabbed a notepad from the antique secretary in the corner and scribbled out a note. The note consisted of three little words: *I'm sorry. Friends?*

Rather than risk infuriating Larry again by going into his room without permission, he slipped the note under the connecting door instead where, with a little luck, Larry would find it on the floor.

Straightening his uniform and ignoring the residual ache in his nuts from where Larry had kneed him, Bo bounced back down three flights of stairs. Ducking through the library, which was a shortcut to the kitchen, Bo slid to a stop in front of the fireplace. He blinked, staring at the painting above the mantle. The painting of the aroused male nude. A self-portrait of the artist himself. Egon Schiele, or so the old man had said. The work was priceless, Bo knew. The old man had said that too.

Bo took in the painting for a moment longer, then dipped his head in a mock bow at the naked painter's rather impressive cock and continued his trek to the kitchen. Popping through the kitchen door unannounced, he startled Mrs. Price, who cried out "Oh!" and slapped her chest.

Two minutes later, he was begging her to share a few more of her famous cookie recipes.

As if he really cared.

But Mrs. Price cared. She cared a lot. Grateful that perhaps things weren't quite as bad as she thought they were between the boys—with Bo in such a pleasant mood this morning, how could they be?—she latched on to Bo's request for recipes with a grateful heart. Especially when Bo told her he wanted to make the cookies for Larry.

LATER, ROGER heard the laughter of his new cook and his old friend floating up the stairs. Accessing the monitor displaying the kitchen, he sat watching them as they giggled and stirred and baked their way through a batch of peach drop cookies, one of Roger's favorites.

WHILE THE smell of freshly baked cookies began to fill the kitchen, Bo kept a clandestine eye on the tiny camera lens in the ceiling. While he watched, waiting for the little red light to blink on, or waiting for it to blink off, a plan began to form.

Chapter Thirteen

So began the Cold War. With Larry and Jimmy on one side, blithely oblivious to everything but each other, and Bo on the other side—plotting, but trying not to appear to be. All parties involved attempted to keep their mysteries hidden from Roger and Mrs. Price. Sometimes they succeeded; sometimes they didn't.

Even in war, time passes. Days blend from one to another.

Three weeks later, Mrs. Price's voice battled with the warbling of the finches nesting in the eaves.

"Larry is sleeping in the trailer every night," she said. "I've been watching. He only goes back to his room to shower and dress."

She and Roger were having tea on the widow's walk. Actually, Mrs. Price was having tea. Roger was drinking a beer, much to Mrs. Price's displeasure, but she'd nagged about it enough over the past couple of weeks. She refused to mention it again. Let the old fool drink himself to death if he wanted.

Meanwhile the finches played on.

Roger grinned at her. "Now, now. You're disapproving inside your head again. I can see it. It's leaking out through your eyeballs."

Mrs. Price puckered her mouth. "Oh pishposh!"

Roger chuckled. He sat gnawing on a snickerdoodle. Staring down at the cookie with a wistful leer, he said, "Funny how well these go with beer."

"Oh, shut up," Mrs. Price huffed. "What are we going to do about the boys?"

"Which ones?"

"All of them!" she snapped.

Roger laughed. "And how is poor Bo handling all this?"

She shrugged. "He does his work. Never smiles. Hardly speaks. Tries to keep up a brave front. I think Larry broke his heart."

"So Larry and the gardener really are…?"

Mrs. Price stuck a fist in her hip. "Well, good grief, man, what else do you think they've been doing in that tiny trailer every night from dusk till dawn?"

Roger stared out over the mountain, watching a hawk circling high in the sky. The storm that had caught them all by surprise a few weeks back was almost forgotten. The summer sun had returned in all its glory, and the day was as hot as blazes.

Mrs. Price eyed Roger suspiciously. "What are you thinking? You're not going to fire them, are you? All three boys are doing their work most satisfactorily, you know. And perhaps all this fooling around business will blow over in the end. Maybe Bo and Larry will get back together. Still, if anyone should go, perhaps—"

Roger tapped his fingernails against the side of his beer bottle. Thanks to the warm weather, his arthritis was in retreat. The graceful rhythm of his tapping fingernails pretty well proved it.

"If you're about to suggest we fire the gardener, I beg you, Mrs. Price, to walk over to the railing and stare out across the grounds. The property has never been so well-groomed or looked so lovely. Our young Indian friend isn't going anywhere. Not if I have anything to say about it. In fact, I was considering giving him a raise. If he quits, I don't know what we'll do."

"Don't worry, Roger. He's not going to quit."

"And why is that?"

Mrs. Price gave her tea a furious stirring with her spoon. "If I have to explain it to you, you're even dumber than I thought you were."

Roger stared at her, happy wrinkles digging trenches in his face. He was obviously amused by her anger. His old eyes squinted merrily. "Ooh. Don't hold back. Tell me how you feel."

Haughtily ignoring the sarcasm, Mrs. Price said, "Old fools are the biggest fools!" and reached for another cookie.

AFTER COUNTLESS couplings, they knew each other's bodies perfectly. They knew each other's smiles. They knew each other's mannerisms. They knew the feel of a knee, the caress of a hand, the heated swipe of a lingering tongue. And they knew what each other's reactions would be to any given stimulus.

When Larry dropped to his knees on the greenhouse floor at Jimmy's feet—Jimmy's *boots*—Jimmy stared down and licked his lips across a sexy smile, which was just the reaction Larry had hoped for. With any witness's view from outside being blocked by rows of blooming plants and stacks of bagged mulch and potting soil, Jimmy lifted his shirttail out of the way and slid his fingers over his smooth belly in anticipation while Larry knelt before him in the dust, hungrily looking up.

"What's on your mind there, Larry?"

The gleam in Larry's eyes told Jimmy *exactly* what Larry had on his mind. When Larry ran his hands up the front of Jimmy's jeans, gently prodding, kneading, his fingertips massaging an ever-growing lump hidden behind a bulge of faded denim, Jimmy was even more convinced he knew what Larry was getting at.

Jimmy dragged his fingers through Larry's ginger hair. Taking a fistful of it in each hand, he pulled Larry's face to his crotch, meeting it halfway with a gentle lunge of his hips.

His words belied his actions, though. "We can't do this right now," Jimmy said. "We've been working. I need to shower."

Larry's words were slurred. They were slurred because his mouth was plastered to that denim-covered lump, which was growing longer and firmer by the minute. "I want you dirty," Larry purred. His hands had found their way under the hem of Jimmy's shirt, and now he was the one who was stroking that flat, warm tummy. Craning his neck to lift himself higher, Larry abandoned the bulging crotch for a moment and slid his tongue over the hot skin just above Jimmy's belt buckle. At the first lick, Jimmy's fingers tightened in his hair.

Jimmy's voice was a frog's croak. If that. "I love your mouth." Sighing, he bent double and plastered kisses in Larry's fiery hair. He slid his hand down the back of Larry's shirt through the neck hole and grazed along Larry's spine with his fingertips, absorbing Larry's heat through his satin skin.

Larry caressed the back of Jimmy's boot, then worked his fingers up under the hem of Jimmy's jeans and glided to the top of the cowboy boots to stroke the bulging calf muscle he discovered there. Then he slid his fingers even higher until he found the silky skin behind Jimmy's knee, always one of his favorite destinations. He smiled and tilted his head back so Jimmy could bend lower and claim his mouth in a kiss. He was rewarded by a shudder running through Jimmy's long frame and a further tightening of his fingers in Larry's hair.

Taking control, Larry pushed Jimmy upright and pressed him against a shelf that held pots of California lilac that were waiting to be rooted well enough to plant along the drive. One poor crockery pot tumbled to the floor and smashed. Luckily it was empty.

"Whoa." Jimmy laughed. "Easy there, cowboy."

"Whoa yourself," Larry growled and went immediately to work with trembling fingers undoing Jimmy's belt buckle and sliding Jimmy's zipper down out of the way.

By this time, Jimmy's bulge looked like he had stashed a kielbasa down his pants. His knees started shaking the minute Larry spread the flaps of his fly wide and buried his mouth in his forest of dark, wiry pubic hair. Jimmy's bush smelled of clean sweat and the remnants of whatever soap he had used that morning. Larry breathed him in like a man who has been short-rationed on oxygen for way too long.

Tugging at the tight pant legs, Larry finally worked the jeans down over the hump of Jimmy's ass, and the minute that obstacle was cleared, the denims slid down to Jimmy's knees without any problem whatsoever. Larry laughed out loud when Jimmy's cock, pumped full of blood and aching for attention, sprang up to say hello. It bounced off Larry's nose once before Larry corralled the fucker and stuffed it in his mouth.

From that moment on, neither man was in charge of the situation any longer. Testosterone took over.

Also at that moment, the little red camera light in the corner of the greenhouse blinked out for good.

"HOLY MOLY," Roger whimpered, his hand on his chest, his old heart banging out a tango against his ribs.

"Holy moly indeed," a disembodied voice said in his ear.

Roger stared at the blank screen for another minute, his fingers itching to turn the damn thing back on, but he did have a *modicum* of restraint left. Not to mention propriety. Didn't he? He spun the chair around to remove himself from temptation and stared about the empty room.

"Where are you?"

"I'm here. On the windowsill," Jeremy said, invisible but for a flurry of curtains and the faintest shadow that moved across the carpet. "I can see down into the greenhouse from here."

Roger's eyes lit up and he said, "Oh my," then corrected himself and barked in disgust at Jeremy's nerve. He leveraged himself from the monitor stand with a shove and rolled his desk chair all the way across the room, planting himself at the window next to his dead lover. Assuming Jeremy was still there. It's hard to tell with dead lovers.

Roger stared down through the glass at the greenhouse below. Yep. There they were. Larry and Jimmy. Joined at the hip. Well, the hip and the tonsils. Jesus, Larry was really going to town.

Roger pushed himself away from the window and dragged the curtains shut.

"Hey!" Jeremy bellowed, outraged. "I'm trying to watch!"

"Well, stop it!" Roger roared. He let fall what tattered remnants of lust remained on his face—after all, he was ninety-three years old—and sat mulling over the problem.

"What the hell are we going to do?" he asked the curtains, the walls, the chifforobe, wherever the hell Jeremy was perched at the moment. Since Roger couldn't see him, it might be anywhere. "Larry's supposed to be falling in love with Bo."

"Bo's a dick," Jeremy said.

Roger froze. Horrified. "Why would you say such a thing? What did Bo ever do to you? He's almost got Mrs. P's cookies down pat."

"Cookies, schmookies. I don't trust him," Jeremy said. "What about the three hundred dollars?"

"Oh, that."

"Yes, that. I think it's time we tested Bo on it. Get Mrs. Price. Let her do it. The cook will know something's up if you tell him *you* dropped the money down in the kitchen. You haven't been below the second floor in months."

"Good lord. Has it been that long?"

"Don't change the subject!"

But Roger wasn't listening. "Months? Has it really been *months*? That's despicable! I can't have *that*! Look out the window!" Roger demanded. "Are Larry and the gardener finished doing what they were doing?"

The curtain fluttered. "Darn!" Jeremy groused. "They *are* finished! Jimmy's pants are rebuckled. I missed the big finale. The money shot. The big juicy kablooey!"

"Good!" Roger snapped. He reached for the alarm around his neck and hit the emergency button.

THE TWO had pretty much pulled themselves together, although Larry could still happily taste Jimmy's come on his tongue and Jimmy's legs were still wobbly. For some reason, neither one of them could stop smiling. Their smiles only fell away—in fact, they hit the greenhouse floor like a ton of bricks, one right after the other—when the emergency alarm on Larry's beeper went off with a clamoring wail. They both almost jumped out of their skins. Two seconds later they were running for the house.

Jimmy and Larry were not the only ones to answer the beeper's call. All of a sudden the mansion was alive with the thunder of running footsteps, coming from every direction: Larry and Jimmy crashing through the back doors from the outside. Mrs. Price pattering hurriedly but carefully from the library and dropping a heavy copy of *William Shakespeare's Greatest Hits* on the hallway floor with a bang along the way. Lastly came Bo, pounding up the stairs, frantically punching the buttons on his beeper to shut it the hell up.

Although it was Roger himself who'd set this ruckus in motion, he still appeared rather startled to find four souls come charging through his bedroom door without so much as knocking.

Mrs. Price was first, since she had been closest. Jimmy and Larry barreled in a second later. Hot on their heels came Bo, a silver spatula still in his hand and a half-eaten carrot stick poking out of his mouth.

Roger sifted through the horrified faces and settled at last on Jimmy, who, Roger could not fail to notice, still had a rather intriguing flush in his cheeks. He was pretty sure that flush hadn't come from running up the stairs.

"Is the Chevy ready to go?" Roger asked.

Jimmy stammered out a reply. "Y-you mean the convertible? Yes, sir. I just tuned it myself. It's purring like a pussycat."

Roger beamed. "Wonderful, son. And how alliteratively poetic. Be so kind as to pull it up to the front door, please. I'd like to go for a spin. And make sure the top's down."

"Uh, sure." Shooting Larry a confused glance, Jimmy weeded his way through the mob still bunched together in Roger's bedroom door and took off for the carriage house. They could hear his footsteps retreating down the stairs.

This was all too much for Mrs. Price. "Just one minute! Why did you scare us all to death? Are you crazy?"

"Oh twaddle, Mrs. Price! I'm not any crazier than you are. And go get your head scarf. We're going for a spin. You too, Larry." Roger gave him a wink. "I think we'll need you to keep the chauffeur in line, hey?"

Larry couldn't have been more confused if he had awakened to find an aardvark ironing his best shirt. "Uh… *huh?*"

Roger's old eyes settled last on Bo. "I'm sorry, son. I'm afraid the car is full. Perhaps next time."

Bo shrugged. "No prob. I'll just go, uh, string some beans."

"Lovely," Roger said, dismissing him with a wave and turning back to Mrs. Price. "We've been cooped up in this house too long, you and I. We need fresh air. Are you game?"

Mrs. Price still looked miffed, but at least she didn't look scared to death anymore. "All right," she said, gazing down at herself as if wondering if she had dressed that morning or not. Seeing everything in order—shoes, dress, hanky tucked in her sleeve in case of a nasal emergency—she made an executive decision on the spur of the moment. Gazing back, she said, "I'm ready."

Roger beamed. "Well, let's go, then."

Roger stuck his arm out in Larry's direction, and Larry took his cue with aplomb, hooking his own arm through it and leading Mr. Stanhope toward the stairs.

"Mrs. Price," Roger said with a laugh. "Fetch the dogs."

"Oh lord," she groused, but she did as she was asked, scooping the two pugs off the floor and cradling them awkwardly in her arms.

The descent was rather time-consuming, but they all made it in one piece, and they were standing under the portico when Jimmy came pulling up in the '57 Chevy ragtop, foxtail stirring in the breeze from the antenna, fat fuzzy dice swaying from the rearview mirror, tailpipe blatting, a cacophony of horsepower rumbling from underneath the hood.

Jimmy looked so happy and handsome sitting behind the wheel that Larry laughed out loud, causing Roger, who was still hanging on his arm, to give a concurring snort. "He *is* an agreeable-looking chap, isn't he?"

Jimmy hopped out of the front seat, raced around the car opening doors, then stood back waiting for the master to decide who would sit where.

"Let's take the back," Roger said to Mrs. Price and the dogs.

"But my hair," she said, staring doubtfully at the convertible top folded back under the tonneau. Then she gave a bleat like a sheep—"Oh phooey. It won't kill me."—and laughing, she climbed into the car with a minimum of grunts and groans while Leo and Max hopped around on the back seat, peering over the doors, barking like seals.

Roger carefully climbed in after Mrs. P and the dogs and settled in among the throng while Jimmy and Larry poured into the front seat, with Jimmy once again behind the wheel.

"Where to?" Jimmy asked, staring into the rearview mirror.

Roger shot him a wink and said, "Destinations are meaningless, son. It's the trip that counts. Just drive."

BO STOOD at the library window staring out at the car heading down the driveway, two young heads of hair and two old ones lashing in the wind. Their laughter flowed back to him, carried on the summer air. The old car really did purr like a cat. Like Bo gave a shit. His eyes were mean. Stanhope had dismissed him. Only him. And he didn't like it one little bit.

He glanced up at the ceiling in the corner where he knew a camera lens lay hidden. The red light was off. Of course it was. There was no one inside the mansion to turn it on.

The meanness in his eyes began to dissolve. It was replaced by a devious gleam. Surprising thoughts began to stir in Bo's mind. Thoughts that perhaps had been there for a while, but ones he had not been willing to face quite yet. Until today.

Turning away from the window, he cast his eyes around the library—the books, the shelves, the teak and leather furniture. His gaze fell on the fireplace and stayed there.

A smile twisted his mouth.

"Later," he said softly.

Climbing two risers at a time, he raced up the stairway to the second floor. With broad, silent strides muffled by the carpeting, he covered the length of the hallway, his heart beating like gangbusters, his mouth dry, eyes darting everywhere at once. Yet he knew he was alone. The mansion was empty.

He stopped in front of the master's bedroom door. Without hesitating, he gripped the knob and pushed the door open, stepped quickly inside, and closed the door behind him.

It must be somewhere in the master's suite of rooms. It had to be. He began searching, opening closet doors in the bedroom. Finding nothing, he stepped into the sitting room, gazed around, checked out a couple of closets. Still nothing.

Another doorway led to the master bath. He left the sitting room, stood for a moment in the spacious marble bathroom, then opened a door leading off to the right.

He knew immediately he had found what he was looking for. In a room that must have once been a huge walk-in closet or dressing room, he spotted the bank of monitors stacked on a built-in island with numerous drawers below that must have once been used for the master's accessories—ties and shoes and miscellaneous crap that rich old farts adorn themselves with.

Bo lowered himself into the rolling desk chair that sat in front of the monitors and took a moment to study the controls. Then he flipped a switch and saw the monitor in the upper right-hand corner of the array blink on. Ha. It was his very own bedroom. Bo wondered how many times the old lech had watched him walk around naked, watched him dress in the morning, watched him in those most private moments when men—*all* men—touch themselves when they think no one is looking.

He experimented with the mouse on the desktop. Using the scrolling button on top, he quickly figured out how to zoom in, zoom out, and pan the camera around.

While he fiddled with the controls, he hummed a song deep in his throat. He was so engrossed in what he was doing, he wasn't even aware he was humming.

His eyebrows knit in concentration, Bo purposely lit up every screen simultaneously. All nine of them. Suddenly he had a major part of the mansion available for private viewing. As he flipped more switches, he accessed other rooms, one right after another, then the outdoors, both at the front of the mansion and in the rear, where the screen was filled with Jimmy's stupid silver trailer. He experimented his way across the control panel, searching for a way to record what was on the monitors—a way to preserve the data.

It didn't take him long to realize there was no way to record what was displayed on the screens at all. Everything was programmed to be seen in real time. Nothing more. The cameras were strictly for surveillance, not preservation of data.

Smiling to himself, Bo flipped all the switches again, turning everything off, darkening every screen. He stood and rolled the desk chair back where it belonged. He even realigned the mouse on the little pad it sat on just the way it was when he'd found it.

When everything was to his satisfaction, he left the room.
Not once did he stop humming his little tune.

"THE AIR feels wonderful," Mrs. Price said, her face tilted back to absorb the sun, her graying locks flapping around her head like Medusa's snakes gone amok.

Roger sat beside her, patting her hand. His eyes were closed, and he wore a blissful expression as he breathed in the air whipping past. In the darkness behind his closed eyes, he saw Jeremy as he had been at the beginning, young and beautiful. Oh, how he would have loved this moment.

Max and Leo stood on the back seat with their front legs hung over the sides of the car—one to the left, one to the right, each anchored with a supporting hand by their fellow passengers—their eyes all squinty, their ears flapping merrily in the wind, tongues lolling, nostrils flaring as they absorbed the smells of the countryside rolling past.

Larry twisted in his seat. Reaching behind him he patted Roger's thin knee. "Are you all right, sir?"

Roger's mop of white hair thrashed in the wind. "Never better."

Scooting forward with a grunt, Roger rested his chin on the front seat, his expression as innocent as a cherub's. His grizzled hands came up to lie upon each of the young men's shoulders before him—the left hand on Jimmy's, the right on Larry's. Roger smiled as he felt the youthful bodies beneath his touch. Their strength. Their health. Their lives laid out before them, waiting to be explored.

And he could sense even more.

"You enjoy each other's company," he said softly, his words barely audible over the roar of the wind rushing through the open car. "I can see it in you both when you're together."

A soft light entered Jimmy's eyes at the words so softly spoken, so unerringly correct. He *did* enjoy Larry. He enjoyed him more than he had ever enjoyed anyone in his life. Without thinking, he reached across the wide bench seat and took Larry's hand. Larry relinquished it happily, squeezing Jimmy's fingers as he did.

While Jimmy never took his eyes from the road, Roger never took his eyes from those two clinging hands.

Mrs. Price sat quietly as Roger spoke to the boys. She wondered what he was getting at, but didn't ask. She sensed these were important matters, at least to Roger, and she didn't want to interrupt. Roger's snowy hair continued to whip around. Even his eyelashes stirred in the wind.

When Roger continued, he spoke as if the words simply came to him on the spur of the moment. Unplanned. And so they did. Still staring fondly at the two young men holding hands across the front seat, he let his memories come rushing in. They washed over him like a flood.

"I'll never forget it, boys. After only one night together, and a drunken one at that, Jeremy and I fell in love with each other in a rented room above a dive in Tijuana. It was back in the days when there were more donkeys on Avenida Revolución than automobiles." Roger's eyes went dreamy with memories. "Don't ever let anyone tell you there is no such thing as love at first sight. I know there is. I've lived it. I'm still living it."

With Roger's words touching his heart, Larry twisted his head to gaze at Jimmy and was surprised to see a tear sliding down his cheek, sluiced sideways by the wind. Roger's words had touched him as well, and realizing it, Larry tightened his grip on Jimmy's fingers.

If Roger saw their tears, he made no comment. He was too busy with the images of the past still surging through him. He had to set those recollections free. He had to explain the way things were. He wasn't sure why, but he did. The young men in front of him needed to know what it was like back then. And how it was no different than now, this very minute. Or next year. Or a lifetime from now.

"I was jealous back then," Roger said. He sighed, giving his head a tiny shake. "We fought once over a man who wanted to bed Jeremy and made no secret about it. Thinking Jeremy was interested too, I told him to go ahead and fuck the stranger's brains out for all I cared. If he came back to me in the morning, I would forgive him. Jeremy wept in my arms that night, refusing to leave my side. We made love with a desperation that I've never experienced before or since. Later, with his tear-stained face resting against my naked hip, Jeremy told me he would rather die than share his seed with anyone but me. He cried again while I held him. Later, as he slept exhausted in my arms—exhausted from sex, exhausted from weeping—I found myself crying too. But I never let him know. Not once over the many years we lived together did I tell him how he touched me that night. Now I wish I had."

Jimmy eyed the old man in the mirror. There was a look of weary defeat on Roger's face, a look of opportunities lost. Without thinking, and with his gaze still fixed on Roger in the back seat, Jimmy lifted Larry's hand to his mouth and pressed it to his lips.

Watching them, Roger smiled. "Larry," he said quietly, his chin still hanging on the back of the front seat, his voice almost lost in the wind. "Is there anything you'd like to tell me about you and Bo?"

Startled by the question, Larry wheeled around, focusing every ounce of his attention on Roger's face. "No, sir," he said, with more intensity in his words than he had intended. He turned back around and stared through the windshield. When he did, Jimmy reclaimed his hand.

Roger tipped his head, studying Larry. He pursed his lips, as if understanding a little more. "About you and Jimmy, then?" he asked kindly.

Larry opened his mouth, but no words came out. His eyes skittered to Jimmy, then back to Roger.

"No," Larry said in a whisper. "There's nothing to tell you."

"All right," Roger muttered, patting Larry's shoulder, then relaxing back in the car seat, once again resting his hand in Mrs. Price's cool fist. If there was any emotion in his face, it was unreadable. Intentionally or otherwise.

He seemed merely untroubled to the others. And oddly pleased.

They rode quietly then, the miles sliding past. Mrs. Price. Roger. Jimmy. Their individual thoughts carried them even farther than the car—not across miles, but across years, across lifetimes. Larry's memories carried him back only as far as that very morning in the greenhouse—when Jimmy stood naked before him, stroked his hair, and freely offered his strong, beautiful body to Larry as Larry knelt before him.

As if hearing Larry's thoughts, Jimmy again brought Larry's hand to his lips. He held it there while he drove. In the rearview mirror, the old man watched them with a beatific glow on his weathered face. Mrs. Price stared out at the countryside, her thoughts lost in reminiscences of her own, Max and Leo now asleep in her lap.

As the afternoon began to wane, Roger reached forward and tapped Jimmy's shoulder. By now, Mrs. Price was sound asleep, her wind-tossed head anchored solidly on Roger's shoulder.

"Best take us home, son," he said. "The old folks are getting tired."

Jimmy nodded, and as Roger sat back and closed his eyes yet again while enjoying the last of the wind on his face, Larry eased his hand from Jimmy's grasp.

Wanting to offer a kind touch where it was perhaps more sorely needed, Larry draped his arm over the seat and trailed his fingers down to rest them on the old man's knee, squeezing softly.

Eyes still closed, Roger patted Larry's hand, lingering for a moment to enjoy the softness of the young man's skin. Roger's heart swelled at the kindness being shown by an employee who was seventy years his junior and who, as far as the employee knew, had absolutely nothing to be gained by showing compassion to the old codger who signed his paychecks.

"You're a good boy," Roger said, the corners of his mouth softly turning up. "You deserve the best." He uttered the words quietly into the wind, freeing them recklessly, knowing they would not be heard by any living creature.

But kindness needs no audience. Often it simply rests on the air, voiceless and profound.

Larry and Jimmy stared out at the road unwinding beneath them. Their hands once again came together, and they stayed together for the rest of the ride home.

By the time they turned onto the long driveway and approached the mansion, Larry knew it was time to say the words. It was past time.

His heart couldn't bear to leave them unsaid another minute.

As the car slowed and the wind died down around them, Roger gave a lazy squeeze to Mrs. Price's hand, easing her awake. Only Jimmy, glancing through the rearview mirror, saw the contented gleam in the old man's eyes as he did.

Chapter Fourteen

"Your hands are sweaty and your eyes are bugged out," Jimmy said. "What's wrong? You look like you're about to throw a tie rod."

They were up against the greenhouse wall, the glass on Jimmy's back warm from the sun. Larry stood facing him, his hands pressed against the glass panes to either side, penning Jimmy in place, not that Jimmy could think of anywhere else he'd rather be. But of course, Larry didn't know that. He might have *hoped*. But he didn't *know*.

Roger had waved them away at the mansion door. Gripping his cane for balance, and with Mrs. Price taking up the slack by holding on tight to his elbow, he had laid a gnarly old hand first on Jimmy's chest, then on Larry's in a thank-you. His white hair stood frazzled on his head from having been exposed to the wind while they rode around for two hours with the top down, but his eyes weren't frazzled at all. They appeared perfectly focused.

Roger had eyed the two young men kindly. "Mrs. Price will help me up the stairs. You boys run along. I believe you have matters to discuss."

To Jimmy's surprise, Larry leaned in and gave the old man a hug. "How did you know?" he asked quietly, but Roger didn't answer. He simply smiled wisely and turned toward the door. Mrs. Price led Roger away. Frankly confused, she wasn't *quite* sure what those two were talking about.

Bo hadn't made his presence known since they'd arrived back at the house. Larry assumed he was down in the kitchen doing what he always did. Plying his trade. Cooking. Acting like an ass. Being a dick. But Larry couldn't think about Bo now. As Roger had said, there were matters to be discussed.

Important matters.

Jimmy enjoyed the feel of Larry's arms trapping him against the greenhouse wall. It stirred all kinds of feelings inside him. As did the cute-as-hell, hesitant way Larry shuffled his feet, like maybe he was wondering how to proceed.

"What's wrong?" Jimmy asked, although he already knew. Jimmy had figured it out twenty miles back on the highway.

"Nothing's wrong," Larry answered quickly, trying to dislodge the lump in his throat but not succeeding very well. "Not yet anyway. Maybe after I say what I'm about to say...."

Jimmy leaned forward and rested his forehead against Larry's, enjoying the connection. Even enjoying the silence. But soon it was that very same silence Jimmy needed to bring to an end. Roger had been right. Things needed to be said. And they needed to be said *now*. Larry just needed a kick in the pants to get him started.

"Come on, now," Jimmy said. "Tell me what's on your mind. It'll be all right. I promise. What is it? Or would you rather I said it first?"

Larry pulled his head back, breaking the connection. "What do you mean? How could you possibly know what I'm about to say?"

A brief glimpse of snowy teeth appeared. The tip of a pink tongue slipped out, then slipped back in. "Maybe I'm psychic?" Jimmy suggested, eyes twinkling.

Larry stared at that teasing smile. He tilted forward and tasted it briefly with his lips. Then pushing himself away far enough to focus properly, he fought not to grow lost and swoony in the tender warmth of Jimmy's gaze.

"Shut up and let me talk," Larry growled.

"Ooh. Huffy," Jimmy said.

Larry narrowed his eyes and glared, then decided all-out snippiness probably wasn't the emotion he should be trying to convey. He remolded his face, aiming for contrite.

Whatever he ended up with, it must have worked. Jimmy's face sobered. The dawning smile disappeared as quickly as it began. He reached up and laid his hand on Larry's cheek, stroking the fragile skin under Larry's eye—feeling the feathery brush of Larry's pale eyelashes on his thumb.

"Talk, then," Jimmy delicately prodded. "Tell me what you need to say. Tell me what I've been waiting weeks to hear."

Larry blinked. "What's that supposed to mean? Do you really think you know what I'm about to say?"

This time Jimmy's smile peeked through, if only briefly. "You really aren't very good at all this romance stuff. You're like a blind man walking through a den of rattlesnakes. You keep hearing the hissing and the rattling but you just keep stomping along."

Larry frowned. "Now you've lost me. How did we get on snakes?"

Jimmy laughed, but his hand never left Larry's cheek. "I'm the snake, dumbass. I keep rattling, threatening to bite, but you just ignore me. Well, you don't *ignore* me. You're always there, you're always open, you're always giving. You're always, ooh, *sexy*. But you don't see what's right in front of your face."

"If I'm the blind guy and you're the frigging snake, then why didn't you strike already? I mean, metaphorically."

Jimmy gave him a tender pout. "There's no great mystery about it. I was afraid I'd scare you off. Simple as that. You used to talk forever about how you never wanted to get attached again. Remember? That every time you got attached, you got hurt. How you're going to be selfish from now on. How you'll never again leave yourself open to being a patsy. You used to say that, Larry. You know you did."

"*Used* to," Larry said softly, his eyes never leaving Jimmy's face. "I *used* to say it."

At that, Jimmy wrapped an arm around Larry's waist and yanked him close enough for their chests to grind together. Jimmy's eyebrows crawled toward each other. A couple of worried furrows split his forehead. He stared at Larry with such intensity that Larry almost shied away, but in the end he didn't. He couldn't.

Jimmy cocked his head, his eyes questioning. "Are you trying to tell me you no longer say those words? Are you saying you're not afraid of commitment anymore?"

In counterpoint to the uncertainty in his eyes, Jimmy slid his arm even tighter around Larry's waist, anchoring him more securely in place. He watched as Larry's expression grew vaguely desperate. Larry's eyes darted back and forth, as he studied Jimmy's face then glanced away.

The muscles in Jimmy's jaw clenched. "No. Don't look away. Don't be afraid of me, Larry. Please. And don't back down either. Tell me what you want to tell me."

The lump was back in Larry's throat. Jesus, maybe he was coming down with something. Or maybe he really was a dumbass when it came to romance.

"I just...."

Jimmy's eyebrows shot up and his fingers gave a drumroll of impatience on Larry's back. He almost made a wisecrack but had the good sense to stifle it before he blew the moment. "Don't stop now," he urged. "You're on a roll. Finish it, Larry. Tell me what you're trying to say."

Larry cleared his throat. Twice. He was terrified, and Jimmy's growing impatience wasn't helping. Jimmy squeegeed a bead of perspiration off Larry's forehead. "My God, you're sweating bullets."

"This isn't easy."

"Screw it, then. I'm going first." Jimmy leaned in and pressed his lips to Larry's ear. "I love you," he whispered. "I love you more than *anything*. So there. Do with that information what you will."

Larry's eyes popped open wide. He stood statue-still, staring. Not only did *he* find himself speechless, he was also fairly certain a wall of stone-dead silence had fallen over the entire Stanhope estate from gable to basement. The bees in the flowers stopped buzzing. The birds in the eaves shut up. Hell, maybe the world had even stopped rotating on its axis for a minute there. Was that possible?

Larry gave his head a shake, dislodging all those weirdass thoughts like he was erasing an Etch A Sketch. "I'm sorry. *What* did you say?"

Jimmy let his smile go. He couldn't corral it any longer. "I said I love you. I wanted to get it out in the open before we both died of old age waiting for you to do it."

Larry's chin scrunched up. "Wiseass. You're making fun of me." He pouted, fighting to extract himself from Jimmy's arms but unable to break the hold.

"Stop it," Jimmy said, grinning broadly now, his hand moving up to lie flat against the small of Larry's back, anchoring him even more firmly in place. Sort of like a scientist pinning a bug to a swath of cotton while its little legs were thrashing wildly. "You're not going anywhere, Larry. Stop wiggling."

"Why did you say that? Why did you say you loved me?"

Jimmy rolled his eyes. "Christ, you're a moron."

Larry frowned. "I know. But, wait. Are you saying you really *do*?"

"Yes, white man. I really, really do. I love you."

Larry suddenly found himself babbling. "You heard me say I did too, right? I had a little trouble getting it out, but you know that's the point I was trying to make, right?"

"I was beginning to gather as much, although not because of any clarity of speech on your part."

"Ow. That hurt."

Jimmy couldn't hold it back any longer. He laughed. Then his laughter died as if somebody had turned off the juice. His eyes misted over. Larry watched as Jimmy's warm brown irises suddenly glittered with starlight. A single tear squeezed out of Jimmy's left eye and slid down his cheek. Then he hiccupped.

"You've got the hiccups," Larry said. "Let me get you a glass of water."

"Shut the hell up," Jimmy said. He took an anguished breath. Then another. "No more jokes. No more kidding around. Tell me you love me too. That was your cue. Do it right this minute or I'm going to break your arm."

Larry's head bobbled up and down. That was all he could manage. There was no voice left in him. Not at that moment. Then he found a remnant tucked away he didn't know was there. "I-I thought I already did," he stammered.

"Oh, fuck it. I'll take that for a yes. At least hold me," Jimmy pleaded. "Please. I'm doing all the work here."

Larry's muscles turned to jelly. He slouched forward and wrapped his arms around Jimmy's neck. Larry buried his face in Jimmy's hair while Jimmy planted kisses up and down his throat.

"I can feel your heart," Larry muttered.

Jimmy pressed his lips to Larry's ear. "It's not my heart anymore. It belongs to you now. I'm just borrowing it. It's like a loaner."

Larry let those words seep in. He snuggled closer. His voice was barely audible. "Holy shit, that was romantic."

"I know," Jimmy said, not sounding *too* conceited.

Larry ignored the attitude. "I'll take care of it for you, Jimmy. I promise. Your heart, I mean. I swear I'll never let it get hurt. Not by me. I'll guard it with my life."

"I know."

"I mean like, forever."

Jimmy rolled his eyes, causing another tear to slip over his lower lash. "I *know*."

The tear sliding down Jimmy's cheek moistened Larry's mouth, and Larry licked it away. "Even your tears taste good," he stammered, as if he'd just stumbled on a vast truth of life he'd never been aware of before.

Jimmy pulled back to gaze at Larry's face. "I'm glad I taste good, but you still haven't said the words," he said.

"You mean I love you? Those words?"

"Them's the ones."

"I'll say them now, then. I love you?"

"Could you say it without the question mark at the end?"

"Oh. Certainly, Jimmy. I *love* you."

"That's better."

"I really do, you know."

"I know."

"You're frowning. What's wrong?"

"That was like pulling teeth," Jimmy said.

Larry blushed. "Thank you."

"That wasn't a compliment."

"Oh."

Just as Jimmy ducked his head to claim a kiss, they heard a booming wail of fury from somewhere deep inside the mansion. Both men jumped, banging their heads together, then spun around, staring at the mansion door.

EVEN AT ninety-three, Roger David Stanhope still had a powerful bellow.

Running full-out, Larry and Jimmy followed the reverberating echo of his cries through the kitchen, the dining room, past the ballroom and the formal parlor, skidding to a stop only after bursting through the library door just off the poolroom. There they found Roger and Mrs. Price staring at the fireplace.

Well, no. They were staring at the wall *above* the fireplace.

Larry was so startled and his heart was galloping so wildly, he couldn't immediately figure out what the problem was.

Bo tore through the library door right behind them.

"What's wrong?" Bo cried. "I was upstairs reading. What's the matter? Who yelled?"

Accusingly, Roger lifted his hand and pointed a trembling finger at the wall above the mantle. The *empty* wall.

Roger's voice no longer boiled in fury. There was only sorrow in it now. "The Egon Schiele sketch," he said. "It's gone."

Only then did Larry understand. He tore his eyes from the vacant wall and settled them on Mrs. Price. The woman was staring at the wall just like everyone else in the room. She was so dumbfounded her lips had formed a perfect O of astonishment and horror.

Balancing precariously on his cane, Roger turned and faced the three men standing at the door. The rage in his face had already slipped away, replaced by weary desperation.

"Do you boys know anything about this? How long has this painting been gone? Has anyone besides us been inside the house?"

Bo hesitantly stepped forward. "I saw the painting was missing yesterday. I assumed someone had moved it. Or maybe it had been sold. That's why I didn't say anything."

Mrs. Price slapped her hands to her cheeks. "Oh my God. The *other* artwork. The Chagall and the Soutine. The Warhol prints." She took a step toward the door, but Roger laid a hand to her wrist, stopping her from hurrying off.

"I'll check when I get to my room," he said.

Jimmy and Larry found the statement confusing. How could he check for the paintings in his room when they were scattered throughout the mansion?

Bo didn't find the comment strange at all. By their expressions, Bo knew immediately neither Jimmy nor Larry knew anything about the surveillance cameras and monitors stashed off the master's bedroom. Too bad for them. *Sometimes a little knowledge goes a long way.*

Roger stared once again at the fireplace wall. His words leaked weakly into the room, his voice wistful. Remembering back. "Jeremy bought the Schiele nude in Munich. He presented it to me for my sixtieth birthday as a gift. It's one of Egon Schiele's finest. A self-portrait of the artist in full sexual arousal, one of the finest examples of erotic art in the world. It's my most cherished possession. And not just because of its monetary value." He turned once again toward the young men standing at the door. He didn't appear accusatory exactly, just extremely disappointed. Wounded. "If there is anything any of you can tell me about the Schiele's disappearance, now is the time to do it."

Wide-eyed, Jimmy shook his head.

Bo stood mute, staring down at his feet.

Mrs. Price, stunned to silence, twiddled nervously at a brooch pinned to her blouse, still gaping at the empty wall above the mantle.

Larry was the only one who spoke. "I'm sorry," he said. He stepped forward and gently took the old man's arm in case he decided to topple over in shock. "Should I call the police, sir?"

"Wh-what?" Roger stammered. He turned away from Larry as if listening to a voice only he could hear. His lips moved, but he didn't speak. His gaze burned. As if still listening, his eyes darted about the room. In stunned silence, he stared first at Bo, then at Jimmy. He held that position for a full minute before slumping in place, as if whatever echoes he had been hearing—whatever shadows from the past had captured his attention—had finally let him go.

With a final glance at Larry, Roger wiped his eyes as if attempting to clear his vision. He suddenly looked ten years older, but that was not the worst of it. The worst of it was that his anger had clearly returned.

"No police," he said through tight lips. "Not yet anyway." Straightening his shoulders, he leaned into Larry and whispered, "Help me to my rooms, please. I want to think this through."

"But the police," Larry insisted. "Don't you think—"

"My rooms, Larry. Please."

"Yes, sir."

Gently, with Larry on one side and Mrs. Price on the other, they steered the old man toward the stairs. Larry was wondering what there was to think through. The place had been robbed. They should call the police.

Shouldn't they?

WITH ONLY Bo and Jimmy left in the library, Bo shot the other man a glare of pure hatred. He then wheeled and strode from the room.

"Asshole," Jimmy mumbled, watching him go. His eyes returned to the spot on the wall where a very expensive piece of art had once hung. He tried to think back to the last time he had seen it there. It was a nude, he remembered. Some poorly drawn guy with a hard-on. Who could imagine anything like that being worth a fortune? He stepped forward and laid his hand to the spot where the sketch once hung, as if that would help him understand what had happened. Poor Mr. Stanhope. He had loved this painting so much. Who would do such a thing?

A hand came to rest on his shoulder, and Jimmy whirled around, his heart thumping. His face softened when he saw who it was.

"You startled me."

"He shut me out," Larry said.

Confused, Jimmy asked, "What do you mean he shut you out? Who shut you out? Mr. Stanhope?"

"Yeah. Roger. When we got upstairs, he told Mrs. Price to go to her room and rest, and then he slammed the door in my face. He shut me out."

"What's he doing?"

"Who the hell knows?"

Larry followed Jimmy's eyes to the fireplace wall. "That's not even the most confusing part," he said absently.

Jimmy studied him. "Why?" he asked. "What's the most confusing part?"

Larry thought about it for a moment, then gazed at Jimmy with a bemused expression. "He wasn't inside his bedroom more than five seconds, when he started talking and yelling at someone. I mean it was like a whole one-sided conversation. It just went on and on and on."

"Who? Who was he talking to?"

"Beats me. There was no one in there besides him."

"Are you sure?"

"I looked past him as he opened the door. The room was empty. When he slammed it in my face, there was no one on the other side of that door but Mr. Stanhope himself."

"Do you think maybe he's getting senile?"

Larry frowned. "No. He's clearer-headed than we are. I think—"

"You think what?"

"I think he was talking to Jeremy. His dead lover."

A gentle heat rose in Jimmy's eyes. "It took you a while to see the light, kemo sabe, but I think you're right. I've thought it all along. I sensed him, you know. The first time I stepped inside this house."

Larry stood there blinking, eying Jimmy. Remembering the weird conversation between Jimmy and Roger the first time they met. He chewed the inside of his cheek. He scratched his nose. He stared back at the empty spot on the wall, seeing clearly the faded rectangle where the Schiele had been hanging for the past three decades. Finally, he gave a befuddled snort.

"So ghosts really exist."

Jimmy gave him an exaggerated shrug. "I'm pretty sure *that* one does."

Larry shot a glance skyward. "Well, I'm full-blown gonzo confused *now*!" Eventually, his eyes wandered back to Jimmy. Rising from the rubble of his troubled thoughts, a smile managed to claw its way to the surface. "Ghost or no ghost, I still love you at least. There's no confusion about that."

Jimmy scooped him into his arms. "Glad to hear it." As quickly as it came, Jimmy's happiness faltered. "I do have one question, though."

"What's that?"

"Just who the hell is Egon Schiele?"

THE FIRST thing Roger did upon entering his suite was turn on the security monitors and check the rooms with other valuable artwork on their walls. He breathed a sigh of relief to see the Chagall, the Soutine, the Warhol prints, all still safely in place.

Reassured on that front—although he was still furious about the Schiele—he shrieked into the empty room. "Where are you? Show yourself! At least cough or something, blast it! Why did you tell me not to call the cops?"

"I'm here," said a voice that sounded like it came from deep inside the bottom drawer of the antique chifforobe that stood in the corner.

Roger growled with impatience. "What the hell are you doing in there?"

"You know all those odd socks you own that don't have a match? Well, I found their mates."

"Wonderful," Roger droned. "You've discovered the graveyard where all the dead socks go to die. Now get your ass out here."

The chifforobe rattled on its four legs, then fell silent. "Fine. Here I am."

The room didn't *look* any different, of course. It still looked empty. But lately, Roger had learned to take certain things for granted. Especially when it came to his deceased lover.

"What happened today?" Roger asked, trying really hard to keep his anger at bay. If he made Jeremy mad, the ghost might scoot off for three days to pout and Roger wouldn't learn anything at all. "What took place while we were out on our little drive?"

"Do I detect a note of desperation?"

Roger's attempt to stay calm fizzled out right off the bat. He banged his cane on the bedroom floor. "The Schiele is missing, dammit! What happened to it? Weren't you watching?"

"What am I? The security guard?"

Roger heaved a long, put-upon sigh. "Of course not, my love. But you're always snooping around, eavesdropping—"

"Why, I *never*!" But there was a chuckle in there somewhere. Roger heard it quite clearly.

"—like I said, eavesdropping, and sneaking around spying on people. I just thought perhaps you might have seen the culprit who did it."

"Did what?"

"Stole the painting, you moron!"

Apparently, Jeremy was having too much fun to get riled up and bustle off in a snit. "My, my. We are in a tizzy."

Again, Roger sucked in some air and dug deep within himself for a bit of patience. After all, he couldn't kill the guy. Jeremy was already dead. Not that he wouldn't have enjoyed trying. He gritted his teeth, trying to remain calm. "Well, *did* you, Jeremy? Did you *see* anything?"

Roger couldn't be positive, but he was almost sure he detected a few arrows of smug satisfaction ricocheting around the room like sonar.

"As a matter of fact, Roger, I did. How would you like to take a stroll with me down to the kitchen? I'll explain it as we go. Here. Take my arm."

"Well, where is it? Your arm's invisible, you know."

"Oh, yeah. I forgot."

"At least tell me if the sketch is safe!" Roger snapped, feeling around for an arm that wasn't there, that would never *be* there. After a while he gave up, rolling his eyes so far up into his head he almost toppled over backward.

Jeremy gave a self-effacing chuckle. "Oh. I forgot. I'm dead. You can't *feel* my arm any more than I can. And yes, the Schiele's safe. Quite an impressive boner that man had too. I especially love the way the only color in the sketch was the reddish glow he painted onto the bulbous head of that magnificent cock."

Roger groaned. "Yes, yes. Big dick. Rosy corona. I know. But where has it gone, dammit? That's what *I* want to know. That sketch is *priceless*!"

"Why, Roger, it's safe and sound, tucked under the gardener's bed."

Roger's mouth fell open. He quietly closed it. "Did you say under the gardener's *bed*?"

"Yes. Out back in that gaudyass trailer that looks like it was made out of tinfoil."

"That gaudyass trailer, as you so indelicately put it, is a classic Airstream."

"Whatever."

"I'm thinking of buying it from the gardener, or at least making him an offer."

"Whatever for?"

"To add to my collection of interesting automobiles. Why do you think?"

"At your age?"

"What does my age have to do with—" Roger suddenly rose to his full six feet two inches, allowing for a certain amount of settling that had occurred during ninety-three years of bucking gravity. It seemed what Jeremy had just told him had finally soaked in. "Wait! *What*? *Jimmy* stole the Schiele? Oh, God, no!"

"Now, now, Rog. Don't jump to conclusions. Come along now. Down to the kitchen. I'll explain along the way."

Roger tried to unclench his fists. It was making his knuckles hurt. Damned arthritis. "Yes. All right. Fine. Lead the way. And tell me everything. Oh dear, what a mess this all is!"

"We'll just stop by Mrs. Price's chambers first," Jeremy suggested. "She can bring the boys up to watch the show on the monitors. They love each other, you know."

"You mean Jimmy and Larry? Yes," Roger said. "I know." He frowned. "Please tell me you're not still trying to tell me what I think you're trying to tell me about Jimmy being the one who stole the Schiele."

Jeremy barked out a laugh. "Magnificent sentence structure, dearest. And of course not! Jimmy's as innocent as I am. Why do you think I'm taking you to the kitchen?"

"Bo," Roger gasped, beginning to see the light.

"I'm afraid so. He really is a greedy prick."

Roger almost smiled. "Well, that's not a good way to be."

"No, indeedy," Jeremy sighed. "Come along now. Let's get this over with. There are still some missing socks I'd like to unearth before the day is done."

"My God, it must be boring being dead."

"You have no idea."

Roger David Stanhope strolled alone between mansion walls, then turned right to descend a long flight of steps, his cane banging along in front of him. Max and Leo trailed behind. Along the way, a disembodied voice whispered continually in Roger's ear. That voice was outlining, step by step, the salient points of what really was not turning out to be the crime of the century after all.

Which is not to say that Roger wasn't thoroughly pissed off by the time he reached the kitchen door. He was indeed.

Even the pugs were growling as they pattered along at his heels.

"Ahem," said a hushed voice behind them.

Jimmy and Larry were still standing in the library, staring at the empty wall. Wrapped in each other's arms, both men were so surprised by the intrusion, they banged their heads together.

"Ouch!" Jimmy said.

"Mrs. Price!" Larry exclaimed, whirling around, while Jimmy rubbed his head and looked surprised. "What's wrong?"

She waited for the two men to separate, a little self-consciously perhaps, and when they were standing side by side instead of front to front, she took Larry's hand. As an afterthought, she took Jimmy's hand too.

"Come with me, boys," she said. "Up to the master's rooms. I want you to see something."

"What is it?" Jimmy asked.

Mrs. Price gave her head a sad little shake. "Just come along and see for yourselves."

Obediently, they followed her out of the room.

Chapter Fifteen

Bo stood in the kitchen. His hands were shaking. He poured a cup of coffee and slopped half of it onto the floor. He left the spilled coffee where it landed.

When the red light next to the ceiling blinked on, he spotted it from the corner of his eye. His heart started hammering a mile a minute. His pulse pounded in his temple as the blood sluiced through his head like white water shooting through a flume.

Why was the camera on? Was the master watching him? Did he know? Did he suspect?

No. He couldn't possibly know *anything*. Bo set the coffee cup aside. His hands were shaking so badly now he was afraid to drink from it anyway. Best to act cool while he was being watched. Best not to look *suspicious*.

To accomplish that, he had to stop cowering in this stupid kitchen. He had to go back upstairs and finish what he started. Finish the plan. Tell the master what he needed to tell him. Get the wheels of justice turning. Well—heh-heh—not justice, maybe.

At that thought, a smile turned his mouth. It wasn't a pleasant smile. There was nothing pleasant about it. If Bo could have seen it, even he might have been shocked by the coldness of it.

Oblivious to his own cruel expression, Bo stared down at himself, nervously smoothing his white uniform, all the while trying to ignore that accusing red light shining down on him.

Then he thought of the money. *All that money.*

He muttered a curse, his eyes bright. His desperation slowly morphed into renewed determination. His fear turned to furious resolve. He sucked in a deep breath. Trying to get a grip. Trying to focus. He could do this. He knew he could. Why should he let the goddamn *gardener* spoil it for him? There was too much at stake. With the gardener out of the picture, everything could get back to normal. He could maneuver Larry back into his bed. He could make Larry fall in love with him. He knew he could. Once he'd done that, it was all downhill. Larry was his.

And so was the money.

Back straight now, jaws clenched, his mind made up, Bo stared through the kitchen window at the Airstream trailer outside. Hatred surged through him. His cold smile turned even colder.

He could do this. He had to. There was no way to back out now anyway.

Strangely, that was the moment when his courage failed completely. His eyes suddenly darted around the room. The terror returned, surging through him. He spun toward the door—the *back* door. The door leading out to the driveway, to his old truck parked beside the carriage house. He had to run. He had to get away. At least for a while. Let the police come. They would find the painting eventually. They would find the painting and that would be the end of the fucking gardener. He just had to not be here when it happened.

He froze with his hand on the doorknob.

He couldn't do it. No. If he left, their suspicions would immediately fall on him. He had to stay. He had to. *Fuck.*

He jumped when the beeper at his waist gave a single ringtone. His call sign. He was being summoned. The old man wanted him.

He whirled and was stunned to see that Roger was already there. Staring at him from the kitchen doorway. His finger was still on the beeper button hanging around his neck.

"Hello, Bo," Roger said.

LIKE A cornered animal, Bo pressed his back to the pantry cupboard. A trickle of sweat slid down his forehead.

"Sir," he said. "You startled me."

Roger eyed him sadly. He tapped his cane with the gold handle at the top shaped like a dragon's head on the tiled floor at his feet. Impatiently, maybe. Or just idly, making noise for no reason at all. Roger was alone. There was no one with him. No one Bo could see, at least. Roger tried to smile as he spoke, but he didn't try very hard.

"You look more than startled, Bo. You look terrified. Is there something you'd like to tell me?"

"Y-yes," Bo said, trying to mold a concerned expression on his face. "I was just on my way up to see you, as a matter of fact."

Roger's eyes flitted to the back door, knowing full well what Bo had been thinking when Roger entered the kitchen unannounced. "You don't say?"

"Y-yes. I wanted to tell you I suddenly remembered something. It's about—it's about the gardener. I saw him with a package wrapped in paper yesterday. The package was the same size as the painting in the library. The one that's missing. I think maybe he's the one who stole it."

"You don't say?" Roger said again, looking even sadder.

Bo fidgeted. He lifted a trembling hand and pointed through the kitchen window. "I was watching from there," he said. "It was yesterday sometime. I forget exactly when. I was working at the sink, and I saw Jimmy take that package into the trailer. A minute later he came back outside, and he wasn't carrying it anymore."

Roger stepped carefully to the kitchen table and slowly lowered himself into a chair, joints creaking—perhaps not audibly, but inside Roger's head they certainly were. From a bowl of fruit on the table, he lifted a Jonathan apple. He sat there, staring at it, turning it over and over in his hand.

"You're the worst liar I've ever seen," he said quietly.

A glint of anger flashed in Bo's eyes. He pointed again at the Airstream trailer sitting outside. "No. You don't understand. The painting's there. I know it is. Jimmy had to be the one who took it. Why else would he have been carrying that package that was exactly the same size as the painting?"

"It wasn't actually a painting. It was a sketch." Roger pointed to a drawer beside the sink. "Hand me a knife, will you, son. I've got a hankering for this apple, but I need to cut it up first. False teeth, you know. Hard to eat an apple with false teeth."

Bo glanced at the drawer, then back to the old man at the table. "Sure," he said absently. He crossed the room and pulled a paring knife from the drawer. Then he carried it to the table, where he stood looking down at the knife in his fist as if pondering what else he might do with a knife at that particular juncture. Surprised by some of his own thoughts, Bo quickly handed the knife over, just to get rid of it.

Roger took it with a quiet thank-you and began peeling the apple over a napkin. He didn't speak another word until the apple was completely peeled and cored and quartered. Bo stood watching as if he had never seen anything as spellbinding in his life.

Finally Roger nibbled at one of the wedges and at the same time returned his gaze to Bo, who once again stepped away, pressing his ass to the counter, his back to the cupboard.

Roger gave the boy a pitying smile. "The Schiele wasn't stolen yesterday, Bo. It was taken today when everyone was out. Everyone but you."

The angry glint in Bo's eyes was still there. He didn't try so hard to hide it now. When he spoke, his voice was measured. Almost threatening. "You're wrong. It was taken yesterday. I just told you. I remember—"

"You were seen," Roger said. He spoke the words as if he harbored no pleasure in uttering them. "You were seen, Bo." He flicked his eyes to the tiny camera lens on the ceiling. The red light was still on.

Bo twisted his head and stared at the red light at the same time Roger did.

The angry fire in his eyes flared even brighter. He turned back to the old man, his fists clenched tight at his sides, his lips a thin mean line slashing across his face.

"What is this place?" Larry asked, staring at the bank of monitors in front of them. "Are these security cameras?"

"Yes," Mrs. Price said. "Roger had them installed just before you came to work here."

Larry turned to her, a hurt look on his face. "Didn't he trust us?"

Mrs. Price laid a gentle hand to his cheek. "It wasn't like that. The cameras were here for a different reason."

"Look!" Jimmy said, pointing. "It's the master and Bo. They're down in the kitchen. Bo looks like he just saw a ghost."

"What an astute observation," Mrs. Price intoned. "Give him a minute. Maybe he will."

Jimmy had to chuckle at that. From his perspective, truer words were never spoken. Even Larry didn't seem quite as surprised by Mrs. Price's statement as he might once have been.

The three of them, two young men and one old woman, leaned in to watch the images on the screen.

"Too bad there isn't any audio," Larry said. "I wonder what they're saying."

Since no one else had claimed it, and since her feet were hurting like a couple of toothaches—lord, being old sucked—Mrs. Price lowered herself into the desk chair. She laid her hands in her lap, as if afraid she'd accidentally bump the wrong high-tech button and blow the whole stupid contraption to smithereens.

"Just watch," she said. "I don't think you'll need sound to figure out what's going on."

BO'S WORDS were cold, erupting from his throat as if carried into the room on a glacial wind. He flapped his hand at the tiny red light on the ceiling. "And don't try to trick me. I know all about your surveillance system. That doesn't alter the fact that there was no one *here*. How could anyone have *seen* me? Your cameras don't record; they merely watch."

"And how would you know that, unless you were snooping around my room when I was gone? And yes, you were seen there as well."

"That's *impossible*! Seen by *who* exactly?"

Roger snatched up another wedge of apple and happily chomped away at it. "You're never alone in this house, Bo. Even when you think you are," he said cryptically. "One might have thought you would have learned that by now. You certainly took enough pains to learn the rest of my secrets." He stopped what he was doing and studied Bo's furiously affronted face with an expression that could only be described as pitying.

Bo felt steady enough with his lies to become sarcastic. Was this old fuck senile or what? "What the hell is that supposed to mean? *Sir*. I think I know when I'm alone."

"Do you really?" Roger asked. "Are we alone now? I mean the two of us. Are we alone inside this kitchen?"

Bo's eyes narrowed. "What sort of game are you playing? I've never done anything but try to be a good—"

"Answer the question, please," Roger insisted. "Are you and I alone at this very minute?"

Bo took a measured step forward and flung his arms around in a circle, doing a pirouette like Julie Andrews on top of that *other* mountain. "Of course, we're alone! Do you *see* anybody else in the room?"

At that moment, Bo was shoved backward by invisible hands. His head hit the cupboard door, rattling the contents inside. His eyes grew as big as dinner plates as he stared about in every direction.

"What the *fuck*?"

Roger flapped an admonitory finger. "Oh, I wouldn't swear if I were you. You'll just make him madder."

Bo glared with hatred at the old man sitting so calmly in front of him, chewing on his stupid apple. "Make *who* madder? There's no one else here, dammit!"

A moment later, the cupboard door flew open, banging Bo in the back of the head. An instant after that, a shower of white flour tumbled off the top shelf, raining down over Bo's head, filling his ears, clogging up his nose, drifting down the back of his collar. His whole body was enveloped in a billowing avalanche of snowy flour dust. As soon as the downpour of flour subsided, the paper bag with Gold Medal Flour written on it bounced off Bo's noggin and landed at his feet.

Roger *tsk*ed. "Just look at that mess." If he was unhappy about it, it didn't show. In fact, he appeared more amused than angry.

Bo sputtered, and a puff of flour dust shot out of his mouth. He sneezed and gave his head a shake, making the downpour start all over again, covering his shoe tops, sprinkling the floor around him in an almost perfect circle.

"Motherfucker!" Bo bellowed from the midst of that billowing white cloud. And then he sneezed again.

Roger gave another *tsk*. "Oh dear. You probably shouldn't have said that. He really abhors cursing, you know."

Bo bellowed when a waterfall of cooking oil—Wesson, it was, a brand-new jumbo-sized jug, sixty-four ounces to be exact—cascaded down over his head, going *glub-glub-glub*, coating his face, burning his eyes, dribbling down his shoulders, filling up his shoes. Blending with the flour, it made a nice thick batter. If Bo had had a few hundred pieces of raw chicken ready to fry up, he would have been in business.

JIMMY'S EYES were as big as dinner plates too. Unlike Bo, he wasn't mad. He was laughing. "Holy cow! Would you look at that. The guy's a dumpling."

Unamused, Mrs. Price clucked. "Jeremy always was short-tempered."

Larry and Jimmy both tore their eyes from the monitor long enough to stare at her. "So you knew too!" Larry exclaimed.

Mrs. Price tapped her mouth with her fingertips as if stifling a yawn. "About Jeremy? Of course I knew." She refocused on the monitor, clucking her tongue again, staring closer at Bo standing there dripping and trembling and puffing out a cloud of flour dust like a snow blower spewing slush. She sadly shook her old head. "Now, who's going to clean up that mess, I wonder. You can bet your billybobs it won't be me. I'm retired."

Larry wiped happy tears off his cheeks. He took a second to wonder what a billybob was, then said, "Hell, I'll clean it up. It's worth it to see the show!"

He grabbed Jimmy's hand, and they stood there happily swinging their arms back and forth like two kids eating cotton candy at a county fair.

"I love you," Jimmy said, apropos of absolutely nothing.

"I love you back," Larry answered without missing a beat.

Mrs. Price regarded them fondly while batting her lashes. "If you boys were cupcakes," she said, "I'd eat you right up."

"Uh, thanks," Jimmy drawled, looking doubtful, and then all three of them turned their eyes back to the screen.

"Just look at that guy," Larry said. "Anybody else getting in the mood for pancakes?"

Jimmy turned to Mrs. Price yet again. "What's all this about anyway? Why is the master's dead lover dousing Bo in batter? What'd Bo ever do to him?"

Mrs. Price was trying to pat her hair in place. It was still a mess from riding in the convertible with the top down. She answered Jimmy offhand, as if she thought he should have known the answer already. "It's not what Bo did to Jeremy, it's what Bo did to *you*."

That made Jimmy jump. "Me? What the heck did he do to *me*, aside from annoy me to death for the past three months and treat Larry like dirt?"

Mrs. Price plucked a bobby pin from her sweater pocket and poked it in her hair. "He stole the Schiele off the library wall and planted it under your bed."

Jimmy blinked. "Oh." The clock in the other room ticked about ten times. *Tick, tick, tick, tick....* Finally, Jimmy shook himself awake. "Uh, why would he do that?"

"You don't know?" Mrs. Price asked, gnawing another bobby pin open and sticking it in her hair alongside the first one.

"Well, I know he's jealous of me and Larry."

"So you don't know about the plan to leave the estate to—oops!" Mrs. Price clapped her mouth shut. She glanced at Larry, but he was too wrapped up in what was happening on the monitor to listen to them. She turned back to Jimmy and eyed him like a schoolmarm staring at the sweetest—and quite possibly dumbest—kid in class. "Well, I guess that's the reason, then," she said. She was lying, of course, although Jimmy was too confused to notice. "Bo did it because he's jealous of you and Larry."

As soon as Jimmy turned back to the monitor, she went through the motions of zipping her mouth shut and locking it with a key. She then proceeded to throw the imaginary key over her shoulder and feign a look of pure innocence.

"Oh, look!" Larry cried. "He's being pelted with Rice Krispies! How cool is that?"

He tore his eyes from the monitor and centered them on Mrs. Price's face. "Is that really a—"

"Ghost? Yes, I'm afraid it is. And he's making a mess." She was distinctly unhappy about the state of her kitchen floor.

"So he really—"

"Exists? Yes, son. Good lord. Catch up."

Larry's eyes drifted to Jimmy. Jimmy was staring at Mrs. Price too.

"Both of you come with me to the trailer," Jimmy said quietly. "I want to see for myself. And I think maybe I'd like a couple of witnesses with me when I do."

"Yes," Mrs. Price said. "That's probably not a bad idea."

Larry was absorbed in the monitor again. "But I want to watch the ghost pummel the crap out of Bo."

"Tough," Mrs. Price said, and taking both boys' hands, she tugged them toward the door.

YEP. IT was Rice Krispies all right. A waterfall of Rice Krispies. They were sprinkling down through the air like the Kellogg's factory had been hit by an air-to-surface missile and been blown to pixie dust. Directly under the waterfall of Rice Krispies stood Bo. The only things *recognizable* about Bo were the whites of his eyes. Otherwise, he was simply nondescript. With no defining characteristics whatsoever. In fact, he was starting to look like a man-shaped mound of clumping cat litter. He stood with his arms and legs akimbo and his mouth hanging open because he couldn't breathe through his nose.

Bo made a half-assed attempt to appear shocked by the treatment he was receiving, but he couldn't quite carry it off. For an asshole *not* to appear an asshole is always an uphill grind.

"You can't prove *anything*!" he yelled, spitting flour and sputtering Wesson oil. The Rice Krispies snap-crackle-and-popping in his ears were *really* pissing him off.

Roger still sat at the kitchen table, chewing on a wedge of apple. He fastidiously flicked a Rice Krispie off his pant leg where it landed after Bo's last sputter. "I don't need to prove anything," Roger said. "I already know. My lover told me."

"Your lover's *dead*, you old fool!" Bo hollered at the top of his voice, then immediately starting coughing and hacking because while he was yelling at Mr. Stanhope, he had sucked in a great glob of cereal and Wesson oil.

Roger nailed him with a pitying frown. "And what about the three hundred-dollar bills you found on the kitchen floor? What about *that*, huh?"

"Wha-wha-what three hundred-dollar bills? I never found three hundred-dollar bills! You're imagining things. You're crazy. You're senile."

"And you, sir, are a liar," Roger said calmly. "My lover planted that money for you to find to see if you would try to locate the rightful owner. Like *that* was ever going to happen. Jeremy, get this creep out of here. I've heard enough."

Bo roared in fury. "But—but—"

With a squawking noise like he was being strangled, Bo shot up on tiptoe when the collar of his chef's tunic was suddenly wrenched up to the back of his head. He looked like an annoying kitten whose mother had snatched him up by the nape to carry him off and shut him the hell up.

"*Wait*," Bo wailed, arms flailing.

But waiting seemed to be off the agenda, at least as far as Jeremy was concerned.

While Roger watched, chewed his apple, and casually bobbed his foot up and down to the rhythm of a tune only he could hear, Bo appeared to tap-dance his way across the kitchen toward the back door, dribbling Rice Krispies and smearing what really did look like pancake batter all over the place in his wake. Leo and Max trailed along behind Bo, licking the unexpected treat off the floor. Roger noticed there was even batter dripping from the ceiling fan. Lordy, what a mess.

At the back door now and still dangling by his collar, Bo weaseled his way around in midair to shake a trembling finger at Roger, who was still sitting there watching his erstwhile chef's ignominious departure, totally unconcerned.

"You haven't heard the last of me, you old fart! I'll sue you, that's what I'll do! I'll take you to court and end up with everything you own. When the police hear how you and your dead lover treated me—"

Roger brushed off his hands and folded his arms across his chest. "Yes, I'm sure the police would just *love* to hear about the ghost who ran you out of my house. And as far as you ending up with my fortune, I'm afraid that's just not going to happen, son. Not in a million years."

"I know lawyers! You'll regret treating me like this. You'll regret it, I tell you!"

In the middle of his latest rant, Bo sucked in another glob of Rice Krispies and gagged for the longest time. In fact, he came just a wee bit short of barfing his lunch all over the floor, which was about the only way he could have made the floor look any worse than it already did.

"Be grateful I don't press charges against *you*," Roger calmly stated, sprinkling a little salt over his latest wedge of apple. "It's a shame, you know. I'm really quite upset about it. You were doing fine with Mrs. Price's cookie recipes. Now I'll have to go the merry round of training someone else."

"Oh, pishposh," said Mrs. Price from the doorway behind him. "You never taught him anything to begin with. *I* did all the work." She was standing there between Larry and Jimmy. In Jimmy's hand hung the Schiele sketch, still framed, still erotic, still safe and sound and worth a fortune.

Roger grunted his way around in the chair to look at them. "Oh, there you all are. I was wondering when you'd join the party. And there's my Schiele. How lovely!"

Bo was still hanging by the back of his tunic with his toes barely touching the floor, dripping and snorting and continuing to sputter fluffy bits of flour dust and clumpy sprays of Wesson oil and Rice Krispies everywhere. It hardly seemed possible, but he actually appeared madder now than he had before. Probably the sight of Jimmy and Larry holding hands and trying not to laugh at his predicament didn't improve his mood any, but that's just one narrator's opinion.

Roger swiveled back toward his newly unemployed chef and gave his fingers a little flutter of dismissal. "Go on now, Jeremy. Get him out of here. Tell him to drop me a note and I'll have all his belongings shipped off to him at no cost to himself. There'll be no severance pay, I'm afraid. He's been far too conniving for that. I doubt if he'll get much of a reference either, but I'll think about that later."

"Noooo!" Bo howled. "Wait a minute—aaugh!"

With that, Jeremy, who was still totally invisible but clearly present nonetheless, dragged poor Bo out the door and booted him off the back step. Bo landed in a spray of rocks and gravel, and it was at that precise moment that Leo decided to take a nip at his leg.

"And don't come back!" Roger merrily called out after him. Scowling good-naturedly, Roger wagged an admonitory finger at the dog. "Leo, go up to your room and gargle. And be more careful in the future what you put in your mouth."

Roger threw his head back and had a good long laugh over that. When he finally managed to calm himself down, he patted the table in front of him and beckoned everyone at the door to come forward.

"Come sit and join me, won't you?" he cried out, as friendly as ever. "These apples are delicious. Maybe we can coerce dear Mrs. Price to incorporate a few into a pie one of these days."

She stuck a fist on her hip and gave an exasperated huff. "So I'm back to being the cook, am I?"

Roger giggled while Leo and Max clamored to get in his lap. "Only until we find a replacement, my dear. Surely a couple of weeks in the kitchen won't kill you."

Mrs. Price didn't look convinced. "Humph."

Jimmy handed Roger his missing Schiele. Roger sat there staring at it, admiring it, making sure it wasn't damaged. With that out of the way, amid the scraping of chairs and the hustle and bustle of everyone getting settled around him, Roger eyed the two young men between himself and

Mrs. Price. Larry had an apple in his hand, and Jimmy was in the process of picking one from the bowl.

"You two look happy," Roger observed. It was as if the drama with Bo had never happened. His old face was as sweet and mild as it ever was. Even the horrendous mess in the kitchen seemed to be momentarily forgotten.

Jimmy and Larry's eyes skipped toward each other. "We *are* happy," they said in unison.

"Lovers, huh?" Roger asked kindly. "You made the commitment, did you?"

Larry blushed.

It was Jimmy who answered. "Yes, sir, we are. And we did. We're going to stay that way too. It won't affect our work. I promise. I hope you'll give us your blessing."

Roger reached across the table and patted each of the boys' hands. "Of course I'll give you my blessing. I think it's splendid."

In the distance, Bo's old pickup truck cranked to life. A minute later they heard the tires spewing gravel as he tore down the driveway, screaming curses out the window as he went.

"It's hot outside today," Mrs. Price observed, twisting around in her chair to peer out the window at the pickup truck disappearing in the distance. "Bo should brown nicely. Coated in batter like he is, he'll look like a fritter by the time he gets to town."

"And no one could possibly deserve it more." Roger grinned, rubbing noses with Max while scratching Leo's ass. "Isn't that right, you little rascals, you?" He lifted his head and gazed around the table at the people who now comprised his life. "Now then, boys, Mrs. Price. Let's all have another apple, shall we? They really are quite delicious. Jeremy," he added, peering over his shoulder, first in one direction, then the other. "You can start cleaning up the mess you made in Mrs. Price's kitchen."

A box of rigatoni toppled out of the cupboard and exploded on the floor. Uncooked noodles shot out everywhere.

Roger smiled. "Or not."

Turning back to his friends, Roger slid the bowl into the middle of the table, and whether they wanted one or not, everyone claimed an apple.

"Say," Larry said, politely interrupting while staring down at the spilled pasta scattered from one end of the room to the other, coated now with flour and oil and Rice Krispies. "Is everybody aware that this house is actually *haunted*?"

While Mrs. Price rolled her eyes up at the ceiling, frowning when she spotted the crap dripping off the ceiling fan, it was Roger who blessed Larry with a most pitying stare. "Oh, now really, my boy. Who in their right mind believes in ghosts in this day and age?"

Chapter Sixteen

They slipped into orgasm together, each young man feeding from the other. They did not cry out. They did not thrash about in Jimmy's bed, tucked away in the little Airstream trailer far from the opulence of the grand Stanhope mansion looming over them in the moonlight. Their juices spilled gently, their explosions of ardor held in check, for once, by the awareness of newly spoken vows. Tomorrow when they made love, the blinding thrill they found in each other's bodies would once again leave them breathless and shuddering. They would arch their backs and stammer and buck and laugh and gasp at the moment of release, fingers grasping, hearts hammering, senses blinded. But for now, on this one night after they first spoke words of commitment—of honest-to-God *love*—the act of sex was less about the moment and more about a grander whole. At this one instant in time, they were too humbled to really let themselves go. Too stricken with the wonder of what it all really meant.

They were no longer alone. They were a couple. They were together. They would face the world on a common front now. Each had been in relationships before, but neither had felt as sure of its success as they did this time. With each other.

Both knew this was something special.

Tonight, impossibly, even a moment of mutual orgasm could not muddy their resolve. Or lessen the importance of the words they had spoken. The promises they had made—and fully intended to keep.

Still, as they lay in each other's arms afterward, the old electricity slowly returned. Nerve endings once again began to spark, to come alive. Even if only to ignite with the last lingering touch of the night. The last taste. The last delicious tremor.

Jimmy's acorn skin was satin under Larry's hands. He lovingly explored the slopes and ridges of smoothly muscled flesh, the warm delicious valleys where he could happily roam for ages, never tiring, never wishing to be anywhere but where he was. Those explorations always left both men shuddering and breathless with need. Even now, even after all that had happened, when Larry's fingers began to explore, Jimmy's body once again responded. He arched into Larry's touch, into Larry's gentle strokes, one drawing the other like the moon pulls the tide. Like a magnet pulls metal.

"My God, your hands are magic," Jimmy whispered, his lips in Larry's auburn curls, made less fiery in the moonlight—almost bronze now, the red in it sleeping. The sweet scent of it, as Jimmy breathed it in, was more intoxicating in the darkness than it ever was in the light of day.

Larry rested his cheek against Jimmy's chest to hear the heartbeat beneath. As he lay there, Jimmy's arms came up to anchor him in place. They lay voiceless, nearly breathless, subdued by their thoughts and the warm silence of the night surrounding them.

Once again their minds filled with the memory of words they had spoken and promises they had made just that day. Mere hours ago. Promises both men knew the other intended to keep. Promises they each *trusted* the other to honor.

Larry had never been happier in his life, and proudly, Jimmy knew it.

"I never thought I'd fall in love again," Larry said, his lips brushing the nub of a coppery nipple that rested near his cheek. He smiled as Jimmy's long fingers buried themselves in his hair. "I never *wanted* to fall in love again."

"Neither one of us did," Jimmy said, his voice a contented rumble. He spoke with his lips still in Larry's hair, ignoring the fact that it tickled his nose. "Roger approves. And Mrs. Price does too. Somehow that means a lot to me."

"Me too." Larry pressed his face to Jimmy's chest and smiled. "But just what the hell happened today? Explain it to me, will you? I'm a little confused. In the kitchen, I mean. What the hell happened in the kitchen?"

Jimmy's gentle laugh echoed through the darkened trailer. He wrapped Larry even more tightly in his arms, one hand at Larry's nape, the other on the silken swell of his hip. Just that simple touch sent a surge of hunger through Jimmy, but he forced himself to ignore it. He was too comfortable. Larry felt too good in his arms.

"Payback, I think," Jimmy said. "Bo tried to pull something, and Roger wasn't having it."

Larry rose up on his elbows and gazed down at Jimmy beneath him. His eyes sparkled in the moonlight as Jimmy reached up to push Larry's hair off his brow.

"But the flour, Jimmy. The cooking oil. The mess. Can ghosts really do all that?"

Jimmy gave a playful shrug. "You saw it as well as I did. Ghosts do what they want, I guess. Just don't try to trick 'em. They seem to be a little testy. At least ours is."

Larry's smile widened to an impossible width. Every tooth in his head glimmered white in the darkness. "No kidding."

Jimmy lay admiring that beautiful smile. He trailed his thumb across Larry's lower lip just to see how it felt. He buried his face in the crook of Larry's neck and slid his hands down Larry's back. The lure of that perfect ass was too strong for him to resist. He cupped it now, claiming it for his own, just as he had done so many times before. The heel of his hand slid along the satiny crevice. His thumb rested softly atop the heated opening he knew so well.

"Oh man," Larry breathed, squirming now, his face still buried in Jimmy's chest, his mouth open, eyes squeezed shut, Jimmy's wonderful smell filling his head like a drug. "Touch me there, Jimmy. Please, don't stop."

And as simply as that, a new round of hunger stuttered through them both. Later, as Jimmy's long cock spasmed deep inside him and Larry arched his back in delight at Jimmy's gasping release, neither one of them was quiet at all. This time they held on tight, crying out, giggling, rocking the trailer, and startling the birds trying to sleep in the eaves.

One old man, lying high above them in his lonely bed, smiled happily at the sounds below.

Remembering back to the days when those sounds had come from him.

AND AS it always does, time passed yet again.

On a morning at the end of August, the coming dawn spilled a cool gray light over the mountaintop. It stirred the finches awake and sent them fluttering from the rooftops, dipping and wheeling. The encroaching light pried open those blossoms in the yard that spent their nights curled up tight, hiding from the moon.

As the day slowly yawned itself awake, Larry opened his eyes and slid quietly from the bed. Naked, he stepped to the trailer window and stared out at the grounds glistening with dew. The window was open because it was summer, and the scent of sagebrush lay cloying on the air.

Mrs. Price would not be happy about that.

A tiny smile played at Larry's mouth as he listened to Jimmy softly snoring in the bed behind him. He turned to watch him as he slept. Jimmy's long, luxurious hair was splayed across the pillow, his lips slightly swollen from their bouts of lovemaking the night before. His elegant bronze neck lay twisted to the side as his broad brown shoulders rested on snow-white sheets. The morning shadows played among the wales of Jimmy's rib cage. The tiny dark puckering of Jimmy's belly button showed itself just above where the sheets, casually crumpled, hid those parts of the man Larry loved even more than all the rest.

One long leg, sleek and finely muscled, had freed itself from the covers, and Larry thought he had never seen anything as beautiful in his life.

It was a big day today. Today they would move into the mansion. Together. The master had asked, and Jimmy had accepted. After all, it did seem rather silly for the two of them to be living in a two-hundred-square-foot tube of aluminum when they had a forty-room brick-and-mortar mansion at their disposal.

Mrs. Price was back working in the kitchen. She seemed to be enjoying it too, now that Larry was the one who had to navigate the stairs. All she did was cook the food. Larry continued to deliver the trays to Roger's rooms. It was part of his job.

After a stranger with a van arrived one day to take away Bo's belongings, Bo was never mentioned again. His departure left not a ripple in its wake. Showing his true kindness, Roger had not pressed charges against him. Larry often wondered if Bo ever took a moment to appreciate that fact.

But at the moment, Larry had more important things to think about.

Today's move, he knew, was practically a formality, since Jimmy really had very little to bring into the house with him. Only his clothes. And his CDs. And his goodness.

Technically he would take Bo's old sitting room and bedroom, but in reality he would be sleeping with Larry. The bathroom doors between their rooms were no longer there. With Roger's permission, Jimmy had removed them and carted them down to the basement. In their place, he and Larry placed curtains that hung from ceiling to floor. The curtains afforded privacy for the bathroom. Nothing more. Instead of each having two rooms, they now both had four, plus the bath. Jimmy swore that never again would there be a closed door between them.

For that, Larry loved him even more.

Thus it went. Larry's and Jimmy's lives rolled on, both of them content, seeing to their work responsibilities while falling more in love with every passing day. Roger remained well tended.

The greenhouse was ablaze with color. Dozens of blossoms sprang to life within the glistening glass walls. Roger could be found there some days, parked in his brand-new (and much-hated) wheelchair, delicately toiling with his beloved orchids. He could still be heard at times speaking quietly to someone who wasn't there, but neither Larry nor Jimmy thought much about it. Larry because he still didn't completely understand, and Jimmy because he did.

"Let him talk," Mrs. Price would whisper, a fond gleam in her eyes. "He may not be here much longer to do it."

Larry feared she was right. For Roger had failed considerably since the battle with Bo. Larry suspected Bo's heartless attitude had left some sort of scar on Roger's gentle heart. While his body weakened, his old eyes grew more introspective. Yet he was always kind, always appreciative. Always admiring of the boys who cared for him. And thrilled by their continuing love for each other.

Sometimes, Larry and Jimmy sat with Roger through long evenings, admiring the stars from the widow's walk at the top of the mansion. Roger always found peace there, chatting casually with the boys, reaching out to touch them now and then, laughing at their jokes, smiling at the devoted way they attended to each other. And between all that, forever spoiling the dogs, who in their own way were beginning to slow with age like their master.

Sometimes Mrs. Price would join them, riding the elevator up to the widow's walk. At all other times, she remained on the ground floor now. Her belongings, her furniture, everything she owned had been relocated to the formal parlor, which was hardly ever used anyway. The massive room had been transformed into her living and sleeping quarters. Working in the kitchen and residing two rooms away, she no longer needed to navigate stairs at all. But since the widow's walk was the one spot in the mansion with an elevator going to it, she allowed herself to be persuaded to visit on occasion.

This warm night in the first week of September was one of those occasions.

"Bring some cookies," Roger had told Mrs. Price.

"You don't want me," Mrs. Price had snipped. "You just want my cookies."

But she brought them anyway. Peach drops, pinwheels, peanut butter crunches, and Roger's favorite: snickerdoodles.

She found Larry and Jimmy there already. Larry sat on one side of the master in one of the wicker chairs, and Jimmy sat cross-legged at his feet with his hand resting lightly on Larry's knee. Mrs. Price parked herself on Roger's other side and placed the tray of cookies on the table between them. She had barely lowered herself carefully into her chair before all three of the men were stuffing cookies in their mouths.

"You're welcome," she said, trying to look huffy but not really carrying it off. She was eying Roger rather suspiciously. She suspected her old friend had more than cookies on his mind when he invited them all up to the widow's walk. She had to admit, it was a pleasant respite from the kitchen. The night air lay cool on her skin. The fat moon overhead cast the grounds below in a maze of blue shadow. Somewhere off in the distance she heard the baying of a coyote, followed immediately by the yip of coyote pups. She smiled to herself as she listened to their song.

Since she was the only one not sampling the cookies, she plucked a peach drop out of the bunch and sat nibbling it along with everybody else.

She was right about Roger, of course. This wasn't just a cookie fest. He had business on his mind.

After casting a glance at Mrs. Price to reassure himself she was comfortable and had everything she needed, Roger stared over at Larry, then down at Jimmy with his chin on Larry's knee.

"You boys are happy," he said softly.

Jimmy spoke for both of them. "We are, sir. Happier than we've ever been."

"You love each other," Roger said. It wasn't a question. It was a simple statement of fact.

"We do," Larry said. He had a lock of Jimmy's long hair in his hand, running it through his fingers. He stroked it with his thumb as he talked. "It's because of you that we found each other. We'll always be grateful for that."

With his eyes never leaving Roger's face, Jimmy planted a kiss on Larry's knee. "Larry's right. We never thought we could be this happy. Thank you, sir. We owe it all to you."

A gentle light shone from Roger's eyes as he regarded the two young men before him. He cast a glance to Mrs. Price. "I told you it would all work out," he said.

Mrs. Price dusted a scatter of cookie crumbs from her bodice before snatching up another. This time it was a snickerdoodle. She'd worry about her weight tomorrow. "So you did. And I thought you were just addled."

"Addled like a fox," Roger snorted, turning back to the boys.

His eyes grew serious. He stared up at the moon for a moment before speaking, as if drawing strength from the night sky, the carpet of stars beaming down. To Mrs. Price's surprise, he reached out and took her hand.

"It's almost time for me to leave you all," he said. "Jeremy's lonely. He wants me with him, and I want to go."

Larry leaned forward, laying his hand on the old man's knee. "No. You're having a bad day is all. You'll feel better tomorrow. I know you will."

Roger laughed at the sincerity in Larry's eyes. It was a sweet laugh. There was nothing mocking in it. "You boys are still young. You don't know what it's like to be tired. Tired to the bone. And I miss him. It's been barely a life for me at all since Jeremy died. I really don't think I could stand another year without him."

"You know he never really left you," Jimmy said. While he spoke the words to Roger, it was Larry's hand he took. It was Larry he tried to comfort. "There are people here who'll miss you if you go. I hope you know that."

"I know," Roger said, his words barely loud enough to carry on the wind.

Roger bent in his chair and extended a hand to gently grasp a long rope of Jimmy's hair. He let it run between his fingers, as if testing its softness. "Lovely," he whispered as the hair fell away from his touch. He sat back in his chair once again. In his other hand he still cradled Mrs. Price's cool fingers. He focused his eyes on Larry.

"I knew you were a good person the first time I saw you down on the driveway that day of the interview. I brought you here for a reason with my silly ad. I'm assuming you know that."

"Bo told me so once," Larry said. "But I… didn't believe him."

Roger cast a sad little smirk at the heavens. "Poor Bo," he said on a sigh. "Greed got the better of him, I'm afraid." Once again, Roger rested his eyes on Larry's solemn face. "But it didn't matter in the end. He fell out of my plan the moment you laid eyes on your young friend here. Not since Jeremy and I were your age have I seen two men fall in love as quickly as you two. It was always meant to be, I think. If you hadn't met here, you would have come together somewhere else."

"I think so too," Jimmy said. "But I don't understand. What's this plan you're talking about? You talk like you had what happened to Larry and me all mapped out. How could that be?"

Roger laughed. "I mapped out *another* love affair. You, my young Indian friend, are the detour that got in the way."

Roger turned to Larry. "You never shared what you knew about the plan with Jimmy?"

Larry gazed from one man to the other. "I never really believed it. Bo told me about what he thought you were doing, but it was too far-fetched. I just thought it was wishful thinking on his part. He really was a greedy shit."

"Do you think he ever really loved you?" Roger asked.

It was Larry's turn to stare up at the moon. If he found solace there, it didn't show on his troubled face. But if it was answers he sought, he apparently found the one he wanted. "I think he would have said anything to get his hands on the money."

Roger nodded. "That's what I think too."

Jimmy stared from Roger to Larry and back again as if trying to work it all out in his head.

Mrs. Price leaned forward and patted his arm. "You poor man. You look lost."

"I *am* lost," Jimmy said. "What the heck are you guys talking about? What plan? What money?"

Roger cast a critical eye at the cookie platter, finally settling on a pinwheel. "Aren't these cute," he said, taking a bite. "Hmm. Delicious too!"

"Oh, for heaven's sake!" Mrs. Price barked. "Put the boy out of his misery. Tell him what's going on!"

Roger grinned, swallowed, took another bite, chewed, and finally swallowed a second time. He was clearly enjoying the tension.

"It's all yours," Roger said, turning first to Jimmy, then to Larry. He made no grand announcement. He merely stated facts. "The money, the house, the cars. A considerable amount in stocks and bonds. Two blocks in the city that rake in a *fortune* every year in rents. Everything." He laughed. "It's yours. I'm glad to get rid of it, actually. What a pain in the ass being rich is! Of course, being poor is a *bigger* pain in the ass. Jeremy and I tested it once long ago on a houseboat floating down the Amazon, and we didn't care for poverty at all." He eyed the two in front of him. "I'm sure you both know all about being poor."

If he was waiting for a response, he didn't get one. They sat as silent as the dogs. More so. The dogs at least moved once in a while. Jimmy and Larry were statues.

"Look at these poor boys," Mrs. Price said. "You've knocked the words right out of them."

Roger seemed to agree. But he wasn't finished yet. He snapped his fingers a couple of times to get their attention, like he might if they had just woken from a coma. "I do have a couple of caveats, boys. For one thing, Mrs. Price must remain here at the mansion for as long as she pleases. This is her home now as much as it's yours. Besides, I don't think you'd want to face the rest of your long lives without a few of her cookies now and then to brighten your days."

"Uh, no indeed," Larry said slowly. He sounded like he was talking in his sleep. Or drugged.

Jimmy added his own two cents by mumbling, "Cookies," which didn't seem to make any sense whatsoever.

"Man of few words," Mrs. Price teased.

Larry brushed a tear from his cheek, wondering where it had come from. "Don't you have any family, sir?" he asked.

"Jeremy is my family," the old man said, with a noble light in his eyes that brooked no opposition, should anyone present have chosen to voice one.

Larry tried again. "No loved ones?"

Roger thought about it for a minute. "Same answer. Jeremy."

Mrs. Price dug a handkerchief out of her sleeve and blew her nose. Her eyes were wet too, but even she knew it wasn't hay fever *this* time.

Larry's gaze fell on Jimmy. Jimmy returned it, his eyes coming alive again. Sparks of moonlight shimmered on their faces. Love shone there too. It was clear for everyone to see. But the only one to voice an opinion about it was the mother coyote, howling down among the boulders.

While the baying of her song still echoed across the mountain, Roger rose on unsteady legs. He patted each young man's head and muttered a quiet thank-you to Mrs. Price for the cookies. She simply nodded in reply.

"I'm tired," he said. "I think I'll go to bed."

Jimmy stood to offer Roger his arm to help him to the elevator, but Roger waved him off.

"Jeremy will help," he said softly.

He took one last look at the moon glowing in the sky, then turned and walked away.

THEY ATTENDED Roger's funeral exactly one week later.

Larry intended to wear the suit he applied for the job in, but Mrs. Price wouldn't let him. She phoned the tailor who had made their uniforms. He came out to the house not thirty minutes later and measured them for new suits.

"But I've never owned a suit in my life," Jimmy argued.

"Well, now you will," Mrs. Price answered.

The suits arrived a day later.

It seemed fitting that Jimmy drive them to the service in the black Mercedes-Benz. On the way home, Larry and Mrs. Price, one as sad and depressed as the other, were ensconced in the back seat, holding hands. Larry was in his new suit, of course, and Mrs. Price had donned a dark gray dress with patent leather pumps and a shiny black purse hanging from her arm. Each quietly endured the ride home, lost in their own private thoughts. They hardly took notice at all when Jimmy told them the town car drove like a dream. He only mentioned it because he was sad too, and he thought he might cheer himself up bragging about the car.

It didn't work.

Jimmy parked the car by the portico out front, and he and Larry helped Mrs. Price navigate the front steps.

"You both look nice in your new suits," she said. "I'm sorry Roger couldn't see you."

"Oh," Jimmy said, his voice subdued, "I'm pretty sure he did."

"Absolutely," Larry echoed. They glanced at each other, sharing a fragile smile.

Even Mrs. Price could find no room to argue. "You're probably right. He never missed anything when he was alive. I seriously doubt if he plans on missing much when he's dead. Come into the kitchen, boys. I'll make us some iced tea. The lawyers are coming later. You'll need your strength. And you might as well leave your suits on too. Have to get used to it sometime."

"Oh God," Larry said.

They followed her through the foyer, where the sunlight leaking down through the skylight ricocheted off the crystal facets of the massive chandelier that hung overhead. Before they were halfway across, Leo and Max came running to greet them, panting, tongues flapping, toenails tippy-tapping across the marble floor.

At the kitchen door, Mrs. Price suddenly spun around and stared at Larry and Jimmy. She eyed them up and down, then poked each of them in the chest with an accusing index finger.

"What happened to your ties?"

Larry and Jimmy stumbled to a stop and stared at each other's chests. Their neckties were gone!

"What the...? But they were just *there*!" Larry said.

Mrs. Price's eyes traveled slowly upward to focus on something high above their heads.

"Well, now, would you look at that."

In unison, Larry and Jimmy lifted their faces toward the ceiling where Mrs. Price was staring. Dangling off the crystal chandelier directly above their heads hung two neckties, one beside the other. The knots were still perfectly in place and snugged up to the exact length where they would fit nicely about their necks.

Mrs. Price shook her head and pinched the bridge of her nose as if she might be experiencing the birth of a headache.

"Jeremy, please don't start. It's been a long day."

"I'm not sure even a ghost can remove two ties at once," Jimmy said.

Larry blinked. "So what are you saying? Now we have *two* ghosts?"

"Oh my," Mrs. Price mumbled. She gazed suspiciously about while her hand fluttered nervously at her throat. "Roger?" she called out softly.

"It couldn't be," Larry said. "Huh-uh. No way. We just buried him. Besides, I don't really believe in ghosts."

The three stood staring at each other. They cast worried glances this way and that at the mansion standing silent around them. When they heard no spooky rattles or moans or thumps, they all gradually relaxed. Their frowns slowly dissolved, turning to expressions of relief.

Then their relief faltered, and they listened some more.

"Roger?" Mrs. Price tried again, her voice as fragile as eggshells.

To everyone's amusement, the only answer came from Leo and Max, who offered up a flurry of happy yips as if they'd just seen an old friend. Stupid dogs.

Larry took one last lingering look at the still-looped neckties hanging out of reach above their heads, all the while wondering where the ladder was so he could retrieve them later.

Jimmy seemed to have forgotten about the ties. In fact, he didn't seem worried about much of anything all of a sudden. He spread his arms in a congenial fashion, draped one over Mrs. Price's shoulders and one over Larry's, and herded them toward the kitchen.

"Iced tea sounds great," he crooned. "Maybe we can round up a few cookies to go with it."

"I think that can be arranged," Mrs. Price answered as the kitchen door swung closed behind them.

Reaching into the fridge for the pitcher of iced tea, she asked, "Do either of you boys know how we can dig all these confounded cameras out of the woodwork?"

They heard the discordant tinkle of piano keys coming from the music room, fifty yards away. Closer at hand, a box of salt fell out of the cupboard and landed in the kitchen sink with a *whomp!*

"Or maybe we'll just let them be," Mrs. Price quickly amended, sticking her head out of the fridge, eyes bulging. "A few cameras never hurt anybody, right?"

Larry took Jimmy's hand while eying the salt in the sink. He leaned toward Jimmy's ear and whispered, "Those two reactions came from different parts of the house. What was it you said about ghosts not being able to do two things at once?"

"That was just a theory," Jimmy whispered back.

Overhead they heard a tapping sound like a cane might make on a hardwood floor. Maybe a teak cane, with a gold dragon's head for a handle. The two pugs took off running toward the stairs.

Mrs. Price and the two young men lifted their eyes skyward.

"Welcome home, sir," Larry said, his face suddenly lit with joy. He pulled Jimmy close with one hand and patted his own heart with the other. "We're so glad you made it back."

JOHN INMAN has been writing fiction since he was old enough to hold a pencil. He and his partner live in beautiful San Diego, California. Together, they share a passion for theater, books, hiking and biking along the trails and canyons of San Diego or, if the mood strikes, simply kicking back with a beer and a movie. John's advice for anyone who wishes to be a writer? "Set time aside to write every day and do it. Don't be afraid to share what you've written. Feedback is important. When a rejection slip comes in, just tear it up and try again. Keep mailing stuff out. Keep writing and rewriting and then rewrite one more time. Every minute of the struggle is worth it in the end, so don't give up. Ever. Remember that publishers are a lot like lovers. Sometimes you have to look a long time to find the one that's right for you."

Email: john492@att.net
Facebook: www.facebook.com/john.inman.79
Website: www.johninmanauthor.com

ACTING UP
JOHN INMAN

It's not easy breaking into show biz. Especially when you aren't exactly loaded with talent. But Malcolm Fox won't let a little thing like that hold him back.

Actually, it isn't the show-business part of his life that bothers him as much as the romantic part—or the lack thereof. At twenty-six, Malcolm has never been in love. He lives in San Diego with his roommate, Beth, another struggling actor, and each of them is just as unsuccessful as the other. While Malcolm toddles off to this audition and that, he ponders the lack of excitement in his life. The lack of purpose. The lack of a man.

Then Beth's brother moves in.

Freshly imported from Missouri of all places, Cory Williams is a towering hunk of muscles and innocence, and Malcolm is gobsmacked by the sexiness of his new roomie from the start. When infatuation enters the picture, Malcolm knows he's *really* in trouble. After all, Cory is *straight*!

At least, that's the general consensus.

www.dreamspinnerpress.com

Chasing the Swallows

JOHN INMAN

Sometimes an entire lifetime can be spent in the arms and heart of one person. It is not so with imaginations, for they go anywhere they wish.

David Ayres and Arthur Smith are about to find that out. When they meet as young men within the garden walls of the Mission of San Juan Capistrano, one man from one continent, one from another, an uncontrollable attraction brings them together. But it is something stronger than attraction that holds them there. It is love. Pure and simple.

After forty years, when the fabric of their existence together finally begins to fray because of David's imaginary infidelities, it is with humor and commitment that they strive to remain in each other's heart.

And turning fantasy into reality, they find, is the best way to do it.

www.dreamspinnerpress.com

MY BUSBOY

JOHN INMAN

Robert Johnny just turned thirty, and his life is pretty much in the toilet. His writing career is on the skids. His love life is nonexistent. A stalker is driving him crazy. And his cat is a pain in the ass.

Then Robert orders a chimichanga platter at a neighborhood restaurant, and his life changes—just like that.

Dario Martinez isn't having such a great existence either. He needs money for college. His shoes are falling apart. His boyfriend's a dick. And he has a crap job as a busboy.

Then a stranger orders a chimichanga platter, and suddenly life isn't quite as depressing.

But it's the book in the busboy's back pocket that really gets the ball rolling. For both our heroes. That and the black eye and the forgotten bowl of guacamole. Who knew true love could be so easily ignited or that the flames would spread so quickly?

But when Robert's stalker gets dangerous, our two heroes find a lot more to occupy their time than falling in love. Staying alive might become the new game plan.

www.dreamspinnerpress.com

MY DRAGON, MY KNIGHT
John Inman

Danny Sims is in over his head, torn between his abusive lover, Joshua, and Jay Holtsclaw, the bartender up the street, who offers Danny the one thing he never gets at home: understanding.

When Joshua threatens to get rid of Danny's terrier, Danny knows he has to act fast. Afraid of what Joshua will do to the dog and afraid of what Joshua will do to him if he tries to leave, Danny does the only thing he can do.

He runs.

But Danny isn't a complete fool. He has enough sense to run into the arms of the man who actually cares for him—the man he's beginning to trust.

Just as their lives together are starting to fall into place, Danny and Jay learn how vengeful Joshua can be.

And how dangerous.

www.dreamspinnerpress.com

Serenading Stanley

THE BELLADONNA ARMS
JOHN INMAN

A Belladonna Arms Novel

Welcome to the Belladonna Arms, a rundown little apartment building perched atop a hill in downtown San Diego, home to the city's lost and lovelorn. Shy archaeology student Stanley Sternbaum has just moved in and fills his time quietly observing his eccentric neighbors, avoiding his hellion mother, and trying his best to go unnoticed… which proves to be a problem when it comes to fellow tenant Roger Jane. Smitten, the hunky nurse with beautiful green eyes does everything in his power to woo Stanley, but Stanley has always lived a quiet life, too withdrawn from the world to take a chance on love. Especially with someone as beautiful as Roger Jane.

While Roger tries to batter down Stanley's defenses, Stanley turns to his new neighbors to learn about love: Ramon, who's not afraid to give his heart to the wrong man; Sylvia, the trans who just wants to be a woman, and the secret admirer who loves her just the way she is; Arthur, the aging drag queen who loves them all, expecting nothing in return—and Roger, who has been hurt once before but is still willing to risk his heart on Stanley, if Stanley will only look past his own insecurities and let him in.

www.dreamspinnerpress.com

JOHN INMAN
SUNSET LAKE

Reverend Brian Lucas has a secret his congregation in the Nine Mile Methodist Church knows nothing about, and he'd really like to keep it that way. But even his earth-shattering secret takes a backseat to what else is happening in his tiny hometown.

Murders usually do that.

Brian's "close friend," Sam, is urging a resolution to their little problem, but Brian's brother, Boyd, the County Sheriff, is more caught up in chasing down a homicidal maniac who is slaughtering little old ladies.

When Brian's secret and Boyd's mystery run into each other head on, and Boyd's fifteen-year-old son, Jesse, gets involved, all hell breaks loose. Then a fourth death comes to terrify the town, and it is Brian who begins to see what is taking place in their little corner of the Corn Belt. But even for a Methodist minister, it will take more than prayer to set it right.

www.dreamspinnerpress.com

JOHN INMAN

TWO PET DICKS

Old friends and business partners, Maitland Carter and Lenny Fritz, may not be the two sharpest pickle forks in the picnic basket, but they have big hearts. And they are just now coming around to the fact that maybe their hearts are caught in a bit of turmoil.

Diving headfirst into a whirlwind of animal mayhem, these two self-proclaimed pet detectives strive to earn a living, reunite a few poor lost creatures with their lonely owners, and hopefully not make complete twits of themselves in the process.

When they stumble onto a confusing crime involving venomous reptiles, which is rather unnerving since they're more accustomed to dealing with misplaced puppy dogs and puddy tats, they take the plunge into becoming real-life crime stoppers.

While they're plunging into that, they're also plunging into love. They just haven't admitted it to each other yet.

www.dreamspinnerpress.com

FOR MORE OF THE BEST GAY ROMANCE

Dreamspinner Press
dreamspinnerpress.com